Praise for *OVER THE EDGE*

"A quick paced read . . . takes the reader through the Trees and over some bumps without destroying any knees."

Dana Dugan
Reviewer/Staff Writer, *Idaho Mountain Express*

"*Over The Edge* is crime thriller, a love story, and a remarkably and compelling tale about skiing."

Richard A. Lupoff
Author of *Quintet: The Cases of Chase and Delacroix*

"Kaplan writes with an eye for visual detail and a breathless style, with punchy sentences that whisk readers through the action."

Melanie White
Jackson Hole News and Guide

The skiing scenes in *Over The Edge* are ecstatic and will make you long <u>for</u> winter."

Betty Webb
Mystery Scene Magazine

"Kaplan makes Jackson Hole come alive. Characters, when not jumping cliffs, jump off the page. Sometimes racy, sometimes violent, *Over The Edge* is nonetheless a compelling read; it resembles pot roast and gravy to the maw of the skier's intellect."

Robert Frohlich
Big Sky Journal

Honorable Mention, 2007 DIY Book Festival
Honorable Mention, 2006 Hollywood Book Festival

Chasing Klondike Dreams

Marc Paul Kaplan

CHASING KLONDIKE DREAMS

iUniverse books may be ordered through booksellers or by contacting:

iUniverse
1663 Liberty Drive
Bloomington, IN 47403
www.iuniverse.com
1-800-Authors (1-800-288-4677)

ISBN: 978-1-5320-1479-6 (sc)
ISBN: 978-1-5320-1478-9 (e)

Library of Congress Control Number: 2017902916

Print information available on the last page.

iUniverse rev. date: 03/10/2017

DEDICATION

To The Lindsay Wildlife Experience, which has kept me connected to the amazing world of Nature for over thirty years—and the thousands of domestic and wild animals sacrificed on the Dead Horse Trail for the brutal search for Klondike Gold.

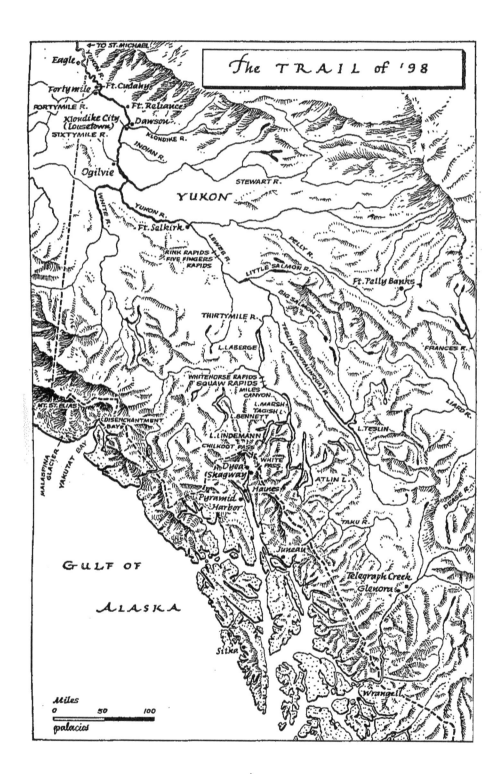

The TRAIL of '98

Chasing Klondike Dreams

"Men were like wolves, they fed on each other."

—Tappan Adney, New York journalist, 1897

CHAPTER ONE

Nerves. Butterflies. More like locusts chewed Jared's guts. A throng of spectators, many Jared recognized from the Boston and Albany electric train ride from downtown, jostled and pushed for a clear view of the race's start in the narrow, dusty street. Race organizers begged and prodded the crowd into two lines the contestants could pass between. No wonder he was such a wreck facing at least three hours of running.

Jared was ready. Beyond ready. Apprehensive and twitching. Tom Burke, sprint champion from last year's revived Olympic Games in Athens, scraped his foot across the dirt in front of the fourteen anxious men. The runners, including Jared, pressed against an imaginary barrier. Jared hadn't taken a single step yet felt winded. And where the heck was Duffy? For once he could use his trainer's prickly presence as a comfort.

"Jared." Duffy's rough, scratchy voice rose above the crowd's noise. His face jutted into Jared's view. "You ain't gonna win your first race, laddie. Pace yourself like I told you. Just finish."

A large busted nose, two ears permanently and unequally swollen, and ridges of scar tissue decorated Duffy's features. The man's battered face resembled a relief map of the Adirondacks. Rough. His personality matched.

But how could Jared compete with the predominantly tough Irishmen from New York and Boston who flexed and stretched their wiry bodies? He stood a head taller than the other runners poised in front of Metcalf's Mill in the small hamlet of Ashland. His birds-eye view of his fellow competitors made him an awkward, vulnerable stork among falcons.

Previous words from Duffy echoed in his ears, "Your family gave you too damn much freedom. Made you wishy-washy." He'd had all of Duffy he could handle. But then again, Duffy was the only one who had ever pushed Jared. Maybe the only one who cared.

"Hope you're a better runner than a boxer," Duffy rasped. "Ya got twenty-six miles in front of you. Goddammit, just finish."

Jared had been doing roadwork for several years at Duffy's insistence. And he'd taken runs of an hour or more with his Airedale, Brutus, on the farm during summers. But a marathon? This inaugural Boston Marathon on April 19, 1897? Shadows of doubt bit into Jared's concentration. Hadn't it been the trainer's suggestion that Jared enter the race? Why did everyone push Jared to follow their own plans? The starter caught the runners' attention. Too late to back out now.

"Go," Burke hollered.

Jared shot forward at a sprint, then slowed as realization of the distance registered. Lanky strides kept him at the head of the tight pack all the way to South Framingham, where a large, boisterous crowd gathered. The pace remained easy, effortless and exhilarating. Jared's mood lightened out of South Framingham as most of the other competitors fell behind the leaders.

A helpful strong wind pushed him onward. But dust from the dirt road, churned by the many accompanying bicyclists, irritated his lungs. Then Duffy appeared out of a murky cloud on a bike too large for the man's stubby legs.

"I told you to pace yourself," Duffy called, his crooked body hunched over the handlebars of the borrowed bicycle.

More cyclists swarmed around the runners, squeezing Duffy away from the contestants. His croaking calls faded into the bedlam of the spectators. Good. Duffy knew only how to criticize, never a compliment or word of encouragement. But his father and older brothers had offered even less. Jared was sick and tired of being browbeaten.

"You may have quick hands," Duffy had once said about his fighting skills. "Good eyes, speed, long arms. Even endurance. But you ain't got passion. No killer instinct." Duffy had spit on the wooden floor of the gym, then noted Jared's obvious distaste. "I'm the one cleans this place. I can spit if I want."

Had it really been two years that the old man had served as Jared's boxing coach at Yale? Jared's boxing career had been less than sparkling. Did Duffy really care? Jared's indecision, lack of aggression, and unrealistic idealism had limited his success in the ring. Though the simplicity and solitude of roadwork had filled some sort of personal vacuum. That was whenever Duffy on his darn bicycle hadn't harangued him along the way.

* * *

Lush spring countryside blossomed in contrast to the nearby congestion of downtown Boston, now sixteen miles ahead. Jared's body reacted efficiently, shifting into a soothing rhythm through the deceptive, gentle terrain. Maybe he could hang onto the front runners. Rise to the occasion. Not just finish, but place. Even win. The thought supplied a wave of energy, softening the edges of any growing physical discomfort.

The veteran Hamilton Gray and Harvard's own Dick Grant bracketed him. Stride for stride they mirrored each other from Framingham to Natick. The leaders offered vague acknowledgment to the never-ending ovations of excited spectators lining the way. Jared couldn't have cared less about supporting the dominance and prestige of his school, Yale, over Harvard. But he wouldn't allow Grant, an arrogant Harvard gentleman-athlete, to beat a humble man of the soil like himself.

Then erratic gasps began to interrupt the consistency of his breathing. A hand-painted sign marked mile eleven on the far side of Wellesley. Not even halfway. An unusual heaviness in his legs and arms marked growing fatigue. Reality surfaced with a swelling tenderness under his right big toe.

The cheering of Wellesley coeds—"Grant! Grant! Rah for Harvard!"—provoked renewed effort. He stuck with Grant and Gray. But the period of cruising had ended. Pain registered with increasing persistence. His agitated mind wandered in search of distraction.

Maybe he'd teach. Jared loved learning, especially the current literature of Joseph Conrad, Kipling, George Bernard Shaw and H.G. Wells. Though exposure to education and the real world had become unsettling. Even those authors wrote of aspects of society he couldn't understand or justify. Too much ugliness, poverty and corruption. Conditions were changing too fast and not for the better. Why couldn't he run as fast as the world now turned?

His father had a master plan for him. Required another year of general studies. Then the challenge of obtaining a Doctorate in Divinity. But to work in the service of the Lord, one needed a calling. Jared had yet to hear even a whisper from God.

Where was he headed in life? His reading had recently shifted to champions of the exploited working class—Henry George, Edward Bellamy and Henry Demarast Lloyd. And dropping out of Yale felt right. Something would work out. He knew one thing for sure. He had grown weary of old men telling him what to do.

* * *

Mile thirteen. Fast-forming blisters balanced the pain in both feet. He felt light-headed with a sore throat. Not a good combination. Aid stations provided unending water, but he had neither the desire nor time to swallow enough. Still he ran with Gray and Grant down the long hill from Wellesley to Newton Lower Falls.

Now another runner was closing fast. Jared knew who it was without looking—J.J. McDermott, the leathery little favorite and winner of last fall's first New York Marathon. McDermott brushed past as the front-runners headed downhill.

"You went out too damn fast." Duffy's gasping voice came from a group of bicyclists. "All you gotta do is finish. Just finish."

Jesus. The gruff old man either battered him with criticism or taunted him with his legacy of failures. He had caught the train from New Haven yesterday afternoon with the crotchety old man and shared a room at the Boston Athletic Association's new quarters. Duffy's snoring had kept Jared awake most of the night. Now every action of the old man brought irritation.

The road stretched forward. Hamilton Gray now faded, but Harvard's Dick Grant gave chase after McDermott. Jared followed, focusing on a pinpoint of anger and pride. Couldn't let that snob leave him behind. Nor let Duffy's skepticism prove to be true.

But a tight web of exhaustion clogged muscle reactions. Rational thoughts no longer registered. Fragments bit into his consciousness. Any sense of efficient flow eluded him. Instead, a seductive, evil presence lurked along the roadway, sneering and screeching for him to quit. Why kill himself for a meaningless race someone else talked him into?

Jared turned back to his fellow runners. To his left, Grant's body wobbled in erratic jerks. The racer toppled onto the rough street. He raised his head to beg the driver of a watering cart to pour moisture over his body. Jared slowed. Grant's collapse caught him by surprise. But the Harvard man's breakdown invigorated Jared. He staggered on, searching for energy and inspiration.

He struggled to regain a degree of rhythm and stumbled down another of the race course's endless hills, feeling empty, dry and brittle. New pains stabbed his lower back. His kneecaps developed razor-sharp edges shooting slicing pain to the surrounding tissue.

Heat enveloped his body, fire licking his feet. His brain searched for diversion but found only the world's worries. Why did he feel so useless? Why was he constantly harassed by the limited vision of annoying old men? Society's messages radiated loud and clear within his head, no way to dislodge them. He couldn't shut out his own troubling doomsday tidings and feelings.

Then, oh God, another hill. His leaden legs kept plodding. Just put one foot in front of the other. Physical, numbing agony pounded on the door of his mind. His legs kept moving without making any headway. A quick swipe at his forehead found no sweat. Too many miles left to be dehydrated. How did his mind still work with his body no longer connected?

Mile twenty. Words pounded upon him without mercy. Corruption, immorality, robber barons, poverty, Godlessness. He didn't need the burdens of the world. His own suffering overwhelmed him now. Spectators leaned forward, farther and farther, their bodies now parallel to the roadway. His legs turned rubbery. The world tilted.

Jared grasped for something, anything of positive substance. And there before him rose the images of his father and brothers, and with them, the security and stability of the prosperous family farm in Ohio. He belonged with his flesh and blood. That hopeful life provided a siren song stronger than any false promise of progress. They would welcome him home with open arms. He could teach. Get a job in town. Work the harvests and take his turn tending the livestock with Brutus. Brutus, his faithful dog. Childhood companion. Maybe now he could even outrun the Airedale.

Then the world tipped at an angle inconsistent with reality. The pull of gravity released him. He sunk into a sucking whirlpool. Everything spun and tilted. Yet the safety and tranquility of his family remained a tantalizing vision before him. The dust that had filled his lungs now floated before his eyes, his cheek against the packed earth of the road.

"Get up," Duffy called.

Where had the old man come from? Duffy was too sharp-edged, too confrontational. He didn't belong on a farm.

"You've got to finish," Duffy screamed. "Get up. Walk in if you have to."

No. He'd go back to the farm rather than give the old trainer any more power over him. Love of his home qualified as passion, didn't it? The dirt that now caressed his lips seemed little different from the soil of Ohio.

CHAPTER TWO

Overworked springs screeched as the wrought-iron bed resisted collapse. Crushing pressure from the beast upon her forced air from her lungs. Ripping agony between her legs blended into a world of bright, exploding flashes. Maggie made gasps sound like pleasure, not tortured wheezes. What else could she do after agreeing to accept this disgusting customer? The kerosene lamp on the adjacent end table rocked an obscene rhythm. Focus on anger, hatred. Couldn't give in to the pain or the shame. Awareness of her vulnerability swallowed her whole.

The rocking increased. The bumpy mattress dug into her back. Opportunities to breathe were too short to provide relief to her constricted chest. Sweat—his or hers—burned her tightly closed eyes.

"Goot, huh?" the farmer grunted.

The words echoed, battering her like a physical force. And the huge Swede's guttural groans rang louder and louder, howls evolving from proud bellows to out-of-control blubbering. The body above her muted her frantic panting, confirming her useless search for escape. The sounds, mournful to Maggie's ears, would go unnoticed at the Prairie Flower. All she could do was listen to her sobs fade into whimpers.

She never should have agreed to such a monster. But $200? The unheard of amount had seduced her into this liaison. Dreams to escape this desperate life shredded. Temporary survival in a brothel had become a life sentence with no way out.

The farmer's intense thrashing jerked to a stop. A brief, unweighted moment of release ended with a thud. The revolting animal sank on top of her. Her lungs collapsed under the load, breathing almost impossible. She was not yet twenty-one, too young to die, especially in such circumstances. The thought shocked her into a frantic clawing and biting attempt to surface.

An unexpected image of her mother appeared, her emaciated body crumpled on a shack's dirt floor. The woman hadn't died, she'd quit living. But Maggie wouldn't give up so easily. She twisted, burrowing through layers of fat, finding daylight under his armpit. Maggie still lay trapped, a tiny bug crushed by a merciless giant's foot. Humiliation smothered her fear of death.

This oaf had traveled all the way to St. Louis for sex. This three-hundred-pound monster with his huge cock had probably slaughtered every whore in the surrounding states. Tears merged with sweat. The pain from her ripped inner lips now dominated all sensations. The damage was done. No new customers anytime soon.

What had happened to her control? To all the defenses she had constructed to avoid just this kind of event? She'd sworn never to be in this position, impaled helplessly to the bed of her profession.

The now snoring hulk lay inert, satiated. Perhaps she could squeeze herself free. One hand pushed against the bed for support and found something terrifying. Dampness soaked the sheets beneath her. Too much moisture. Blood? Lord help her.

She stretched her head and arm to the edge of the bed. His massive head rolled toward her, reintroducing the putrid stench of whiskey. Saliva bubbled in copious quantities from the corners of his thick-lipped mouth. Her stomach churned. Maggie gagged. Her body flexed into rigidity, then into spastic movement.

Involuntary convulsions gave her unexpected leverage. She lunged from beneath him, off the bed and hit the floor, landing on her shoulder. She struggled to her knees, dry heaving. Intense heat and a thick blanket of humidity—1897 the hottest spring on record. Maggie quivered on the floor, unable to regain her feet.

Crimson liquid flowed from between her legs. So much blood. Could she be seriously damaged? She might still die. Or did more than just her own life stream from her body? Did her unborn child have a prayer of surviving? Had this bastard destroyed that too, unrealistic though the very thought of a baby might be?

"Never again," she gasped.

The familiar refrain ricocheted through her mind. Necessity had overwhelmed all her resolutions. She reached for a towel on the floor by the nightstand and pressed it between her legs. Pain continued to dominate her senses. She struggled upright and shrugged into her robe, compelled to cover her nakedness, afraid to take stock of her bruised body. Her body. One that had functioned so well. Until today.

Tears dripped down her cheeks, dizziness clouded her vision. She checked the towel. Red drenched the white fabric. Where was her strength, pride, the will to survive? A sick sliver of irony registered— so much for the best house in the Midwest, best room, Maggie the star attraction.

She soaked a fresh cloth with scented water from the decorative bowl sitting atop the maple dresser. The delicate painting on the vessel mocked the gross pig unconscious on her bed. She opened her robe, tentatively touching her wounds with the wet linen, cleaning her bruises, scratches and torn flesh. Her large breasts, of which she had been so proud and utilized with great effect, hung in creased defeat. How had Maggie become so defenseless?

She pulled her stiletto, sheathed in velvet, from the top drawer. The feminine blade looked silly compared to the brute on the bed, a peashooter to protect her from a bear. But the touch of the weapon— her finger caressing the razor-sharp edge—brought a small sense of security. She tied the thin leather straps around her thigh and tightened the elegant Chinese silk dressing gown.

His overalls hung over the expensive ottoman, dwarfing the piece of furniture just as the Swede's bulk had overwhelmed her. Objects bulged in the many pockets and flaps, but she knew where he kept his money. A furtive glance back at the farmer told her he wouldn't be waking for some time. An inside seam held his pouch. She again looked back at the bed. This son of a bitch had taken her out of circulation. He'd wiped out her plans to escape from her demeaning servitude as a whore. At least her price should rise to cover her future lost wages.

Nervous fingers pried the bag from the rough denim. The amount of gold coins crammed into the fabric confirmed the farmer's loud boasts. Such wealth. Her stomach churned to a different rhythm now—a sharp-edged, metallic fear. She fumbled into the pouch, eyes whipping between the Swede and his money.

Fingertips wormed out two $10 gold coins, then a third, a shiny $20 double eagle. Then two more coins, a $5 half eagle and another $10 gold piece. This $55 added to the original $200 would be closer to the true price of his destructive appetite.

Maggie replaced the pouch in the farmer's clothing and limped over to the wall by the dresser. She took another quick peek over her shoulder, then pried the baseboard loose. The gold slid into the hidden compartment, joining two years' worth of savings—close to $2,000. An amount that would allow her to forge a new life.

Maggie moved to her padded chair, collapsed onto the cushion, and stuffed the linen snugly between her legs. Her robe parted, allowing a clear glance at her knife. If she stabbed him, would he deflate like a balloon as he had punctured her hopes of freedom? Or would fluid gush from the overstuffed animal like the breach in a dam? Didn't matter. She knew she couldn't kill him.

If her parents could see her now. Of course, if her parents could see, Maggie wouldn't have been forced into this position. They'd left her an orphan struggling for survival. Well, she still had a dream, far-fetched as it might be. And perhaps now she had enough cash as well. This could still be her time to move on, if only she still possessed the physical strength necessary. One thing was for damn sure, she'd never allow herself to again be destitute, hopeless and alone on the pitiless streets of any city.

CHAPTER THREE

San Francisco morning fog from the Pacific chilled and invigorated Alex. The usual commercial activity swirled around him as he made his way to the middle of the block. He caught himself whistling last year's most popular and now most appropriate song, "There'll Be a Hot Time in the Old Town Tonight." There sure as hell would be. Images of the night's pleasures brought a grin to his lips, ending the song. Couldn't whistle and smile at the same time. A long-suppressed laugh burst from his swelling chest.

Goodman would be the perfect manager—honest, experienced, but with little ambition. Wiggens had negotiated the rent below market, needing only Alex's father's signature on the lease. Alex had purchased passage to Seattle on the *Excelsior* next Thursday, a first-class berth at that. He had the last piece in place. He hurried down Montgomery Street to the store, excitement lending speed to his steps, and pushed through the substantial oak door of Stromberg Mercantile. His new life would be that of a successful businessman, free from his father's destructive grasp and the unrelenting guilt of past events.

Noisy customers pawed at the piles of dry goods that showcased the wide selection for which the store was famous. Alex dodged two salesmen waving purchase orders at him. With a smile and a tip of his hat, he moved too fast to invite conversation. But Max grabbed him at the foot of the polished wooden stairs leading to the second floor offices.

"Watch yourself, Alex," his uncle warned, large features crowding his eternally worried face. "Your father seems upset about something. Wouldn't confide in me. As usual."

"For a change, it's nothing I've done," Alex said, patting Max on the shoulder.

He flew up the stairs two at a time. No more sneaking like a petty thief to the activities that any normal male gravitated toward. No longer would he play the sham game of conforming to a restrictive, reactionary community of social misfits. Sweet release was right around the corner. Four years of waiting and he would get his opportunity—welcome space and freedom from the iron, often irrational, grip of the old man.

He entered his father's small but well-appointed office. Mordecai Stromberg sat erect and formal behind his large desk, impeccable. The older man's serious, lined face was clean-shaven, unlike most of his contemporaries. Even his large nose did little to tarnish the image of a handsome gentleman, aged but dominant.

"Father, the deal's done," Alex said.

Don't smile. Maintain cool control. Mordecai disapproved of outward emotion. Never let anyone know what's on your mind. This lesson served him well in his nightly poker games. He could thank his father for at least that.

"Sit down, Abraham."

Why did the old man insist on calling him Abraham? No one ever called him anything but Alex. Mordecai knew full well his son's distaste for his given name. Max had been correct. Mordecai did not look happy—instead, more sour than normal.

Once again Alex sat in the large, hard green-leather chair angled in front of Mordecai's desk. He hated that chair. An inquisitor's chair. He had often been reduced to a powerless child in the grasp of that armchair, humbled before his father.

"I'm headed for Seattle Thursday, Father, with the signed lease," Alex said with more confidence than he felt. He shrank under the old man's glare, always less of a man here in this office. "Wiggens found an excellent location two blocks from the wharfs. You couldn't come close to a spot like that here in San Francisco."

"I don't understand why you're driven to such risks," Mordecai said. The patriarch's clothes sheathed his slight body in a perfect fit, every strand of his thinning hair in place. "We have a profitable, secure business in the city. You'll inherit all of it. You're the only one left."

A wistful note stole into his father's stone-cold delivery. Alex's older brother, Samuel, dead but not forgotten. Never forgotten. Guilt crept up Alex's spine. Fifteen years had passed since San Francisco Bay had swallowed his brother and spared him. Fifteen years battered by unrelenting nightmares, further fueled by his smothering father's too obvious preference for Samuel. The son who no longer lived.

"I've survived in this city for almost fifty years," Mordecai continued, "because I've resisted temptation. I persevered through gold fever, fires, the erratic supply of goods, the lure of the stock market and real estate speculation."

Amazing the intensity the old man brought to a message delivered a hundred times before. So damn sure of himself. The old man had never shown him one sliver of gratitude or respect for any of Alex's hard work. And Mordecai refused to acknowledge his own mistakes, even after Alex had scrambled to cover his father's shortcomings.

"There is no easy way to grow. You, Abraham, must also control your urges. Be patient, build slowly, consistently and at the right moment."

"We've been through this a hundred times," Alex said, unable to meet his father's eyes. "I admit last time you were correct. Timing was bad. The Panic of '93 would have put us in jeopardy if we'd expanded to Sacramento."

Four years ago he'd been ready to erupt when his father, at the last minute, vetoed the new Sacramento location. Alex had to stay calm. Just surviving in San Francisco working for his father was not enough. He craved success and freedom from the grisly bonds of his past. This was one battle he had to win. Today new hope filled him.

"But this is 1897," Alex said, struggling to keep his excitement under control. "We're in much better shape."

"We are not in better shape." The old man opened his arms in a gesture of peace and understanding. "It isn't time, Abraham."

Mordecai now folded his hands on top of the empty desk. A predictable, earnest expression pursed his father's lips. Here comes the goddamn lecture. Again.

"The economy hasn't recovered. In fact, it may even be in worse condition than it has been the last several years. Millions are out of work. Gold is still being hoarded. Store sales are flat at best, despite price increases—"

"We're committed," Alex hissed, rebellion building within him.

Sparks in the hard brown eyes, a tightening face sent a not so subtle warning to Alex. Interruptions were a cardinal sin. Bracing air flowed from the open window, bringing the ring of bells, horses neighing, hawkers squawking. But the refreshing breeze couldn't staunch Alex's instant perspiration from fear-induced heat.

"No." The old man's voice intensified in depth and timbre. "We're not committed. And we are not opening in Seattle."

Not again. Not after all his work, his promises to Wiggens and Goodman. Panic roared through Alex's body.

"You gave me permission," Alex said, embarrassed by the pathetic squeak of his voice. Would he forever be a slave to this man? "I've arranged everything. Given my word."

"You're too inexperienced to understand the dangers." His father slapped both palms on the immaculate surface of his desk. "Too willing to risk what I have built at such a terrible price."

"Goddamn it." Alex lunged to his feet, his long, taut torso levered over the desk, knuckles white. "You can't do this."

"Don't you dare raise your voice to me," his father said, pointing a shaking finger at Alex. Steel laced the old man's words.

This was the point of no return. Alex had to make a choice. One more word of anger, one more hint of disrespect, and his father's temper would crash down upon him with its usual devastating force and consequences. Should he fold his cards, retreat to the role of the good son? Was there even hope that he could become the good son? When his own survival convicted him of his brother's death?

Mordecai sat stiff, frail. His eyes looked through Alex, gazing at some painful memory that had to encompass Samuel's death. A tide of violence flooded toward the surface. He would be humiliated within the entire West Coast business community. Nothing but a high-priced errand boy with no authority. His reputation destroyed. Alex wanted to kill the ancient son of a bitch. Just snap his ornery neck.

Mordecai Stromberg appeared an ancient rock, inflexible and sharp-edged. Their roles cemented in place: Mordecai, the grieving father; Samuel, the favored son even in death; and Alex, the perpetual disappointment crucified to the damn green chair, forever cursed for living.

"Sit down," his father demanded, refocusing on Alex.

A desire to crush his father seared hot and deep. Alex could never act out his fantasy, the urge to destroy snuffed by a lifetime of subservience and demanded duty. He swallowed his pride, disgusted with his weakness, his inability to break loose from this old coot.

How many times had he been humbled in this goddamn green chair? How many great ideas reduced to useless kindling? Expand the store's assortment to include housewares items to attract women customers—not necessary. Increase newspaper advertising—too expensive. Promote a week-long annual sale liquidating slow-moving items to create space for new merchandise—too many markdowns.

Why was he so intimidated? He eased back into the chair, anger and frustration simmering. Why couldn't he tell his father to go to hell? Just walk out the door and start a new life free from the old man's suffocating control? One day his father would die. But not soon enough. Today, once again, his father crushed any hope of freedom. Was he really so incompetent he couldn't be trusted to run the business, any business? No, the bustling activity on the floor beneath him rekindled his confidence.

CHAPTER FOUR

Jared stepped off the Cincinnati, Hamilton and Dayton Railroad carriage and onto the familiar avenues of Eaton. Eaton, Preble County's only city, was an upward stretch of the word "city," even if the place was the county seat. Yet dirt streets littered with manure, slow-moving wagons, warm late-May sun, all flooded him with a comfortable sense of security. Jared jumped to the buckboard bench of the hired wagon that contained his two large trunks and single battered suitcase. The vehicle bumped from the train station through downtown, beginning the ten-mile trip to the family farm.

Ohio enveloped Jared like an old shoe. The agricultural community even smelled like worn, sweaty footwear. Three miles from the farm Jared dropped from the wagon, giving instructions for the driver to follow on behind him to the homestead with his luggage. Jared would jog the last few miles.

The creaking and groaning of the bouncing wagon faded behind him, replaced by musical calls of Baltimore orioles, warblers, robins and waxwings, interrupted by the ever-obnoxious screeches of blue jays. The birds joined the humming of cicadas to form a rough symphony. A distant red-tailed hawk circled, probably contemplating which musician to pick for dinner. The purity of the countryside brought a lightness to Jared's comfortable pace.

The sky shone a liquid blue. Light, white clouds strung across the horizon. Then an image of his father's face appeared in his mind. Morgan would not be pleased with his son's decision to drop out of college. Nervous energy added to Jared's increasingly discomforting thoughts. The sooner Jared got the unpleasantness over with the better. He shifted into a ground-swallowing run, moving through the dust and heat of the late afternoon.

Concerns eased as Jared observed ancient groves of McIntosh apple trees reaching into the thick, scented air. Leaves radiated vibrant, late spring green with new fruit only a hard, tight promise. Evidence of the legendary John Chapman, better known as Johnny Appleseed, grew in great abundance.

Jared would soon see the borders of the family's property—over twelve hundred acres with five hundred in orchards of Goldens and the recently introduced Rome Beauties. Middle brother Tom ran this fruit operation with the same dogged intensity he brought to all his actions. Tom, large and gruff, hid his true feelings behind a surly countenance. Love and warmth had to lie beneath his brother's icy exterior, even if Jared had rarely glimpsed it. Certainly Jared loved his brother and was loved in return.

But the anticipated pleasure and comfort of home, the relief, couldn't overcome the disquieting images of the world he so desperately desired to escape—the gaping chasm between rich and poor, an economic system rewarding the connected corrupt, crushing the mass of the miserable laboring class. At least he had fully recovered from his marathon, and fresh legs picked up speed and momentum. He longed for peace in this lush farmland.

He reached the top of a low ridge. The panorama opened to Tom's orchards and the cropland nurtured by his oldest brother, William. Monroe land stretched both east and west: apple trees to the east, and, to the west, unending rows of green corn sprouting from the fertile soil. Surrounding pastures merged with the far ridgeline, stocked with cattle, sheep and fat Poland China hogs. Below him spread the ancient farmhouse, barns, new machinery shed, corrals, windmill, large chicken coop, corn cribs and the grassy mounds under which harvested apples lay in cool protection. The Garden of Eden.

Jared slowed, savoring the order and familiarity of the scene. The simple, solid values and compassion of Jared's family served as a comforting relief from the chaos and cruelty of rampant change.

Movement rippled the pastoral scene. Tractors, wagons and four or five hired hands plodded through what resembled a small village. His father's large, prosperous farm had never looked more inviting.

A large brown dog charged around a flock of sheep, herding them from a pasture to a fenced enclosure. The animals surged toward the open gate, cowed by the ferocious barking that rose to Jared's ears. Brutus. When Jared had progressed halfway down the slope, the dog whirled from his task to face uphill, nose skyward.

A tall, thin man, Jared's father, yelled at his distracted four-legged assistant. Several wayward lambs veered away from their destination. Morgan snatched the straw hat from his head and scrambled to keep the sheep headed into the holding pen. The lanky man waved his hat and yelled at the dog. Brutus ignored him and began a stiff-legged, rocking-horse lope toward Jared, a quarter mile away.

"Brutus," Jared called.

The huge, kinky-haired animal shifted from his awkward-looking trot into fluid, powerful flight, a dusty cannonball blasting up the road. The ninety-pound Airedale mix closed the distance with amazing speed. Jared felt his broad smile stretch his face with a pleasure absent for months.

He misjudged the animal's progress. A thick, curly coat added the illusion of another thirty pounds and hid the dog's muscular body. Jared sidestepped too late, and the huge dog hit him at the knees, knocking him off his feet. Brutus smothered Jared with a flurry of tongue and paws. Jared grabbed the dense tangles around the dog's neck and levered himself off the ground. Brutus spun around his legs, threatening another takedown. Jared's eyes filled with tears. This could be the only unqualified and affectionate welcome he would receive.

* * *

Conversation swept from subject to subject, continuity irrelevant. Nerves curbed Jared's appetite, but his brothers and their wives showed no such restraint. Morgan directed the late supper in honor of his returned son, although "prodigal" might soon define his father's feelings. Jared had yet to share the decision to end his formal education.

"Just think," Julie, William's slender childhood sweetheart, bubbled. "Mr. Graden promised telephone service no later than next spring. I even used one for the first time last week in town."

"These wonderful technological changes," Jared said, unable to contain his dark thoughts concerning progress, "in science, industry and transportation come at a terrible price. And the impoverished immigrants and downtrodden Americans are the ones who pay."

"Jesus," Tom spat out. "Now you sound like a damn bleeding-heart socialist."

Brutus jerked his head erect. The dog's body stiffened. Ears pointed at Tom, reacting to the vehemence in the man's voice.

"So might you," Jared said, as surprised at his brother's reaction as his dog. "You haven't witnessed two thousand women and six hundred children strike the Hartford shoe factories. Middle of winter. Freezing in deep snow. Risking their humble lives for 95 cents a day, and that barely enough to survive."

"That's a shame," William said with a condescending smile at Jared and a smug wink at Tom. "But the world's a cruel, difficult place. It's up to you, as an individual, to make your own way."

"Spoken as a fortunate, well-born landowner," Jared said, unable to hide his anger.

"Fuck you, you spoiled little brat," Tom snarled.

He surged to his feet, pointing a threatening finger at Jared. Brutus rose between them. The Airedale's roaring snarl froze the Monroe family, including Jared. He directed a silent plea to his dog to calm down.

"Tom," Morgan shouted above Brutus's warning. "Watch your language. There is no reason we can't comport ourselves in a civilized manner."

Tom collapsed back into his chair. Brutus toned his snarl down to a low rumble.

"I'm sorry, Tom." Jared also sat back hard into his chair, shocked by the unexpected emotions flooding the room.

Tom nodded, eyes locked on the Airedale.

"I don't know about that dog," Morgan said. "Got an edge to him."

"No, Father," Jared said. "He's just independent."

But Jared knew better. Brutus did have an edge. Only he could control the Airedale. And even that relationship was more of a negotiated partnership. He swallowed a smile.

His father's brusque attempt at discipline when the five-month-old dog had first arrived resulted in an unpuppy-like bite to his father's rear end when he had turned his back. If Morgan hadn't been so shocked, Brutus would have become pig food. Instead, the family had laughed it off, and the name of the back-stabbing Roman became that of the new dog.

"That animal's worthless," Tom snarled. "Only thing he'd be good for is a rug. And even skinned and on the floor, that mutt'd trip you with his scroungy, tangled coat."

Once again the unmistakable click of Brutus's teeth echoed through the room. The snap of teeth indicated Brutus paying attention. The volume of the clicking rose and fell, reflecting the Airedale's excitement, whether pleased or wary. Tom scraped his chair back to face the threatening dog.

"He thinks," William said, his sarcastic smile evidence of his enjoyment at Tom's discomfort, "you're a bit too aggressive toward his buddy."

"I'll kick your ass from here to Indiana, Brutus."

"Brutus," Jared called in a reasonable tone. "Give me a break. It's my first day home."

The Airedale flashed an irritated look at Jared, then lay down, eyes focused through matted brows on Tom. If only his dog could talk, Jared could have better insight into the swirling, unexpected agitation surrounding his homecoming.

"And he's far from worthless," Jared said. "He's a great hunter. This is probably the only rat-free farm in Ohio. He can herd cows or sheep. You can't argue that he's an exceptional watchdog."

"Trouble is," Morgan spoke up, "he works part-time. When he feels like it. He's supposed to be a working dog, not a pet. And I wish you'd teach him to dispose of all those rats in one place 'stead of leaving their bodies scattered all over the farm."

"Only reason," Tom said as he eyed the dog, "we haven't shot that sneaky son of a bitch is 'cause of you, Jared."

"Last time I'm warning you about your language," the old man said, eyes flashing in displeasure like the old Morgan.

What was this animosity between Brutus and Tom? And why Tom's lack of respect for his father and siblings? Brutus was an excellent judge of character. His hostile, unflinching gaze at Tom gave substance to signs of change. Tom's normal surliness extended deeper below the surface than Jared had realized.

Jared glanced at Tom's new wife. Thelma's large, square head hovered over her plate, uninterrupted by the tensions surrounding the table. She shoveled in large mouthfuls of chicken and vegetables. Her beady pale blue eyes focused on her food, powerful jaws a threshing machine devouring crops. She already approached her husband in both girth and sullenness. No wonder they had built a new home on the far side of the orchards.

Tom had always been prickly. But what had happened during the past months to undermine the consistent warmth of the family? Some new barrier of entangling relationships kept him from connecting with his loved ones. And Morgan seemed to have lost control of the family. Perhaps staying on the farm wouldn't be as comfortable as Jared had thought. He felt an interloper in his own home.

Conversation returned to the dinner table. Other subjects filled the space. Morgan had made an offer for an additional seventy-five acres adjacent to Tom's orchards, taking advantage of depressed land values. William pushed his brother to plant peach trees rather than more apples—diversify. Tom resisted, stubborn to the core. William pointed out the value of rotating crops between corn, wheat, hay and oats. The oldest brother became animated, describing the introduction of tobacco to the Monroe farm. Tom scoffed at the plan.

The topics and emotions kept Jared out of the conversation, his opinions unwanted. Perhaps he was imagining things. Perhaps the long train ride had dulled his senses. But Morgan also seemed to be ignored—more of a referee between the brothers than a contributor. Enough. Jared could stall no more.

"Father. Why don't we step outside? I have some news."

"You don't mind," Tom interjected, standing up, "if your two brothers share your news, do you?"

Yes, he did mind. His confessional would be difficult enough with only his father present, but now he couldn't avoid including William and Tom. All the disturbing undercurrents of anger and stress undermined Jared's confidence. How would his brothers accept his change of plans? What should he expect?

CHAPTER FIVE

Maggie propped herself against the wall. No four-poster bed with carved headboard in this pathetic excuse for a bedroom. No extra satin pillows or seductive art work on the walls. Another late-May heat wave produced a thin sheen of sweat over her lightly clothed body. The thick leather-bound novel slipped in her wet fingers, difficult to keep propped in her lap. Even her favorite white cotton drawers with their intricate embroidery, crocheted edge and pink ribbons felt uncomfortable.

What a son of a bitch that farmer had been. The damage he had inflicted cost her dearly. Madame Davidson had turned on her, offering no sympathy and yanking her from her prime bedroom into this cell. Even charged Maggie for the room, food and doctor's visits. Another girl slept in her old spot.

Inaction had eaten into her savings. She should escape now with the amount she still possessed. The pig could have at least offered extra gold once he'd regained consciousness and discovered his bloody damage. But he hadn't. Instead he'd staggered past her without a word.

She should have stolen more than a measly fifty-five dollars. That amount hadn't even covered two weeks of work. Anyone else would have recognized the true cost of his pleasure. Well, maybe not anyone else. Her fellow whores, as always, kept their distance. This dysfunctional community of women was like no other, selling their bodies to survive, yet having no compassion or patience for their sisters in crime.

And she found little solace in anything, even her normal escape into literature. Her latest novel, *The Mill on the Floss*, proved too thick and daunting to penetrate. Once more, she struggled to regain focus on the print. The weight of the novel supported the rumor that authors got paid by the word. So the verbose George Eliot must be wealthy. All she had in common with this story of sibling rivalry was a shared name—Maggie.

She had grown a bit stronger. But gentle probing between her legs confirmed flesh too damaged to perform. She would have to do something else soon. Her customer's attack had diminished her, made her less human. The chipped mirror tacked to the rough pine wall did reflect a healthier body than the one from two years ago, before the Prairie Flower. But looks were deceiving. Soon nothing would be left but a colorful shell. And that too would soon be ground into diseased ugliness if she went the way of most whores.

Motherhood was the only way she could bring something of value to her life and the world. The farmer's lust had taken that from her as well. Birth and rebirth—to become part of that circle would bring a degree of peace and respectability. Was that why the working women of the Prairie Flower treated her like a leper? Because she held tight to hope of a better life?

Who knew which disgusting lecher got her pregnant? Next time, please let there be a next time, she'd have a choice in the father. Someone with character and strength. Little likelihood she would meet him in a brothel. No choice but to move on. But when and more important, how? Torn flesh healing at a snail's pace and dwindling resources, that's all she had now. How could she read? Deliverance from this dead-end nightmare occupation was slipping away.

She had to get out. Moisture trailed down her cheeks, dripping onto her nightgown. Start a new life again. Did she still possess enough money? Tomorrow she would begin a serious search for some job, if any were to be found. The Panic of '93 had been devastating. St. Louis, as well as the rest of the country, had failed to regain any economic vitality. Few people had dreamed things would stay so depressed four years later. Whoring at least paid a living, even in times like these.

And where was God's help when she needed it? Well, He had never been there. She had only to call up her nightmare memories of the past. Why expect the appearance of a guardian angel now?

* * *

A thumping noise outside made her look up from her book. The last thing she wanted was a visit from anyone. Besides, who would use this side entrance to the Prairie Flower?

The small door to the back alley burst open with a loud crash. The massive farmer from Minnesota filled the room with his bulk. In an instant he had blocked any escape. Shock smothered any attempt to scream. This bastard had almost killed her once. What else could he possibly want?

"I haf already paid for another session, you thieving slut," the farmer lisped. "But I haf better idea. You come home wit me. If not, I tell Madame and whole town how you stole my gold."

A flush of anger checked Maggie's fear. Take her to his home? Was she just another cow or pig to be possessed? A piece of meat?

"I'd rather die," she blurted out.

The farmer's eyes widened. A smirk enveloped his grotesque features. A backhand blow slammed her against the wall. He lunged toward Maggie, pinning her to the bed.

"I can do that," the man sneered.

He ripped off her camisole and drawers with a single clawing motion. His powerful hands gripped her throat, crushing her to the mattress. Maggie wrapped her legs around his waist, squeezing tight, her fingers tearing at the Swede's forearms and face. He tried to shake her loose. Maggie struggled to breathe and bit at the huge arms now forcing her toward unconsciousness. How long could she hang on?

"You think you can steal from me?" he sputtered. "You think I don't know when my gold is missing?"

Was this brutal attack to be the end—such a degrading death? She was helpless against such size and strength. The stiletto on her thigh. Maggie reached up and pulled out the thin blade. She slashed at the man's trunk-sized forearms. The razor-sharp edge sliced through fabric and into flesh. He jerked his arms in pain and surprise, releasing her neck. The movement took away his leverage, and he collapsed forward onto Maggie's bosom. And the stiletto disappeared into the bulk of his body, her wrist swallowed by flab and flannel. Then strange, unexpected silence.

He moved his lips. An eerie whistle escaped his mouth. A bovine look of astonishment spread across his grimace. Maggie saw her own disbelief mirrored in the shocked stare of the Swede only inches from her face. His mouth worked like a dying fish, wide-open eyes still unbelieving. She couldn't look away from the twitches. She didn't dare stir, couldn't with the giant crushing her.

She wasn't sure how it had happened, but she understood what had occurred. The knife buried in his flaccid flesh had been deep enough to cut some vital organ. His own weight had impaled him.

How could this be happening? Her racing heart thumped in her ears, listening in panic. Where was everyone else? Could he truly be dying?

The normal house noises continued in uninterrupted rhythm. No one came. How could the world not know what she had done? She'd accidentally killed a man. Lord, she was only trying to defend herself. Could this insane act be just another nightmare like the many others during the last few weeks? The last four years? If she didn't move, maybe she'd just wake up.

The gigantic man's chin pressed into her forehead. His weight bore down, generating uncomfortable heat. Her twisted wrist ached. Maggie couldn't just lie there, a victim. Couldn't allow this pig to crush her.

She'd been here before, trapped by this same overpowering hulk. First he'd ripped apart her body. Now he trapped her with his death. So heavy she couldn't cry out even if she wanted to.

She used both hands, one still wrapped around the knife, the other beside it. She shoved at the inert body. Maggie had to get him off. She took another breath and pushed again. The body moved.

The farmer spilled onto the worn wood flooring. An unpleasant odor permeated the air.

She rolled on her side toward the body. The incongruous shaft of the stiletto protruded from the farmer's chest. This creature had not only raped and assaulted her, but now her knife lodged in his body would lead her to jail and a hangman's noose. People will say she murdered the man. The cruel consequences of her actions swept through her. Heat engulfed her body with rage at this new injustice.

She dropped on top of the dead man, knees buried in his overfed belly. A red-hot whiteness enveloped her, blocking out the weather, the noises, the tragedy that was the Prairie Flower. Maggie clenched her fists and pummeled the inert body. Tears poured down her cheeks. Maggie struck at every drooling, violent, selfish customer she'd been trapped into servicing; at the lecherous sweatshop supervisors and their dead-eyed bosses; and finally an even harder swing at the dark heart of her father.

Then Maggie's fist smacked into a hard, solid object. The farmer's pouch of gold. Money. He would certainly never need it again. She had to think, be calm, figure a way out.

But what about the police? What would the authorities assume? Who was the victim? The dead, rich landowner or the surviving, sinful whore? Self-defense was an irrelevant excuse. Who would defend her? Not Madame and her dependent ladies. Gaye, her only friend, was in California. Was there any hope for justice—a whore who had stabbed and killed a citizen? Maggie had no parents, no friends, no support. She was alone, damned if she ran, doomed if she stayed.

She wiped blood off her breasts. How could he have died with so little bleeding? Her unborn baby's death had come in a torrent. Where was the guilt she knew she should be experiencing? She had murdered another human being.

She drew her fingers over the rough denim that covered his money bag. The outline of an outrageous scheme materialized. She would exact her own justice. How long before someone knocked on the door? When would she be discovered? No one yet. She willed her hands to stop quivering.

Maggie had spent the last weeks in this dump with hardly a person acknowledging her existence. She had time enough. She again knelt on his body. Her stiletto sliced through the overalls. She yanked out the heavy leather sack, her hands shaking once more.

The weight of the pouch gave her comfort. She loosened the rawhide drawstring and poured the contents onto the man's stomach. There had to be hundreds, maybe thousands, of dollars in a shining array from $5 to $50 gold coins. She stifled a gasp. Add that to her own dwindled stash, and there'd be more than enough for her needs.

* * *

How could Maggie sneak out of St. Louis? And which way? South to Mexico—doubtful. Single women didn't travel there alone. Where would the coppers expect her to flee? East or west probably. So she'd head north, back where this pathetic slob came from, then to Canada and Winnipeg. They'd never expect her to head toward the farmer's home. She stuffed the gold coins back into the pouch.

What would be the best way out of town? River routes would be too slow. She could catch the trolley to North St. Louis and connect to the train depot. Trains ran north into Iowa and Minnesota several times a day. If not Canada, a train anywhere north. Then perhaps she'd work her way west and back down to California. There she could hook up with Gaye. She had to start moving. Now.

First, she needed a disguise, a different look to blend into a crowd, to become an altogether different person. Why not a man? Better yet, a boy. Her thick auburn hair, hanging loosely below her shoulders, would be her first sacrifice. Gorgeous hair, which had been one of her greatest assets, could prove her undoing. Identify her as the wanted woman.

Maggie stumbled toward her painted dresser and grabbed scissors, then hesitated. She couldn't leave a pile of hair on the floor. The authorities would guess her new identity from such an obvious clue. She snatched the soiled sheet off the bed and spread it underneath her.

Sharp, tapered scissor blades sheared handfuls of dense, lustrous curls. Her treasured locks cascaded to the sheet. Each clump of hair brought new sorrow and disorientation. But she kept slicing. The action calmed her. She would dispose of her hair and bloodied clothes on the way to the trolley.

Then a look in the cracked mirror at the ragged haircut undermined her confidence. At least she recognized that her dark skin glowed a solid shade beyond a woman's popular pale. But almond-shaped brown eyes held a hint of the exotic, a bit too pretty for a boy. She'd have to rough up her flawless complexion with makeup.

She pulled out a pair of old riding pants. She hadn't used them in months. Also a denim blouse cut similar to a man's shirt. Unsteady fingers worked the buttons and anxious eyes reflected back from the faded mirror. Her shape wasn't right. Large breasts were evident even without support. Hardly a boy's profile.

She snatched the single pillow from the crumpled bed, shrugged out of the blouse, slapped the pillow under her bosom, took the fabric belt from her robe and secured the sack of feathers to her stomach. She replaced the blouse and looked again in the mirror. A fat clown with a butchered head of hair. Fluid formed in her eyes. A better disguise could be purchased if—when—she made it out of Missouri.

She cleaned her face with a damp cloth, wiped away the tears and scrubbed irregular coloring into her skin. With trembling hands she struggled to pull on her pants, boots, and a medium-brimmed cowboy hat. She grabbed the gold-filled pouch, added it to her own stash, lifted her denim blouse and wedged her newfound fortune inside the pillow. Finally, she stuffed a small valise with a random selection of clothing.

Again she turned to the mirror. Now the frameless glass reflected a boy with little resemblance to the Prairie Flower's high-priced star. Who was this new creature? Was there hope for a better life? She had to believe. She had no choice. She had to try. No way would she face the hangman or prison in St. Louis framed as a murdering whore. She'd die first.

An irreverent thought stuck in her mind. Could this bloated, sadistic monster lying on the floor be an answer to her prayers? Could he and his money free her from this life? This creature could be the ugliest and most unlikely angel ever to visit the earth.

CHAPTER SIX

Alex sipped a watered-down beer and considered an early exit from the luxurious card room at Bertha's brothel. He knew the odds, exercised discipline, rotated strategies and followed his refined tactics religiously—the very characteristics his dear father felt his son lacked. Here he sat in total control of the poker game and his life. What a difference.

The small room's rich draperies, soft, seductive furniture and expensive oriental carpet emphasized his escape from the realities of retail. The fragrance of some delicate perfume still rose above invading odors of cigars, liquor and nervous perspiration. The money was easy. Good thing. He needed winnings to supplement the stingy salary his father paid him to operate Stromberg's Mercantile.

Two kings for down cards and a nine showing. Stealing candy from babies. But if he wanted to continue to enjoy the comfort and security of Bertha Kahn's fine establishment, he'd have to limit his winnings. He needed to fold. And he needed his late-night distractions, anything that protected him from the terrors waiting to ambush him in vulnerable sleep. What the hell. He took a deep breath and folded his arms across his chest.

That evening Bertha had not offered Alex the warm hug of welcome that only a 250-pound woman could provide. He siphoned off too much money from customers who would normally partake in the women and liquor of the parlor house. That's where she made her profit. He didn't want to piss her off. Alex was a merchant. He knew the importance of cash flow. Bigger stakes and more action could be found within the Barbary Coast but not with the safety Bertha provided.

The other indisputable advantage of Bertha's, the sensual, gorgeous Gaye. She floated around the poker players, wearing an outrageous low-cut white nightie trimmed in lace with red sandals and a red velvet cap somehow attached to a full head of frizzy red hair. Gaye. She also lived up to her name in bed. A real screamer. Certainly a possibility this evening. Hell, a necessity. Living without the touch of a woman was as impossible as life without food and just as important as winning at cards.

That was the beauty of his parlor-house circuit. No commitments. No family entanglements with the local overly protected society girls. No gossip and manipulation within the tight-knit community in which his father held such a prestigious position. Wherever Alex was headed in life, he did not intend to be trapped with any of the local empty-headed debutantes.

Alex examined the four faces around the table. The presence of a new, aggressive stranger, Jim Sizemore, might provide a decent challenge. He seemed to know how to play, just couldn't draw any decent cards tonight. But Sizemore broke the first commandment of poker: Don't try to beat the other players, let them try to beat you.

The three regulars already looked a bit discouraged. They had good reason to be. He was already up $75 in only an hour. How could these losers expect to do well against someone who obeyed the laws of poker? Got a great hand, make everyone pay. But not this time. He sighed and folded, kissing off a potential twenty-five dollars.

"Keep your damn hands on the table," Sizemore barked at Herbert Malvean.

Alex snapped to attention. The belligerent stranger was focused and angry. Anger was a liability when up against the unalterable odds of the game. Herbert, the fur trader, looked hurt, like he'd been slapped. Tension enveloped the table.

"You gotta be kidding, stranger," Jack Connelly said. "Poor Herbert's such a lousy player. He couldn't win even if he cheated."

The fur trader could no more hide his feelings than swim after the seals his livelihood depended on. He might as well play his cards face up. And Connelly should talk. He violated another poker law, much to Alex's pleasure. The man loved to play and couldn't resist hanging in the game, even with lousy cards.

"Well, he's winning now," Sizemore said, throwing his cards on the table, "and his hands are twitching all over the place."

"I resent your implication, sir," Herbert stuttered.

Sizemore's verbal attack could be a prelude to violence. Alex welcomed the shot of adrenaline, realizing just how boring these poker games had become. He'd never used the derringer tucked in his right sleeve. He'd practiced often, loosening the constraining cord and shaking the small pistol into his hand, ready to fire. Tonight he just might need the little gun.

Sizemore said no more, and the atmosphere stayed electric. Alex straightened and concentrated on his new hand. He relished an opportunity to take out his embarrassment and frustration on someone worthy. Mr. Sizemore would be a more appropriate target than the other suckers at the table. This evening had become a hell of a lot more interesting.

Herbert and Connelly folded. The antagonistic stranger added five dollars to Alex's raise. Well, well. What did we have here? Alex had two jacks showing but nothing else of value. Couldn't tell how good a hand Sizemore held. Let's see if we can't bluff Mr. Sizemore.

"I'll meet your five," Alex said, "and bump the pot another ten."

Sizemore hesitated, checked his down cards, slammed his fist on the felt table.

"You lucky son of a bitch," the stranger snarled.

He threw his cards down and rose. His stained fingers reached into his shirt pocket. Alex once again concentrated on the derringer up his sleeve. But Sizemore pulled a business card from his coat pocket and spun the creased paper across the felt to Alex.

"Come play with the big boys at the Empire instead of these stiffs," he said in disgust, heading out the door. "And next time, my luck won't be so bad."

Alex's energy flowed unchecked. Maybe the threat of violence was better than sex. He was sorry to see the man stomp out of the room. He checked out Sizemore's calling card lying face up on the table. A large embossed "E" filled the center, with the name and address listed below—The Empire on Jackson Street, right on the edge of the Barbary Coast. Alex might one day take him up on his offer. But now his thoughts returned to Gaye and the pleasurable diversions she would provide.

* * *

Once more sitting on the bed in Gaye's overstuffed room, Alex couldn't shake a surge of emotion and feeling of danger. He again looked at the card Sizemore had tossed down. His ticket to freedom from his father might well be found in the big-dollar games at the often deadly saloons of the Coast. The potential of both, escaping from Mordecai and winning at cards, struck a strong resonance within him. Sizemore's introduction might serve him well. Maybe he'd discover quality competition at the Empire. Win some real money. Then he wouldn't have to deal with the petty harassment of his old man. But what about the crooks and cheats drawn to the big games and the Barbary Coast? Another ripple of excitement worked through Alex.

Gaye's fingers teased the buttons of Alex's shirt. He grasped her hands, a calming squeeze to slow her down. Then he kissed her slender fingertips. He needed time to put his swirling emotions into some kind of order. And he couldn't shake Mordecai's disconcerting presence from the room.

His father's inflexibility, second-guessing, and vetoes made no sense. The old man's actions seemed counterproductive. Was Mordecai so blind? Alex now handled all the buying, merchandising, displays, personnel problems, and supervised the selling floor. Why couldn't the crocky son of a bitch acknowledge his son's back-breaking contributions? Hell, he was Stromberg's. But he was treated as nothing but his father's whore.

Gaye slipped behind him, lips and tongue caressing his neck. Her sensual attempts at seduction became more and more difficult to ignore. He wanted to savor the excitement of the poker game. Follow the thought process that could aid him in understanding Mordecai. But she was so damn pleasantly persistent.

Then a lightning flash of revelation jerked him off the bed. Of course. What a fool he'd been. His father had squelched expansion to Sacramento and Seattle for one reason. He didn't want to free Alex from his direct duties at Stromberg's in San Francisco. No wonder Mordecai had refused to pay for talent to come into the business. Why pay when Alex assumed all the job functions? The old man wasn't going to return to the selling floor, let alone assume the responsibilities he'd delegated to Alex.

Mordecai's plan was now crystal clear. He'd keep his son in place so that the father could enjoy the fruits. The bastard had total control over Alex and would use his undeniable tenacity to maintain it. Alex took better care of his painted ladies than his father treated him.

"Alex."

Gaye's sweet voice and tapping foot returned him to the silk-draped room. She pushed him back onto the bed with a seductive smile, then stripped in two fluid motions. She thrust her thick patch of bright red pubic hair in his face. Alex no longer wanted to resist. He allowed himself to be swamped by the woman's flagrant sexuality. He fumbled with his buttons and clasps.

She knelt upon the bed, proudly stroking long, hard nipples that compensated for a more frugal gift of breasts. Gaye moved her fingers between her legs. A strange, distant eroticism colored her fine features.

Alex rolled toward her, luxuriating against her satin skin. Her frizzy head disappeared between his legs, and Gaye's lips closed around him. A different kind of sensation took possession. He stroked her long leg, light-colored fuzz sparkling under the influence of the Tiffany lamp on the bedstead. His hand traveled up her flanks, fine hairs thinning as he reached her sculptured buttocks.

The wild tangle between her legs beckoned, only inches from his face, as she continued her oral assault. Great to give back the pleasure she gave. Tempting. More so tonight, with the evening's momentary confrontation still a potent force. No respectable lady he would eventually marry would willingly offer a similar opportunity, let alone enjoy the act.

But did any woman enjoy sex? Did Gaye only play games? Were her moans and cries arousal or theatre? He would like to bring total satisfaction, uncontrolled passion to a lady. But women could be the most wonderful of God's creatures or a constricting pain in the ass. Could an emotion such as love make the act any more enjoyable? Did it matter? He was as addicted to the sexual attraction and warm companionship of women as some were drawn to drugs and alcohol. Only the power of a winning poker hand could compete with a lady's lure. Then a surge of pressure released him into unquestioning bliss.

CHAPTER SEVEN

T he sun slid on into Indiana, thin pink splashes evidence of its exit from the Monroe homestead. Jared's eyes took in the colors of sky, shades of earth. The air remained soft, gentle, with a strange bouquet of blossoms, grass, fertile soil and fresh manure. Brutus patrolled the perimeter in the growing shadows. Jared was home and safe.

He followed his father and brothers to the giant elm between the house and main barn, the family conference area. Three battered benches sat around the stump of a broad buckeye. Morgan settled on the shortest bench, while William found a place on another. Jared settled on the third, near his father, and offered the other end of his worn wooden seat to Tom. His brother ignored the gesture, first looming huge, then merging with the shadows at the base of the elm.

"Father, William, Tom," Jared began and leaned forward, intent, hands on his knees. "I am not meant to be a man of the Lord. To be a man of God one needs a calling. It is clear to me that I have none. Along with my fine education at Yale, I have witnessed the horror that is life for millions in America. I want out of the voracious onslaught of progress, a force that eats its own. But I have also learned an even more important lesson—the value of family and farm." A smile creased his lips as his eyes made a quick sweep of the surrounding land. "I want to live and work with you."

"No." Morgan's immediate response came close to a shout. Frantic glances flew from William to Tom, then settled on Jared. "That's not going to happen."

He must have misunderstood his father. Alarm bells rang, first at a distance, then a growing clamor. Jared was no longer stable on the hard bench.

"What are you talking about?" Disbelief raised Jared's voice.

He searched his father's face. Jared swung toward his brothers and thought he saw a nod directed from William to Tom, maybe even a wink. Brutus came into view, alert, tail down, head dropped below his broad shoulders. Involuntary clicking of the dog's jaws crackled through the thick air.

"Jared," Morgan said, eyes wide, fingers running through his thinning hair, "you ever wonder why you were the only one who went to college? Why William and Tom been working the farm since they were kids?"

"Father." Jared tried to keep the whine out of his words. "I've worked every summer with you. I carry my own weight. I can put out as much effort as William and Tom. I've done everything you asked."

"That's true," Morgan said. A shift in his father, a tightening of his jaw.

"I don't care what chores you give me," Jared pleaded. "I just need to be here. You're my family."

"Jared," his father said, rising to his feet, hands clenching the straps of his overalls. "Let me explain. There's a plan in place. The days of the small farmer are numbered."

"We've got a large farm," Jared said, opening his arms to encompass his childhood home. "Fertile land, mature trees..."

"Exactly." Morgan released his grip on his overall straps, rammed his calloused hands into oversize pockets. "But if I divide the land three ways for each of you boys, we'll have three small farms. Lose the economies of scale. Splitting the farm in two still leaves us with over five hundred acres of orchards and seven hundred in crops and grazing. Tom runs the apples, William the balance. Both share in the livestock. Both parcels can stand on their own. Understand?"

Jared sagged onto the hard bench. He searched for some response, stunned. The encroaching evening seemed lit with sparks of disaster. Brutus moved closer, his huge head poking protectively against

Jared's leg. Jared grabbed at Brutus's kinky hair. His mind fought to hold onto the images of his love of family, the farm, the values. This was his life here. What was his father telling him? That he no longer belonged?

"William and Tom have been paying their dues." Morgan's eyes bored into the rich earth. "They've done well. I'm confident they'll keep the land producing. They've worked hard and made sacrifices. No college. No traveling. They're men of the soil, and I'm proud of them."

"I understand that, Father," he protested.

How could an object as hard as the primitive wood bench seem so precarious? His free hand grasped the smooth, worn surface of the seat, searching for security within the flow of overpowering confusion. Brutus nudged him again, this time with more force.

"You, Jared, have the opportunity to choose a different path." Morgan took several steps around his bench, speaking with increasing confidence. "Become a man of God. This family could sure use one. That's what your mother, God bless her soul, wanted. Now you're telling me you want to come back to the farm? No, son, that's not why I invested in your education. I knew long ago there was only room for two sons here."

"But, Father." Jared jumped from the bench. "My education has convinced me of the value of farming and the importance of family. The world's unraveling. It's become an evil place. Why are you punishing me?"

"You're not thinking straight," Morgan said. "I'm not throwing you out. You're always welcome here. But you can't live here full-time. It's not fair to your brothers."

Jared's mouth became too dry to speak. Where was he? Where was he going? What had he done wrong? He'd always treated his family with love and respect. Assumed whatever responsibilities that had been placed upon him. Only Brutus seemed real.

"We're not sending you away without resources." His father's voice came from far away, looking almost apologetic for bringing up the subject. "We'll stake you to any enterprise that makes sense. You still have a third share in the family's assets. Less, of course, what's been spent sending you to Yale."

"You can go anywhere you want," William said, another comment from some distant place. William's lean, foxlike face sat like an exclamation mark on his thin shoulders. "You're lucky. You've got freedom, little brother. Heck, I wish I was in your shoes."

"Take my shoes," Jared said, struggling back to earth. "Take my great opportunity. Enjoy whatever adventures are ahead. I'll stay here."

"Maybe that's not a bad idea, William," Tom said, words thick with venom. "We should check with Julie. She might not mind a change."

"I'll go live in Eaton," Jared tried again. "I can get a job with the bank. Teach school."

"Things aren't going too well in Eaton," Morgan said, now only a silhouette against the encroaching darkness. "City folk, the clerks and salesmen, are unemployed now. I don't know how the Farmers and Citizens Bank has survived. They sure aren't hiring. There's no jobs I know of, not even for teachers. Things are grim. You're fortunate you got some cash and a line of credit with us."

"Very fortunate," Jared said, his bitterness a foul taste in his mouth.

"Quit your whining, you little baby," Tom growled from the semidarkness.

He resembled a fairy-tale giant, shoulders as wide as the tree trunk he leaned against. Brutus stiffened, clicked his teeth louder, swinging his shaggy head back and forth between Tom and Jared. Jared again placed a trembling hand on the dog's shaggy head, searching for support, some comfort.

"Think about it, Jared," Morgan said. "You'll realize you've got a chance few men have. Pick a direction—east, west, whatever. Understand we do love you. We'll always be here for you. But you've got to head out. Your world's waiting."

Morgan stood and walked toward the house. Jared couldn't believe the discussion had ended. William followed his father. But Tom kept his position against the tree. Jared remained anchored on the bench. Brutus lifted his head and tail back to attention. A squirrel scurried across the dirt between trees. Brutus gave chase, dust from his charge floating in the air. Tom now shuffled from the elm, stopping before Jared as the Airedale blended into the murky night.

"You always been babied." Angry heat radiated off Tom's flushed features. "You got the world by the balls, and all you can do is bitch. The old man always protected you, gave you whatever you wanted. Be good to get your ass permanently out of the way."

Tom's eyes and nose compressed into one piece, teeth clenched. What had he ever done to Tom to generate such animosity? Yet another blow to Jared. How could all the stability and security Jared hungered for disappear in one brief evening? He leaned toward his middle brother.

"I thought you loved me," Jared spoke with soft, shocked sadness. "You taught me, protected me—"

"Are you kidding?" Tom interrupted. "I pretended all that crap, or the old man would have kicked my ass. And I've had to play second fiddle to William. He's got the best part of the farm."

Jared's mind went back to supper. He saw the pleasant features of Julie and the silent, sullen Thelma. Maybe Tom's growing ill humor and unhappiness was tied to a poor marriage.

"Maybe if I had a wife like yours," Jared said, "I might want to trade places also."

An explosion lit the darkness, slamming Jared to the packed earth. Tom stood over him, shaking with rage, his clenched fist threatening Jared like a blacksmith's hammer.

"Get up, you wimpy bastard," Tom hissed. "Thought you were some kind of a boxer. Show me your stuff, or I'll stomp you right where you're lying."

Jared tucked himself into a fetal position, not caring what Tom or anyone did to him. Then Tom kicked him in the back. The blunt weight of the field boot knocked him breathless. Jared rolled with the blow, anger joining confusion and sadness. Tom followed with another foot that glanced off Jared's shoulders.

No more. Enough. Jared sprang to his feet and jabbed at his brother to keep him away. Four, five, six stiff punches caught Tom in the face. The lefts bought little time. Tom charged. Wild but powerful swings rained upon Jared's forearms and elbows. Jared tightened into a protective defense. Just keep moving, dodge and bob.

Most of Tom's haymakers missed or bounced off. Then one flying roundhouse snaked through Jared's shell, smacking him in the mouth. Jared staggered. Sharp pain awakened survival instincts. His technical defense wouldn't be enough to hold off his brother's maniacal charge.

Tom's swings somehow picked up speed. His brother had wasted his time on the farm. He should have become a professional boxer. Jared stepped inside the vicious swipes and rocketed punches to Tom's midsection, burying deep, beyond the fat to bone and organ. Tom paused.

"Let's stop this craziness right now," Jared gasped, still shaken at Tom's brutal attack.

"Fuck you," Tom hissed.

An unexpected monstrous left knocked Jared sideways despite the protection of his forearms shielding his head. Tom pressed the fight, crashing his fists against Jared's arms and shoulders. Jared absorbed so many punches that early stars appeared before him in the gathering darkness.

Jared kept shucking and weaving. The threat of Tom's anger and size now overcame any thought of letting his brother keep swinging. Would he never tire? Tom backed Jared against the thick elm. No way out except to fight. Another wallop staggered Jared. He punched back. Urgency supplied added energy. He was battling for his life.

Jared had been in many bouts, controlled and civilized. Tom's attack was the street fight Duffy had always warned him about. The image of his ornery coach brought discipline. Jared no longer had time or inclination to take it easy. He shot sharp jabs to Tom's face, setting up opportunistic crunches to the chest, stomach and ribs.

The damage Tom had inflicted became submerged in a driving desire to smash his brother into the ground. Jared's skills took over. One didn't kiss a charging bear. The tide turned.

Jared responded with wild uppercuts and overhead blows. Unlike Tom's, they landed. Two brutal shots to the temple by each fist sent Tom crashing to the earth, his head snapping as it landed on something solid. Tom lay motionless.

A trickle of blood from Tom's ear frightened Jared. How badly had he hurt his brother? Jared dropped to his knees, head close to Tom's face. Blood oozed from Jared's mouth and nose. Hands hung by his side, swelling even as he looked down at them.

"Tom, Tom," Jared cried, "are you okay? I'm so sorry. I didn't mean to—"

A huge arm snared Jared into a paralyzing headlock. Tom rolled on top. His free fist pummeled Jared. And he kept pounding. Jared lay trapped, overpowered by his brother's strength, weight and rage.

Tom finally released Jared's head and sat on his chest. But his brother was far from finished. He used both hands, free to swing with more punishing force into Jared's head. A roaring snarl, then a lifting of weight. A depthless blackness enveloped Jared.

* * *

A wet nose and tongue were the next sensations Jared experienced. Barnyard debris and earth mixed with blood into a paste clogging Jared's mouth, nose and eyes. He couldn't separate the physical agony from surprise, misery from rejection. Heavy footsteps faded into the distance. Tom headed for his new home on the far side of the farm? Every negative emotion Jared had ever experienced made raucous entry into his stunned body and soul. He lay disabled in the Monroe dirt.

Jared forced himself to his feet and staggered toward the lighted house. Brutus's solid body provided a crutch. Each breath became an agonizing challenge, the discomforts of his marathon now seemed inconsequential. Pain, frightening in its intensity, drove him to the earth at the side of the building. Jared couldn't reach the front door. He curled his body into a ball, his back against the foundation of the farm house.

The voices of Morgan and William, foggy and indistinct, carried through a nearby open window. Sounded like they were discussing the price of apples. Didn't they know what Tom had done? Didn't they wonder where Jared was? He wiped blood from his mouth.

More flowed. Not good.

House lights reflected on steady brown eyes. Loyal Brutus stood above him. An incongruous whine accompanied the Airedale's rough tongue. Jared welcomed the heat of the dog's thick body.

"Sorry, boy. Not even one lousy run." Pain laced each word, each syllable. "But we're leaving. Go somewhere we can run. Let the rats take over the Monroe lands."

CHAPTER EIGHT

How much time did she have? The question rolled through Maggie's mind as the train rumbled north into Iowa's infinite fields of sprouting corn. Telephones and telegraphs traveled faster than any damn railroad. News of the farmer's death could arrive anywhere once the body was discovered.

Maggie kept her eyes glued to the dense text of *The Mill on the Floss*. A dull ache spread across her back from holding the heavy book. She hadn't read a word since St. Louis, anchored to the seat, afraid to look around, attract any attention.

Her empty stomach growled behind the feather pillow strapped to her body. She twisted her neck, relieving stiffness. Random waves of fear and unexpected guilt had imprisoned her to an unnatural position bent over the novel. But now Maggie experienced an expanding exhilaration. For better or worse she had broken from the past.

The little round man sitting across from her, an anonymous traveling companion since Hannibal, stood and stretched. The railcar lurched, and he stumbled against Maggie. His forearm almost knocked her hat off.

"Sorry, son."

How would a boy react to this situation? A bolt of despair shot through her exhausted body. She had no clue how a boy would respond to any situation. How would she ever pull off this charade?

Maggie gave a grunt and refused to meet his eyes. She didn't trust her voice or her clumsy disguise. She'd lie low until refinements could be made to her costume. In fact, she'd remain in her protective shell until Canada. Shiny black shoes peeked out from under the well-fed, pink-faced passenger's spotless trousers. He must be a man of substance. Her eyes squeezed tight, forcing out the image of the privileged path she had once expected to follow.

Her birthday was in two days, May 15, 1897. Maggie's life had unraveled fast and in many directions over the last five years. Seemed more like her thirty-second rather than her twenty-second. Once again she was faced with crisis, forced to act.

She did have the vague idea of a plan. Unfortunately, she'd hit a detour before she'd even started. And her first adjustment would take her right into the dead farmer's Minnesota home and on to Canada. She hadn't wanted to choose this train or her path. Tragedy and the country's crumbling economy had driven her to this mad dash, and now there was no turning back. She would be forced to re-create herself. Somehow she would regain self-respect, quiet the tremors that shook deep within her body. Had her exile into prostitution stained her soul forever?

* * *

Sunrise brought light, but Jared lay in shadow. The gray dawn revealed a pile of six dead rats ten feet away. The Airedale could snatch a rodent by the neck and snap its spine in one movement. A normal night's work for Brutus, but the dog had never before deposited the carcasses in one place. Did the Airedale sense Jared's helplessness, showing his loyalty to his young master?

Jared's fingers traced the damage to his face. Limited vision in his left eye and several missing teeth as best he could determine, with a tongue the size of a sausage. If his jaw wasn't broken, it was at least dislocated. All injuries attested to the job done by his brother's ham-sized fists and well-placed kicks. And who knew what internal damage existed within his throbbing frame?

For the hundredth time he asked: What had happened, and where would he go? The question of "when" he could answer. He'd leave as soon as he could stand. His original plan had been to return home. Now he needed a new one. And why hadn't either his father or William come looking for him? Disappointment and frustration grew. The sudden demand for change overwhelmed him, prodding him into considering anything—any place—other than here.

Not east. The worst evils of the Industrial Revolution overflowed the cities and infected the countryside. He'd been there and never wanted to return. Nothing to the north but desolate wilderness and even less opportunity. The south, after over forty years, was still mired in the Civil War, unable to shake itself from the sins of the past. West had to be the answer. Head as far west as the continent allowed.

What was the golden lure of California? Probably prove to be false promises, but better than the alternatives. West it would be. False promises with blind hope were better than the bitter rejection of his family. And he'd take Brutus.

Then he tried to stand.

* * *

Jared held tight to the back of a heavy wooden chair in the family's main room. Lunch dishes littered the scarred dining-room table. A metallic, bitter taste filled his mouth. An overwhelming tide of pain almost swept him off his feet. He faced his father and two brothers across the wooden floor, worn smooth from memories he now refused to share or recognize. Everyone's eyes roamed the room, no one willing to look the other in the eye. Only Brutus, anchored by his side, seemed in focus. He no longer felt connected to his brothers, father but a ghost of the past. Somehow Jared remained upright.

"I'm leaving," he said, speaking a painful challenge.

"My God, Jared," his father said. His voice full of a concern Jared no longer believed to be sincere. "You can't travel, hurtin' like you are."

Jared ignored him. Concentrated on standing. The hell with the old man.

"And I'm taking Brutus," Jared added.

"Good," Tom said through split, swollen lips.

His older brother's forehead bulged with a massive, disfiguring blue and purple bruise. Blood red washed out the whites of both eyes. Jared felt no satisfaction from his fist's destruction of Tom's face.

A lone, battered traveling case sat by the door, as disconnected to the proceedings as Jared. William had helped him pack, prodded by his father and, probably, his family's desire to rid themselves of an unfortunate incident. Preparations hadn't taken long. Jared had shed any possession reminding him of his family.

"We could stake you in most ventures. We're asset rich and cash poor," William said. Time to depart, and Jared's oldest brother, not his father, did the talking, trying to make peace. "There's enough to go around, if you're conservative. The value of your share, one third, less the cost of your education, will be honored by me. And Tom."

Jared's body swayed. Nausea rose from pain, betrayal or revulsion at the hypocritical attempt to buy him off. He didn't care.

"Jared," William said, his voice soft and calm. "We'll give you traveling money of $500. Plus another $750 to draw from. And an annual sum dependent upon the price of crops and profits of the farm. You can access your funds with a bank draft. Nothing huge, but you'll have freedom."

The $500 amount registered through the growing fog—a year's worth of toil for a factory worker. He'd have his freedom, and they'd all be free of him. William's words rang hollow.

The old man rose and stepped forward. He thrust a worn, heavy money belt into Jared's swollen hands. Then he attempted an awkward embrace. The emptiness of the gesture confirmed the end of any relationship with his family. Jared jerked back.

* * *

Maggie stood exposed on the station platform in St. Paul. The late-morning sun beat down on the roofless landing, bringing stifling heat. The warmth of the feather pillow strapped below her breasts added an additional layer of discomfort. The bright daylight reinforced her need to refine her disguise. She could use the two and a half hours before the departure of a new coach to Canada to remedy the problem.

She headed downtown to the retail center of the city. No one took much notice. Her weathered hat rode low over her eyes as she made the rounds to a general store, haberdashery, and druggist. A few coins purchased a man's full-fitting shirt and pants, plus a bolt of lightweight cotton to replace the pillow. She changed clothes, cowering behind the store's dressing screen. The drug store's theatrical makeup darkened the skin of her hands and face and thickened her eyebrows. A pair of wire-framed reading glasses would further her masquerade on the train.

What about her hair? Her butchered haircut looked like a flock of sheep had been grazing on her head. But a barber could become suspicious and discover she was a woman. Too bad she couldn't find a wig for a boy. At least she had the hat.

She wolfed an early lunch, then worked her way back to the station. Furtive glimpses at her reflection in storefront glass showed a boy indistinguishable from the locals, except for the crispness of new clothes. At least her hat and boots were old. Still, she avoided the station lobby, walking around the edge of the building and taking one step onto the platform.

Three men in suits hovered outside the telegraph window that opened onto the loading area. Their animated conversation and quick movements were inconsistent with the oppressive weather. One of the men held a piece of paper, a poster. Maggie knew two of them were police even before she saw the badges pinned on their black vests.

But who was the third man?

He appeared more ominous––tall and thin, with sharp, angular features reddened by heat and sun. No expression on his tight face. Her stomach twisted behind the folded cloth of her disguise. He was no ordinary lawman.

Maggie made a slow turn and exited the platform. Panic lay like a snake in her gut, poised to destroy her from the inside out. They were looking for her.

* * *

If pain could kill, Jared would be dead. Only one thought at a time struggled through the maze of his agony. He needed Doc White's help in Eaton before heading west. The hired driver tried to help him off the wagon at the doctor's office. But the man's arm around Jared only increased the searing spasms roaring through his body.

He staggered to the porch, then the front door, Brutus by his side. Edie Mae, the doctor's assistant, took one look at Jared and fled through the glass partition door, screaming for Doc White. Jared swayed in the center of the waiting room. He couldn't breathe, focus his eyes.

"Sweet Jesus," Doc White said, appearing from the back. He ushered Jared to an examination room and sat him on a table. "What the hell happened to you, boy? I'm getting you to the hospital."

"No. Noon train," he wheezed. Dread that he wouldn't be physically capable of heading west, that he might die from his injuries engulfed him. "Help me."

"You're nuts," Doc White said.

"Got to. Please."

Doc White hesitated, a strange expression on his face. Then he began a slow, methodical search of Jared's face. Gentle fingers unbuttoned Jared's shirt and repeated the process over his chest, sides and back. A trail of pain followed the doctor's probing. Individual injuries sorted themselves out from the single dense cloud of torment that had been swallowing Jared's entire body.

"Damn," Doc whispered after his cursory check. "You've got broken ribs, don't know how many. Jaw's all cockamamy, fractured in several places, and half your teeth are loose, two gone. Left eye may be damaged. Can't tell for sure until the swelling goes down. Got more bruises than a barrel of rotten apples. Internally, there could be serious damage. Especially if you keep moving around."

"Need help with pain." Jared struggled with the words and attempted to rise.

"I'm sending word to Morgan. You're in trouble."

"No."

"You are seriously hurt," Doc White said. Anger and frustration clouded his features. "Don't move. You either let me get you to the hospital, or I won't help you."

One more old man, no different than Duffy or Morgan, telling him what to do. He'd rather die. He struggled to his feet. Nothing could keep him here. Doc White swore, then placed a hand on Jared's chest. Minimal pressure forced him back on the table.

"You're a fool," the doctor said. "I expected there'd be problems if you moved back to the farm, but nothing like this."

Surprise registered through his agony. Doc White knew, even understood. Jared had been clueless. How could he have been so blind?

"Okay, then," the doctor said and left the room and returned with three vials. "Don't take any of this until you're lying down. You won't be able to function with the doses you'll need to ease the pain. And easing is the best I can do."

"Thanks," Jared whispered, fighting back tears of relief.

"I don't think you're going to get very far, son."

Doc White was wrong. Somehow he would distance himself far from Eaton and Ohio. Jared had no choice.

CHAPTER NINE

"**F**ilet of sole," Alex ordered as he took a seat at the long polished bar. "Don't have much time."

He swiveled to his left and right on the tall stool. No other customers at the bar. Thank God. The glossy dark wood paneling of his favorite restaurant, the Tadich Grill, calmed Alex. He needed a break from the intensity of business at Stromberg's. Alex wanted something to take the edge off an aggravating morning of waiting on two of Stromberg's most important customers.

"Beer, Adolph."

Abigail Braun had performed her customary hour-long soliloquy on the harrowing challenges of operating one of the largest and most profitable bakeries in the city. Avery Goodwin had spent an hour and a half questioning, prodding and doubting the quality and quantity of goods for his barrel factory he had been purchasing for years. The bigot would never feel comfortable dealing with Jews. At least Miss Braun had no such issues.

The Seattle fiasco, although a month old, still sucked out his usual inexhaustible energy. Mordecai's restriction on expenses meant unending responsibility for Alex. No man would work as hard as he did at such low wages. The barman set a large chilled mug before Alex. He drained half of his Golden Gate beer. The drink brought him neither relief nor calm.

Then he caught a glimpse in the mirror of three men sitting in a nearby booth. Damn. Isaac Snyder and two cronies. One he recognized, the second remained indistinguishable in the corner.

Isaac and his father owned the Great Western Auction House, the biggest schlock joint in San Francisco. Sailors were their main customers, buying flawed and distressed merchandise at ridiculous, overvalued prices. The Snyders fleeced them without pity. He had hoped a late lunch meant fewer business and fellow associates to deal with. Nothing he could do now to avoid Isaac lurking in the corner.

The fish arrived. Alex focused on his meal, forcing down his food. The large mirror behind the bar reflected movement at Isaac's booth. The chances of Snyder ignoring Alex were about as good as an Irishman hugging a Chinaman.

"Hello, Alex," Isaac said in a voice too loud. "How's business?"

Isaac's flunkies chuckled, standing a respectful half-step behind their leader. Their cheap gray business suits fit too tight over their broad shoulders. Isaac wore a ridiculous multicolored plaid sack suit. His large belly bulged beneath the obligatory gold watch chain attached to the top button of his white vest. More food decorated the vest than remained on Alex's plate.

"Haven't seen much of you since your Seattle deal blew up," Isaac said with a greasy smirk. "Heard Mordecai cut you off at the knees."

This bastard knew the difficulties Stromberg and the rest of the honest merchants had faced since the crash of '93. Several store owners had attempted legal maneuvers against the Snyders, but that was a joke. Old man Snyder had the resources to outbribe Stromberg and their allies.

Anger flamed. Isaac's supercilious tone struck the anticipated raw nerve in Alex. He left the last forkful on his plate but finished the beer. He pivoted off his stool to face his tormentor. All he'd desired was to be left alone. No hope of that now.

"Nice to see you, Isaac."

"Have you met my associates, Conner and Brian?" Isaac said, puffing up with confidence and pointing at his bodyguards.

Isaac dwarfed Alex's six feet in both height and flabby girth. Please, Alex thought, insult me. Give me some legitimate excuse to kick your ass. This doughboy needed to be pounded into the size of a biscuit.

"Too bad about Seattle," Isaac said and smiled. He checked the two men backing him up and gave a calculating look at Alex. "Should have left town before we drive you out of business."

"You mean before they throw your thieving ass in jail," Alex said, every muscle tensed to strike. "You're a bigger crook than your worthless old man."

Color flooded Isaac's face. He closed the distance between them. The man's red face now matched the dominant color of his tentlike plaid outfit. The group tightened around Alex. "You squeak pretty loud," Isaac said, "for a boy still wearing his daddy's diapers."

Enough. Alex drove his knee into Isaac's groin. The man bent over in pain, and there, bobbing large as the harvest moon, was Isaac's spud-sized nose. Alex couldn't resist. He fired a rock-hard punch. His fist splattered Isaac's dominant feature into mashed potatoes. Snyder crumbled to the floor.

One of the so-called associates, Brian, stared frozen in place; the second, Conner, made a move toward Alex with his hand in his coat. A glint of steel sliced at his stomach. Alex swept his heavy beer mug from the bar and crushed it against the man's temple in one smooth motion. Isaac's companion hit the floor in a shower of glass.

Isaac and his flunky lay side by side on the hardwood floor. Isaac rocked back and forth groaning. Blood poured from what was once his nose. The other fallen man made no movement. A warm glow of satisfaction spread through Alex's chest. He hadn't even damaged his hand. Why couldn't old Mordecai be as easy to handle as these overmatched incompetents?

Isaac's other cohort hesitated, then dropped to his knees. He put his palm against the fallen man's nose and mouth. Anxious concern contracted his pale face. Frantic shakes brought no life to his immobile comrade. The injured man's face had lost all color. Fear nibbled at Alex's gut.

"I don't think Conner's breathing," Brian said, panic lacing his voice. "We need help, quick."

The man couldn't be dead from one blow, could he? Alex backed against the counter, adrenaline leached by growing unease. Still no movement from the motionless body. Serious trouble, no question.

Was he dead? Alex had wrought much damage to his fellow man over the years, but he'd never killed anyone. Now what? Could he claim self-defense? The man had threatened him with a knife. Still no feeling of guilt or remorse. The crumpled heap brought no value to the world in life, but he might bring Alex grief in death. How could he slip out of Tadich's without further trouble?

Then an uneasy finger of guilt and fear tickled his throat. Had he never killed anyone? How would one describe his nightmare on San Francisco Bay so many years ago? The echo of his brother's screams and the harsh slap of chilling salt water tore at his composure. Panic crept into his consciousness, squeezing the air from his lungs.

Crowd noises grew in intensity, forcing him to focus on the unconscious Conner. Men swarmed into the Tadich Grill, several police included. A quick sweep of the restaurant confirmed the absence of an easy exit.

An older gentleman, maybe a doctor, knelt and placed his ear next to the inert man's nose, hand on his chest. Isaac's moans lifted above the sounds in the crowded restaurant. Why hadn't he permanently shut the bastard up? The doctor felt for a pulse at the prostrate man's neck. A serious expression tightened his features.

"He's dead," the doctor said, looking up.

A tall, almost elegant policeman stepped forward and pushed the assembled crowd back several steps. He conferred with the doctor and the barman. Questions the officer directed at Isaac went unanswered. The fat man, still propped against the foot of the bar, gasped for air. Isaac's crony had more to say, pointing a shaky finger at Alex. Finally, the policeman turned to address Alex.

"You're Alex Stromberg?" he asked, no answer required. "I'm going to have to ask you to come to the station."

"What's going on?" Alex wiped away emerging moisture from his forehead. His gut twisted, and the filet of sole threatened to reappear.

This idiot cop was taking him to jail for defending himself. "Isaac and his thugs attacked me. Why don't you check for a blade? Where is it?"

The dead man's hands were empty. His partner gave a blank look. He must have disposed of the weapon. Alex felt sick. A salty, sour taste filled his mouth.

* * *

Alex found himself once again in the clutches of the damn green armchair in Mordecai's spotless office. But he couldn't blame Mordecai for his brutal actions at Tadich's, and that generated his current squirming discomfort. Mordecai needed little help in assuming the judgmental frown he so favored.

"You gave Judge Terry $500?" Alex gasped. "For what?"

"Son, you killed a man," his father said, his voice more muted than usual, his face an unhealthy gray.

"They attacked me." Alex couldn't believe the old man had caved in to the crooked judge. "Don't you know what self-defense is?"

"It was your word against the two of them," Mordecai said. "Your temper is not unknown within our community. Judge Terry said you would be locked up until a trial."

How would Mordecai have reacted to Isaac's disrespectful comments? Would his father be spouting accusations at Alex if he'd been present at Tadich's? Mordecai's lack of support came as no surprise—always criticizing, never satisfied. But frustration and betrayal boiled within him anyway.

His long-dead mother had always backed her husband, driven into total submission by the man's power and temper. Only his brother had stood up against the old man's domineering negativity. Young Samuel had stood resolute against the torrent of Mordecai's abuse.

"Do you know," Alex replied, "what that fat tub-of-lard Isaac said about me? About you? He's the one I wish had died."

"Abraham." His father jumped to his feet. "What are you saying? God forgive you. Trouble and tragedy follow you. Your bad luck has already taken my firstborn."

So damn predictable. Every problem, every crisis always prompted Mordecai to bring up the eternal nightmare—Alex's brother's death. He had expected the response by his father. Still, uncontrollable fury consumed him.

"That's bullshit."

"And now you spout blasphemy at the memory of my boy?"

"I'm your son, too." Alex rose from the green chair and met his father's hard stare. "You always blamed me for Samuel's death. It was an accident. I almost drowned with him." Alex moved toward the door. "Sorry the wrong son died."

Mordecai let fly a flow of strangled words. None registered as the apology Alex hoped for. Why couldn't his father offer that which Alex desperately sought? Support and approval would be too much to ask for. Forgiveness was what he craved. How could he shed the guilt of brother Samuel's accident with Mordecai's continual innuendos?

He stomped out of the office, shaking off the tremors of his own body, gasping for air. His hands made an involuntary pass over his sides. The hard-ribbed ridges of the half-submerged dinghy no longer dug into his body, but the marks still scarred his soul.

CHAPTER TEN

Maggie ducked back into the shadow of a freight company warehouse. Had they seen her? She eased around the corner of the station, ready to run if the men appeared. A quick glance over her shoulder gave her a moment's hope. She stumbled into a protected alley, well out of sight of the three men on the platform. What to do?

A sheen of sweat threatened to streak her carefully applied makeup. The stolen gold-filled pouch, hidden beneath her breast, became a burning ember, hot to the touch. Why hadn't the tragedy at the Prairie Flower been about some poor married slob who'd been embezzling the St. Louis Guaranty and Trust?

Authorities would be checking all the major rail centers. She took the train schedule from her pocket. So Canada and Winnipeg were out. Suicide to head back south. Omaha might have appeared to be the natural gateway west, but the Union-Pacific crossroad would also be obvious to the police. The farmer must have been very important for this kind of vigilance.

Even if she determined a probable rail escape, how would she sneak by the men at the St. Paul station? They were definitely on a serious quest if they remained unfazed by the crippling heat. She hoped they would relax their attention after the Canadian coach departed north.

Then a new possibility caught her eye. On the next to the last line on the page, a train headed west to Sioux Falls and Rapid City, South Dakota, down into Cheyenne and then west. The Great Northern line left at 4:00, well after the departure of the Minnesota train to Canada.

Maggie lugged her bag back downtown and counted minutes by drops of perspiration. Lord, the humidity crushed like a physical presence. Was the whole world this uncomfortable? Would there be any difference in California? Would she ever find out?

* * *

Several hours later she worked her way back to the station and followed the dusty path to the corner of the station. She peeked around the building. Only the hawk-faced man remained patrolling the loading area. The intensity with which he observed his surroundings sent a stab of anxiety through her overheated body. She should have stayed downtown until the last moment. No way to purchase a ticket unobserved. Maybe her disguise would work. But she wasn't ready for that test. Failure was too frightening to consider.

The platform shook as the westbound coach made its rumbling arrival. Action increased on the station landing. Maggie's plan would have to be simple. Climb the stairs to the platform as the train began to pull out. Jump aboard at the last minute. Tell the conductor she'd been too late to buy a ticket, then pay him.

Maggie leaned into a sliver of shade. Heat drained some of her fear and left her semidazed. How would she jump on the car with her awkward valise? Right now she had difficulty standing. Well, consider the consequences of inaction—life in prison, if not a quick hanging. Sure enough, the cost of capture brought a welcome surge of nervous energy.

The train clanked to life. Now or never. Maggie ascended to the loading area, head down, eyes focused on the metal steps of the next to last passenger car. The noisy, smelly locomotive strained with its burden. Two, three, four paces. Movement in the crowd to her right. A dark image crossed the periphery of her vision. The tall man moved toward her. He must have seen her. Terror overwhelmed her. Maggie made a desperate lunge.

She grasped the metal handrail. One foot found the step, the other missed. The weight of her body and the valise in her other hand threatened to pull her from her perch. The train picked up speed. Sweat greased her palms. Steel wheels ground a song of death. Her hand slipped, impossible to even push away and avoid the crushing danger.

Maggie's foot flapped in the wind. Would her body soon follow? Was this how her life would end? At least there'd be no more crises, no more deceit or betrayals. An end to her futile attempts at freedom from the depths of moral degradation. Then powerful hands grasped both shoulders. Strong arms applied a forceful jerk, and she was snatched to the companionway. Her feet found solid footing and safety.

"You all right, son?" the conductor said, his hands maintaining a tight grip on her quaking shoulders. Her savior was as wide as he was tall. Kind eyes lay buried in a florid, well-fed face. A mouth too small for the head smiled a cherubic grin. "Funny, you don't weigh as much as you look."

"I've got to buy a ticket," Maggie gasped. The absence of air and the presence of fear contorted her voice into a squeak. "Got to the station too late."

"Not a problem, young man," the conductor said. "I can sell you one. Now I've impressed myself. Been on this job over twenty years and never had so much excitement. You know, son, there's easier ways to get on board."

Her sudden deliverance left her stunned, but at least she was safe. Wasn't she? She kept her face averted and mumbled a thanks in as rough a voice as she could muster. Boy or girl would have been embarrassed by this clumsy arrival on board. And the hawk-faced man couldn't have caught the train. Could he?

* * *

Each jolt of the ancient railcar and the poorly maintained tracks sent shocks to Jared's ribs and stabbing spasms through his damaged head. A cry escaped his split lips. Typical of the country's blind march of progress. Overbuild the railways, then run out of capital to keep them maintained. Another lurch against the side of the decrepit train with its splintered benches, stained floors and encroaching layer of rust. In a year or two everyone would be back on horses.

Morphine and laudanum left him benumbed and stupefied on the rickety train's hard bench. Every breath brought swirling reactions. Disconcerting thoughts and ragged fragments crept through the thickness of Doc White's medications. His head bumped against the glass. Where in the world was he? Had to be somewhere in southern Indiana, halfway to a more comfortable Pullman sleeper in Omaha.

Monroe memories assaulted him. Faces floated, then faded before his eyes. Jared had vowed to banish all thoughts of his traitorous family—another failed plan. Sadness and self-disgust reinforced the pain, competed with the drugs.

Jared found himself slumped forward. Lord, he was miserable. Why couldn't he just pass away into oblivion? Brutus provided the answer, imprisoned in the baggage car. Jared had to survive to take care of his dog. But the purchase of a ticket to San Francisco seemed futile, a way station in purgatory.

He fought to clear his mind, and his surroundings took shape. Amazing how one could travel in close, knee-knocking proximity to fellow passengers for hundreds of miles without any meaningful exchange. A greeting, a nod, an occasional comment camouflaged a life with thoughts no less complex than his own. And what must they think of his ravaged face—a monster's mask, molded by Tom's beating? The less said, the better. He barely had enough energy to breathe, let alone converse with strangers.

And no position proved free of pain. Nothing could be more uncomfortable than the torture of the rock-hard bench. Jared rose from the seat and embarked on the slow, agonizing process of standing. He drifted through two passenger coaches to the freight car, where Brutus lay in a large, slated crate. He limped to the cage and, with disconnected movements, lay down, back to the floor, face against the wood bars.

Brutus's familiar rough tongue licked his face. The dog's touch brought at least a slim degree of soothing comfort. But feeding and watering the Airedale served as an unwelcome responsibility, chaining Jared to continued existence. Had to be more to life, didn't there?

CHAPTER ELEVEN

Jared arranged his large suitcase between the facing seats on the Union-Pacific Pullman out of Omaha. This car, new in contrast to the ragged equipment of his journey's first leg, afforded more space. The extravagant purchase of two facing seats would allow him to stretch out. One space for his head, the other for his bent legs, the suitcase to prop up his back. Night would be even better. He could rest his broken body on the friendlier surface of the Pullman's converted bunk.

The train rumbled through the great valley of the Platte River, abundant with crops. The vast expanse of natural grass on the Laramie Plains supported uncountable herds grazing on the land's plenty. Another anomaly of progress: Overproduction and increased productivity had dropped the price of a bushel of wheat from $1 in 1870 to $.75 today. Farmers couldn't afford to grow and harvest their bountiful yields.

He'd been too long on the train. His mind needed other thoughts. The weight of his bag reminded him of the recently purchased books he had packed. Yes, Edmond Rostand's *Cyrano de Bergerac*, Joseph Conrad's *Nigger of the Narcissus*, and H.G. Well's *The Time Machine*, as well as two of his older favorites, *The Adventures of Sherlock Holmes* and a collection of stories by Oscar Wilde. At least he'd been strong enough to lug the bag onto the train, but the silent recital of the titles exhausted him. Pain continued to dominate his senses. Easier to take more drugs and retreat into the twisted reality of the medicine.

* * *

Four days on the run with little or no sleep. Maggie had spent an interminable five hours in Rapid City, waiting for the train south into Wyoming. Then the creaking, smoke-filled trip through Buffalo, Casper, and, finally, almost to Cheyenne. Wagon trains could have gotten her there faster than this circuitous route. She ached with fatigue. Thank goodness no stalking cops had appeared.

Now the critical crossroad neared. Would the police be waiting? Ragged, abused nerves brought the taste of bile to her mouth. The improvements to her disguise as a young man should work, shouldn't they?

The memory of another costume from another life drifted before her. An angel in a white silky, flowing gown, gossamer wings slightly bent out of shape, and a wire halo. Her parents' beaming faces, bright within the gathered crowd. She'd been seven years old or maybe eight. Life back then had been perfect. Her parents had immersed her in love and showered luxuries upon her. A violent shake of her head freed Maggie from the image of another lifetime. She was no one's little angel now.

* * *

In Cheyenne, the westbound Union-Pacific Pullman she hoped would take her to California had already arrived. Passengers, porters and baggage handlers surrounded the train. Clouds of steam engulfed sleek railroad cars. Maggie had less than twenty minutes to make the connection. She waited for a majority of her fellow passengers to disembark, then stepped onto the platform.

Activity swirled around her. Shouldn't it be easy to lose herself in the rush of harried travelers? She scanned the area. The unmistakable tall figure stood above the moving flow of passengers. Her heart stopped in midbeat.

Her worst nightmare stood guarding the area between the two trains. The hawk-faced hunter hadn't changed expressions since St. Paul. He'd probably headed back south to Omaha and then Cheyenne, beating her here by at least a day.

Maggie darted behind a large luggage-filled cart. For the moment, the pile of suitcases and crates shielded her from discovery. But how to get to her train? Silhouettes of passengers within the Union-Pacific Pullman filled every window. Were there any available seats?

She placed her valise on top of the pile and tried to move the heavy cart from the side. Nothing. She needed more leverage, but moving to one end would expose her to the tall man. He now talked with several other cops in unseasonable wool uniforms. Maggie put all her diminished strength into moving the loaded wagon. It swayed, then grudgingly began to roll.

She pushed the cart within several feet of the Pullman. Maggie jumped aboard and crowded into the first bathroom she came to. Shaking hands slammed the locking bolt home. Now what? The train was scheduled to pull out in five minutes. Again no ticket, and this time maybe no empty seats. Only five minutes. All she could do was stay put until they were underway.

She allowed herself a brief moment of relief, even satisfaction, at her escape. She checked herself in the mirror. Little comfort there. A small window provided a view to the activity outside. Tension returned with a vengeance.

Her pursuers maintained a steady presence on the platform, unaware of her movements, she hoped. Her train shuddered and surged out of the Cheyenne station. Did she detect a tightening of the hard-faced one? He took several rapid steps toward the departing Union-Pacific. Then another man in a dark suit grabbed his arm and motioned toward the station lobby. The Pullman picked up speed. Immediate danger slid out of sight.

Maggie slumped against the door, safe for now. A loud banging interrupted her brief respite. She unlatched the door and stepped around a plump, well-dressed woman. The matron's face lit up in shock. What was happening? Why was she so upset? Did the woman somehow recognize her? The woman brushed past and slammed the door. Maggie glanced at the gold lettering on the bathroom door. She'd been hiding in the Ladies Room. Her disguise had worked this time.

A slender, dignified Pullman porter approached, his uniform immaculate. Questions creased his coal-black face. He stood before her. A careful, courteous smile took shape.

"Can I help you, sir?" the porter asked.

"I didn't have time to purchase a ticket," Maggie began. "Got to the station too late."

"I'm afraid the train's full," he answered, an edge of irritation in his voice.

A new surge of panic swept through Maggie. All seats taken? She searched the crowded car, hoping for a miracle. And there it was. Two spaces empty by the window in the middle of the car. She pushed past the porter. Thank God. This was cutting things close.

"What about one of those?" she said, walking toward the open seats.

But as she approached, she realized the empty spots were occupied. To her dismay, a man lay stretched between the two seats on top of a large suitcase on the floor. The man used the two seats and the case as a makeshift bed. His battered face looked like a wagon had driven over it. Her hope dissolved.

The slumped passenger stirred, his tight-lipped, pale face painted with pain. The prostrate man opened one eye. Maggie returned his look with a flood of tears. He shifted his body to a sitting position.

"Please, sir," Maggie pleaded. "I'll pay you twice what the seat cost. Any price you say."

"Listen here, young man," the porter stepped forward, grabbing Maggie's arm. "Can't you see this gentleman's injured. You have no business on this train."

Desperation engulfed her. She cast a pleading look at the man. Their eyes made contact.

"Wait," the man sighed. "Let the boy have the space. Need to get something from my case first."

The damaged traveler struggled to pull out several books from his suitcase. The uniformed man moved forward to help him and then shifted the bag under the chair. The porter stepped back, flashing a disapproving glare at Maggie. She ignored him, dropping onto the cushion, grateful, but now unwilling to look the injured man in the eye. Her survival depended on this seat.

* * *

What had he done? The boy's problem wasn't Jared's. The intruder looked healthy. Let him solve his dilemma on his own. Why did Jared assume any responsibility?

The smooth-faced, stocky young man sat staring down at his lap. The man—no, boy—wore fresh, clean cotton pants and long-sleeved shirt. He seemed a worn-out, nervous wreck, probably his first trip from home, purchasing new clothes for his adventure. Jared gave the new arrival a brief nod. Even that small movement of his head brought added pain.

A mistake. Jared should never have given the boy his second seat. If he was going to survive this miserable journey, he'd soon have to find the freight car with Brutus and once again hope for relief on the floor. He turned his attention back out the window.

The engine labored to the top of Sherman Pass, 8,242 feet. No railroad in the world traveled at such a lofty elevation. Ahead, great coal and iron fields stretched between Carbon and Evanston. And then the long train would move into the giant bowl holding the Great Salt Lake. Even through his medicated haze, Jared found his education connecting him to a world he wished to escape.

Blurred brown was the dominant color, the wide-open, barren landscape a fitting companion to his desolate mood. He glanced again at the boy. Worn leather boots peeked out from the baggy cuffs of his tan pants. A medium-brimmed cowboy hat worn low and wire-rimmed glasses almost hid dark brown eyes. The depth and beauty of those eyes startled Jared. The boy pulled a large, heavy volume from his valise, *The Mill on the Floss*. Not expected reading material for a callow youngster. In fact, probably the most boring book of the nineteenth century. The young man seemed to struggle to keep those intelligent eyes focused.

"Try this," Jared mumbled through swollen lips, surprising himself with his unsolicited offer. He reached down and picked up *The Time Machine*. "Might be a little more interesting."

Jared handed the new leather volume to the youngster. The boy reached out and accepted the book. Hands as smooth as the face, fingers long and shapely didn't match the body. This child had avoided hard labor. Spoiled? Privileged? Did he have a father like Morgan who had undisclosed plans for this boy's future?

A wave of nausea interrupted his thoughts. He fought back dizziness and the metallic taste of bile. Jared couldn't endure the discomfort from his sitting position. He rose and struggled down the aisle toward the freight car. Time to check out Brutus. Focus on his dog. Don't pass out. Frightening that an animal and the cold, unforgiving freight-car floor promised his best option for survival.

CHAPTER TWELVE

M aggie watched the slow-motion stumble of the injured man. Where was he going? He hesitated at the Pullman-car door, then pushed out of sight. The dining car was in the opposite direction. Only the freight car and locomotive were at that end of the train. Strange. Then unexpected guilt pricked.

She shouldn't have taken his extra seat. She had added to his discomfort. Silly to compare this moment of guilt with the killing of a man, accidental and deserving as the death may have been. Still, she had to do whatever it took to escape.

The goal had to be to keep to herself, hold conversation to a minimum and blend into the background. The last thing needed was any personal entanglements. Stay calm and concentrate. She put down *The Mill on the Floss* and opened the stranger's offering. Less than two paragraphs of *The Time Machine* proved the story to be more interesting than George Eliot. The magical tale swallowed her whole.

She looked up from the book, surprised that she'd reached page fifty. Several hours must have passed. The stranger hadn't returned. For once, minutes weren't crawling as slowly as sap down a tree. But where was the battered man? It shouldn't matter. None of her business and an unnecessary interruption to her plan of maintaining anonymity. She had enough to worry about.

Then discomfort from her growling stomach demanded attention. Only four in the afternoon. Maggie would be early for supper, but fewer passengers would be eating. The less people the safer. She headed to the dining car.

She grabbed a discarded copy of yesterday's *Omaha Tribune* at the small end table inside the door of the dining carriage. The banner headline with its accompanying drawing of a woman slapped her in the face. Damn. The murder of the Minnesota farmer was front-page news. At least the crude drawing was a poor likeness of her face. A white-hot knot in her stomach killed her appetite. But she had to eat something. She sat down at the nearest table.

"What can I get for you, young man?" Maggie jumped at the sound of the purser's voice.

"Well," she stuttered. Maybe she could keep simple food down. "Chicken soup and bread would be fine, thank you."

Her clenched fist held the newspaper. She didn't have the willpower to read beyond the headline. Instead, she stared trancelike out the window at the desolate, burnt-dry landscape until her order arrived. But the dry dough of the bread stuck to her mouth. A sip of soup fared better. The heat of the liquid eased the cramps in her stomach.

Maggie scanned the dining car. Only one couple sat three tables away. She took several deep breaths and turned back to the bowl. She lifted the spoon to her lips, and to her relief, the liquid continued to slide down her throat. Then two men burst into the dining car in animated conversation, and her next serving spilled from the spoon. A family of four—father, mother, daughter and small son—followed soon after. She had once belonged to a happy family like this. Now she huddled alone in her seat, a hunted criminal. The unexpected melancholy caught her by surprise.

Now a steady flow of hungry passengers entered, filling up the dining car. None looked like Hawk Face. He couldn't be among the passengers. Hadn't he been left at Cheyenne? Curiosity overcame her trepidation. She opened the newspaper and scanned the page.

Swen Nadar, one of the wealthiest landholders in the Midwest, had been murdered by one Maggie Saunders, a prostitute working at the Prairie Flower brothel. Poor man died with his pants around his knees—a lie. Money stolen. The woman a ruthless killer. Long auburn hair, large brown eyes, olive complexion, full figure. Dangerous. The Nadar family offered the unheard of reward of $1,000. She threw the paper on the table beside her. Anyone could start a new life in these times with that large a stake. My God, couldn't she purchase a hotel for that amount of money?

Now what? Such an enormous reward would attract every policeman and bounty hunter in the country. Again the snake of panic coiled in her stomach. Did she have a prayer of reaching California? She shuddered, thinking of the cruel-faced stranger left in Cheyenne. Would San Francisco be far enough from Hawk Face's search? And what of the threat of all the other pursuers whipped to a frenzy by the size of the reward?

Maggie stared out the window. More barren terrain. The bleakness outside mirrored her state of mind. How long could she keep up this act? A hand on her shoulder sent a stab of fear through her body. Maggie jumped in her seat, the soupspoon spilling its contents again.

"Young man," an elderly gentleman said. "You finished with the paper?"

She answered with a disjointed grunt. Maggie handed the damning newspaper to the gentleman, tilting her head toward the window. He settled in a seat across the aisle. She kept glancing at him, scrutinizing his face as he read. Could he or anyone connect her to the story? No, not if her disguise worked.

* * *

The soup had cooled. The bread was as appetizing as a lump of coal. Maggie felt exposed at the table. Every unknown face became a threat, danger growing everywhere. The longer she sat, the more the poor excuse for nourishment took on a menacing aspect. She stood, shoulders slumped, hat brim level with her eyes, ready to make her way out of the dining car.

"You hear what happened to that farmer Nadar?" she overheard an older man say. "Killed in St. Louis by a whore. Can't trust them hookers."

"I don't know," his companion said. "Met as many decent sporting women as straight ones."

"You're kidding yourself," his friend retorted. "One thing you can be sure about, all whores hate men."

She'd had enough. Maggie escaped the crowded dining car and made an unsteady return to her seat. The injured man still hadn't returned. Her seat was safe.

What had happened to the man? His hands had been as swollen and bruised as his face. Was he a boxer? If so, he couldn't be that good. More likely he'd been assaulted and fought back to protect himself. And he had sacrificed his seat to her. She felt drawn by his kindness. Then another thought calmed the turmoil of her stomach.

What if she helped him? He was severely injured. He could hardly walk down the train's swaying aisle. If he was going to San Francisco, Maggie would be his crutch, carry his bag, and arrange transportation to wherever he was headed. He could provide perfect cover disembarking the train. The idea had promise. First, where was he? Maggie rose and walked toward the front of the train.

Only one car separated her from the engine. What if he wasn't headed to San Francisco? What if he recognized her from the newspaper? No, he seemed far too injured to care much about anything. She entered the freight car. Shadows shrouded the boxes and luggage piled high. Several small windows near the ceiling offered muted light. Her potential benefactor lay sprawled on his back by a large wooden container.

Something moved in the crate. A small brown bear. No, a dog. One of the young man's hands grasped the wooden slats, the animal's nose pushed close to the fingers. A rumble and loud clicking sound arose from the cage. Maggie stopped, startled. She had to get closer to the immobile body. Then, with care, she lowered herself to her knees.

"Hello, boy," she said in a soft, comforting voice to the dog, and waited for a response.

The dog's eyes followed her every move. She expected a growl, a whine, some action. Instead, the animal reacted only with a light clicking of his teeth. She put her palm on the man's forehead. His flesh was aflame. The poor man was unconscious. The dog shifted his body, yet kept his nose by the man's hand and made no aggressive moves. Maggie gained confidence.

The animal's bulk seemed too large for the crate. His owner could provide little care. How long had the poor dog been caged? She was trapped just like this imprisoned dog. Compassion tinged with anger made an unexpected appearance. Still, the animal could be dangerous.

The man groaned. She turned from the dog. The young man might look vulnerable now. But when he recovered, would he be no different than every other male son of a bitch? But the boy wouldn't be a threat for some time. This was her last chance to avoid getting involved. But didn't his potential usefulness overcome any potential risk?

Again her attention shifted to the cage. Almost two more days locked up if their destination was San Francisco. She couldn't do much about her own dangerous predicament, but she could help the dog. She turned toward the front of the freight car. A pile of tools sat in a corner. Maggie grabbed a large claw hammer and returned to the crate.

"You're not going to make me regret this, are you?" Maggie whispered to the brown-haired mutt.

No answer from the prisoner. Maggie applied the hammer to the end of the box. She pried the side off. The clicking of teeth increased. The animal rose on unsteady feet. A pause, and then the dog stepped from its cell. It looked even larger and fiercer free from its constraints. Maggie froze. The dog glanced her way, then scrambled over luggage and boxes into a corner of the car and squatted. A laugh burst from her lips like a jailbreak. When was the last time she'd found any humor in her life? Too bad for the unfortunate porter who discovered the pile of shit deposited by the dog.

The animal returned to his prone master and lay beside him, panting. Both owner and dog could use some water, as well as a cool, wet towel for the injured boy. First, she needed to confirm his destination. Her fingers searched his breast pocket and found his ticket. Headed for San Francisco. Thank God. She gave a tentative pat to the massive head of the dog, then rose and walked back toward the dining car. Tension and panic eased a notch. Yes, this just might work.

CHAPTER THIRTEEN

The rhythmic clacking of the train's steel wheels had lulled Maggie into a semicomatose state. The consistency of the sounds and vibrations created an aura of security she hadn't felt since her escape from St. Louis. Her body nestled into a pocket within bundles of freight and mail sacks. The small windows created a restful, permanent twilight. If only this dreamlike journey to San Francisco could continue forever.

The train slowed, then stopped with a sharp jerk. Maggie's eyes flew open. Panic brought instant awakening. The freight car moved in jolts and shakes like some monster playing with a toy. Was she already in San Francisco? A chill raced through her body. A chill? Refreshing air filled the freight car. A surge of energy accompanied the recognition of long-missed goose bumps.

The injured young man lay in a fetal position on the floor. Half-lidded eyes gave no sign of awareness. The large dog remained passive beside him, now freed from the cage, nose still pressed as close to his owner as possible.

Another delightful shiver shook her. Lord, how long had crushing heat been her unwelcome companion? Strange rocking motions became more apparent as she stood. What the hell was happening? She climbed over the young man and hurried to the freight car door. She stepped out onto the apron connecting with the first Pullman.

Cold drafts swirled around her. They were on a boat, a ferry. Must be the last leg of her journey. The cars had been separated into two parts. A third rail sat unused between the two lines of Pullmans. She'd had no idea the train didn't roll into the city uninterrupted.

Passengers strolled along the empty space. Large wooden barriers blocked any view of what had to be San Francisco Bay. Too many passengers. And no way to escape if Hawk Face or other authorities discovered her. All the old paranoia and fear flooded her thoughts. Here she was on the edge of the continent, and she couldn't see a damn thing. The motion beneath her feet increased. Only the frigid air kept her from total alarm.

What would be the best way off the train once it reached its final destination? Should she use the boy as a shield? What about the dog? Could it become vicious? The best plan would be to forget the dog and the boy and sneak off the train with as little attention as possible.

One thing was for sure. She hadn't traveled over 1,500 miles to arrive in San Francisco trapped in a box. Maggie leaned around the edge of the car on the side facing the wooden wall. A metal ladder gave access to the roof. She stood on the edge of the apron, reached around and grabbed the iron crossbar. Her body swung onto the frame, feet searching for the security of a ladder rung. Her hands tightened on the bar, uncomfortable images returned of her near-death experience jumping on the moving train back in St. Paul. But this train wasn't moving, and no one chased her. Her foot gained purchase, and Maggie swallowed her fear. Just calm down.

The ladder led to the top of the freight car. In her attempt to stand, she was driven off balance by a powerful blast of wind. She hit the steel roof, banging both knees and scraping one palm. On hands and knees she looked over the edge of the wooden wall of the ferry.

Shades of gray surrounded her. San Francisco Bay stretched beneath her in roiling white caps. Billowing fog and clouds filled the sky. A rugged thumb of an island rose from the rough waters before her. Several miles away beyond the island protruding skyward, San Francisco glowered a frigid welcome. Steep hills and mountains ridged the shoreline back to the north, a monochromatic outline no friendlier than the hilly city. And directly to her right, the fabled Golden Gate opened the door to the Pacific Ocean and the Far East.

The smell of the saltwater saturated the air. Invigorating, freezing temperatures awakened her entire body to tingling sensations. Soon the once refreshing chills and shivers evolved into teeth-chattering discomfort. Light clothing provided little protection, but warm clothes would solve that problem. Would that all her new challenges be so easily met. Wind whipped at her shirt, threatening to tear away her buttons. How could such uncomfortable cold fill her with hope and giddiness?

She crawled back to the ladder, the only safe way to retreat. She worked down the rungs and swung back onto the apron. Even more passengers ambled along the ferry. Maggie slunk back inside the murky freight car. Decision time.

The young man stirred on the floor. Maggie knelt beside him, offered some water from the cup wedged into nearby luggage. The boy accepted her help, more liquid dripping down his chin than his throat. God, he was so helpless and pathetic. How was he going to get off the train and find shelter and medical care? He might provide cover, but he'd also be a royal pain in the ass. And his wild-looking dog? What the hell was she supposed to do with that creature?

The young man watched her with eyes veiled in pain. He raised a hand to grip his dog's side. The animal licked his fingers. Low rumbling sounds emerged from the huge kinky-haired body. At least she'd had the presence of mind to drag both her own and the injured man's luggage into the freight car. And they both traveled with only one bag, but the boy's weighed a ton. Must be his books.

"Do you have any money?" Maggie asked.

The young man patted his waist. A money belt? She opened the buttons of his shirt and lifted the flaps of the belt. She didn't have to count the coins. There was more money than she expected. She wouldn't have to invade her own much larger stash for him. Still the conundrum—dump him or use him. She couldn't leave him like this. Was it her conscience or necessity that drove her to help the damaged man?

"What about your dog?"

"He'll be fine," the boy whispered. "He'll stay with me."

Sweat broke out on his forehead from the effort of only a few words and despite the bracing air now filling the freight car.

"All right," Maggie said. "I'll get you to the closest hospital."

"No," he cried out. Concern warped his damaged features. He tried to rise. "Won't let Brutus in a hospital. Hotel. Doctor."

His efforts sucked him dry. He collapsed back into a fetal position. Damn. She would need help loading him into a wagon. Asking for aid could bring unwanted attention. Or turn the focus to the boy and his dog. Her fingers tapped her lips.

"I'll pay," he murmured. "Use my money. Please."

Money meant nothing. Safety was the issue. Still, her pursuers would be looking for a single lady, not a boy attending to a seriously injured friend. And who bothered to look at humble caregivers? Guilt and practicality blended. Get the boy to a quality hotel where she could arrange medical care. Let them make the decision to get him to a hospital and deal with the dog from which he refused to be separated. She'd be safely hidden within the city.

CHAPTER FOURTEEN

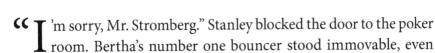

"I'm sorry, Mr. Stromberg." Stanley blocked the door to the poker room. Bertha's number one bouncer stood immovable, even bigger than Bertha. No fat, all muscle.

Had Alex overplayed his hand? If Alex was no longer welcome at Bertha's, word would quickly circulate through the parlor-house circuit. Without these card-game winnings, how could he afford the lifestyle he now lived?

"But, Stanley."

"Bertha gave strict instructions," the huge man said, leaving no alternative for Alex.

He'd been warned about siphoning cash from potential customers. If they lost everything at poker, nothing would be left for liquor and women, the high-margin profit items of Bertha Kane's parlor house. Alex couldn't say he was shocked. And where was the good Madam? Alex felt rather than heard the woman's approach. The hallway rattled with each of the massive Madam's steps, despite thick carpeting and fabric-covered walls. He turned and faced Bertha. She wasn't smiling.

"Alex," Bertha said. "Let me buy you a drink."

The offer provided no comfort. Was this the prelude to ejection? He followed her toward the parlor room. Instead of entering, the wide woman veered into her office. Alex had never entered Bertha's headquarters. He expected elaborate decor similar to the poker and parlor rooms, but the sparse furnishings—sturdy oak desk and faded leather swivel chair, two worn burgundy wing seats, one-shelved sidebar—caught him by surprise.

Her large hand motioned for him to close the door and sit down. She moved to the small sidebar and offered him a drink. He chose whiskey, no reason to keep a clear head now. And no way in hell would he again sit the supplicant in a goddamn chair—green or any other color. Didn't seem to bother Bertha that he stood. She offered him his drink at eye level.

"I like you, Alex." Her hard stare gave away little emotion. But the scowl distorting the lower third of her jowl-encased face left no questions. She poured herself a double. "Unfortunately, you're bad for business."

Bertha ran the largest and probably most successful high-class whorehouse in the city. She hadn't achieved this pinnacle of success through kindness. She protected her business with as much tenacity as a mother wolf.

"I've explained this situation before," she said. "It now appears that you also have a problem with your temper. Bad enough taking my clients' money. But I certainly wouldn't have many customers left if you beat one of them to death."

"Bertha," Alex said, keeping his voice calmer than he felt. "It was an accident. Self-defense."

"That doesn't make the gentleman any less dead."

"Be honest." Alex fought back an immediate flare of anger. He had to control his temper if there was to be any hope of salvaging his welcome at the brothel. "You don't give a damn about that. It's strictly a business decision."

"You're right." Bertha's lips parted in a grin showing mangled teeth better left hidden. "I've always liked you. You're a businessman just like me. So I'll cut the bull." She tilted her head and drained the large whiskey, her triple chins jiggling with the motion. "You're welcome to partake in our specialties. Just no more poker."

Alex thought of Gaye. That woman could make him hard even while he stared at this obese, bulldog-faced bitch—a testament to the redhead's powerful allure. He needed Gaye. Or someone like her. But this lady just put a hole in his supplementary livelihood. How would he afford Gaye in the future?

"Okay, Bertha," Alex said. "I understand. Since you think I'm dangerous and such a great poker player that I'm a threat to your customers, why not stake me in a high-roller game near the Coast? Split the winnings fifty-fifty."

Bertha's mouth opened wide with guffaws that turned to chuckles, then coughing. She regained her breath, but her fat face was gray and sad.

"You got balls. If I didn't hate all men, I'd make a move on you, cutey. But I'm going to have to pass."

A firm rap on the door cut the conversation short. The door opened. Stanley filled the doorway.

"Got a live one, Miss Bertha," Stanley said from the doorway.

"Excuse me, Alex. Gotta get to work." She shifted her body with a ponderous effort and thumped out of the office. Her voice gained volume. "Company, girls."

Alex swallowed the remainder of his drink and fought back surging frustration. Now what? His options were disappearing. Goddamn his father. Would he never let go? Yes, his old man had survived fires, earthquakes, cyclical oversupply and bankruptcy. But the world had finally passed Mordecai by. Now his stubbornness and conservatism would drag Alex down with him. And Alex would run out of opportunities long before Mordecai departed this world.

Time to find Gaye.

* * *

A black maid opened the ornate front door of Bertha's and escorted Maggie into an oversized parlor room. Elaborate-detailed Persian carpets, burgundy-flocked wallpaper, paintings of full-bodied Rubenesque nudes, velvet couches and divans, and heavily gilded chairs and tables filled the large room. A brand-new self-playing piano plunked out a cheerful tune. She had expected a fashionable establishment, perhaps a notch above the Prairie Flower. But the grandeur of this interior was pure opulence.

"Well, well. What have we here?" A monstrous woman clothed in an acre of cotton greeted Maggie with a self-pleased smile. "How can we help you?"

The huge lady considered Maggie with an unconcealed expression of doubt. Had to be the Madam, Bertha Kahn. Maggie was speechless. A good thing, the fewer words the better.

"Look, laddie." The Madam's curves threatened the seams of her clothing. "This isn't a cheap establishment. Only the best, and it costs the most. You got the wherewithal to partake?"

At least her disguise fooled the glint-eyed Madam. Now on to her critical mission—find Gaye. The former headliner of the Prairie Flower had been Maggie's one-time friend and protector. Her high-spirited co-worker had been the only person she could trust. The only person she now felt she could turn to.

Then Maggie saw Gaye approaching from the bottom of the stairs. Red hair and high energy radiated around Gaye Fitzsimmons. The lady stood out from the group of painted working women. Maggie, hat low over her eyes, pointed at Gaye without a word.

"You picked the best." The Madam placed a huge arm over Maggie's shoulders and whispered, "You got twenty dollars?"

Twenty dollars? Such an exorbitant price. Twenty dollars would have bought the company of a woman for an entire evening at the Prairie Flower. Maggie nodded hiding her shock.

"Good," Bertha said, a note of surprise laced her comment. "Got to buy Gaye a couple of drinks first. She performs best when she's happy. Excuse me now, young man. I've got some business to attend to."

The Madam winked at Gaye and lumbered down an adjacent hallway. Gaye motioned Maggie to a bar tended by a tall, elegant black man dressed in coat and tails. The irony of Maggie posing as a nervous youngster, probably a virgin, almost brought a smile to her lips. How many times had she been in Gaye's position?

"Buy me some champagne," Gaye ordered, "and I'll put some hair on that sweet, smooth chin of yours."

Maggie nodded, keeping her face averted. This was not the place to be recognized by Gaye. The barman produced champagne and two fluted crystal goblets. He opened the bottle with a flourish.

"Five dollars, please."

Again the price gave her a start. She fumbled in her pocket and pulled out a shiny new $5 gold Liberty coin, then turned to Gaye and lifted the crystal to her lips. Gaye drained her glass and so did a nervous Maggie.

The redhead had a questioning look on her face. Did she recognize Maggie? Maggie snatched the bottle and moved toward the stairs to the upper floors.

"Horny little fella, aren't you?" Gaye said and giggled. "Okay, let's go. It's your money."

Gaye led her to an upstairs room, grabbed Maggie's wrist, pulled her in, and shut the door. Gaye hung onto Maggie's hand, running her fingers over soft, unblemished flesh. Maggie jerked her hand away.

"Nice hands," Gaye said.

The woman moved closer and pulled off Maggie's hat, exposing chopped hair still untouched by a proper barber. Maggie could no longer hide her identity. Gaye's mouth dropped open. Then she let out a squeal.

"Maggie!" Gaye wrapped her arms around Maggie in a crushing hug, smothering her face with wet kisses. "My lord," Gaye gasped. "Are the stories true?"

* * *

Maggie told her of the farmer's two visits, his death, her escape through Minneapolis and Cheyenne, the reward, even about the battered young man she'd used to avoid detection upon arriving in San Francisco. Everything, except the amount in the farmer's pouch.

"Gaye, I'm so glad I've found you," Maggie said, still on her feet, hands gripping Gaye's thin arms. "I'm not sure where to turn. Will you help me?"

"I don't know, Maggie." Gaye's eyes sparkled with mischief. "I could retire with that one-thousand-dollar reward. Very tempting. Hell, Billy the Kid was only worth half that." She pursed her lips, serious thoughts playing across her gorgeous features. Then Gaye giggled. "But I just couldn't live with myself."

Gaye pulled Maggie to her, placing a firm kiss on her mouth. Gaye's lips lingered on Maggie's, the redhead's tongue flicking between Maggie's lips. The kiss grew passionate. Maggie pulled away, shocked. Then Gaye's fingers caressed Maggie's cheeks with a tenderness not at all unpleasant. Maggie had heard rumors of women, especially whores, drawn to the softer, sensual allure of their own sex—but Gaye? She had always been affectionate.

"Why don't you work here?" Gaye asked, a hoarseness deepening her normal light, lilting voice. "I've really missed you. We could perform two on ones. We'd make a fortune. And we'd enjoy it."

Heat built within Maggie. An arousing, prickling sensation enveloped her body, generating confusing emotions. She looked into Gaye's bright eyes, now filling with moisture. Tears? Or passion? Maggie trembled, then shuddered. Men had never generated an emotion like this. Could Gaye provide more than friendship? But Maggie didn't want this distraction. She was searching for a companion—a business partner—who would help her build a new life. A safe life far from the degradation and dangers of prostitution.

"I can't," Maggie said. Thickness clogged her words. "First place they'll look will be the high-class houses. There's not much disguise available in a parlor house. And other than you, damn little loyalty among whores."

"True," Gaye answered, taking a step back. "But you'd have better success hiding in a whorehouse than me. All they'd have to do is check out my pussy to find the real me."

With a languorous movement, Gaye lifted her nightgown above her pubic area, exposing the same bright red hair as on her head. Maggie again felt a strange allure. She tore her eyes away and wiped a thin film of sweat from her forehead. This expensive champagne must have more kick than the watered-down slop in St. Louis.

"Now, if I was married," Gaye said, a lewd smile on her lips, "my husband wouldn't be one of those poor, horny slobs. You should hear my poor customers' pathetic tales. Their respectable wives are such prudes they take baths without removing their petticoats. One poor sex-starved soul admitted his wife had given birth to three children and neither he nor the doctor had ever seen her undressed. Sad, isn't it?"

Gaye laughed and dropped her gown. Was Maggie expecting too much from her friend? Whatever pull Gaye exerted only complicated matters. Did Gaye have any concept of a future, or was she only chained to the moment?

"If you're not interested in working at Bertha's or another parlor house, forget it," Gaye said. "It's all downhill from here to absolutely disgusting dead falls and cribs where women are used up and spit out like garbage. At least Bertha will take care of you. She's not the easiest to deal with, but she hates men."

Maggie could understand those feelings. It had been easy to block out any warmth or emotion with customers after what her father had done to her. Customers served one purpose: survival. And now, maybe deliverance.

"Let's leave town," Maggie said, a familiar thought solidifying. "I have enough to open our own place. We can go anywhere. Prostitution might provide secure profits for the Madam but not the poor whores like us working for wages. We would treat the women better and with more respect. Protect them from monsters like the farmer that assaulted me. If we took care of the girls, they'd, in turn, take better care of the customers. Gaye, we couldn't sink any deeper into sin as a Madam than as a working whore."

"Jesus, Maggie," Gaye said, an incredulous expression twisting her pixyish face. "Where'd you get all these crazy ideas? There's plenty of money to be made without such fancy plans."

"We could charge more," Maggie answered with growing frustration, "and deal with less trouble with our own operation. Once we generated enough capital, we'd open a classy boarding house or hotel and get out of the whoring business altogether. That's how we'd gain security and control."

"Where?" Gaye asked, hands on her hips like she was dealing with a small child. "Should we head to Bolivia like those robbers Butch Cassidy and the Sundance Kid?"

Why was Gaye toying with her? Maggie had the means, education and desire to free Gaye from a dead-end existence. She offered her friend a way out. And Gaye's physical magnetism perplexed her even more. Had her distaste of men drawn her naturally to her own sex? Gaye was certainly more sensual and compassionate, more alluring than her smelly, prickly customers.

"No," Gaye said, twirling in a full circle. "I think I'll stay at Bertha's. I've got a few good years left. What do you think?"

Gaye again closed the distance to Maggie. Maggie held up both hands to stop her, but Gaye's extended fingers caressed Maggie's breast. Even through the thick fabric Maggie felt a sharp jolt. She pushed away.

"I'll be in touch," Maggie said as she retreated to the door.

"What about my twenty dollars?" Gaye asked. "I've got to give two-thirds to Bertha. But if you like, I'll take it in trade."

Money and Madams. Some things would never change. Maggie crammed her hand into her pocket and pulled out two $10 dollar gold coins. Bertha would be all over Gaye, demanding payment. What better example could there be to break free of the brothel?

"I was just kidding," Gaye said, but Maggie wasn't so sure.

The redhead took a rare step backwards. But her eyes remained fixed on the money. Maggie forced the heavy gold into her hand. Gaye's fingers clamped down on the coins.

"I'll be back, Gaye," Maggie said. "Come with me before something terrible happens to you, like it did me. I'll figure out a place to go."

Maggie edged out the door, disappointed. Gaye followed, pinching Maggie's behind and giggling. Had Maggie made a mistake placing so much trust in her friend? The thudding sound of boots on carpeted stairs caught Maggie's attention. A man approached from below, taking two steps at a time. Tall, handsome, piercing eyes. His proud bearing held a degree of aggression. He focused on Gaye.

"I've been waiting for you," the man said, annoyance evident by his tight lips.

"Well, Alex," Gaye said, grabbing his arm and turning her back to Maggie. "I'm ready now."

Alex placed his hand over Gaye's as they ascended the last few stairs, exhibiting a courtliness despite his impatience. His eyes reflected excitement and energy. This man displayed a different attitude than any customer Maggie had serviced. Her spontaneous attraction to the man came as a relief, answering some of the disturbing questions Gaye's actions had aroused. For a brief, irrational moment she wished her disguise hadn't been good enough to fool him.

CHAPTER FIFTEEN

Bells. Constant ringing. Also a cool touch on Jared's cheeks and exposed hands. Almost a smell but not quite definable. Then comforting wetness on his fingers. Brutus's prodding nose. Hell or heaven? Wasn't there a boy? At least his dog remained with him.

Now he felt the intrusion of pain. Rough hands raising his head. Warm fluid forced between his lips. Liquid flowing down his throat. Swallowing. Like an evil demon, a choking cough—excruciating pain ripping through the surrounding shield. Terrifying. How could he live with such unimaginable agony?

The last spoonful brought a bitter taste. Then the curtain again descended, heavy but gentle. Forcing out the bells, the breeze, Brutus, the pain, memories of his family, Jared's torturous journey west and the depressing collapse of society.

* * *

Force-fed fluids became soups with unknown flavors. He waited for his feedings with anticipation, just had to swallow with care. An uncomfortable stab in his side even with miniscule movements, made him freeze in shock. Then too, the sounds. Always clanging, ringing bells. And a chill, gentle wind that kissed him and gave him hope. Also Brutus. Always Brutus. Wet nose and tongue, a welcome connection.

"A young man brought you here." A harsh female voice answered a question that somehow had passed through his lips. "Got you set up, then left."

What young man? The boy on the train? Jared remembered the boy's eyes. Deep brown, almond-shaped. He had given up his seat to him. Those eyes didn't belong on a boy. Who did they belong to?

"Who was he?"

"The boy?" she answered. "Don't know. Didn't say."

"But where am I?"

"You're at the Leemont Hotel. Nicest place in town."

"Money? My money?"

"Safe. Safe as money can be. The boy took nothing."

First the boy. Now this woman. Who was she? What did she look like? But the curtain was falling. Find out another time. Another day.

* * *

What kind of place was this? Jared's eyes focused in the muted light of morning. Or was it afternoon? Walls covered with red velvet. Ornate drapes. Ceiling painted with gold leaf. A plush chair and matching chaise also in red material. Big room. Someone in the room. The woman? The fleeting memory of a name. Gertrude.

He eased his head to the side and caught sight of a wizened lady. She sat reading a book, her body buried deep into the arms of the large, elegant chair. A clumsy craftsman had taken a grown woman and whittled her down to half-size. Effort had been spent etching deep creases and gouges on a pale, lifeless face. No way to determine her age. Whatever force created such a visage had been without pity.

"Excuse me," he murmured.

"Yes?" she said, glancing up at him.

"No more drugs. Please."

* * *

Ragged images and comforting darkness had kept him in a cocoon of mixed dreams. Now sounds of the city seduced him back to reality. Why did he even want to return to the real world? Maybe the drugs were good. No, medicine had shut down his system, drug-induced darkness fueled depression.

Today his mind and body approached familiar territory as long as he kept activity to a minimum. Fifteen days, Gertrude had told him, of drifting within a sharp-edged tide of sensations. Two weeks flat on his back. Finally an urge to move. Clarity came with a price.

"You better this morning?" Gertrude asked. Her curt tone of voice seemed to have changed from previous days. Her truculence had faded into tolerance.

This woman, Gertrude, had been by his side from the beginning. Days before he could focus on her face, he'd felt her forceful hands, kind at times, but also producing sharp discomfort—a nurse. She hadn't deserved any of his anger and disrespect. And she'd made no response to his rudeness. She must have been forged under the pressure of abuse. Embarrassment warmed his face.

"Yes, thanks." Jared's words sounded hollow, an echo of what he used to be—a grateful and polite son, a future minister of God.

Then the click of Brutus's teeth. Jared shifted. The Airedale rose from his spot by the door, stretched and stepped to the bed. Jared felt the dog's rough, wet tongue. His eyes filled—an unbidden, uncontrollable wave of gratitude and vulnerability.

"What about Brutus?" Jared asked.

"What about him?"

"How does he get out to do his business?" How had he done his own "business," helpless in bed? Another embarrassing thought. "He's never been in a city. Wouldn't know how to take care of himself."

"Had no trouble I know about. 'Cept for the first time."

"First time?"

"Went to the front entrance and barked. Started tearing the door apart when nobody opened it for him. You gonna have to pay for the damage."

"He okay now?" Jared moved his hand to the dog's massive, kinky-haired head.

"He gets what he wants. Comes and goes as he pleases. Eats in the kitchen." Gertrude glanced at the Airedale. Her rough expression softened. "Cleared the damn rats out in a couple of days. Don't ask for much. Takes care of himself."

A faint tone of respect laced her last comment. The first deviation from her normal flat delivery. He again considered the care required of a man incapacitated for two weeks. Heat again flooded his face.

Brutus stirred, drifted back to the door, but remained standing. Jared levered onto an elbow. A stab in his ribcage tempered his urge to rise. How long before he could free himself from the prison of this bed?

"You ain't quite ready to move about," Gertrude said.

"Can you get me a map of the city?"

"Why?" Gertrude said.

"Need to get the lay of the land. Find some decent routes to run."

"Run? Hell, you can't even walk. And this city's nothing but steep hills and too many people."

Steep hills? What kind of city was this? Not that it mattered. It would be a while before he would be strong enough to explore the surrounding streets and neighborhoods, let alone run again. But at one point he would have his strength back. And he needed to focus on something positive to occupy his mind.

"Tell me about San Francisco," Jared asked.

"I ain't a damn tour guide." Gertrude bent over her book. The black cover was embossed with gold lettering. A Bible. "I'm a nurse."

Jared could still hear the embarrassing echo of his past groans and complaints. How rude had he been? Still he craved information. He'd traveled through hell, or at least purgatory. And his progress across the country had been shrouded by pain and depression. He hungered for information about San Francisco, the western edge of the continent.

"I'm sorry if I've been disrespectful, Gertrude. Not the perfect patient. I apologize."

Jared turned his head toward the nurse. She looked back at him. Faint color brought limited life to her features. Had his apology meant anything to her? Maybe rare that anyone considered her feelings.

"You gotta be careful in this devil's playground," she said. "More places you shouldn't go than should. It's a mean, nasty city. Full of dreams turned to nightmares."

"Can't be worse than back East." Jared could only hope.

"Stay away from the Barbary Coast, Chinatown and the waterfront," Gertrude continued. "Boy like you wandering down Pacific Street wouldn't last two blocks. Best thing could happen you'd be mugged and robbed. Leave you buck naked. Worst thing, shanghaied."

"Shanghaied?"

"Kidnapped and dragged to some Far East heathen hellhole for a couple of years."

"Can't Brutus protect me?" he asked.

"Hell. They'd club your dog to death. Sell him to the damn Chinamen. Those bastards eat dog. Assuming there's any meat under all that fur."

Jared flinched at the woman's foul language. Ladies didn't cuss. And neither did gentlemen. But this was a new land, new times.

"Little hoodlums roam around the Barbary area," Gertrude continued. "They're young, but they can create grown-up grief. You best be healthier than you are now 'fore you test the waters of this foul place."

He couldn't quite believe her vivid descriptions of gangs of youths terrorizing the downtown area. Nothing could be as painful and depressing as his past. San Francisco couldn't be that bad. Not after what he'd witnessed on the East Coast. And additional unpleasant thoughts of Ohio and family jumbled Gertrude's tales of apocalypse.

CHAPTER SIXTEEN

Finally. Jared stood with Brutus at the entrance to the Leemont Hotel on California Street. A bracing wind blew off the bay, bringing a confusing chill. This was June, wasn't it? The month always brought miserable heat and humidity, whether in Ohio or New England. But this was a new world with a new, heartening climate. Still, refreshing as the crisp air might be in June, what must this place be like in January?

A multitude of grays layered the city from the swirling mist to the waters of the bay at the foot of California Street. To his left, tracks and brightly painted cable cars filled the avenue that dropped toward the water. Buildings and congestion clogged the roadways below him. To his right, California Street soared several blocks, then crested and disappeared beneath looming mansions. A small swarm of pigtailed Chinamen, all clad in black pajamas, hovered at the mouth of Grant Street a half block below.

More activity could be seen down the steep drop of California Street. Jared turned in that direction. One jarring step on the sloping sidewalk brought back painful reminders of his unhealed injuries. Would he ever run again? Then the bustling activity and excitement of a new city swept away his discomfort.

Brutus dodged into an alley. His erect tail evidenced familiarity with this new territory. Curiosity prodded Jared to catch up. His dog had found a comfort level with the alien but stimulating surroundings. Now he too could finally explore this new world.

Within two blocks, buildings rose in height, making the wide street feel narrow. Horse-drawn carts and carriages competed with clanging cable cars. Constant wind supplied an unending source of energy and crispness. Well-dressed gentlemen, more Chinamen, laborers, craftsmen and merchants filled the sidewalks, all headed with purpose toward unknown destinations. The relative calm that had surrounded the Leemont Hotel became spinning activity.

A woman's occasional smile or greeting toward Jared, or more probably Brutus, shocked him. Such friendliness. Elaborate dresses and outrageous hats in colorful and contrasting fabrics reflected the difference between East and West. These ladies possessed an allure and openness that contrasted with the stiff, stodgy, stone-cold aloofness of women in the East. Jared walked forward in amazement.

He turned left on Kearny. Brutus drifted closer to his side. The stores and office buildings were really not that different from back East. But a different atmosphere of expectation hung around many of the bustling men and women. Jared also caught glimpses of a familiar world of poverty and despair partially hidden in alleys and doorways.

Four blocks down Kearny, on the other side of Jackson, the atmosphere changed. Jared sensed an invisible border. He had entered a tawdry, more edgy area of the city. Dirt and grime dominated the sidewalks and streets. Increasing pain and the return of a feverish headache added to his dislocation. But curiosity again overcame his doubt and discomfort.

Bars named The Cave, Dolphin Club, Galloping Cow, St. Charles, crowded an avenue with a mosaic of stains covering its worn cobblestones. Large, new-fangled neon signs lined the streets. Their intricate designs seemed dead in the gray afternoon but like vampires, ready to come to life in darkness. A new smell of stale beer and human waste filled his nose. The parade of respectable citizens melted into a motley assortment of drunks, bums, harlots and rough thugs.

Jared glanced up at the street signs on the corner—Kearny and Pacific. Women lined doorways, their gaudy silhouettes frayed and shabby in the filtered light. If this was what sex was all about, he could do without it. Perhaps the life of a celibate cleric had merit.

A disreputable character with a top hat towed two stumbling sailors. Action moved in slow motion, a disgusting array of the flotsam and jetsam of humanity suffering from a massive hangover. The two sheep being led to slaughter disappeared into the uninviting maw of the Golden Eagle, the scene a caricature of evil.

A conflicting stink—raw sewage and sickly sweet perfume—tainted the air. A cacophony of ominous sounds accompanied the stench. Dim echoes of drunken laughter, curses and music from every conceivable instrument provided a muted preview of evening to come. Gertrude's warnings made a belated appearance. Jared had blundered into the frightening and disgusting world of the Barbary Coast.

A ragged, scarred bear was chained to the entrance of a deadfall bar appropriately named The Bear. Brutus froze. All aggression had been beaten from the pathetic animal, but Brutus had enough. The Airedale refused to move further into the hellhole of filthy sidewalks and dark alleys. Jared stopped.

A pack of ragtag boys emerged from a narrow, garbage-filled lane signed Dead Man's Alley. Their loud curses tormented two miserable, bloated prostitutes in scraggly outfits and an advanced state of drunkenness. A low growl from Brutus prodded Jared to turn back toward the hotel, sanity and safety.

Too late. The hoodlums' feral faces lifted, seemed to catch the scent of his vulnerability. One shoved the whores aside, and the gang swept toward him. Alarms rang. Jared needed to make a speedy exit, but his weakened condition made the attempt futile. Stabbing sensations in his side and growing weariness slowed him to a fast shuffle. The threatening group of toughs closed.

Proximity exposed various-sized punks dressed in a wild assortment of outfits, the common denominators—foul mouths, filthy faces and depraved eyes. A few feet ahead lay the world of the civilized and security. Might as well be miles. Jared released a sigh of fearful resignation.

The pack's taunting grew louder. The largest man-child, wearing a crimson-sashed woman's hat, plucked at Jared's jacket. Pressure from a club digging into Jared's back pushed him forward. The circle tightened. Trapped. Jared had little strength to fight back. But Brutus tensed at Jared's side.

A roar erupted from the mass of brown curly hair. The Airedale whirled into action with pavement-shaking barks and snarls. The dog snapped at legs and arms, ripping garments. Screams and curses met his charge. A frantic dance of legs and wildly swinging arms erupted, ruffians scrambling to escape the flashing teeth.

Brutus continued to drive the boys back toward the alley as if they were balky lambs. The sound of their retreat faded into the thick, pungent air. The abrupt absence of danger kept Jared rooted in his tracks. Then Brutus trotted back to a protective spot by Jared's left knee. A sickening sensation settled onto Jared. Could San Francisco be even more evil than the East?

CHAPTER SEVENTEEN

T he dealer, attired with eyeshade, arm garters and large moustache, wasted no time between hands. The house pulled its table-time tithe from each pot. The more hands dealt, the more take for the Empire. Alex followed each move. So far so good. Maybe the dangers of these big-dollar poker games were overblown. But there was still that slick-looking gambler to Alex's right. Over the last two hours Alex had developed a somewhat guarded comfort level in the Empire's high-stakes backroom poker parlor.

"You in?" the dealer asked.

Yes, he was. He tossed in $20 worth of chips, which included a $10 raise. Alex certainly felt more secure now than when he first had entered the raucous music hall-casino. It helped that he had exchanged his normal dress attire for rough seaman's clothing. He'd been frisked before entering the back room, but the bouncer had failed to detect the hidden derringer in his sleeve. Wouldn't this be a perfect time to dump the retail prison of Stromberg's for the life of a professional gambler?

Alex surveyed the up cards, then the expressions of the remaining two players still in the hand. The old, gnarly sea captain folded, but the slick gambler to his right met the raise. Alex had parlayed his $50 initial buy-in to over $250, depending on the outcome of his current hand. But anything too good to be true wasn't, and he waited with wary anticipation for trouble to surface.

The gambler wore a dark suit, vest and beaver-skin top hat. His lean, clean-shaven hard face seemed almost ascetic. In another life the hustler could have played the role of a fire-and-brimstone preacher. But his stone-faced expression was inconsistent with any offerings of salvation.

The dealer flipped the last card of the seven-card stud game face down to Alex and the gambler. Alex peeked at the last card. Nothing of value. Three tens would have to suffice. The gambler displayed a possible diamond flush. The man checked his hidden seventh card and flashed a quick glance across the table at a rough-looking thug who was down to his last $30 in chips. Did Alex catch a nod between the two men? They hadn't said a word to each other since Alex's entrance into the game.

Alex, with two tens showing, opened the betting with two $5 chips. Three tens would be a great hand, and Alex was on a roll. But three of a kind would be crushed by a flush. He couldn't get too aggressive. To Alex's surprise, the gambler folded.

"Cards comin' your way, ain't they?" the rough character said from across the felt-topped table.

Alex nodded, scooped up his winnings and leaned back into his spindle-backed chair. Little conversation and no camaraderie. Every man for himself.

The small poker parlor reeked of flat beer, stale smoke and the usual odor of nervous men playing for keeps. When he first sat at the table he'd ordered a whiskey—breaking one of his cardinal rules. But he couldn't afford shaky hands.

The game appeared civilized, the six men facing him at the table not much different from the suckers he had fleeced at Bertha's. Except for the gambler and the thuggish brute, who neared the end of his funds. Winning seemed too easy.

The door to the Empire's ballroom opened. The sound of chaotic, screaming activity accompanied the entry of the lanky body of Jim Sizemore, the angry stranger from Bertha's. Alex was not surprised.

"You're a little late," Alex said, directing a skeptical look at the new arrival. "No room at the table now."

"There's plenty of time," Sizemore said in a tone of sarcasm and satisfaction. "Won't be long before a seat opens up."

Alex nodded at Sizemore to keep things civil, then returned his concentration to the game. Sizemore found a spot against the wall, eyes focused on Alex. Was the man sent in as a distraction? Maybe. But it didn't matter now. The cards were falling his way. Had he finally made it to the big time?

After taking yet another large pot, Alex lost three close hands in a row. Was this somehow Sizemore's doing? Then Alex won a small amount when everyone folded by the fourth card. Not much, but what the hell, winning was winning.

The gambler kept pulling out his shiny, gold pocket watch. Each time he would flip it open, twist the watch around as if he had trouble reading the time, then put the large timepiece back in his vest pocket. Why was he having so much trouble remembering the time?

Within half an hour Alex had given back $100. Cards were fickle, but something else smelled. He was being worked. He glanced at Sizemore, expressionless, leaning against the wall. Still up $100, the time had come to depart. He surveyed the small room—a tiny, boarded-up window and a worn, chipped door leading to a back alley. He needed to know if the door to the alley provided a possible escape.

"I've gotta take a piss," he said and stood. "I'll just go out in the alley."

Alex left his chips on the table to keep everyone calm. No one objected. He took the few steps to the door. Not locked. He stepped into the dark filth of the alleyway. The rotten stench of fish overpowered all competing smells. Alex gagged as he opened his fly. Welcome light shone at both ends of the garbage-strewn street. He should just walk away. But he needed the $150 still on the table.

He returned to the room and noticed several photographs hanging on the wall. Pictures of cheap-looking women and the Empire's main room filled to capacity. Then, from the reflection off one of the corners of the framed pictures, he saw a small narrow mirror angled over his shoulders. At his cards. His suspicions had been correct. So was the whole table in on the scam? Or only the gambler and the scruffy man sitting opposite him? What about the dealer? He had been the one who had directed Alex where to sit. Why had they let him win at all? Sizemore's presence became more ominous.

Once again cards sailed across the table. He couldn't pull out of this hand soon enough. Didn't like the odds. No longer comfortable with the cast of characters. And he had to be careful of the damn mirror, hanging like a hungry vulture behind his shoulder. Last hand for sure. But he wanted, needed, the earnings he'd worked so hard for. If he hadn't been so absorbed in winning, he might not have ignored all the warning signs.

The beat of his heart brought a quiver to his fingers. He lifted the corners of the two down cards he'd just been dealt—a queen of spades and ten of clubs. The up card was the nine of hearts. Alex bet, and no one dropped out. Another card—jack of spades. One card from a straight with three chances to fill it. Again no one folded, and the pot grew. The fifth and sixth cards, a deuce and a five, were worthless.

The stack of chips continued to swell, but none of the other players' exposed hands showed much promise. Why was everyone still in the game? Granted, he couldn't see the other players down cards, but he had a potential straight. And of the possible kings or eights that could fill that straight, only the king of clubs showed on the table.

Sparks of light reflected off the pile of chips. The pot looked huge. Rare for all six players to remain in the game with only one card left. Alex had committed $70, his biggest bet of the night. He checked his tablemates, all expressionless. Something felt wrong. Something was wrong. What?

The last cards flew from the dealer's hands. Alex peeked at his, careful to lift a corner for only a moment. He also kept an eye on the table. Several players didn't check their final card, including the rough one. A king gave him a straight. But warning signs flashed through his mind. Far too late to fold.

A small, squirrelly-looking man had the high hand showing. He raised a paltry $5. But by the time it was Alex's turn, $20 was required to stay in. Tension tightened his back, his stomach turning taut, heat building. Alex didn't raise, just called and threw in $20.

The tough fellow smiled for the first time. He flicked in his money and flipped up his three down cards. All aces to go with the ace he'd been dealt face up.

"Four aces. Looks like you're a loser," he said. His crooked smile showed broken teeth.

That was enough for Alex. He didn't know how his fellow gamblers controlled the game, but no question that he was trapped. He was in way over his head. He needed to bail out. Now

"I'd like to cash out," Alex said.

"Not yet," the gambler on his right said. "You've got some chips left. Lady Luck's a bitch, and she flops around like a cheap whore. Hang in there."

"I'm done," Alex insisted, fighting back a tremor creeping into his voice.

"What's the matter?" the rough one snarled. "You think we're cheatin' you just 'cause you lost a few hands?"

Did they want more than his money? Alex shook his wrist, making sure his small pistol was free of fabric. Sizemore remained against the wall. He wiped his mouth with his sleeve in a predatory gesture. New animation reflected on his gaunt features.

Alex swept the faces of the other players. Bright eyes betrayed increased interest in the proceedings. And again the questions. Were they all in this together? Did they want more than his money?

"You leavin'?" the ruffian said. The man rose from his chair, pulling a large revolver from his waistband. "Don't think so. You're headed for a nice long boat ride."

Alex pushed his chair back. But instead of standing, he dropped to his knees. He snapped the derringer from its leather restraint. The tiny weapon dropped neatly into his hand. A silent prayer of thanks registered within the flash of motion. All his practice had paid off.

The thug's wicked-looking revolver arced back down toward Alex's face. The barrel looked the size of the Broadway trolley tunnel. Alex had no time to aim. His small caliber pistol made a surprising loud crack.

The bullet smacked into the crook's throat. The man dropped his gun on the green felt table, scattering cards and chips. Both hands flew to his neck. Blood flowed as if by magic from between his fingers. The tough collapsed, body glancing off the heavy wooden poker table, hitting the floor gagging.

Alex gave brief thanks for his lucky shot. He couldn't believe so much damage could come from such a small shell. Could he have killed yet another man? Still, this would be his one and only chance to save himself. Only one shot left in what now felt like a puny weapon. He had to make his escape fast.

"Nobody move," Alex cried.

The surrounding men scrambled to their feet and stepped back from the table. The large .45 lay seductively on the green felt. Alex needed that added firepower. The gambler twisted his body away from Alex, hand reaching inside his coat. Alex pointed his small pistol at the gambler's temple.

"You move, you die," Alex said.

"You got only one shot," the gambler said, but his hand emerged empty from his coat. "You can't stop us all now, can you?"

"Only plan to stop you."

So damn many of them. And why hadn't anyone entered from the music hall? Had the muted roar of the customers muffled the noise of the derringer? But hands moved toward hidden weapons.

Alex lunged for the large weapon on the poker table. Fingers snatched the gun. He leveled both barrels at the hovering players. The heavy pistol provided a hell of a lot more comfort. He dropped the tiny derringer into a coat pocket. Still he had little chance against six men. All they had to do was rush him together.

"Everyone against the wall," Alex said, "next to my good friend, Mr. Sizemore."

The carved wooden cigar box that held the buy-in gold sat on the edge of the card table. The wounded man made loud, ominous gurgling sounds from the floor. The man's struggles distracted his companions, buying a few more precious seconds. But time had almost run out.

Alex fired two shots into the wall, inches above the players' heads. The men jerked back against the wall. He reached into the case and snatched a handful of money. Then thought, *Screw it,* and seized the entire container.

The exit was only steps away. Alex crashed open the door with his shoulder, whirled and triggered one more reverberating bullet into the wall. This shot rang louder against the silence of the players. Then the door to the Empire's main room burst open. Too late. His feet flew over the rough cobblestone alley. Fear propelled him down the fetid passage. The dim light at the end of the lane promised safety. That was all he needed.

CHAPTER EIGHTEEN

J ared turned left on the relative flats of Stockton Street. He cursed his plodding pace. Damn his slow-healing body, and damn brother Tom and the rest of his cold-hearted family. Unfamiliar foul words flowed from him, shocking his senses. Quite a transformation from the pious, naïve expressions of a Yale divinity student. He never dreamed he'd be accusing God of a lack of benevolence and an abundance of imperfections.

Dim street lamps exposed less of the depressing elements of San Francisco and not as much traffic and commotion. But even in the darkness of evening, he could glimpse huddled bodies littering doorways and alley mouths.

Jared shuddered. His previous visit to the disgusting hellhole of the Barbary Coast remained vivid in his mind. But he was safe here, keeping a one-block buffer from the degradation and violence. The rhythmic breathing of Brutus close to his side provided additional security. Thank God for the dog. Frustration tormented him as much as his injuries.

But pounding downhill proved more than his tender ribs and jaw could handle. Too many hills in this city. Long, slow jogs would have to suffice. Jared struggled against his limitations. He needed some plan of action. If he could regain strength, maybe he could address this overpowering depression. Or would even physical recovery be able to combat the pervasive, spiritual emptiness of his soul? At least the cold weather with constant waves of gray fog provided energy. Only at night could he find a degree of peace.

But the blackness also hid dangers. Brutus could hold his own, but not Jared. He would have to stay close to the Airedale. No place in this rough-and-tumble city for a semicripple. Dependent on his dog—a pathetic situation at best. He needed more time to heal before he could defend himself.

Boisterous shouts and off-key music floated from nearby bars, dancehalls, and the deadfalls of Hell's colony on earth. Brutus halted, ears up. Jared stopped beside him. A tall blur of a man burst from the shadows of an alley, loud obscenities and cries not far behind.

The man ran past, desperate eyes locking on Jared. His workman's clothes looked incongruous against a handsome, clean-shaven face. The stranger hesitated, then made a sharp turn into another alley twenty feet farther up the street. As he disappeared back into shadow, a mob of seven or eight disreputable-looking ruffians emerged in hot pursuit.

"You see anyone running by?" a bearded, wild-eyed rogue screamed at Jared.

"Yes," Jared said. Then he made a split-second decision. He wouldn't be party to helping this rough-looking crowd find its victim. "He's a couple of blocks ahead of you. Just turned up Green."

"Let's go," the bearded leader shouted and led his unruly swarm down Stockton to Green. But three of the men stopped, one so out of breath he had no choice.

"Tough-looking dog," a scar-faced marauder said.

Brutus maintained his wary stance. Jared smelled trouble. What had Gertrude said about the danger to dogs? Food for the Chinamen? He again swore at his feeble state.

"We'll buy him," another of the men said. "Big money in dog fights. Looks like it could hold his own in the pit."

"Not for sale," Jared said. His helpless condition lent a tremble to his voice. These thugs had to smell his weakness.

"Buy him, hell," someone in the group snarled. "Let's just take the mutt."

More threats, and no way out. A tremor gripped Jared. Brutus stiffened, tail sticking straight behind. The familiar light rhythmic clicks of the Airedale's teeth now turned to solid, steel-trap snaps. Brutus's neck extended like the head of a spear. Lord, not another battle where he couldn't defend himself.

Two of the men lunged for Brutus, a blade glimmered in one's hand. The other attacker, the winded one, closed on Jared. The previous rumble of the dog blossomed into bloodthirsty snarls. A leaping bear-shaped image was the last he saw of Brutus. Jared had his own problems.

Jared lurched into a stumbling dodge to avoid his assailant. Every shift brought a stabbing, painful jolt. His body wouldn't perform. But he could at least move to avoid a wild punch. Fortunately, the thief threw useless roundhouses. Then screams of pain and terror echoed against the brick walls. Jared's attacker hesitated and turned toward the ruckus.

Jared looked over the man's shoulder. The other two thugs were in rapid retreat back to their holes in the Barbary Coast, the dog at their heels. Beams from the dim street lamps reflected off the bloody face of one. Jared's adversary turned and frowned at him, then scrambled after his fleeing associates.

Brutus stopped, tail down, watching the retreating men. The third tough approached Brutus. He veered toward the Airedale. Brutus shifted his hindquarters and tucked his head to the side. The fool performed a sloppy pivot and kicked at Brutus. The dog shoved back, using his butt as a massive club. The thief bounced away, stumbled and hit the ground. Brutus roared as he dove on top, ripping at ankles and legs. Fabric, blood and tissue filled the air. Jared blanched at the dog's viciousness.

"Brutus!" He ran to the flailing victim. "Stop!"

Jared grabbed Brutus with both hands. The Airedale shook him off like a flea. But the dog let up and stood above his now helpless victim. His terrorizing snarl slid back down to a rumble.

Then Brutus whirled to face an alley twenty feet away, back on full alert. Jared could see nothing but had no doubt of new dangers. The dog crept several steps from the writhing crook. Once again his body braced, his neck an aggressive ramrod. A figure emerged from the shadows, hands raised. The same man the mob had been chasing.

"You saved my rear end," the stranger said.

"Put your hands to your side." Jared gazed at the man, thankful for Brutus's protecting presence, lowering his own voice. "My dog would be more comfortable."

Had Jared helped a criminal escape? Was this tall man, dressed in rough waterfront clothing, just a higher level of slime? Certainly he was a different variety than the mob that had chased him.

"I'm Alex Stromberg. Tell your dog I'm a good guy."

"You tell him," Jared said. "He makes up his own mind."

Brutus took another step, placing himself between Jared and Stromberg. The Airedale relaxed the massive muscles of his neck. His tail dropped into wariness. No longer in attack mode. Watchful, fifteen feet from the stranger. Jared was surprised by his dog's acceptance of the new arrival.

"Those men wanted more than money," Stromberg said, pointing at Brutus's crumpled, bleeding victim. Emotion brought more volume to the man's voice, no longer the cool customer. "The bastards had planned to shanghai me."

The memory of brother Tom's sucker punch reappeared. Jared remained silent. Suspicious. Then he had a question.

"Why didn't you help us?" Jared asked.

"Two reasons," Alex said, a smile softening his features. "First, your dog finished the fight before it started. Second, those boys deserved what they got."

Who was this man materializing from the dark alley? Jared's mind dictated caution, but Brutus's acceptance contradicted the possible threat. The stranger spoke with a degree of cultivation inconsistent with his seaman's clothing.

"That animal's performance was an amazing sight." A small smile drifted across his lips. "But the others will be back. Here's my card. I owe you. Now leave. I'll figure out what to do with our injured friend."

Jared met Alex halfway, Brutus shadowed. Alex stuck his hand out, ignoring the dog. Jared hesitated and then grasped the man's hand and the card in its palm. Brutus remained alert, seeming to accept the stranger. But the Airedale matched the movement of Alex's rapid glances, both searching the surroundings for additional danger. Enough. Once again slapped with a vivid reminder of his vulnerability. Jared wanted to get as far from this violence as possible.

* * *

Jared headed down Stockton and turned up Union Street at a fast walk. The attack had erased fatigue. Adrenaline had overcome much of his pain. But his mind whirled with uncomfortable thoughts. San Francisco, New York, Philadelphia, all cities stunk with the depravity of mankind, to say nothing of his own consistent and considerable failures.

He'd now traveled as far west as the country allowed. Here also wealth was being strangled out of the common worker into the bloodied hands of the robber barons and their political hacks. This distant end of the North American continent was consumed by the same misery and exploitation as the East. Maybe worse. Merchant, banker, accountant, lawyer—all were futile professions mired under the manipulation of the rich. No occupation seemed desirable, certainly not religion or education.

What would he do? He had no idea. Where could he find a new world, a utopian society not yet infected by greed, hatred and fear? This world sickened him. He glanced down at the dog. Brutus rewarded Jared with a snarl-like smile, lifting his upper lip, exposing a quantity, size and sharpness of teeth that seemed more appropriate in a prehistoric man-eater. The long hair surrounding the dog's mouth stuck in clots, wet and matted from blood and saliva. And the Airedale frightened him.

Then Jared noticed drops hitting the street below Brutus. He moved closer, touched the animal, weaving long, gentle fingers through the thick coat. An ugly, ragged wound sliced the dog's shoulder. And Brutus favored his left front leg, a limp becoming evident. Wounds could explain the Airedale's ferocious behavior. Or perhaps the violent actions of the assailants had brought out Brutus's true nature. Either way, a new, almost intimidating respect swept through Jared. He led his only friend up the murky avenue. The wound needed attention.

* * *

Alex waited for his benefactors to disappear. Nerves twitched, feet itched to run, but he had to wait. That mutt had been mythical. He didn't know why the dog accepted him. Couldn't animals smell evil? Alex didn't believe he was wicked, but unfortunate things kept happening to him. An example lay at his feet. He recognized the dog's victim. Time for a short conversation with Mr. Sizemore. Alex needed some answers.

"Well, well," Alex said. "Mr. Sizemore, I do believe. You're more than just a gambler, aren't you? Long ways from Bertha's now."

The assailant huddled in a fetal position, clutching his ankles. Blood pooled around him, flowing enough to give birth to a small stream, moving in a crooked path between the cobblestones. The man only whimpered. Alex examined the shredded tendons and muscles in one leg, white bone sparkling through the damage.

"You're never going to walk normal again," Alex said with little sympathy. "Fact is, now that I look more careful, you're going to bleed to death anyway."

"Damn you to hell, Stromberg. Snyder will get your ass. Send you to hell where you belong."

Isaac's handiwork. That chicken-shit bastard. If someone had to die at Tadich's, it should have been that fat slob. But why the elaborate poker game? Why not have a mob of hired killers mug him from behind? Alex pulled out the heavy .45 he'd appropriated at the Empire. Too many questions.

"I don't think you're giving me the whole story, Mr. Sizemore," Alex said, pointing the gun at the man's forehead.

The injured man spit at Alex, then grabbed the barrel of the revolver. But the blood and gore on his fingers couldn't control the gun. His hand twisted without purchase. Alex jerked back, and the .45 roared to life. Sizemore slammed back to the wet cobblestones, a bullet between his eyes. Shit. Alex hadn't meant that to happen.

His eyes swept the surrounding street and alley. Still no one in sight. He no longer had a future in San Francisco. Snyder knew everything about him: where he lived, where he worked, played. Wouldn't take long to figure this out and find Alex. Time to leave the city. Goddamn Mordecai. If not for the old man's eternal stubbornness and selfishness, Alex would be safe in Seattle. He tucked the gun in his belt and took off in a fast trot.

CHAPTER NINETEEN

The familiar hum of activity drifted through the open door from the selling floor. The stack of inventory sheets before Alex demanded attention, but inventory was the last thing on his mind. He couldn't run a retail business hiding in the back room. What the hell was he doing here like a prisoner in his small office under the stairs of Stromberg Mercantile?

Alex was a marked man. How could he escape the reach of Isaac Snyder in San Francisco? That well-financed porker could hire an army to finish the job. Packing a Colt in Stromberg's would sure as hell cause questions. But he kept the loaded revolver close at hand in the stockroom. Maybe he should march over to the Great Western Auction House and strangle the nasty bastard. Another claim of self-defense. Ridiculous thoughts. Alex snarled at his own impotence.

An explosion of cries prompted him to peek around his stack of merchandise out the door. From the opening of his office he could see the selling floor. A shabby dockworker stood at the store's entrance.

"Gold! Gold in Alaska," the man yelled, puffed up with rare importance. "Tons of gold. Bunch of miners on the boat *Excelsior* got millions in gold."

Alex jerked to attention. Gold in some godforsaken wilderness of Alaska could be a wished-for miracle. The miracle that might save his ass. He snatched his coat and strode out of his office.

"Max," he called to his uncle, "cover the floor."

At the front door he stopped, then turned back to the stockroom. His precipitous actions of the previous evening had created a new world of jeopardy and peril. He had to remain vigilant at all times. He tucked his dearly earned .45 into his waistband, then ran out to the street.

A flow of excited men and women carried him down Montgomery Street toward the waterfront. Every representative of the San Francisco community, from top-hatted gentlemen to ragged laborers, hurried to join the crowd. Alex slowed his pace, checked each face, searched for possible threats. Any one of them could be hired by Isaac to put a bullet through his head. He cut right at Greenwich, shedding the current of frantic humanity still rushing toward the docks.

The *Excelsior*. Alex remembered receiving several shipments of furs from the well-traveled ship that now docked at the foot of Beach and Dupont. Rumors of gold from a distant river valley called the Yukon had circulated for weeks. Few had paid attention, but Alex had. The news had fueled bitter disappointment. A northern bonanza would explode upon the West Coast. Seattle had been the perfect location to capitalize on the predictable gold rush. Damn Mordecai. So insecure. So afraid of his own shadow.

Alex avoided the piers and headed straight to the offices of the Alaska Commercial Company on Battery. A constant roar drifted from the *Excelsior*'s berth. Alex ducked into the trading company's office. No clerks, no customers. Deserted. The counter was vacant, and Alex prepared to wait. Movement on the second floor sounded above him. He turned from the counter and catapulted upstairs. Louis Sloss, Alaska's president, sat behind a battered desk, puffing a cigar the size of a banana.

"Morning, Alex." The businessman's wiry, silver-gray beard merged with the cigar smoke, thick as the bay's impenetrable fog. "Why aren't you stampeding down to the *Excelsior* with the rest of the idiot cattle?"

Alex hesitated. Stromberg's was a valued customer, using Alaska's aging fleet for furs, fish and building materials. Why was the old man filled with such bitter sarcasm? The discovery of gold would allow Sloss to triple, quadruple, the price of passenger and freight traffic.

"I want to book passage and freight space on your next boat north." This time Alex would be the one shipping product, and Alaska would be the destination.

"Alex, my boy," Louis said, a sad frown developing beneath the forest of hair and smoke. "Thought you were a little sharper than the rest of them sheep. Not going to be enough gold in all of Alaska to satisfy the crush of fools that'll be heading north. And the ones that do make it to the Klondike are going to starve to death."

Damn. Another old man blind to the opportunities available. Sloss and Mordecai were two withered peas in a pod. Both could only see the glass half-empty.

"I've been telling anyone who'd listen about William Ogilvie's Yukon Survey Report," the ship owner said, bitterness creeping into his words. "The place is so damn isolated it takes months for news to travel from the interior. Every valuable claim's been staked since last summer."

"I'm not going for the gold in the ground," Alex said with a smile. "I want to pull the gold out of the pockets of that mob of fools. Prospectors need equipment and provisions. I'm going to open a branch of Stromberg's at the end of the Lynn Canal."

"How'd you know the Lynn Canal's the gateway to the Yukon?"

"I've been studying the geography for some time," Alex said. "What with the discoveries from Circle City to Juneau, I knew it'd only be a matter of time. Question is specifically where should I set up shop?"

"Two choices," Louis said. "Dyea or Skagway. Dyea's at the foot of the Chilkoot Pass—shortest route into the Yukon Territory. John Healy's already got an established trading post there. Problem is the difficulty of unloading goods. A thirty-foot tide creates havoc. Lots of sand bars blocking any landings."

"What about Skagway?" Alex asked, dancing from foot to foot with growing excitement.

"Better choice," Sloss said, nodding with approval. "An associate of mine, a tough old coot, Captain James Moore, has staked out a town site and runs a sawmill. Building a wharf across the tidal flats near the mouth of the Skagway River."

"How well do you know the area?" Alex asked, grasping for every piece of information he could get.

"It's rugged country," Louis replied, a skeptical expression pursing his lips. "The Captain discovered another trail over the coastal mountains into the Yukon Territory. Called it the White Pass. Longer than the Chilkoot but, according to Moore, easier to travel. He's been waiting for the mother lode just like you."

Doors slammed. Voices rang out loud and aggressive. Activity had returned downstairs. Sloss remained motionless, ignoring the commotion below. Alex didn't share the old man's calm. Anxiety tightened his chest.

"I want on that first boat, Louis." Alex lowered his voice. He had to control his impatience. So much at stake. "I need two or three bunks and as much cargo space as you can give me."

"The *Al-Ki* is scheduled for St. Michaels in six days," Louis said, his face twisting into an ironic smile. "I believe we'll be changing the destination to the Lynn Canal."

All the days and months spent developing the model inventory for Stromberg's in Seattle hadn't been wasted. Bypassing Portland, Seattle and Vancouver to open a location in Alaska required only a few adjustments to his inventory model. Those thoughts and calculations might have once appeared to be wishful thinking. But not now. He would not pass up this incredible opportunity to escape.

* * *

Jared stood on a crate above the waterfront crowd. His height gave him a birds-eye view of the tumultuous dynamics surrounding the *Excelsior*. The whirlpool of movement below him brought dizziness, and he struggled to stay upright. The rapid current of people stoked his uneasiness and naked vulnerability. He wanted Brutus with him, but his dog remained at the rooming house, immobilized by twenty stitches.

A swirl of cries and comments rose from the mass of humanity, blending into an unintelligible roar. "Gold from Alaska" was one phrase that rose above the noise. The names Yukon and Klondike also flew through the air. The excited throng waited with growing expectation for the new Alaska millionaires to disembark.

The *Excelsior*, stubby and rusted, with one black smokestack and two masts, looked unimpressive. The vessel certainly didn't resemble a treasure ship. A roar erupted from the crazed mob. Activity on deck. The newly rich hovered on the ship preparing to journey down the gangplank. The raucous throng below roiled in a threatening wave, eager to swallow the disoriented prospectors. A mixture of excitement, compassion and hope swelled within him.

The passengers disembarking didn't look like wealthy men. Their clothes were tattered and soiled. Broad-brimmed miners' hats couldn't hide faces blackened by the Yukon sun. But each grizzled and unshaven Argonaut staggered under loads of gold carried in every imaginable manner, from bulging suitcases to fruit jars and coffee tins. The arrivals, stereotypes of rugged miners, all had one thing in common—eyes bright with the fire of life. Unexpected envy swept Jared.

No privileged aristocrats or capitalist tycoons in this group. No question these men and the several women among them had scrapped and clawed for their gold. These people had struggled against all odds, shaken off the bondage of a depressed economy, had overcome the monopolies and tyranny of the times. This was the Common Man trooping down into the anxious crowd of curious, excited onlookers. The wealth these miners carried off the ancient *Excelsior* wasn't only gold, but also optimism. Positive emotion returned, sweeping over Jared, his lungs filled, his heart beat with a long-absent energy.

What was Alaska? The Klondike? The Yukon? Every man for himself. No boundaries. A new life untouched by the stifling structure of the country's economic rulers. Alaska could be his utopia. A powerful hunger for information pierced him.

He dropped from his place on the crate. Questions flew from his lips toward anyone who might respond. The array of contradictory information confused him. He'd heard enough. He needed facts. The library downtown would provide answers. He used his arms to protect his ribs as people glanced against him. The occasional blow that evaded his defenses couldn't wipe the smile off his face.

* * *

Once again Alex stood before Mordecai. This time Alex wouldn't back down. No more questions, no more doubts. Mordecai couldn't use reason to argue away the discovery of gold and the imminent stampede. And he wouldn't sit in that damn green chair. But why did Alex have to fight for the obvious?

And he had to leave San Francisco without telling the old man of his life-threatening predicament. He'd killed Sizemore, another accident, but another death that left blood on his hands. And the gambler at the Empire? Another killing in self-defense? Jesus. Three deaths in a matter of days. His life was spiraling out of control. All the more reason to take advantage of this chance to flee the city.

"Your inventory demands will clean out Stromberg's," Mordecai said.

No argument on whether to open in Alaska. No question about Alex leaving. Mordecai had capitulated with one statement. Alex relaxed for the first time. Didn't matter why his father had given in. And he wasn't going to ask any questions.

"It'll be much eaiser to restock here than up north," Alex said. "And the markup we'll get in Skagway will finance all the inventory we'll need in both locations."

"We'll have to borrow in the short term." Mordecai spit out the words as if poisonous. "I don't like placing us in that kind of danger."

Didn't his father realize this great opportunity? The veil shrouding the depressed economy of San Francisco, Seattle, the entire West Coast, and perhaps the nation, was about to be lifted. Just look at the space Alex had booked. Already those tickets could now be resold for five times the original price. And only twenty-four hours had passed since the *Excelsior* had landed with its cargo of hope.

Loss of control shriveled his father into a smaller, older man. Finally. Leverage Alex had only dreamt about. One serious question remained. How much would Mordecai commit to this venture?

According to Alex's plan, the initial inventory investment, freight charges and capital for building in Alaska would cost close to $5,000, limited only by the available space on the *Al-Ki*. He laid out his plan for Mordecai. The amount frightened his father. The old man turned grayer than his normal pallor.

"Why can't you be satisfied with the increased volume that will come here to San Francisco?"

"Portland, Seattle and Vancouver," Alex said, attempting to mute the triumph in his voice, "will be the greatest beneficiaries of Klondike gold. If we had opened in Seattle, then we would indeed be in a good position. San Francisco will receive only indirect benefits."

Alex also wanted an agreed-upon credit limit once he arrived in Alaska. If business proved to be as spectacular in Skagway as Alex assumed, he'd sell product in tremendous quantities. He'd already booked freight space for fill-in merchandise with Louis Sloss to be shipped weekly from San Francisco to Alaska. But he didn't want to push his luck with Mordecai. When sales went through the roof, or tent, more probably, even Mordecai would be willing to gamble.

CHAPTER TWENTY

Maggie fought her way through a vibrant, jubilant crowd. San Francisco boiled with excitement, news of the Klondike gold strike as widespread as morning fog. Gaye waited for her at Boudine's restaurant. Maggie stole a glance through the café's large plate-glass window. No one suspicious-looking. She entered and made her way among the crowded tables to her friend. Thank God for Gaye. She needed her, but did she completely trust her?

"Maggie, I'm full of news," Gaye said, then gave a nervous laugh, her fingers flitting over the chipped china place settings.

Maggie had insisted on meeting Gaye at public restaurants. She made a habit of appearing several minutes late for every encounter. Her friend's street attire, though less audacious than her working outfit, still attracted attention. Too much attention. A risk for Maggie, who attempted to be as inconspicuous as possible. But better than another private face-to-face with Gaye. The burning memory of Gaye's touch disturbed Maggie almost as much as the threat of Hawk Face.

"I thought you'd never get here," Gaye burbled, fingernails tapping a manic rhythm on the cloth-covered table.

Gaye's enthusiasm crackled even more than usual. Could this mood be a reflection of the heightened anticipation within the city itself? The *Excelsior*'s arrival yesterday with news of the rusted boat's load of new millionaires had spread like wildfire. A quick sweep of the lunch crowd discovered an animation previously unseen: waiters moving faster, conversations louder, movements quicker, smiles and laughter at every table.

Why couldn't she join in the excitement swirling around her? She straightened in her chair, focusing her attention on Gaye. Strange how full of drama her life had been, struggling every moment for survival or performing at the Prairie Flower. The required intensity of those activities had demanded too much energy, no time for the luxury of mood swings. Now, after weeks of indecision and unsettling fear, her spirits were fading. Maggie had to shake off her growing depression.

"Alex is headed to Alaska," Gaye bubbled. "The Lynn Canal, wherever that is. He's going to open a branch of Stromberg's. Alex says there isn't even a town yet. That man's got bigger balls than a stud bull."

Alex had been a consistent topic during Maggie's several lunches with Gaye. Gaye had told Maggie everything she'd ever need to know about the man and much information she could live without. Most disconcerting was her friend's graphic description of Alex's manhood. Gaye had attributed the Jewish custom of circumcision to explain his thrilling and erotic performances in bed. Maggie's brief encounter with Alex at Bertha's confirmed a certain attraction. But men were nothing but commodities. They stood out only when obnoxious or dangerous. Still, Alex had made a positive impression, incongruous though it may have been, on the stairs of a whorehouse.

But weren't Jews also supposed to be good with money? That's what her father had said in a backhanded way—"hoarded" had been her father's word. She saw value and necessity in hoarding her gold, spending only what was necessary. She knew all too well how difficult it was to make money, let alone save it.

"Maggie," Gaye said breathlessly, bright eyes bouncing through the lunch crowd. "I have a friend I want you to meet, Gardner Taylor. He wants to open a hotel in Sacramento. He's completely trustworthy."

Gaye's nervous laugh burst forth sharp-edged. Why was she so tense and twitchy? And who was this "completely trustworthy" man?

"I told him your parents had died--and that's the truth--and you've inherited a comfortable sum," Gaye said as her body twisted in her chair. "Didn't tell him you were considering a brothel."

Gaye's clutching fingers crept from her teacup in an unending assault on Maggie. Maggie stiffened, withdrew her hands to her lap, and tried to catch Gaye's eyes as they roamed the room. A growing frustration appeared on her friend's face. What was the problem?

"He'd partner with a woman?" Maggie asked.

"He'd partner with the devil. Needs capital. But I'd trust him with my life."

The comment brushed up against Maggie's overstimulated survival instincts. Who could she trust with her life? Gaye? Someone Gaye recommended? Her friend had made it clear she was interested only in the moment. Did Gaye even have the ability to recognize a business opportunity?

"Look, Maggie, you're not going to find the perfect circumstance. Just meet him at your hotel," Gaye said with growing exasperation. "You'll feel the same way about him that I do. Where are you staying now? I know you've been moving around."

Gaye couldn't sit still, petite hands fluttering, an uneasy tightness contracting her lips. Did Maggie's doubt reflect on her face? But she had to trust Gaye. Gaye was all she had. No reason not to tell her good friend where she lived now, but why take any unnecessary risk? She would meet this stranger someplace other than where she currently lived.

"The New Meridian on Post," Maggie said. "You'll be there with him, won't you?"

"No," Gaye said. "I have an early appointment with a regular. I'll send Gardner to your hotel. At four this afternoon. He's short, round, balding. Dresses well. He's your ticket to safety."

* * *

Maggie was already a few minutes late for her meeting with Gaye's potential investor. She'd spent too much time at the display windows of the White House Department Store. The women of San Francisco enjoyed fashion, luxuriated in colors and styles never seen in St. Louis. She had also long ago tired of playing the role of a young man. The act demanded constant vigilance, always on stage, draining her of any spontaneity.

Once her beauty and grace had been assets. Now she sat stifled under a large man's hat and an uncomfortable, ungainly disguise. Gaye was right. Time for Maggie to do something, anything. Opportunities were limited under any circumstance. She'd see what Gardner Taylor was all about.

Maggie increased her pace up Post Street toward Van Ness and her meeting place. She had become a connoisseur of midpriced hotels in the city and had spent a week at the New Meridian. Maggie pushed through the hotel entrance. Excitement flowed through her body at the possibility of finally making some progress. Two steps into the lobby Maggie froze in mid-stride.

A tall, dark figure from her nightmares paced back and forth before the reception desk. Fear erased the smile from her face. She dropped her chin to her chest, hat covering her features. How had he found her? He wore the same black suit. The same sunburned hawklike features. No coincidence could account for his presence in the lobby of the New Meridian.

Maggie spun in an agonizingly slow circle back toward the door. Quick movements would attract attention. Spasms of terror mocked her attempt to appear calm. She stumbled through the entrance, afraid to look back. Her path became a rapid zigzag between pedestrians and vehicles. How had he tracked her down? Who knew she would be here? Her heart pounded, a painful beating that left her winded, her internal organs bruised.

Gaye.

* * *

Gaye had introduced Maggie into the demimonde at the Prairie Flower and taught her the techniques and attitude required to please men. They had become sisters in crime. When Gaye headed west for greener pastures--fatter pocketbooks--Maggie had taken her spot as the star of the St. Louis parlor-house circuit. She had hoped for a new partnership to begin once she found Gaye in San Francisco. Terror resurfaced. Now Gaye had made different plans.

She staggered toward a bench in a small, block-sized park. Uncontrollable tears trailed down her cheeks in the fading light of afternoon. Emotions overwhelmed her, fragile security and exciting plans shattered. She'd held everything together for so long and under such incredible pressure. Was she now doomed? Finally crushed? Well-constructed walls of defense, denial, and delusion crumbled at her feet. The plaza's lush green foliage, folding around her, mocked her soul's dying hopes.

Crippling events of the past years had swirled too fast for her to consider good versus evil. Morality had become subservient to survival. But now the rush of the past crushed the air from her body. Gaye had betrayed her.

But then Maggie had been betrayed at every step. Her father with his precipitous drop into hopelessness, degradation and death. Her mother huddled in a corner of their filthy hovel, never to move again. Madam Davidson turning her back on Maggie after the Minnesota farmer's assault. And Gaye, the only person left Maggie thought she could trust, another tragic disappointment. Completely alone. No one gave a damn about her.

The hard unyielding wood of the bench dug into her back. Cool air washed around her, the return of evening fog as dependable as breathing. She couldn't sit here much longer without attracting unnecessary attention. She had to pull herself together.

She had survived. Options remained open. She had tried to never look back. Never let her past frighten or weaken her resolve. She had battled to justify her every action. She'd had no choice. Morality belonged to the well-fed, those surrounded by family and security. God had deserted her long ago.

Once again she forced back the despairing images of her past and sucked fresh air into her lungs. She still lived. Still had hope. Even possessed most of the gold strapped to her body. She had survived worse.

Her tears dried. Her stomach eased its cramping. She would use her parents as a dire warning to the threat of surrender. She would fight back. One step at a time. The same steel discipline required. What she needed was a new plan.

* * *

Her disguise was worthless. As worthless as her friendship with Gaye. The thousand-dollar reward, months of dehumanizing work in even a high-class San Francisco brothel, must have been too much for Gaye to pass up. Gaye's electric touch had been the caress of the devil. At least Maggie had been sold out for a high price. How far would she have to travel to escape Hawk Face? To the end of the world?

The Klondike.

Every story placed the Yukon Territory at the edge of civilization. Alex Stromberg. He was headed to Alaska. Not in blind pursuit of gold but to establish a business. Miners would need more than supplies. Prospectors wanted lodging and meals—and female companionship. Had Gaye's tongue, loosened with liquor and passion, shared Maggie's secrets with Stromberg?

Rumors told of difficulties obtaining passage north. Cabins were now impossible to purchase. All space had been taken within twenty-four hours. But, according to Gaye, Stromberg had been smart and quick enough to secure tickets. What did she have to offer the merchant? More than money, she guessed. But offering her body would provide no lasting leverage. Maggie would have to play a new game. She'd have to capture Mr. Stromberg's romantic interest without physical touch. She would maintain her independence and mix business with sexual allure.

The idea spun without clear steps. But somehow, some way, she had to manipulate Stromberg into aiding her escape to Alaska. And Hawk Face would be searching for a boy, not a woman.

Maggie would shed her male disguise. She could function better as a woman. The female Maggie had far more tools than a callow boy. If she couldn't connect with Stromberg, perhaps she'd head to South America, Australia or Africa. The emergence of a plan brought a degree of relief, calmed her.

CHAPTER TWENTY-ONE

The Airedale lay on the frayed carpet of the boarding house, a far cry from the luxury of the Leemont. An unusual calm had enveloped the dog as he recovered from the knife wound of two nights ago. But Jared's mind was anything but calm. His library research had filled him with excitement, a positive restlessness as unfamiliar as Brutus's peaceful repose.

"You won't believe what I've learned at the library," Jared said. His fingers twisted the tangled hair of Brutus's head. "Regardless of the rumors and lies, one thing's for sure. Alaska's huge." He jumped to his feet, too excited to sit.

"The Yukon and Klondike," he continued, "cover over 2,000 square miles of frozen wilderness and forests, with one wonderful advantage—empty space. Brutus, Alaska's as large as the Great Plains."

When had Jared first spoken out loud to the Airedale? Probably lying in the dirt of the Monroe farm. Until now he hadn't had a lot to talk about other than to bemoan the sad, corrupt state of society. The dog proved to be an excellent listener. Always attentive, always present. Good thing. Jared had no one else to talk to.

"You should have seen those new millionaires stumbling from the *Excelsior*," Jared said, clapping his hands, the image fresh in his mind. "I was right. Those miners sure weren't privileged aristocrats. They were the salt of the earth. The *Call* and *Chronicle* confirmed my suspicions. Talk about improbable pedigree. Mutts just like you, Brutus. Merchant, blacksmith, laundryman, fruit farmer. There was even a YMCA instructor, a preacher, a teacher and an artist. You should have seen those dreamers struggling down the gang plank. And they weren't weighed down only by gold. They're now burdened with sudden fame they didn't desire."

These miners had originated from Norway, Nova Scotia, Stockholm, Sydney, Seneca Falls, Colorado, and Chicago. Had they come of their free will, searching for new adventure and fortune, or had they also been driven from their homes like him? Jared felt connected to this group of misfits—disillusionment and a need to escape had provided his motivation.

"I'll tell you this, Brutus, they made one critical error. Those rugged, hard-boiled, hard-working miners won't have a chance. They'll be swallowed by the swarm of grifters, grafters and new friends they never knew they had."

Klondike gold. Jared wanted to make a strike. He wanted to discover gold. To succeed. But wealth would be incidental. The promise of clean, vast emptiness could prove a reward greater than riches from the earth. A trembling, positive energy—an emotion long absent—swept over him.

Nervous trepidation also flowed through his system, just like the beginning of the Boston Marathon. No doubt life would be brutal. That was the price of wilderness. A challenge where success was measured by survival. Yes, chaos might reign north to Dawson, but the human void beyond the stampede would be broken only by the crazy, eccentric nomads who, like himself, also wanted to be left alone.

"No laws, Brutus. No need for them."

His hand patted the slight bulge in his shirt's breast pocket—one-way passage to Alaska for man and dog to leave in four weeks. His ribs and Brutus's wound could use the healing period before their voyage. Thank God he'd reacted with uncharacteristic quick action in purchasing his tickets. For once he hadn't procrastinated or been paralyzed by indecision.

Tickets for the next two months' sailing were selling fast and at a growing premium. He'd paid $150, only twice the face value for a cabin on the *Eugene*. They'd be worth ten times that when he set sail in four weeks. He'd been able to squeeze Brutus aboard for another $50. No space for much luggage. He and Brutus would require fewer provisions than others. They'd be moving faster. Jared estimated he'd need an additional $500 for a grubstake.

Jared had wired $500 from the Farmer and Citizen Bank to go with his remaining $185. That still left $250 safe in Ohio. More to be deposited at the conclusion of harvest season in late September, if he was to believe his family. Now he could head into a new life with enough cash for whatever supplies and equipment Alaska would require.

A lightness lifted Jared's spirits to unfamiliar levels. Maybe his plan for the Klondike did belong with his old books of fantasy and fiction. But he'd traveled the rational, measured course of education to discover the truth about this crumbling, corrupt country. Perhaps this move was only a dream, but he was out of options. Energy continued to surge through his body, eager fingers again working Brutus's curls.

"Heal fast," he whispered to his dog. "Time for us to have those runs I promised."

* * *

Maggie stepped into the filtered sunlight, wearing her new feathered hat. The familiar application of makeup opened the door to the reappearance of an old friend—a face most definitely female. A contentment, inconsistent with the unchanged threats of reality, swelled within her proudly displayed bosom. Her image in shop windows added to her confidence. Several men paused to steal a glance, others smiled with an unashamed directness. So why did her knees shake as she set out on her mission?

She moved down Montgomery to the entrance to Stromberg's Mercantile. But she couldn't summon the courage to enter. What would she say to Stromberg? She had given no thought to anything other than her appearance and the unequivocal need to escape Hawk

Face. She didn't know enough about business to even ask intelligent questions. Well, she did have one great asset. Alex Stromberg needed to be bewitched, and that she hoped she could achieve.

She hesitated again at the threshold, then stepped into the bustling general store. Customers swirled around the well-organized merchandise, but no Stromberg. Gaye had said he spent most of his time on the general store's sales floor helping customers. But he was nowhere to be seen. She approached an older gentleman, round, bald and ruddy-faced.

"May I speak with Mr. Alex Stromberg, please?" Maggie said.

"Let me see if he's available," the man said.

The man backed against a stack of shoe boxes, knocking several to the floor. Mounting crimson colored his face with each clumsy movement. His wide-eyed gape confirmed her ability to hold a man's attention. He turned and scuttled through a curtain to a back room.

Alex Stromberg appeared within seconds. His quick, furtive glances toward the storefront evidenced a nervousness that surprised her. Both Gaye's many comments and Maggie's own brief observation at Bertha's had prepared her for a man with total self-confidence, even arrogance. Then he focused on her, and she witnessed again the familiar pull she exerted over men.

Hadn't she played this role hundreds of times at the Prairie Flower? She had forced herself to perform many disgusting and depraved acts; this part should be much easier to perform. Maggie swallowed hard, attempting to control her agitation and discomfort. Focus on the physical attraction she projected. And at this point, the less she said the better.

"My name is Sophia Alverson." She spoke in a voice low enough to require Alex to lean closer. "I have a business proposition you will be interested in."

"Ah." His wide-eyed stare confirmed that, yes, he was interested. "Why don't we step into my office?"

"Certainly."

So far so good. She trailed him through stacks of merchandise reflecting the wide range of products offered by Stromberg's, then into a cramped office beneath the stairs. A blackboard with indecipherable notes and numbers covered the wall behind a small scarred desk. Papers and notices were tacked onto every available surface. Ledgers lay piled on the desk's surface. Sample products littered the floor—everything from two-headed shovels to women's light-blue long underwear.

The tall man moved a pile of material from the chair that faced the desk, but taut nerves and insecurity kept her standing. Stromberg's intense gaze took an unabashed inventory of her. What did he see?

She knew that with the tan undertones to her clear complexion and bottomless brown eyes, she didn't look like his favorite, Gaye—light-skinned and light-hearted. Maggie straightened her broad shoulders, stretching the velveteen fabric across her prominent bosom. Could he imagine the promise of long legs hidden beneath the folds of her expensive dress? Did he think she might be a countess or other royalty or just a well-dressed hooker? No matter. She had his full attention. Time to attempt her plan.

"Miss Alverson. It is Miss, isn't it?" Alex nodded his own answer. "Just what would you be proposing?"

"Alaska," Maggie said, then settled onto the seat in a smooth, graceful motion. "I am planning to open a hotel in Alaska."

"Would your business encompass man's more basic interests?"

Alex spoke with spontaneous suspicion. Maggie understood. Her arrival here in his office, her desire to travel to Alaska to build a hotel, her poise and beauty were the stuff of fairy tales. Both she, and probably Mr. Stromberg, knew fairy tales didn't exist. Especially ones with happy endings.

"Room and board, Mr. Stromberg," she said. Thank God for her olive skin, which hid her embarrassment. "I find your implications rather rude."

Redness traveled from Stromberg's neck to his cheeks. Her quick response had rattled the man. She regained a degree of confidence. But did he suspect who or what she was? Had that treacherous Gaye already told Stromberg about her dear friend Maggie? At least she had had the good sense to change her name.

"I apologize for my crude comment," Alex said.

For the first time a hesitant look clouded the smooth contours of his strong features. She allowed the thin suggestion of a smile to flit across her full lips. How long had it been since a woman or man had left Mr. Stromberg speechless? She gave him her best seductive smile. Let him recognize that she possessed intelligence as well as beauty. She certainly was no empty-headed debutante like those Stromberg had complained to Gaye about.

"Where in Alaska are you planning to open your hotel?"

"That brings me to why I'm here, Mr. Stromberg," Maggie said. She hoped her expression reflected a calm she didn't feel.

"Please, call me Alex."

"Mr. Stromberg." She needed whatever tools available to keep the relationship as formal and distant as possible. "I require advice and protection. I've been told you are an aggressive merchant and a man not to be trifled with."

"Do you have capital?"

Ah. The question she knew would come. Good looks, no matter how powerful, couldn't overcome the absence of money.

"Funds are not a problem," she said, her eyes boring into his.

"You'll find," Alex said, "that in a stampede such as is about to sweep Alaska, gold may not buy as much as you think. Certain basic items will become priceless. Others, such as timber, will be cheap. You might build a structure easily enough, but where would the furnishings come from?"

Alex seemed to be checking his emotions and, she hoped, any physical arousal. Could he establish a business relationship with someone he might find sexually attractive? Now for the critical portion of her plan. She smiled, shedding the role of aloof goddess for that of interested business woman and potential partner. She was becoming more and more comfortable with this act.

"I want a partner with your expertise," she said. "I also need safe passage to wherever is the best location for your store. And my hotel."

Stromberg stared at her, stone-faced. What if he realized how little experience she had? What if she'd overestimated the power of her physical attraction? The challenges of opening a business in the wilds of Alaska could require his total attention. Maybe he didn't want to be bothered by any physical or emotional distractions. What would she do if he said no? Panic seeped back into her belly.

"Mr. Stromberg." Maggie's body tightened. She struggled for control. She was so close. "I'm willing to trade partial ownership for your experience. And just because I'm a lady does not mean I can't work as hard as any man."

A strange expression crossed Stromberg's face. Had he sensed her vulnerability? Had she been unable to hide her weakness and fear? Had he made up his mind?

"All right, Miss Alverson. Let's see if we can't iron out some of the details required for your interesting proposition."

Relief washed through her. She'd captured Mr. Stromberg. But the momentary comfort dissipated as the limitations of her inexperience and ignorance resurfaced. Yes, she was out of her depth, but now she at least had a chance at escape.

CHAPTER TWENTY-TWO

The well-worn boards of the pier vibrated under Alex's feet. A sea of animated spectators clogged the surrounding wharfs, frustrating the frantic loading of freight and animals. Before him, the *Al-Ki* quivered under a swarm of teamsters, sailors and passengers. Near him, hawkers offered food and beer. Scalpers screamed last-minute prices for tickets on the first ship headed to guaranteed riches in the Klondike. Alex couldn't believe the skyrocketing values—a $50 steerage pass snapped up without question by crazed gold seekers for $500. He shifted with apprehension.

People swarmed around him, faces a blur, noise filling his ears. Events had opened the door to unimaginable opportunity, and here he was, twitching in fear. Isaac Snyder would pick just such a crowd to exact vengeance on his enemies. The fat pig was capable of wreaking havoc at any moment. Although Alex had no confirmation that Snyder could connect him to Sizemore's death, only a fool would ignore such possible deadly consequences. The heavy revolver strapped to his waist brought some comfort. Not exactly the way he'd imagined his triumphant escape from the strangling clutches of Mordecai and San Francisco society.

And where the hell was Sophia? What an unnecessary complication she presented. Why had he consented to be her nursemaid to Alaska? The memory of beautiful hazel eyes, strong-boned features and overflowing bosom answered that question. But how would he find her in this craziness?

Thank God his assistant, Horace Ingram, had loaded his crucial merchandise before the frenzy of the last hours. Without the help of a capable assistant he'd be swamped. He'd fought hard to pry the clerk from Mordecai. He didn't expect much aid from his mysterious traveling companion.

The crisp air, laced with the normal morning fog, did little to cool the rising heat of his nervousness. He could no longer remain a sitting duck in the maelstrom swirling through the waterfront. Damn Sophia. Alex pushed toward the *Al-Ki's* gangplank. Bodies banged against him. He struck out blindly, keeping his gun hand free. Angry voices bounced off his back as his aggressive action maneuvered him forward. Finally, he reached the dense crowd struggling to board.

"Mr. Stromberg," an anxious voice called out.

Alex whirled toward the sound of his name, hand grasping the butt of his .45. A young boy, slouch hat pulled low, stood before him. A surge of activity pushed the boy against him. Large, firm breasts pressed into Alex's chest. This was no boy.

"It's me," the figure yelled above the strident calls and shouts of the anxious throng. Her full lips silently mouthed her name.

"Where's your luggage?" Alex asked.

Sophia motioned with her chin at the single valise trapped at her side.

"Traveling light, aren't you?"

Sophia offered no answer. No time for pleasantries. Too much action and danger on the docks. Alex grabbed her worn valise. Not many gowns crammed into that bag.

What kind of lady embarked on such a long voyage with so little clothing? Did she feel safer among men who thought her a boy? Could she be on the run from something or someone? He'd ask her once they reached the relative safety of the boat.

Alex struggled to the foot of the gangplank, Sophia close behind. Alex flashed his tickets at the two armed sailors controlling entry. No easy task as a steady stream of passengers, longshoremen hefting freight and luggage, and potential stowaways clawed toward the ship. The large, gruff crewmen swung the butts of their rifles with brutal skill, cracking the skull of a sloppily dressed supplicant in front of them. But they allowed Alex and Sophia to squeeze up the wooden plank and onto the *Al-Ki*.

A massive, bearded deckhand pushed both of them aside, manhandling a flailing man. The desperate fellow, cursing and spitting, kicked at his tormentor. He was rewarded with a violent shove that sent him stumbling off the boat and into the fetid waters of the bay.

"No ticket, no ride, ya little bastard," the rough sailor called down to the figure thrashing in the debris and filthy bay water washing against the dock's pilings.

"That man'll be crushed," Sophia screamed. "He'll drown."

"Every man for himself," Alex said.

He pulled her away from the railing and dragged her toward the stern of the tramp steamer. Nerves short-circuited his normally cool demeanor. He searched the wharf again for any of Isaac's flunkies. Then a new, uncomfortable realization—they could already be aboard. He backed against the bulwark of the boat's superstructure, eyes darting up and down the crowded deck of the *Al-Ki*. Distraction came only when he realized Sophia also scanned the crowd aboard.

"Why a boy's costume?" he asked.

"Do you think it's safe for a woman?" Sophia answered. Her mouth hovered close to Alex's ear. "Simpler as a man."

Amazing how, even in her rough clothing, Sophia's attraction remained strong, disconcerting. He again felt the press of her body, a faint smell of lavender. Everything about this woman generated questions. Didn't matter how she dressed, Sophia was all woman.

* * *

The *Al-Ki* crew cast off its thick lines after an eternity of frenetic action. Alex let out a sigh loud enough to register above the final climactic roar of the crowded docks. Giddiness replaced anxiety as reality sunk in—they were underway. He found himself waving and cheering along with his fellow fortunate shipmates, although Gaye would be the only person he'd miss. But his lighthearted joy disappeared with the rocky motion of the tramp steamer succumbing to the grip of the wind-chop of San Francisco Bay.

The once stable deck came alive with dips and jerks. He'd mentally anticipated this first moment afloat, but his preparations had been in vain. His dread of water, memories of desperation, the death of his brother in these very waves, all flooded back. His older sibling had been a leader, Mordecai's favorite and blessed with many skills. Where would Alex be, what would his life be like if Samuel still lived and worked in the business? Would his older brother have shielded him from Mordecai's unreasonable demands? Would he ever have needed to escape San Francisco?

No. Concentrate on Sophia. On the promise of a new world free of the claustrophobic control of his father and the strangling social structures. No, he would be the first merchant to the Klondike with tons of goods secure in the *Al-Ki's* hold. No more stifling hypocrisy. And, unless Snyder's men had snuck on board early, no more looking over his shoulder at every shadow. Then, of course, this beautiful young woman who was indeed worthy of his attention stood at his side. Based on her own wariness, she would also provide an extra pair of eyes, if not more.

The boat chugged toward the Golden Gate. He turned his attention to Sophia. Despite the *Al-Ki's* distance from the wharf, Sophia's watchfulness remained evident as well. Time to see if he couldn't shock a few answers out of his new, mysterious partner.

"Who are you running from?" Alex watched Sophia's eyes widen. She swallowed hard and glanced up and down the deck for the hundredth time—a deer caught in the crosshairs.

"What makes you think I'm running?" she responded, her pause long enough to confirm Alex's suspicions.

"If we're going to be partners, don't you think we should be honest with each other?"

"The absence of information isn't dishonesty," she said in a tone of annoyance and anger that took Alex back a step. "And you seem to be rather unsettled yourself."

"I'm uncomfortable on the water," Alex said.

That was no lie, although the words lay lame on his lips. Sophia's face softened, but doubt still shaded her expression. He'd pursue this line of questioning again once—if—he could find his sea legs.

"Let's see to our accommodations," Alex said. "There are many more passengers than berths. I'm sure we've got roommates."

He led her on a tour of the boat. Their stateroom held one double bunk and several other people's gear already crammed into the small space. It would be difficult to secure private time with Sophia here or anywhere else aboard this ancient derelict. But the sway of the ship upon the deep waters of the bay cut into his confidence, turning his thoughts from sex to survival.

* * *

The boat's erratic motion flushed Alex back on deck. The fresh tang of salt air provided momentary relief from the churning discomfort within his stomach. His mind also cleared, registering confidence. He felt increasingly certain Isaac had not planted any killers aboard.

But what about his enigmatic companion? Did she have any connection with Isaac? If she was what she represented to Alex, then he could be in the clear. Alex had done his best to keep his Alaskan plans quiet. He hadn't wanted to alert his competition, especially Synder. Without prior knowledge of Alex's presence of mind, Isaac would have had a difficult time getting tickets at any price. Alex couldn't worry about imagined problems when the immediate threat of open ocean was upon him.

The tramp steamer eased through the Golden Gate, and the shuddering beneath his feet increased. The *Al-Ki* cleared the headlands, and wind ripped across the decks. A slow, roiling turn to the north toward Alaska brought an unpleasant increase in the ship's movements. The bow rose and crashed into the Pacific current.

Each rocking, smashing plunge into the eternal ocean undermined Alex. A disconcerting queasiness grew within his body. Sophia stood close to his shoulder. But he had no interest. Thoughts of wealth and a new beginning drifted into the sharp wind. Nausea gripped his guts, sweeping away any remnants of excitement.

Alex bit down the taste of bile rising from his belly. Deep swells kept the sickening motion of the *Al-Ki* constant. Reflex action in his throat couldn't hold down the foul brew threatening to exit his body. God, Alex felt terrible, out of control. His body had been kidnapped by a cruel force twisting his insides out. He dove for the rail, and the contents of his stomach erupted, fragments of puke blowing back into his face.

He gasped and folded to his knees, his own stench competing with salt air. Embarrassment registered, then another series of cramps drove him prone to the wooden planks. A faint awareness of others glued to the gunnels in similar agony brought no comfort. Weakness overpowered him. Hadn't he heard somewhere that this rough-water misery could last for days? How did one overcome such a nightmare of sickness and helplessness?

CHAPTER TWENTY-THREE

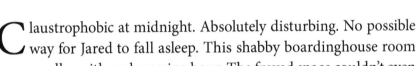

C laustrophobic at midnight. Absolutely disturbing. No possible way for Jared to fall asleep. This shabby boardinghouse room grew smaller with each passing hour. The frayed space couldn't even be considered a poor cousin of the luxurious Leemont Hotel. And the healthier he became, the slower time crawled.

Still two weeks before sailing north. Brutus at least kept him company on runs through the city. That was using the term run euphemistically—more like a fast slog. But getting out cleared his head, gave him a degree of control.

"Okay, Brutus, let's get out of this cage," Jared said, slipping into a wool shirt.

Didn't take any begging. His dog already had his nose crammed against the thin wooden doorjamb. Jared pulled the door open and walked out of the cramped cell, descended two flights of stairs and into the welcome wet, frigid air of a San Francisco summer night.

Muted sounds of civilization echoed through almost empty streets. Corner lamps fought a losing battle against the midnight darkness. Halos of moisture added a dimension not experienced in daylight. San Francisco never slept, but by the midnight hour, the hustle and bustle lost its edge.

Jared trotted with Brutus down California to the relative flats of Stockton Street and turned right. Human shadows shifted in doorways and alleys. At least he could leave these ghostlike figures behind him, unlike the unwelcome, unshakable faces of his family.

An occasional pack of drunks paused. Jared kept focused on the street before him. Words, insults floated to his ears, but Brutus's presence provided a comforting shield. The Airedale had recovered from the slashing knife wound much faster than Jared's bones or self-respect.

Broken or malfunctioning street lamps left ponds of blackness. Jared's pace took him through the empty spaces before any potential threats could materialize. He wouldn't be outside in the middle of the night without his long-haired protector. And impossible to make his way through the chaotic congestion of the workday.

Activity picked up when Jared turned onto Market Street. Occasional wagons rattled along the uneven pavement, and horse hooves clopped in a comforting rhythm. Lights reflected from multiple bars. Cries and shouts extended out the entrances, meanings indistinct as Jared picked up his speed. Brutus pulled away with a trot more efficient than Jared's long strides.

"Slow down, Brutus," Jared whined.

The dog looked back. Jared imagined an expression of irritation. Jesus, not only was he talking to his dog on a regular basis, but assigning expressions to the dog's shaggy face. Ridiculous. He could barely distinguish the animal's eyes through the matted hair, let alone detect the difference between looks of irritation or pleasure. Didn't matter.

Fewer citizens of the night this far from the city center. Maybe two miles into his jog. A left turn after another five blocks, then left on Bryant. He'd take the street parallel to Market for ten or twelve blocks before swinging back to the main drag. Fewer lamps. Pools of darkness expanded into small lakes free of humanity, injustice and danger. Head down, arms and legs in smooth coordination. Contentment overcame his confusion, anger and dislocation with life. By the time he and Brutus reached Alaska, Jared should be fully recovered. Confidence leaked into his consciousness. Time to reconnect with Market.

Fingers of fog played above the streets, breaking the symmetry of the streetlamp glows. Loud noise to his right on Fifth. The rowdy bar Argonaut sat halfway down the block. Loud, abrasive catcalls and harsh off-tune music emanated from the open doorway.

Most of the jarring noise came from a group of drunks surrounding a lamppost near the Argonaut's entrance. Hard to count how many, but more than Jared wanted to deal with. Still, he paused, attracted by the strange swaying of the crowd. Words became distinguished in bits and pieces.

"Goddamn Chink"..."curfew"..."sucking up white man's jobs"..."worse than lice"...

Jared took several steps forward, struggling against the magnetic draw of the action. The mob parted enough for Jared to see the object of the crowd's anger and abuse. A small Chinaman bounced between rough hands.

The besieged little man in dark pajama-like clothing flew haphazardly within the circle of rowdies. The Chinaman's head jerked like a puppet from vicious yanks of his pigtail. Jared took another step toward the group, then thought better of it. He could count at least fifteen roughnecks pummeling the defenseless Chinaman. He'd been ensnared by barbaric drunks in the Barbary Coast and barely survived. What chance did he have against this rabid mob?

"Let's hang the little fucker." A loud, slurred voice rose above the melee.

One man moved to a nearby store and with a paving stone broke a display window. The crash of glass brought louder howls and curses. Conflicting emotions swirled through Jared. The man reached through the fractured window and withdrew a coiled rope. Restraint and self-preservation competed with guilt and cowardice. Screams and garbled cries again blotted out individual words.

To Jared's horror, the rope seemed to climb over the light standard of its own volition. Several men lifted the helpless Chinaman. He should step in to protect the poor overwhelmed victim. Yes, he should. They held him aloft while one of the drunks fumbled with the end of the rope. They were going to hang the poor man. Right there in the street. Right now. His head throbbed, blood pounding his temples demanding he do something.

Cops always patrolled Market Street. Jared tore his eyes from the mayhem and sprinted the five blocks toward the main thoroughfare. If only he could get there in time. He had to move faster. Pounding down the rock-hard street brought pain to his ribs and even his jaw. Jared hit Market, arms pumping, gasping for air. Brutus kept by his side in an effortless lope. He swung around the corner and swerved, almost crashing into two patrolmen.

"Easy, laddie." An Irish brogue emitted from a cop as tall as Jared and twice as wide. The hulking officer's powerful hands held Jared. "What's your hurry? You wouldn't happen to be some thief running from trouble, would you?"

"Quickly," Jared squeaked, gasping for breath, pointing back the way he had run.

"What's your problem, boy?" the bulky man asked.

"A mob of drunks is hanging someone outside the Argonaut." Jared snatched at an arm. "Follow me."

Jared wheeled and retraced his steps. The two officers followed. Within seconds Jared outdistanced the two men. This was taking too long.

"We have no time," Jared shouted over his shoulder.

He reached Fifth Street and hesitated. A figure swayed under the ghost-white glow of the streetlamp, while the mob danced at the victim's feet. Their curses had turned to laughter. Jared froze in shock. A sickening emptiness brought instant nausea. Pounding feet approached from behind. The two gasping cops stumbled around the corner.

"Hey, you," the larger policeman cried. "What the hell ya doing?"

"Time to move on, boys," came a laughing voice.

The men split off in two directions. Half retreated back into the Argonaut. The other half took off down the road. The cops didn't move. Jared ran to the figure hanging in the damp air like a child's rag doll.

Slippered feet twitched an arm's length above Jared's head, then stopped. The last movement loosened one of the man's slippers. The black cloth shoe floated to the ground in peaceful contradiction to the brutality of the moment. Jared's eyes closed, the image of the fluttering slipper like a dead leaf seared his mind.

"Help me get him down." Jared had no knife and nothing to stand on. "He could still be alive."

"You didn't tell us they was only hanging a yellow bastard," the big copper rasped.

A man hung by his neck. No attempt to cut the Chinaman down. Had to be dead now. What difference did his color make? He'd been murdered. For what? Breaking an unenforced curfew? Being in the wrong place at the wrong time? What was the matter with these animals? Jared stood in shock.

"He's a human being, just like you." Jared turned on the cops.

The bulky, fat-faced officer bent over, catching his breath. No trace of interest showed on the faces of the police. Both officers surveyed the empty street, animation fading into boredom.

"There's plenty more of the little fuckers around," the larger policeman spit out in disgust. "One dead one won't make no difference one way or another."

"I'll tell ya what ain't right," the second cop said, speaking for the first time. "Those damn drunks never should a' broke old man Holbrick's hardware-store window."

Jared glanced at the broken glass of the store front. Diamonds of light sparkled off the scattered shards. A man's life meant less to these apes than the damaged window. The cops would show more concern over an injured horse. He wanted out of this so-called civilized society.

CHAPTER TWENTY-FOUR

Alex remained pathetic and helpless by the *Al-Ki*'s railing on the second day of their voyage. How could she reconcile this green-faced, crumpled figure with the image she had of Alex Stromberg, handsome, dashing capitalist? Where was the romantic gentleman that was going to save her?

"I have some water for you," Maggie said above the roar of sea and wind.

She handed the cup toward Alex between the rhythmic, crashing rise and fall of the boat. His quivering hand waved her away. The sour smell of vomit filled her nose. How could this man handle the challenges and pressures of opening businesses in Alaska when he couldn't even survive the first day of a boat ride?

"Just leave me be," Alex said.

He must be too weak. Her initial attempts to comfort him with the offer of a water-resistant mackinaw, food or drink had been rejected with the same force as the contents of his stomach had emptied. Dry heaves were all that Alex could now offer the blue-gray waters of the Pacific. Maggie's distaste now turned to concern.

She pulled away from the stricken man and returned to pacing the crowded deck of the tramp steamer. Maggie had found release in the northbound journey. Hours scouring the *Al-Ki*'s packed decks had uncovered no trace of Hawk Face. The chilling, salt-flavored gusts had torn her past away, cleansing her body and soul of crushing fear and guilt. A new world beckoned. With or without a healthy Stromberg. She allowed hope to seep back.

Now on the second day, Alex's deathlike immobility generated anxiety. Reality slapped at her face in concert with the tangy, sharp-edged spray of the waves. Maggie knew nothing about operating a hotel, whorehouse or any other business. Her homemaking skills were nonexistent. She'd never cooked or sewn. She had forced herself onto Alex in desperation, opening her to new feelings of helplessness. If Alex died at sea, then where would she be?

And she was the lone woman on the boat. How long could she keep her sexual identity from her all-male companions? What would happen once they landed in Alaska? Surely she faced anarchy and barbarity on the edge of the civilized world. Who could she turn to for protection and guidance if not Alex? Chills chased the remnants of hopeful anticipation.

Another uncomfortable set of memories formed unwanted concerns—her father's incessant and bitter accusations against the three Jewish merchants in town. Greedy, clannish and dishonest. Jews used their outsized intellects to fleece good Christians. Jews intended to take over the world on the backs of others. They would drive down the values of businesses and property, stealing them when prices reached rock bottom. His last rant blamed Jews for the Panic of '93. Never trust the Jews. But trust her father?

He had proven to be more despicable than any man she'd known, Jew or Christian. Besides, who the hell was she, whore and accused murderer, to put on airs, become picky? She was stuck with Alex Stromberg, angel or devil, and would watch him closely. Assuming he didn't die on the decks of the *Al-Ki.*

The image of another damaged traveler she had ministered to popped into her mind—the boy on the train. She felt more like Florence Nightingale than a female Billy the Kid.

"Alex." She returned to his spot by the rail and knelt at his side. "If you don't drink some water, you could die."

The first mate had made rounds, warning the sick of the need to keep some fluid in their convulsing bodies. She again thrust the tin cup under his chin, bracing for an angry rebuff. Instead, Alex accepted the cup, trembling hands encircling the container. The surging motion of the steamer splashed as much water on his face as he swallowed. He offered the half-empty cup back to Maggie.

"No, Alex," she said. "You've got to force the water down. All you can. Maybe some soup would help."

"Damn it." Alex's curse carried little conviction. "If this keeps up, I'd rather die."

"You won't die," she said softly. "You have too much to live for."

And so did she. Their eyes connected, his distracted expression faded, replaced with a look of interest. Relief filtered through her at signs of Alex's limited revival. Only four or five more days before they reached calmer waters beyond Seattle. If she could deliver Jared and his dog to San Francisco, she could nurse Alex through this rough boat ride.

* * *

The explosion drove her backwards into Alex. Five days from San Francisco and he had at last regained control of his body, granted, a body many pounds lighter and weaker. She felt his arms around her, unnecessarily helping her maintain balance on the main deck of the tramp steamer. The welcome calmer waters beyond Seattle had allowed Alex to return to the living.

"Nice shooting, Sophia," Alex said, laughing.

A throng of surrounding spectators joined in his amusement. A blush warmed Maggie's cheeks. Her disguise no longer fooled anyone. Several called her by her new name as well. The sound of her newly adopted identity was disconcerting. From now on she would have to think of herself as Sophia. Maggie no longer existed.

"Even you couldn't miss this target," Alex smirked, then spread his arms wide. "The whole Pacific Ocean."

She threw an angry glare at him and fired again. The cumbersome .45 bucked, despite her two-handed grip. Another bullet flew harmlessly into the sea.

"You're concentrating mighty hard," Alex said, a smile plastered on his face. "You trying to shoot us a fish for dinner?"

She didn't bother answering, just aimed. Her targets became faces appearing, then dissipating within the crest of unending waves. It was a good thing Alex didn't know how badly she wanted her targets to be real, fish being the last thing on her list. And she had unlimited possibilities—all the bastards from the factory to the Prairie Flower who had harassed and abused her. One face kept reappearing, that of her father. She focused with all her senses at this last apparition and squeezed the trigger. Click. The hammer fell on an empty chamber.

"Let me reload for you," Alex said.

Sophia spun from the rail to face him. No reason now for his arms to enclose her. No reason before either, but she didn't want her withdrawal to appear as a rude rejection.

"Thank you," Sophia said, trying to muffle her irritation, "but I need to learn to load myself."

He handed her the bullets. They rolled against her palm, pleasing in their cold smoothness and symmetry. For some reason the shells supplied a sense of power and control over Alex. Any earlier dominance he might have exercised over her had blown away on the decks of the *Al-Ki*. Now when they discussed future business opportunities in Alaska, and Sophia's inexperience became apparent, her hunger for knowledge overcame her lack of confidence. Alex seemed disconcerted by Sophia's intelligence, let alone her beauty. Those emotions mirrored Sophia's new doubts about Alex's strength and abilities.

"When we land, I'll dig out a smaller pistol from my inventory," Alex said. "Now let's try again. Straighten your arms. Be ready for the kick."

She resumed her position at the railing. He again reached around her body before she could react, placing his hands over hers on the revolver, extending her arms. His chest pressed against her back. Her body stiffened and jerked forward. She couldn't help recoiling. Any physical contact, regardless of how random or brief the connection might be, compelled her to pull away. And she wouldn't apologize. Hadn't she come aboard as her own woman?

"We've got another week," Alex said, releasing her arms. "By the time we get to Alaska, you'll be much more comfortable."

She reloaded, clumsy fingers dropping one cartridge to the deck. She stopped it with her foot. Picked up the bullet and placed it in the cylinder. She fired another six times into the oblivion of the sea, focusing on the jerk of the barrel, flash of gunpowder, roar of sound. Faces dissolved on the waves as if from the force of the shot. Alex gave her another half hour to blast her way through a full box of shells. She couldn't hold back her expanding smile.

"Time to go back to our serious homework," he said.

He took the revolver, replaced six shells from his pocket into the empty pistol and holstered the .45. She felt defensiveness flood back when he repossessed his weapon. She would master this skill and keep her own gun with her at all times. She would learn from Alex as quickly as possible. The sooner she gained required knowledge, the sooner she could establish her freedom from her mentor and gain the independence she craved. And if she could keep Alex at arm's length, perhaps he wouldn't become another face on the waves that she wanted to shoot.

* * *

The Lynn Canal spread before the *Al-Ki*. The journey neared its end. Sophia stood close to Alex on the windswept bow of the ship as it cut through the calm black waters. Twinkling stars and the silver sliver of a quarter moon played hide and seek among scattered clouds. As she leaned against the bow rail, the dim birth of daylight at 3:30 a.m. threatened the brief Alaskan night. Thousand-foot cliffs, solid dark sentries, hugged the dark inlet. She snuggled into the thick wool coat Alex had given her. The thick-weaved fabric cut the chill to a refreshing breeze.

Her heartbeat matched the throbbing pulse of the steamer's straining engine. In only hours her feet would be on solid ground. The new territory would provide the opportunity to allow her dreams to come true. Opportunity, not the man beside her, generated the thrill within her.

"We'll reach Captain Moore's settlement soon," Alex said.

She stood with him alone in the darkness of early morning. What a strange, wonderful part of the world. Days stretched beyond understanding. Sophia shivered. But winter would bring brief days of bleak, extended darkness—the flip side to today's phenomenon.

Sophia felt Alex's eyes upon her. For a sophisticated man-about-town, his emotions radiated with transparency. The cool distance she kept between them only served to fuel Alex's obvious desire for her. At some point she would have to find a way to deflect her teacher's amorous emotions without alienating him.

"Let's be clear on our plans," he said in a soft voice, a feeble attempt at drawing her closer. "Stromberg's opens under one of the oversized tents we packed. You work with Horace and me until we begin erecting permanent structures for my store and your boardinghouse."

Sophia had come too far, worked too hard, to be shunted into a sales-clerk job. More important, she'd be visible and vulnerable to the hundreds of unknown customers flowing through the store. Her picture remained plastered on wanted posters throughout the country she left behind. Who knew when that picture or someone who'd seen it would turn up in Alaska?

"We've worked out," he continued, "an estimated cost of construction and a budget for your operation. I'll warn you again, these expenses are guesswork. Building materials, fixtures—every product will initially be hard to come by. Prices could rise."

At this point she had no alternative but to cooperate with her new partner. But no reason not to negotiate for quicker progress.

"You have more than one large tent, don't you?" Sophia asked.

"Yes."

"Why not use one for my temporary location?" she asked in a reasonable tone. "There'll be immediate customers if it rains as much as rumors have it."

"A tent is not enough," Alex said. "What you need more than shelter is a cook. These crazy prospectors will pay plenty for a decent hot meal."

"Let's compromise," Sophia said. "We'll set up the tent as a temporary hotel. Easy money. Then we'll add a restaurant as soon as I hire a cook."

"And just where do you plan to find a cook?" Alex said, irritation surfacing. "Every able-bodied man is hell-bent for the Klondike."

"I'll find one," Sophia said, determined to defy him. She softened her tone. "Until then, I agree to spend most of my time working with you and Horace at Stromberg's."

Alex shifted, arranging his lanky frame to make contact with her shoulders and hips. Sophia allowed him to remain tight against her. This wasn't the time to play coy. She would no longer need Alex at some point, but she was dependent now.

"We agreed," he said. "You invest your money, and I serve as your agent to purchase land, build, teach you to operate and manage, set up your books and provide whatever protection and aid that become necessary. Your gold and my experience and effort makes us equal partners in...What are you naming your venture?"

Fifty percent sounded like a high price to pay for Alex's help, but she was in no position to bargain. But her plan was no longer just a dream. She was about to take her first step upon the soil of her new life.

"The Star."

The name sprung spontaneously from the romantic star-splashed heavens above. And a hotel it would be. No brothel, regardless of how profitable Alex promised that venture would be. The very thought of opening a whorehouse had become as repugnant as thoughts of her father. She would never return to that nightmare profession as either whore or Madam.

Listening to him brought a tingling excitement from fingertips to toes. Her exhilaration contemplating The Star did not extend to the man pressed next to her. Why was there no attraction? The thought of a relationship with any man seemed as unappetizing as spoiled meat. And Stromberg appeared to be the closest thing to a knight in shining armor that any woman could dream up, even if he was a Jew. And a whore on the run couldn't be too picky.

Sophia bit back that last thought. She was no longer a whore. Hadn't she been forced into prostitution to survive? Hadn't her bastard father driven her into abuse and despair? Hadn't men proven over and over again to be disgusting animals? And let her not leave out the betrayals of Madam Davidson and Gaye. She didn't just hate men, she mistrusted all of humanity.

"You're a great student, Sophia," Alex said. "I can't believe how quickly you've picked up the business principles thrown at you the last week. You've also become a pretty good shot. Could become another Annie Oakley."

"Thank you."

She allowed a smile to break through her reserve. She'd like nothing better than to have the reputation as a deadly shooter. She moved from foot to foot, hands clenching in the deep pockets of her borrowed coat. She glanced at Alex, met his unwavering eyes. Would she ever feel an emotional charge for the man? Not likely, even if most romantic novels contained a dashing love interest. His arms slipped over her shoulders. She half-stepped sideways. His arm stretched awkwardly, then dropped to his side.

"Any other questions?" Alex's voice registered irritation, even anger, in the dense, brisk air.

"No, Alex. We have a clear understanding. I guarantee you I'll work hard. We'll make Stromberg's and The Star successes."

He nodded, made an abrupt turn and stomped from the bow. Again she asked herself, why so little spark. Why couldn't she generate more warmth and interest toward him? Standing alone, heading toward a new world, she knew the answer. She had tasted independence. Hawk Face could show up in Alaska, but no longer would she be a helpless pawn, a sex slave imprisoned beneath the predatory, disgusting lust of any man. As for Alex? She could finally say no. That sweet power of choice was worth more than any potential relationship with a man.

CHAPTER TWENTY-FIVE

R are bright sunlight bathed the meeting on Skagway's tidal flats in a clear, warm light. Captain Moore ranted and raved under the temporary, crystal-clear weather, acting as if some terrible, dirty deed were being committed against him. Alex looked on in disgust. What bullshit. The old man couldn't have it all. Alex's new ally, Frank Reid, large and ominous-looking, stood beside Alex, emphasizing the danger to the overwhelmed captain.

"This is my land," Moore roared for the tenth time. "I've owned this spot for years. I've claimed 160 acres here on the valley floor where you're standing. Filed in Juneau. Already named the town Mooresville."

Alex faced white-haired Moore, ignoring the injustice playing out before him. The ancient adventurer already owned the only working sawmill and had made much progress constructing the only deepwater dock at this end of the Lynn Canal. Alex only wanted a cheap lot to build his store, but the captain wanted to hold Alex and the other anxious business operators hostage.

"I'm willing," Moore cried out, "to sell the lots at a fair price."

Moore was a pig, claiming to have staked out the whole town site. But Moore's concept of a fair price differed substantially from the value Alex and the mob he led placed on the property. The frantic sea captain paced and stomped in front of the assembled group of men, an ancient, ragged bull moose harassed by a pack of hungry wolves.

The aggressive throng, drawn by potential drama and violence, could not care less about land. They smelled blood. Their only real concern was to secure unlimited booze and food, a dry place to gamble, and supplies for the Yukon trek.

"Captain Moore," Alex interrupted. "We've heard enough. You don't understand. You can't stand in the way of progress. It's not the American way. We've got the same rights as you do. This wilderness is virgin territory. We're building a city for everyone. One man isn't going to block us from our destiny."

Impatience vibrated in the moist air. How long could Alex keep the throng's attention focused on the action at hand? He stood close to the furious old explorer and glanced at his compatriot standing beside him. Frank Reid looked more like the hardened Indian fighter he'd once been rather than the surveyor he represented himself to be. Alex glanced back at Sophia, dressed like a man with a large slouch hat, standing at the edge of the crowd. She also examined Reid's cold, narrow eyes, small, no-nonsense mustache and large frame. Sophia had agreed with him that Frank would not be one to cross. They'd work with him instead.

"Look, you damn fools," Moore shouted. A rush of blood reddened his face, blue eyes blazing, wild, wispy white hair and beard flying in the constant gale blowing down the river canyon. "I ain't trying to stop you. I'm willing to sell these lots for a reasonable price."

Moore pointed a long, gnarled finger in Alex's face. Alex stiffened, then snatched the old man's finger and twisted. He hadn't made this miserable trip to be strangled by an incarnation of Mordecai Stromberg. He levered the proud sea captain to the wet dirt and released the weathered man's finger. Moore knelt before the group, no fear evident. The captain exhibited bravery but little common sense.

"Don't stick your finger in my face," Alex snarled, standing above the beleaguered man.

His rage matched the captain's. Alex felt the veneer of civilization draining from his face. He struggled to control a desire to crush the old man into the dirt. A glance at Sophia, her expression undisguised shock, brought him back to reality.

"Are we going to keep listening to this old coot?" Alex shouted at the throng. "Are we going to let one decrepit old man rule our future?"

Agreement echoed off the surrounding cliffs. The men rose as one from the barrels, crates and tree stumps. Irate gestures and foul curses showered upon the captain. But Moore didn't flinch. He struggled from the packed mud with dignity. Brushed the debris from his knees. Reached into his coat pocket.

Alex put his hand on the butt of his holstered .45. The big pistol fit nicely as a permanent attachment to his hip. He'd not hesitate to blow the old man away if he drew on Alex. Again he noticed Sophia, saw her flinch. Why in the midst of threatening danger did he keep looking to her? He had to focus on the crisis at hand.

"You're all fools," Captain Moore said. He made a theatrical gesture of opening his coat and pulling out a folded paper. "This document is called a deed. This little piece of paper proves I have ownership of this land. You idiots want to ignore the law, it's fine with me. I'll see every one of you in jail."

"Stick that paper up your ass, old man," Frank Reid said. "We're the law here. You best skedaddle or Stromberg here might lose his temper. We'll string you up for obstruction of real justice."

The crowd roared their approval, and the captain spit at their feet. Alex laughed and spit back, more than ready to wreak violence on the selfish, obnoxious Moore. Such unbelievable anarchy would provide great opportunities for strong men such as Reid and himself.

Activity swirled behind the old man's back, where, in only a few days, a new town of tents had blossomed amidst ever-growing piles of equipment. Men, dogs, horses, goats, oxen flooded the low mudflats at the base of towering, cloud-shrouded peaks. Captain Moore's dignified battle stood no chance against such odds.

Vibrations of pent-up energy and violence ran through the assembled rabble. Good reason to advise Sophia to carry the small pistol he had supplied. The gun seemed to add a greater level of comfort to the complex beauty. What kind of woman derived such pleasure from handling weapons? He bet she also carried a knife hidden in her men's clothing. But she did appear uneasy with the threatened conflict.

The crisp winds of the canyons surrounding Skagway reinforced Alex's resolve. Smells of the loamy earth, both life and decay, gave a texture to his excitement. No wonder Captain Moore hung with tenacious energy to his claim. Alex, too, would accept the risk of brutality for the sake of establishing Stromberg's in Alaska.

Moore stomped back toward his cabin, the small structure the only building among the erupting city of tents and raw building frames. Alex watched somewhat disappointed but now glad he hadn't done something stupid to the grizzled adventurer, who would not be destitute at the loss of his claim. Let him go back to his sawmill and deep-water wharf in the bay. The combination was worth a fortune, with the expected rush of prospectors and goods. Moore didn't need to own all the land as well.

"And your cabin's sitting in the middle of Broadway," Alex yelled at the captain's back. "Move it, or we tear it down."

Moore's exploration and discovery of the White Pass from the shoreline over the threatening Coastal Mountains were why they now stood in this god-forsaken spot. Moore had been waiting for the Klondike bonanza for eight years. He had opened the trail in July, before the *Excelsior* had landed in San Francisco. A surprising stab of guilt pricked Alex. The captain had staked out the town with the fervent belief that a stampede to the interior would have to pass through this very spot. Now a rude, rough group of disrespectful, irreverent newcomers ripped the land from his grasp. But the man had overreached.

"Frank's a surveyor." Alex pointed at Reid, then turned back to the crowd. The audience was already thinning without the promise of a good fight. "He's offered to lay out our new town. And our future city isn't going to be called Mooresville. We're naming this metropolis Skagway, Indian for windy place. Appropriate, don't you think?"

Few showed any interest in building a town. The men milled around mumbling. Most were concerned only with gathering gear and hitting the trail to the Yukon. And Alex would be more than happy to fill their needs and send them on their way. The mob was looking to escape civilization, not build it.

"There'll be nice wide streets," Alex continued with waning enthusiasm, "with lots fifty by one hundred feet. Anyone willing to put down five dollars a parcel is in business."

Crazy. Five dollars bought a prime piece of property while a pair of rubber boots cost nine dollars. Even a broken-down horse fetched one hundred dollars and up. Few would trade their dreams of wealth for humble real estate. These give away land prices would work just fine for Alex and his new partner. They could now buy multiple parcels on the main street—two lots for Stromberg's and two for Sophia's Star Hotel.

Sophia should recognize the method to Alex's madness as he squeezed out Moore. But she continued to resist his pressure to open a brothel. Why? He didn't expect her to sell her services. Although he'd be the first in line to buy. Alex just wanted her to manage the whorehouse. So much more profitable than a fleabag hotel. Business was business. But money was freedom, and Sophia would do as she wished.

Alex had explained to Sophia during the voyage the logic for the purchase of two pieces each if possible. They would be able to open temporary tented locations while constructing their permanent wood-frame structures. Keep that flow of cash rolling in. Location was everything, he'd preached. Alex wanted the visibility of a prime traffic location on the main thoroughfare. His foresight and business expertise should blot out some of the doubt he knew Sophia had developed at the beginning of their voyage.

And why did she maintain such emotional distance from him? She used unending questions to provide a foil against his persistent advances. Alex had prepared her for this whole unsavory scene with Captain Moore. Recognizing the resemblance between Moore and his father and losing his temper had not been part of that plan. Color had drained from her face during the dispute. Evidently, this woman wasn't big on public confrontation.

This was just an example of Sophia's unfamiliarity with business if she felt so uncomfortable. At least she'd been honest enough not to try and fool him. Her inexperience and ignorance were staggering. She'd need much more than capital to survive in this wild settlement. Once he helped her establish her hotel, she'd owe him more than gratitude, although 50 percent ownership was pretty damn good.

And he couldn't resist her magnetic, visceral pull. She was indeed different from any woman he had ever met. Was this how romance began? His only experience was with prostitutes. Now he would need to take care if he were to break through Sophia's aloofness and defenses.

Moisture accumulated on his face. The usual mist, turning to rain, replaced the sunshine of only one hour earlier. Skagway had to be the wettest place on earth. Time to get back to business. He pulled a handkerchief from a pocket and wiped his forehead, then closed the distance between Sophia and himself.

* * *

The roar of rain on the giant canvas tent top competed with the questions and demands of twenty or more customers desperate to complete their equipment list and hit the White Pass Trail. Merchandise flew out the tent flap, price and quality irrelevant.

"Sophia," Alex called out.

Her temporary presence seemed as much a distraction as help. But Alex felt the same panic the harried prospectors projected as their fevered eyes swept the diminishing pile of goods—too little product for sale. He knew and had prepared to provide a complete array of goods for prospective miners, but the crush of sales had caught him off guard.

"Take this gentleman's money," Alex yelled to Sophia. "I've got two guys fighting over our last shovel."

"Come on, Joe," a sallow-faced tenderfoot cried out. "This damn place's out of beans, rolled oats and soap. And we're running out of time. There's gotta be more grub over at Keller's."

The two men headed out the entrance, and Alex wanted to head for the nearest saloon. Where the hell was Mordecai's shipment? He could picture his father procrastinating in San Francisco. Pointing his crooked finger just like that ornery Captain Moore. If Mordecai diddle-dawdled too much, any initial advantage Stromberg's achieved at opening first would be gone. He definitely needed a drink.

"Sophia," Alex said. "I'm going to check out construction. Be back soon."

Moore had had no trouble selling Alex lumber despite their conflicts. The old captain was no babe in the woods. The tough old goat had fought in the Mexican War, mined in two continents, run riverboats and stomped with tireless energy through the wilderness of Alaska and Northwest Canada. At least his lumber prices would rise no higher, thanks to the limitless forests surrounding the mudflats of Skagway. Both Sophia's Star Hotel and his new general store rose rapidly from the rich soil. Although he didn't know what good it would do if his flow of fill-in merchandise didn't soon arrive.

He glanced back at his partner maintaining her composure in the chaos under the tent. She wore baggy trousers and a wool shirt, and she looked beautiful—thick hair piled on her square head, heart-stopping dark eyes and a bosom that could start a war. To his ultimate frustration, Alex had had trouble coaxing even a smile, let alone a kiss, from her full lips. He'd had relationships with both the stuffy, sophisticated Jewish Princesses and the high-class whores of San Francisco. Nothing had prepared him for Sophia Alverson. Aloof and calm.

Who was she? Where had her money come from? Was she an experienced con artist or a respectable woman of the world? Still an enigma, even after three weeks on the boat and days of back-breaking labor establishing their businesses in Skagway. But he didn't give a damn. Alaska provided a new start. All the archaic rules had been crushed by the brutal hardships of the Yukon Wilderness. Or sunk in the unforgiving Pacific. Those chill, merciless waters of the *Al-Ki's* long, miserable passage brought an unwelcome shudder from the past.

He slogged through the eternal mud, dodging wild-eyed men and their equally frenzied livestock. Once things settled down, he'd make a serious attempt at capturing Miss Alverson. If this insanity ever slowed. Alex paused at the entrance to the large tent housing the Nugget Saloon. Frank Reid appeared from the maze of temporary structures.

"Another batch of swindlers and con men just landed," Frank said. "More crooks now in Skagway than prospectors. What the hell are us honest merchants going to do?"

"Accommodate them," Alex answered. As long as his customers paid, he wasn't about to make judgments. "There's enough loose gold to go around."

"I'm not too excited about dealing with the devil."

"You got any other suggestions, Frank?" Alex asked. "There's no lawmen, no troops, no permanent city officials but us. This swarm of thieves is pouncing on the same opportunity we are. It's every man for himself."

"And every woman," Frank said, "too."

A thickening in Frank's voice left no doubt of whom he was thinking. A stab of jealousy caught Alex by surprise.

CHAPTER TWENTY-SIX

P recipitous cliffs, smothered by forests of infinite greens, cascaded into the turquoise, mirror like waters of the Lynn Canal. Jared vibrated as much from excitement as from the rickety boat's struggling engines. An incongruous sight of thousand-foot waterfalls sharing space with massive shelves of glacial ice breaking off into the blue-green sea captured him. Crowded ceilings of solid gray clouds hid peaks on both sides of the waterway.

Moose and bear traipsed along the narrow shoreline. Whales, otters and seals frolicked like gay tourists around the rusted bucket *Eugene.* Irregular engine beats echoed against steep mountains as the ship labored to its destination. Was Jared the only one appreciating the grandeur surrounding them?

Raw beauty stood in stark contrast to chaotic activity aboard the tramp steamer. He'd recoiled from the misery of hundreds of horses below deck, crammed into two-foot-wide roped enclosures, too little space to breathe, let alone lie down. Then the incessant howling of dogs of every breed and mix crated in boxes so small they lived in their own excrement. And most important, he'd struggled to ignore the pack of humanity roiling in anticipation of their imminent arrival.

An unrelenting flow of questions had flooded him during every segment of his exile from Ohio. They had begun with his pain-shrouded train ride west. He couldn't shake the need for answers during the weeks of semiconscious recovery or jarring rehabilitation in the hills of San Francisco. Now they appeared again as he was completing an almost mystical sea voyage to Alaska. What had caused his family to turn on him? Why was he no longer loved as he had embraced them? How could his life have unraveled into such lonely despair? The questions appeared in his dreams as he ran, and even now as he stood on the deck of the decrepit ship *Eugene*, given a reprieve, a pardon, an opportunity for rebirth in a new world.

The Airedale stood close at Jared's side, aloof from the frenetic activities of the wild-eyed gold seekers. Brutus had escaped the indignity of a cage thanks to the extra twenty-five dollars Jared had slipped into the first mate's willing fingers—a small fortune, but worth the price.

"We're almost there, Jared."

Jared tore his eyes from the spectacular scenery. David Jefferies moved beside him. David had befriended Jared two days out of San Francisco during the brutal first week of the voyage. His new acquaintance reminded Jared of a coyote, with his sharp, extended nose and long, pointed ears poking through scraggly, shoulder-length hair. Patchy, thin growth fronted for a beard. His eyes forever wandered, no eye contact to be made. Jeffries could lie and boast with the rest of his passengers on the *Eugene*, but at least in private he admitted his exaggerations to Jared. The man offered friendship and decency.

Now the same electric excitement glowed within Jeffries as Jared felt nearing their destination. But did Jeffries share Jared's motivation? Jared had tired quickly of his fellow passengers' constant gambling, swearing and cock-and-bull exaggerations. Their actions were inconsistent with his hopes of discovering a new world of virtue and equality. None of his shipmates seemed steeped in any philosophy other than the desire to get rich quick. Well, the land was vast, and this gang of grasping, wishful capitalists would be swallowed whole by the unforgiving elements.

The *Eugene* rounded one of the endless forested points. The settlement of Skagway appeared as a white line bordering the shore, standing out against stands of spruce, hemlock, white birch and cottonwoods. Cries and cheers erupted from the wild collection of prospective miners. A similar exultation filled Jared, but his awe at the surroundings kept him silent.

Five other ships lay anchored close to land. A grim reality tugged at him. He knew what they lusted for—the opportunity for wealth. Jared prayed for utopia. Somehow he would carve out his own piece of paradise.

Indian canoes and rowboats swirled around the *Eugene* once she dropped anchor, each operator offering passage to shore for twenty-five cents. The cacophony of men and animals rose to thunderous levels. One look at the desperate, scrambling men fighting to offload tons of equipment and animals reassured Jared that he'd made the correct decision: Travel light and purchase what was needed in Skagway.

Jared shouldered his large pack and elbowed aboard the second dinghy to nudge against the rusty steamer, paying the rough boatman fifty cents. Brutus followed with a clumsy leap that almost capsized the unsteady craft. Men cursed Jared, wanting the dog's spot. Verbal taunts were all the fortune hunters could muster. No one attempted to physically dislodge the huge, kinky-haired dog.

The craft headed toward land, finally grinding onto shore. Jared jumped into freezing, knee-deep water, more green than blue. Brutus followed with an undignified belly flop. A stumbling slog through the lapping waves brought Jared to dry land. Brutus shook off the clinging waters of the Lynn Canal, then began a reconnaissance along the cluttered shoreline.

There seemed little difference between the cramped discomfort of the boat and jumbled piles of provisions, angry men, nervous horses and hungry dogs on the rocky beach. The existing low tide exposed driftwood and debris littering the ground, giving evidence of major tidal shifts. The threat of returning high tides panicked arriving passengers, prodded them into desperate activity to move their goods from harm's way. Beyond the beach, one-half mile away, a town appeared to grow before Jared's eyes.

Tents of every size and shape surrounded wood-frame buildings sprouting from the wet earth. Frantic miners on the beach struggled with the logistics of staging all their goods. Jeffries had recommended an outfitter in Skagway, Reliable Packers, which could fill his every need on the trail to the Yukon. His new friend knew the proprietor and would introduce him to Jared.

Brutus wandered a hundred yards away, toward an almost completed wharf jutting into the deeper waters of the Canal. Jared whistled for his dog. Brutus glanced back, but didn't turn around until Jared screamed his name several times. Then the Airedale meandered back toward Jared. Barks and snarls from leashed and roped animals greeted Brutus's progress as he strolled unconcerned, neck extended to absorb the new smells, sights and sounds. How could his dog maintain such calm surrounded by such insanity?

Only ten feet separated Jared from Brutus when motion erupted from the crowded tidal flats. Three large mongrels charged Brutus. The lead dog, a shepherd mix, wild-eyed, teeth bared, closed with frightening speed. He and his two pack-mates tore across the sand, making a direct line for Brutus. The Airedale dropped into a crouch, facing his attackers. He appeared passive, submissive. But Jared heard the rapid clicking of primeval teeth, saw the arrow-straight tail. Oh God. Jared stood paralyzed, mouth open.

The shepherd streaked toward Brutus with a ground-swallowing gallop. The frenzied gray-brown mongrel was as large as the Airedale, if not bigger. Jared couldn't be sure. He tried to call out. His mouth moved, but no sound emerged. Brutus contracted into a tight curly-haired ball, the shepherd a step away. At the last second Brutus lunged forward, powerful legs propelled him like a Jules Verne rocket ship, body angled close to the ground.

The shepherd overran his target. Brutus's jaw clamped on the mongrel's throat. Momentum toppled both dogs. They rolled and thrashed in a blinding, snarling thrash of fur. And with each turn, Brutus chewed deeper into the other dog's neck.

The shepherd must have sensed disaster. The animal twisted and jerked in panic, Brutus holding tight. Movement stopped, Brutus on top, a primitive roar surging between clenched jaws buried in the aggressor. Blood and fur flew as the unfortunate animal made one last twitching, futile attempt to escape. Death came in only a moment.

The attack and fight had seemed instantaneous—the devastation total. Brutus released his death grip. Jared watched horrified, several feet from the slaughter. The other two dogs slunk back into the maze of stacked equipment.

Jared tore his stare from the dead dog, caught the shocked expressions of other bystanders. Brutus stepped to Jared, brown eyes clear and untroubled, killing not registering as anything out of the ordinary. Nature had played out its own version of self-defense. Comments from the witnesses of the terrifying violence grew in volume. Brutus fell into place beside him, no longer interested in exploration, acting normal. Would anything in Jared's life be normal again?

CHAPTER TWENTY-SEVEN

Sophia's new Star Hotel resembled a thin-walled, two-story barn more than a classy hotel. Still, pride swelled within her chest as she stood hands on hips near the front door. The speed with which her life had been transformed was breathtaking. Or perhaps the backbreaking, twenty-hour days contributed to her giddiness. Within minutes of opening her establishment a week earlier, miners, misfits, conmen, and even two families had checked into the first lodging available in Skagway, filling The Star to capacity. In addition, the large tent next door that had been The Star's temporary location also remained close to full—only six available spaces.

And now through a door to her left, a complete kitchen added to the overflowing income that would, incredibly, pay for the new structure within several weeks. Hiring Jacob Tredaway, an experienced chef, had been a most fortunate event. The irascible old man had broken a leg transferring from his ship, the *Pacific Argonaut*, to a barge in Skagway Bay. He'd been unable to make the trek to the Klondike, stuck in Skagway. Sophia had little difficulty capturing the cook with charm and money.

She jerked herself from reverie and glanced through the entrance of The Star into the crowded lobby and reception area. The first floor held a small counter serving as the front desk, two long wooden plank tables with pine benches providing enough seating to serve her hotel guests and a growing number of walk-in diners, and a functional kitchen with sheet-iron stoves and no frills. Large nails had been hammered onto a two-by-six board and attached to one wall—the coat rack. Laughter threatened to erupt at the primitiveness of her new establishment. The Star might not be San Francisco's Palace Hotel, but her guests could enjoy Jacob's food in at least some comfort.

A crude ladder against one wall provided access to the sleeping quarters. Single mattresses covered the upstairs floor. Canvas curtains hung from the flat ceiling. Even Sophia couldn't call the accommodations rooms. But the coarse mattresses provided much more comfort than the pine boughs making up the tent floor. There might be visual privacy with the hanging fabric, but the noise and smell of exhausted, agitated men ignored the artificial boundaries.

The Star's kitchen had become a wild, hectic, day-and-night enterprise. A limitless demand for decent home-cooked meals brought a horde of new arrivals. Sophia often found herself a prisoner in her own establishment, filling in for the constant shortage of staff. She could no longer help her partner at Stromberg's—a welcome blessing. The gold flowing into her coffers for The Star's supply of tasty meals proved much more valuable.

And when would she tell her partner that her plans included replacing the tent with another new hotel? Capital was no problem, thanks to the promise of The Star. Finding labor, construction materials and fine furnishings would be the real challenge, one that Alex had proven expert in solving with the rapid, efficient completion of Stromberg's and their hotel.

The newly finished Star would also soon provide enough financial stability to address Alex Stromberg's unrelenting and unwelcome advances. She maintained the same dispassionate distance from him as she had all her disgusting clients in St. Louis. But Alex had proven to be an honest and invaluable partner, deserving of her respect.

Satisfaction and security, unfamiliar sensations, nestled within her soul. No regrets or guilt could displace the pleasure of her accomplishments. Here life blossomed for the first time in many years, her new identity as Sophia Alverson solidifying, muting the unpleasant images of her past. A smile of happiness threatened to spread across her face.

Sophia wiped her hands on her men's trousers and took several steps toward the bustling kitchen. She wouldn't want a mattress upstairs above the cooking activity. But her guests would overlook the noise and smoking odors for relief from the incessant wind and rain. Alex had been right again. Restaurant service already contributed three times more income than lodging.

At the door a tall young man with a dog approached Sophia. She turned to the stranger. Oh, my God. Shock jolted her body. Her hands flew to her mouth. No mistaking the huge, brown, kinky-haired animal. The man and dog from the train—Jared and Brutus. She stood immobilized.

"Good morning," the man said. "Need a place to sleep. Do you have any space?"

Swelling had subsided, but one cheek bone remained depressed within his face, a pothole of skin and tissue. His nose had enough crooks and bends to remind one of a meandering creek bed. Several missing teeth in his lower jaw detracted from the intelligence radiating from dark eyes, although one eyelid hung half-mast. Despite the damage, Jared's face looked much improved.

"Miss?" Jared said, his voice soft and respectful. A questioning expression played across his irregular features.

Did Jared recognize her? She continued to wear men's clothing, for function as well as disguise. But up close, no one would confuse her for a man. The Airedale extended his neck and stuck his muzzle into her privates, tail wagging back and forth in relaxed rhythm.

"Brutus." The embarrassed man pulled his dog back, but with a tentativeness unusual in an animal/master relationship. "I apologize. He usually keeps to himself."

"That's okay," Sophia stuttered. "I can't let your dog in the hotel. Couldn't climb the ladder anyway. But I can rent you a corner of the tent for two dollars a night."

"Thanks. That'll be fine." Jared struggled to pull a $5 gold coin from the money belt beneath his Mackinaw. "Don't know how long I'll be here. Need to hit the trail soon."

"You and everyone else," Sophia said. This man didn't seem the prospector type, but many other men trooping through town didn't either. "So many people and horses headed to the Klondike, you'll have to wait a while just to get a spot in line."

She reached her hand out and Jared dropped the coin in her hand. Again a puzzled expression crossed his crooked features. Still no recognition? Sophia felt the urge to tell him the truth, to recount their train ride and arrival in San Francisco. But how would she answer questions her admission might generate? And if Jared and his dog could show up in Skagway, how far behind could the hawk-nosed bounty hunter be? One thing was for sure. She'd die before falling into the unkind hands of the law.

* * *

Today, excitement and joy warmed Jared. His new landlady had radiated everything the woman of his dreams would possess and more. Despite her bulky man's outfit. Foolish thoughts, though. Even if a beautiful lady fell into his lap, he'd have no clue. Jared had never kissed a woman, held no memory of a woman's touch. Yet as ridiculous as the fantasy of this frontier goddess appeared, he felt more confidence, more hope. No, he felt...happy.

"Brutus," Jared called. "Let's get our gear."

He threw his pack into the corner of the tent and scrambled out. But Brutus poked his nose into the shelter, then headed out on his own. Far too many distractions for the Airedale. Well, Jared also had business to tend to.

He stepped from his canvas lodging and onto Broadway, Skagway, Alaska, doorway to Yukon wilderness and Klondike gold. And into thick, clogging mud. Traffic flowed both ways in jerky motion down wide ruts. Saloons, packers, druggists, photographers, tents, frame buildings thrown up as he watched. Uncleared tree stumps littered the road in irregular patterns, obstacle courses for humans and animals. Such craziness. Where could he find Jeffries?

"Ahoy, mate." The familiar rasp startled Jared, the man right on his shoulder.

"Mr. Jeffries." Jared managed a smile as he spoke. "Good to see you."

"Well, Jared, I promised you I'd direct you to the right outfitter. There they are down the street, Reliable Packers. At the end of the block. Where's the dog?"

"Exploring."

"Dangerous for loose dogs. 'Specially one as healthy as your animal. He wander away, someone will snatch him, guaranteed."

"Brutus can take care of himself," Jared said with a rueful smile. His dog's viciousness no longer frightened him as much as put him in awe of the Airedale. "Does what he wants. We're more like partners."

"Here we are," Jeffries said after a short walk.

Jared stepped into a small, recently completed crowded store. Smoke floated thicker than the rain clouds outside. Men milled around the tight space. Well-written signs adorned the rough walls, lists of essentials for a trip to Dawson and instant riches. Jared appreciated the clarity and organization of the signs. Prices were even grouped by category of goods: Foodstuffs, clothing, mining equipment.

A multitude of articles necessary to survive a trek to the Klondike gold fields lay displayed before him. The food list began with 200 pounds of bacon, 100 pounds of beans, 25 cans of butter, 24 pounds of coffee, 75 pounds of evaporated apples, peaches and apricots, 40 pounds of rolled oats, and ended with 15 pounds of salt and 60 boxes of matches. Mining and carpentry equipment covered a range from 16 pounds of various-sized nails, 200 feet of 5/8 inch rope, to axes, handsaws, sheet-iron stove and tent. Lord. He could no more carry this much gear than fly.

The total sum of $500 was as expected. But the required pile of equipment might as well be a mountain. He would need packhorses. Air seeped from his lungs along with any previous elation. He had never considered the realities. He'd convinced himself that he had more than enough money. Another failure to think things through.

"Pretty daunting task," said a florid-faced clerk, whose vest stretched in desperation around the man's full body. Mutton chops and fat hands added to the substance of the salesman. "Tough to carry a thousand pounds of goods four thousand feet over White Pass and six hundred miles to Dawson."

"I couldn't have said it better," Jared said, a touch of sadness muting his enthusiasm.

"Jeffries explained to me your needs. I'm sure we can give you the services you need. Name's John Trelfant. Reliable Packers is the correct choice for you, young man."

Jared half-listened to a barrage of rapid-fire information. It was enough that Trelfant knew his business. Jared's goods could get to Lake Bennett with Reliable's own crew of packers at a price of ten cents per pound—only a third of the tariff charged by most freight companies. Total cost of goods and services $650. Reliable also provided boat space at a reasonable price once he reached Lake Bennett. Jared's funds would be stretched, but he was happy to pay. The bustle in the room, professional signs on the walls and Trelfant's obvious expertise reassured Jared. Excitement returned.

"Where do you keep all your supplies?" Jared asked.

"We store some product in the back. But we give you the best deal by buying what you need at the best price from the other stores and outfitters in town."

Other milling customers and clerks paid little attention to the elegant signs. They moved about in what seemed aimless steps. Why weren't they as anxious as Jared to buy their goods and hit the White Pass Trail?

"When do we close this transaction?"

"Soon as you give me a 50 percent deposit for the goods." Trelfant opened his hands. His red face broke into a wide grin. "Can't get a more complete service anywhere in Alaska. Mr. Monroe, we are the best. We tell you what you need for your trip and procure the items at the cheapest price. Our customers always come first."

The merchant gave a slight bow. Jared fumbled under his shirt, opening the money belt. He pulled out his leather pouch containing his funds. The noise level rose several notches, the movement of customers sped up, bodies closed around him. Someone stumbled into his back, pushing him hard against the counter.

"Sorry," a voice said.

Jared turned toward the sound. A large, rough hand grabbed at his pouch. Arms wrapped around his body, holding him tight. Strong fingers clawed, then ripped the pouch from his hands.

"Hey," Jared yelled, panic overpowering him. "That man stole my money."

He lurched forward in the small, crowded space, then bounced from body to body, the swirling, confused customers blocking his progress toward the door. Cries of "Thief" and "Stop that man" rang out in the tight quarters. Jared whirled his arms with frantic gestures, fighting to reach the door. Every bounce gave the crook an extra step.

Jared stumbled through the entrance after an endless series of starts and jerks. His legs struggled to bring him balance on the rough boardwalk. His eyes caught a man dashing down Broadway—the man with his money. He sucked in a deep breath and took off sprinting. No one could outrun Jared, especially with this much at stake.

A solid force slammed him from behind, crashing him forwards. He flew off the primitive wood-plank sidewalk, pinwheeling out of control. He crashed to the ground, landing spread-eagled, sprawled in the grasping mud.

"You clumsy ass." A huge man, full beard, potato-sized nose and angry, blazing eyes loomed over Jared, then stepped back sneering. "Damn cheechakos got no sense and no manners."

The huge man towered above him, making no attempt to help Jared to his feet. The thief was long gone, dreams stolen with his money. Reliable Packers. The set-up now became clear. His good friend David Jefferies had turned out to be the conniving coyote he resembled. What a complete and total failure. Jared was a clumsy, stupid chump. A fool. All energy drained from his body.

"I should teach you damn tenderfoots a lesson," the monster bellowed. "Stomp you back to where you belong."

Jared lay in the dark mud disillusioned, broke, helpless and now stuck in Hell. An errant thought slipped by: He'd been spending too much miserable time in the dirt, from Boston to Ohio to Alaska.

He sensed Brutus before he heard the thick, locomotive breathing. The snarling animal closed on Jared, mired in the sticky slime of Broadway. But his dog was too late, the damage done.

"I been warned about your dog," the large, bearded thug said, drawing a huge revolver from his belt. "Can the mutt dodge bullets?"

Jared raised his hand and waved at Brutus in a feeble attempt to prevent the dog's attack. Helpless again. Couldn't control the bully above him or his charging dog. Panic swallowed him. All the damage wasn't done. Would a bullet take away the only living thing he cared about?

CHAPTER TWENTY-EIGHT

D ark shadows filled the primitive wood crib. Alex looked at the lady lying on the rough mattress. He could see only the outline of her oval face. Embarrassing what his overpowering hunger for a woman's touch could drive him to. The unquenchable demand had ruled his life since a young teenager. Even this plain, stocky lady of the night brought him a degree of pleasure.

"Why don't you visit more often?" she asked in a hoarse voice. "Wish all my customers were as considerate as you."

"Well, even a whore should be treated like a lady," Alex answered, dropping several gold coins on the woman's stomach.

She hadn't even taken her clothes off, just raised her skirts. Too damn cold to do anything else. Poor woman. Seemed a million miles from Bertha's and Gaye. And from out of nowhere came a pang of guilt. Sophia. He paused pulling on his pants, the unexpected emotion a shock. What the hell was this all about? Sophia's image spoiled what little satisfaction he'd achieved from the completed sexual encounter. He climbed out of the Fourth Street crib. He took several quick steps, then blended into the frantic crowds of Broadway.

This muddy swamp was in dire need of a decent whorehouse. Sophia should turn The Star into one as he had so often suggested. She'd been adamant in her refusal. Hell, maybe he'd open his own. Hard to resist the enticing economics of supply and demand. And it was that woman's beauty and aloofness that drove him to the whores in their crude crate-sized hovels tucked off Broadway.

For the first time he felt both under a lady's control and willing to be under her influence. At least he thought so. But he was becoming a more eligible bachelor every day as business boomed. Everyone needed his goods, whether a complete outfit or only necessary fill-ins. If only Sophia realized the seriousness of his advances.

Alex sucked in the smell of wet decomposing earth, sawdust, horseshit and overripe, overdressed miners. A beautiful, pungent scent. He turned to catch his reflection in the display window of Keeler the Money King. His hands straightened his fox-trimmed coat and beaver-skin top hat, both items accepted in trade for mundane beans and waterproof boots. An involuntary smile creased his lips. He looked like a New World nobleman. Should enjoy wearing the clothes now, for they'd be off and hanging in his closet the moment he entered Stromberg's for another endless shift there.

Sophia's unbidden image reappeared. He'd miss more than her beauty now that her new hotel consumed her every waking hour. Lack of employees presented the greatest challenge at Stromberg's. The newly arrived idiots wanted only to gather their gear and head to the false promise of the Klondike goldfields.

A commotion close to Stromberg's down Broadway caught Alex's attention. A figure lay prone in the mud. Alex moved swiftly through the muck. As he approached, he made out the lanky body of a young man. Those scrambled facial features became familiar. His Barbary Coast escape. And he'd be damned, here came the dog. Alex also recognized the large, bearded pistol-waving brute gesturing above the sprawled boy—a Reliable Packer bully.

The Airedale swallowed the ground between them, aiming body and teeth straight at the thug. The Packer pointed his .45 at the fast-closing dog. The kid didn't move. Just lay there, stuck and dazed with his arm in the air.

This boy's help in that San Francisco alley had probably saved Alex's life. He rushed the final distance and thrust the long steel barrel of his own revolver deep into the thick man's bulging neck.

"Drop it," Alex spoke into the crook's ear. "Now."

The tough released his gun. The weapon fell to the ground. Alex bored his barrel deeper into the man's massive neck.

"You'd kill me for a dang dog?" the thug said, twisting his neck in a feeble attempt to see Alex.

"I don't need the excuse of a dog," Alex answered. "I should pull the trigger as a service to the community."

This damn horde of thieves plagued the city, sucking cash from unsuspecting fools before they had a chance to buy goods from legitimate merchants. Now he and Bertha had something in common—outside forces stripping their customers of cash better spent at her brothel and his general store. But shooting the bastard would be as useless as swatting at the infinite swarm of mosquitoes harassing Skagway's inhabitants.

The Airedale stopped between the man in the mud and his tormentor. The dog's rumbling growl and snapping teeth commanded Alex's attention. The animal looked as big and as dangerous as a canon, with his neck stretched out, tail stiff behind him. The cowering criminal pushed back into Alex.

"You be a good boy," Alex said to the large ruffian and danced back several steps.

"My gun?" the bully whined.

"I'll return it to the rightful owners."

Alex stooped, picked up the heavy Colt and tossed it toward the entrance to the crooked outfitter, Reliable Packers. The humiliated flunky went to fetch his mud-clogged pistol and disappeared into the building. The small crowd moved on, the man still lying spread-eagle in the wet Skagway earth.

"You hurt?" Alex asked, towering over the prone boy.

"No."

The young man lifted his arms from the muck. He shook some clods of dark mud off his sleeves, then dropped his long limbs back to the ground with a resigned groan. The fallen man's eyes tracked Alex. This boy looked pathetic.

"Why are you just lying there? Let me help you up," Alex said, grabbing an arm. The mud made a sucking sound, and Alex yanked him upright. "We've met. I'm Alex Stromberg. You and your dog saved my hide from a long miserable cruise to Shanghai. Or worse."

Alex brushed some of the dirt off his hands. Damn small world. How the hell could such a coincidence occur? Maybe there was some overlying plan in the world.

"You think we're even now?" Alex smiled. "Never got you or your fine hound's name."

"Jared Monroe. And Brutus."

Brutus remained an intimidating sentinel. His thick neck rotated at the surrounding flow of traffic. Alex had seen this same alert stare in that San Francisco alley. Impressive animal.

"I'm sure you remember me, buddy," Alex said, taking several slow steps up to Brutus.

Alex stuck out his hand below the dangerous rows of teeth. The Airedale sniffed, then snapped his head toward a motley team of seven sled dogs roped together traveling down the ruts of Broadway. Brutus wheeled to face the pack. Must have been too close. The malamute mixes veered to avoid him.

"They stole everything," Jared moaned, his mud-encrusted hands flapping in the air. "What can I do, Mr. Stromberg?"

"I'm afraid there's nothing you can do," Alex said, "short of buying two .45s and storming Reliable Packers with your dog. With Brutus you just might have a chance to take those bastards down. Not that I'd recommend it. I'd head home. Fare's a lot cheaper with all these ships dead-heading back to the States."

"I told you," Jared said in a flat, lifeless voice. "I have nothing. I deserve nothing. An educated fool. A complete failure. Don't know what disgusts me more, mankind or myself."

An educated boy? This young man's predicament could be an answer to Alex's manpower shortage. Take a while for the boy to save enough cash for another grubstake. Especially in the penny-pinching world of retail. Alex should take advantage of this unlikely coincidence.

"I need help at my store." Alex tested the possibility. "I'm desperate for a strong back and a sharp mind. The impatient fools I hire work a week or two and split for the Promised Land."

Jared stared hard at Alex. Contradictory emotions swept across his battered face. Intelligence reflected in the boy's eyes, despite the apparent physical damage. Wonder what had happened to the kid?

"I'll even let you and Brutus sleep in the back of the finest and newest emporium in Alaska," Alex offered. "If you clean up the store each night. You take this job, you'll learn where the real wealth's going to be flowing."

"Thank you," Jared said in a muted tone. "I guess that's the best offer I'm going to get."

"Put everything in perspective, young man," Alex said. "Best thing that could've happened to you is to lose your money up front, instead of struggling 600 miles only to find out you're too late. That's assuming you don't die on the trail. Want to know what I'll pay?"

"No. I don't care." Jared wiped his muddy hands on his pants, eyes downcast. "I'll get my pack. Unless someone stole that too."

CHAPTER TWENTY-NINE

Jared levered the last crate off the wagon. The wooden box of mackinaw jackets teetered on the narrow loading dock of Stromberg's. The grizzled teamster snapped the reins above his two horses and rolled away without a goodbye. Jared turned to the clogged dock—clothing, foodstuff, mining equipment and other assorted gear in danger of tumbling into the wet slop of the alley. Now the difficult job—distributing this inventory across Stromberg's ever-shrinking sales floor and overwhelmed storeroom. The only thing holding the emporium together from this onslaught of merchandise was Alex's business expertise and organizational skills.

"Damn Mordecai," Alex cried out the back door to Jared. "Any more clothing and we'll have to make mattresses with them. The old man's not filling my orders, he's shipping whatever he can find on sale."

That seemed the only rational explanation Jared could come up with for the duplicating flow of merchandise shipped from San Francisco. He also realized that as the White Pass clogged in mud, misery and death, sales would soon slow. Discouraged tenderfeet would discard more goods than they bought. Only food would keep selling, along with a swelling demand for liquor, gambling and whores. The retail business of Skagway was not so hard to comprehend.

"Jared," Alex said. "You'll need to move this excess product to the old tent next door. We'll have to turn the space into a warehouse. You and Brutus need to move over there nights. Thieves would love to get their hands on that merchandise. Fools wouldn't realize there's no current market for this stuff."

Dizziness and near exhaustion from the heavy lifting made Jared stumble along the dock. At least Alex didn't look any fresher. The owner of Stromberg's would never be accused of being a fat, lazy capitalist. He worked shoulder to shoulder with Jared and a growing crew of employees.

Unlike Alex, Jared's first priority continued to be his life-sustaining runs up the steep mountains. Those charges up Mount A B provided release from the primitive city's centrifugal force of greed and desperation. The draining physical effort proved much more effective than laudanum or other drugs in escaping the troubles of the world.

Also, infinite opportunities offered themselves for fantasizing about Sophia Alverson. He knew his daydreams were absurd and ridiculous, but they supplied him with one of his few pleasures. Despite the proximity of The Star, Jared only saw her when she met with Alex. No reason to think she gave any consideration to his existence. But her image couldn't be shaken. He held tight to some hopeless, pitiful connection. Why?

A loud disturbance at the store's entrance snapped his mind back to the task at hand. He made his way onto the selling floor and stopped. Two filthy prospectors stomped through Stromberg's, scattering product and customers. The men held armfuls of worn, damaged goods—boots, coats, a randomly folded tent and a sled-dog harness. Horace Inman moved to intercept the ruffians in the middle of the general store. Jared stepped behind Horace.

"This crap didn't hold up for two weeks," a wild-eyed, scraggly-bearded man roared and made straight for a quivering Horace. "Give us our money back, or we'll rip this place apart."

The frenzied prospector doing all the talking spluttered, spit flying in all directions. His liquor-laced breath swept over Jared. Customers, especially lowlifes such as these two, were the Achilles heel of working in Stromberg's, and why Jared avoided waiting on trade. Still, Alex paid him to assume responsibilities just like this.

"Hold it," Jared said and pushed the helpless clerk to the side.

One quick glance at the thug's load of cheap goods and Jared knew they had not been purchased at Stromberg's. He faced the two men. Violence radiated from them. They wanted to fight as much as defraud Stromberg's. From their expressions, the two drunks seemed quite sure they could make short work of Jared. They very well might, but a surge of anger and frustration engulfed Jared. He had had his fill of being buffeted by his fellow man.

"Give them something," Horace whispered in his ear.

"You didn't purchase this merchandise here," Jared said, stubbornness keeping his voice steadier than he felt. "We don't sell inferior merchandise like this."

"Calling us liars?" the lead man bellowed. "You son of a bitch."

A flash of realization jolted Jared. These crooks were nothing but empty scarecrows compared to the threatening mass of Brother Tom. He could take both of these clumsy bums. Dissect these slobs with his boxing skills as easily as gutting dead fish. Jared imagined firing two, three solid blows at the first pig, flooring him within an instant. He'd close swiftly on the second one, punching skill and new-found power destroying his worthless opponent. No reason to accept any more humiliation and physical bullying. Weeks of heavy lifting at Stromberg's and constant brutal runs had added strength. His confidence soared. Jared wanted to fight them.

Adrenaline dissolved the stupor that had gripped him since he'd been buried in the Skagway mud of Broadway. Contrasting aromas of wool, burlap, coffee and sawdust filled his nose. Previously unacknowledged colors from hundreds of product labels filled his vision. A cacophony of sounds poured from the streets. His acceptance of his own weakness had begun in the rich dirt of Morgan's Ohio farm. Now he welcomed an awakening.

He raised his fists and balanced on his toes. Both men quieted, then took a half step back. The scroungy thieves dropped their armloads on the floor. Snarls creased their dirty faces, but they shuffled backwards. Amazing. Jared's stance had stopped them cold.

One man spit into a display containing cans of evaporated fruit. This was too easy. Then Jared noticed their eyes focused over his left shoulder. He swiveled his head.

"Gentlemen," Alex said. "Don't leave without your garbage."

Alex's salesman's smile graced the lower half of his face, but his eyes gave no comfort to the frightened miners. A steady hand wrapped around the butt of his revolver. His legs flexed forward, tense and ready like a runner at the start of a footrace. Stromberg's gaze, cold, and cruel, had lost any glimmer of life.

The men inched forward. They gathered the motley gear into their arms and slunk out the front door. Alex took several swift steps to catch them at the threshold.

"Don't even think of dropping that junk in front of my establishment," Alex called out, pointing his finger like a pistol at the retreating prospectors.

Alex stepped toward Jared. Light and warmth returned to his face. Jared exhaled, confusion and emptiness replacing the tension within his body. Alex had an uncanny ability to defuse dangerous situations.

"I do believe you would have fought them," Stromberg said. He patted Jared on the shoulder, a haunting expression interrupting his grin. Then a weaker smile returned. Alex presented an enigma, his moods wild fluctuations. Would Jared ever understand his prickly, complex boss?

"Maybe," Jared said and turned on his heel.

* * *

Jared returned to shifting boxes from the dock to the battered tent that once housed Stromberg's. His hands trembled from unexpended energy. Conflicting emotions swirled without form or rhythm. Usually raw labor provided unending escape from his troubled thoughts. His daily runs sucked up whatever strength remained. Only physical collapse allowed sleep. But the opportunity to slip into bed was hours away.

And the ethereal image of Sophia Alverson once again materialized to further unsettle him. To be truthful, she didn't just ignore him, she looked right through him. The woman was as difficult to read as Stromberg.

What a total fool he was. And still a virgin. He didn't even know how to kiss. He should pay for the finest whore in Skagway. Admit his ignorance and get educated. Couldn't be as boring as theology classes at Yale.

But what was a woman like Sophia doing here? She didn't belong in Skagway, this mud-encrusted Dante's inferno. Hadn't he thought he'd witnessed the worst abuses of civilization in the factories of New England and the grinding poverty and desperation hidden in the shadows of San Francisco? Just another example of his naiveté. Nothing could compete with the degradation and cruelty swamping this Sodom and Gomorrah. How could a woman such as Sophia arrive in such a place under her own volition?

The unending thoughts of Sophia required escape into fresh, wide-open freedom. The sky's lifeless gray threat of approaching winter required a shift to midday in his running routine. A wet, chill wind whipped through the alley behind the general store. The days had shortened. Darkness that in August held off until 9:30 now swallowed the lawless community by 6:00. How would he ensure exhaustion once snow choked the mountains? Would he be imprisoned within the claustrophobic confines of this hellhole? How would he then handle Sophia's haunting presence?

"Mr. Stromberg," Jared called out after two more hours of backbreaking effort. "I'm going to start my runs during the day. It's getting too dark too early."

"Do whatever you need to do," Alex answered. "Just let me know, so I can cover your hours. You know you're my best worker."

"Thank you," Jared called out. Why didn't Alex's compliments mean more to Jared? "I'll make up the time by working later in the evening. I can catch up on paperwork after the store closes. Be back later this afternoon."

Jared went into the tent to change into thicker pants and shirt and to pick up medium-weight leather gloves and a stocking cap for today's bushwhack up the mountain. Several steps from the tent and he merged onto the muddy ruts of Broadway and into the flow of desperate miners and terrified, overloaded packhorses headed to the base of White Pass. How could these fools ignore the returning empty-eyed men and the remains of their beaten, bloody animals? Didn't they realize they were fresh fodder for the disastrous route already referred to as "Dead Horse Trail"?

CHAPTER THIRTY

For the life of him, Alex couldn't figure out what motivated his assistant. Alex stood at the entrance to Stromberg's, watching Jared retreat down Broadway to flail himself once again in the wilderness. Jared returned from his insane runs looking like a broken pack animal. That boy was definitely missing a few spokes. Would the skinny kid really have fought those two drunk scoundrels? Great worker but crazy as a loon.

Jared might be dour and downbeat, but he worked hard. Damn hard. What a relief having trained the young man to perform the grinding paper work. The cockeyed kid was smart as a whip. Alex would not want to run Stromberg's without Jared.

Fading light outside reminded Alex how little time was left in the day. He had to get back to work in his tiny office crammed into the back of Stromberg's. Sophia should appear any moment for their scheduled meeting.

A section of shelving filled with sales and inventory journals took up one side of his hole-in-the-wall. A thin wooden bulletin board covered a second. Purchase orders and notepaper were tacked up in four columns—Due Immediately, Two Weeks, Four Weeks, and Pray For. The last column, Pray For, held the most paper. He pulled down the few filled orders, updating the board. Didn't take long. Mordecai's latest shipment had solved few problems. Alex had even been forced to buy basic items at retail prices from his competitors. He shuddered just thinking about the loss he would take on those goods. No way Alex could maintain a balanced inventory using that strategy.

Yet business continued to boom. Stromberg's had become a gold mine, as he had predicted—an endless supply of desperate customers flowed through his doors. Commerce moved in Alaska with incredible speed. Stromberg's San Francisco was a major player. And that was true even if the profit margin sat mired at a pathetic 4 or 5 percent in a good year. In Skagway Alex was producing an obscene 50 percent. Yes, he'd never worked harder in his life. But every dollar Alex invested in inventory returned tenfold here in Skagway.

His father had long ago received the thousands in gold dust, nuggets and bills sent south with his loyal senior clerk, Horace. Far more than the cost of the new orders requested. Alex hoped the shock of all that cash killed the crotchety old man. Why didn't the tight son of a bitch feel confident now in shipping the ever-larger inventory orders Alex demanded?

A prickly uneasiness brought a tightening in his back and shoulders. Storm clouds, both physical and financial, threatened in the immediate future. The tight office walls and his dependency on his stubborn father trapped him. Could the old bastard be deliberately undermining Stromberg's in Skagway to force his son back to the San Francisco store? Should he be sending the excess profits to his father? Next time he'd keep a much higher percentage of his proceeds for potential opportunities. Why did he continue to put himself into such financial jeopardy?

Hot flames of guilt gripped the back of his neck, providing an answer to that question. He shook his head, a feeble attempt to escape slate-gray images of San Francisco Bay. He couldn't afford that high a price for guilt much longer. The bottle of whiskey beckoned from his desk drawer. A little early for a drink, wasn't it? Still, he pulled the liquor out and took two large hits directly from the amber-colored glass.

The booze failed to relax him or disperse a disturbing odor filtering into the room. Should he sail back to San Francisco to confront the old tightwad? The image of a month on the merciless Pacific Ocean drowned that idea. Hell, he had no desire to venture even onto the protected Lynn Canal. Let Ingram shuttle the cash back and forth.

"Fire!" Horace cried out from the selling floor. "Mr. Stromberg, fire."

Shit! The smell of fire was recognizable now. Smoke curled beneath the wall separating the store from the adjacent storage tent. He snatched a miner's shovel and several heavy blankets as he sprinted through the selling floor.

"Coming from the alley," Alex called to Horace. "Follow me."

Alex dashed out the front door, reached the corner, and turned into the alley. A pile of material flamed, scorching the wooden walls of the general store. Fire. The most deadly threat in Skagway. Not only his establishment was at risk, but all the wood-sided buildings on the block would be destroyed.

Alex threw down the blankets and dug his shovel into the wet muck between the old tent and his store. Horace and another clerk clambered into the narrow opening. Frantic shovelfuls of moist earth flew onto the flames. Several passing miners joined the struggle in the constricted space. Someone slapped a thick blanket at the burning wall, now more smoke than flame. Alex kicked at the pile of clothing and leather straps, scattering the smoldering items. Swift action with mud and blankets extinguished the blaze.

Jesus. How close was that to total disaster? Frightening images swept through Alex, as terrifying as his San Francisco Bay nightmares. Soot covered his hands. Three more minutes, maybe only two, and Stromberg's would have been engulfed. His shovel pawed at the smoking material that had caused the fire—discarded goods the drunken prospectors had tried to return. Horace's expression showed he had come to the same conclusion.

"Son of a bitch," Alex cried out. "Where are the bastards?"

Would they try again? Chances of finding them would be slim. Not much Alex could do about the danger. No police to take a complaint. Cowards' tactics.

More and more defeated prospectors limped back to town to dump their gear and head home. Scavengers swarmed the trail, gathering up discarded items and increasing the flood of used merchandise on the market. Soon the trail would become impassable. Then even more goods would be unloaded at fire-sale prices. Alex grimaced at his poor choice of words. If only Jared's dog had been roaming the area. Nothing more to be done now.

"Horace," Alex directed, "clean up this mess. I'm meeting Miss Alverson in my office."

Sophia would appear any moment. The whiskey bottle sat seductively on Alex's desk. He took another welcome hit. How would he survive the next months once the pass was forced to close? The answer, ironically, could be his investment with Sophia in The Star. His half-interest in the hotel-restaurant already supplied more income than Stromberg's. And his father took no cut of that. If only he could convince Sophia to turn The Star into a brothel. Talk about filling a need.

And that brought him to his final problem, Sophia Alverson. How could he be so obsessed with a woman so aloof? A woman who buried her beauty in men's clothing? He held tight to the vision of a sexy, sophisticated Sophia the day she had entered Stromberg's in San Francisco. A lady who could appreciate and benefit from his years of experience and technique.

Hell, sex, like poker, required the same demands of education and practice, just different rewards. How much more his sexual pleasure would be enhanced if his partner became equally excited and sensually satisfied. He had come close with Gaye, but part of the whore's response had to have been an act. But Sophia was no sporting lady. He tried to suppress the swelling pressure in his groin. Damn.

CHAPTER THIRTY-ONE

Sophia made one last check of the projected expenses for her new hotel, the Alverson House. No matter which way she figured the numbers, she could come up with only two-thirds of the required funds from savings and her share of the Star's profits next month. She looked up from the papers on her small primitive desk. At least for the first time in many years, she felt a degree of warmth and security in this small log cabin awkwardly attached to the back end of The Star.

The purple-and-gray velveteen gown, worn once to woo Alex in San Francisco, hung in wrinkled elegance in one corner. What a shame to waste her many feminine wiles. She wished she could use the dress again this afternoon when she met with her partner. But even wearing bulky men's clothing, her remaining visible charms worked all too effectively on the many prospectors, crooks and businessmen thronging Skagway. Would her looks provide good enough leverage on Alex today?

Sophia stood, assembled her papers in a tight roll, slipped on her gloves and shrugged into her heavy parka. The weight of the .44 in the right pocket reassured her. She had long ago traded in the small-caliber pistol Alex had given her for more powerful protection. This would be the perfect time for her almost daily reconnaissance walks around Skagway. She needed an escape to gather her thoughts, even if it meant abandoning her overworked staff at The Star. First, a quick check of the bustling restaurant where activity never seemed to slow.

One of her cabin doors opened into the alley. She used the other entrance, leading into The Star's small stockroom and cooking area.

The saturating scent of the kitchen inundated her senses. The dining room, crammed with customers as usual, forced her to squeeze through tight spaces. No obvious problems. Never enough workers. But any lingering guilt at leaving The Star short of help faded.

The fractured wooden sidewalk awaited her when she stepped out the front door. Wet, bracing air washed over her body, a wonderful relief from the oppressive memory of the St. Louis heat and humidity. She made a rapid but thorough inspection in all directions. Two prospectors pushed their way past her into the hotel. Her hand tightened on the revolver. No lurking Hawk Face on the streets of Broadway. No hints of threats to the delicate balance of a woman in a man's world of gold, gambling and whoring.

Freedom. She would move unobserved, traveling a loop that covered downtown, the waterfront and the approach to the mountains. Her height, the hat tipped low on her brow, and worn men's clothing provided invisibility in the crowds. Her right hand remained anchored in the oversize pocket of her deerskin parka, the smooth butt of her .44 adding security.

Something cold and wet brushed Sophia's exposed left hand, launching her sideways into a group of startled miners. She scrambled to keep her hat on and maintain her footing. The familiar large dog leaned into her. Couldn't Brutus just walk up and greet her rather than scaring the hell out of her?

She placed her hand under the Airedale's chin. As usual, the dog accepted her attention for a moment, then set off on his own rounds. She received as much affection as his owner, Jared. Although "owner" seemed an inappropriate description of their relationship. Boy and dog were more like traveling companions, like Daniel Defoe's Robinson Crusoe and his native, Friday.

She admired the characteristics of the Airedale, independent and aggressive. She too would no longer accept the role of helpless victim. But the animal also generated thoughts of Jared, which in turn brought a familiar stab of fear and insecurity, despite her grip on her revolver. The poor man posed no threat, but his unexpected arrival in Skagway had reinforced her vulnerability. Rekindled the fear of an unexpected appearance from Hawk Face.

How long had she been in Skagway? Three months felt like a lifetime, and still so much yet to do. She had to sell Alex on her plan for a new hotel—this one to be an actual high-class establishment, her dream. She wouldn't feel safe until she had established security in her own place. All her progress could evaporate in a heartbeat if she let her guard down. No, the dog was an example of why she must maintain constant vigilance.

Brutus crossed the mud of Broadway with a purposeful gait, then darted in front of a two-horse wagon. Crates of dogs barking, snarling or beaten into unconsciousness crammed the wagon bed. A crude sign on their wagon read Skagway Dog Collection. The dog collectors were another disgusting profit-making scam initiated by Alex's friend Soapy Smith. The operation served only as an excuse to steal any hapless mutt not chained to its owner and then sell them to newly arrived, ignorant fortune hunters, cheechakos. Why did her partner associate with this slimy scoundrel, as crooked as the White Pass Trail?

Two burly, bearded thugs dropped from the cart's bench seat and stalked Brutus from two sides. Sophia caught her breath. One wore a dented top hat and held a large, wicked-looking billy club. The other, clad in a filthy mackinaw jacket, gripped a metal-linked choke chain and leash.

"Brutus," Sophia called, alarmed.

The scraggly men closed on Brutus. Sophia's concern mounted. A billy club swept down with vicious velocity toward the Airedale's unprotected head. Brutus lunged sideways against his attacker. Sophia freed her pistol. The club's blow glanced off the dog's shoulder. Brutus's thick body cut down the man at his knees, and they toppled together to the ground.

The mackinaw-clad assailant stood confused, watching the man and dog roll and thrash in the mud. The animal's snarls filled Sophia's ears. Then a high-pitched screech—a human sound—rose from the struggle. The fallen man scrambled to escape, top hat cartwheeling off his head. Blood flowed from a face wound. The desperate dogcatcher threw up his arms in futile defense.

The wounded man's companion whipped the chain toward the dog. He missed the dodging Brutus and slapped the linked metal against the side of his partner's face. The besieged man's features exploded into a rough pattern of red blood and raw flesh. Sophia gasped.

Brutus swiveled toward the second attacker. The man dropped the chain and clawed a gun from his waistband. Where should she point her gun? Should she shoot? The Airedale smashed into the man, knocking him backwards onto his butt. His drawn pistol fired into the air. The bullet whistled over the heads of the collection wagon's horses. The startled animals took off, Brutus at their legs, driving the panicked horses around the corner of Fourth and Broadway.

The wagon hit the deep ruts crisscrossing the intersection and tipped on two wheels, then crashed on its side. Wooden crates spilled out in an avalanche of barks and shattered cages. Several dogs shook loose of the wreckage and scattered. The uninjured man, his yellow mackinaw encrusted with mud, staggered to his feet and made an unsteady path to his partner, lying in a bloody fetal position.

Sophia relaxed. No action had been required that would have brought attention to her. She settled her revolver back into the parka pocket. Brutus disappeared into a nearby alley. What a joke. The Airedale needed no human help. Quick steps took her to the street corner, then down Broadway toward the waterfront. Her reconnaissance walk could continue.

The movement of men and animals increased at the shoreline. Confusion ruled as new arrivals struggled with gear and their own overheated emotions. It was one thing to imagine the promise of gold and adventure, another to be plopped down on the Skagway beach without a clue how to proceed. But she held no sympathy for this frantic, bewildered mob. Her gloved hands pulled her parka collar tighter. Suspicion was the only emotion Sophia could generate.

Tense, feverish conversations swirled among newly arrived Stampeders and the thieves, packers and suppliers poised to fleece them. She filtered words and conversations. Most fragments flowed by her without registering. Information was her key to survival, and here by the shore much could be learned. When would the words she most dreaded reach her ears through the cacophony, "I'm lookin' for Maggie Saunders—whore and killer."

But today brought nothing new. War with Spain over Cuba seemed inevitable. The latest miners' strike in Colorado had been brutally crushed, using federal troops and scabs. San Francisco agitated for even harsher restrictions on the Yellow Peril. The country's economy, stumbling along, showed signs of life, thanks to the exhilarating discovery of Klondike gold. Same news as two days ago. Sophia relaxed—no apparent dangers.

"Goddamn waste," a well-dressed man said, his bowler crammed on his head.

He nodded to a grizzled packer who stood before him. Moisture dripped from pant legs soaked from the gentleman's slogging arrival through the shallows of the Lynn Canal. Something in their edgy grimness caused her to hesitate.

"I remember her from Bertha's," the packer said. "Wilder than any two whores combined. A true redhead all the way between her legs. You say some customer killed her?"

A woman murdered? Sophia came to a halt. Who were they talking about?

"Yep," the man with the bowler said. "Tied her to her bed and cut her up something terrible. Why would any son of a bitch do such a thing? Unnecessary waste. Hell, there wasn't nothing Gaye wouldn't do for money."

Gaye? Sweat broke out under Sophia's layers of clothing. Gaye dead? Desperation filled her. She needed details, additional confirmation. But the two men's voices melded into the shouts and cries of the swirling multitude. She could no longer distinguish their words.

Tears blurred her vision. She forced her legs to move back toward downtown. The Minnesota farmer's huge hands were once more around her neck, his stinking breath and arrogant sneer in her face.

She fought off the image of Gaye tied to a bed, slashed and desecrated, then of the hawk-faced man pursuing her, Sophia. A cold, unnerving awareness registered. No one gave a damn about the woman, a prostitute, a disposable commodity. Another whore's death, only this one took place in a high-class brothel.

She hated Gaye. Had hated her. The treacherous bitch had betrayed her. Now those thoughts seemed hollow. Why had Gaye been killed? Who had committed such a despicable act? It couldn't possibly have been Hawk Face, could it? Had he tried to get information from Gaye about her? Gaye had known Sophia planned to meet Alex Stromberg. No, Gaye wouldn't have died for her. Gaye would have talked before being tortured.

A surge of insecurity added to the discomfort roiling in her stomach. Sophia shrunk deeper into her heavy clothes, jerking her slouch hat even lower over her eyes. She had already escaped to the end of the world here in Skagway. Where else could she go? Was there any safe place left?

Alex. Alex could help her build a fortress she could hide behind. She had to regain control before her meeting with him. She'd need calm calculation now more than ever. Could she still manipulate him? She had hoped to keep their relationship at a level of business only and failed. His hungry eyes and growing frustration distracted and annoyed.

But then she could no longer ignore a softening of her own once-solid shell of uninterest. Why couldn't he find satisfaction with the expanding population of whores in Skagway? She hesitated at the back door of Stromberg's. He was handsome and fearless, with the exciting edge of a gambler. How long could she avoid a man she respected and maybe even trusted? Did it matter if he was a Jew?

CHAPTER THIRTY-TWO

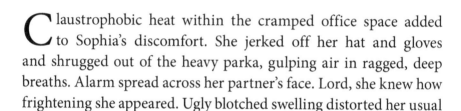

Claustrophobic heat within the cramped office space added to Sophia's discomfort. She jerked off her hat and gloves and shrugged out of the heavy parka, gulping air in ragged, deep breaths. Alarm spread across her partner's face. Lord, she knew how frightening she appeared. Ugly blotched swelling distorted her usual flawless complexion. Redness ringed lusterless eyes. Bad timing. She needed every feminine asset she possessed.

"Sophia?" Alex stood, then wedged himself around the cluttered desk. "What's wrong?"

She struggled to rein in her emotions. Now was not the time to let her guard down. But his concern touched an empty corner of her heart.

"I received some bad news," she said, her voice strained and tight. "A dear friend of mine has passed away."

"Is there anything I can do?" Alex said.

"No, thank you, Alex," she answered in a more normal voice.

She had heard that Alex was a great poker player, but even he couldn't have hidden knowledge of Gaye's brutal death. He must not yet know the terrible news.

"I apologize for the distraction," she mumbled. "We have much to discuss today."

He guided her to the room's single chair, taking the opportunity to place his hands on her shoulders. Then he squeezed around her and took his place at his desk. To her relief, Alex proceeded with their normal agenda, covering the problems of supplies, personnel, repairs and marketing, now that both Stromberg's and The Star faced major competition. Alex became all business. The concern in his eyes faded as the meeting moved forward. She gained confidence as they slipped into their routine. Soon time to present her plan.

"Alex," Sophia said, gathering her composure as they neared the end of their discussions. "I have plans to build a new hotel. A first-class establishment. Like I've always dreamt and talked about."

"What the hell are you thinking?" Alex's eyes widened, hands raised, palms out. "Are you crazy? A new hotel? You can't even control the flood of business at The Star. The restaurant's packed all day, and you haven't had a vacancy since you opened."

Sophia was not surprised at the array of emotions transparent now on her partner's face—shock, anger, then frustration. She'd have to slow down, start again. She had to make him listen.

"There are no rooms in The Star," she said, sparks of temper supplying welcome energy. "Only stalls. People are crammed in like animals. You know I came to Skagway to open a fine hotel, not a barn for humans."

"The place's a cash machine." Alex's body swayed, hands waving in the air with each word. "Too much risk opening a new luxury hotel. Especially at a time when my future sales are threatened."

Blood rushed to his face. He slammed a fist on the desk. Sophia flinched.

"The damn trail's going to be forced to close." Unexpected anxiety painted his words. "New businesses are sprouting like mushrooms. Winter's coming. I haven't ironed out our supply problems from San Francisco. Every dollar of my share of the profits from The Star is critical. I need your madness like another load of useless clothing from my father." He pointed an accusing finger at her. "Don't you see what's happening around us?"

She'd expected some degree of resistance but not flat-out refusal, even fear. Her fingers straightened wayward curls crushed by her hat. How to respond? First, slow everything down. If she presented her plan as a fait accompli, Alex's objections might seem futile. Her breathing calmed.

"I've purchased a double lot near the corner of Fifth Street and Broadway." She spoke in a low, controlled tone. "Mr. Liddicoat has drawn up plans. From that we can determine our costs. Construction of the building will be cheap. The expense is in the furnishings required."

"God Damn," he said, fingers plowing through his thick hair. "Property tied up. Architectural plans and interior design already laid out. You sound like a San Francisco capitalist. The Star's been open only two months. You've concocted this fantasy without even consulting me."

"You've taught me well," Sophia replied, attempting a gracious smile.

Why was he so adamantly opposed? Didn't Stromberg's and his share of The Star provide an abundance of income? Look how much she had already saved. Heat rose to her cheeks. This was her life. She had earned this opportunity. What was wrong with him?

"Your project," Alex said, lurching to his feet, "will devour cash like Skagway devours hope."

"I'm not asking for additional money, Alex." Sophia's hands lay clasped in a death grip in her lap, any attempt to calm herself swept away by Alex's intransigence. "I've projected The Star's profits from rentals and the restaurant for the next four weeks. If we both contribute, there'll be more than enough to fund our new investment. And I'm offering you a 30 percent interest in the new venture in addition to your half of The Star."

Sophia would invest her time and money—and his from The Star's operation—and her reasons all made sense. If only her face wasn't in such a disgraceful condition. Now what argument could he come up with? Beauty and charm would certainly help overcome Alex's objections.

"I don't have time to build your ridiculous dream," Alex said, collapsing back into his chair. "Stromberg's is eating me alive."

She did know the pressures of his overwhelming workload. His exhausting schedule was no different from her own. But not enough time in the day was a different challenge than generating profits. And this was her dream. Somehow, some way, she would convince Alex to help her. He had to understand how much this new hotel meant.

"I told you, you've done an excellent job of training me," she offered again with another weak smile. "I only need a little of your time. And your experience."

"Sophia." Alex's skin flushed, jaws clenched, and eyes narrowed. "There are already ten hotels in Skagway. Five more are under construction as we speak. Soon there'll be twenty more. You want my experience, then listen to what I'm telling you."

"Alex." She leaned forward, with her elbows creating space on the cluttered desk, enthusiasm building. "None will be as fine as the Alverson House. When the trail closes, the town will fill up. There's no slowdown in ship arrivals and no vacancies now. Even once the trail reopens, many would rather winter in Skagway than camp in freezing conditions at Lake Bennett, waiting for the spring thaw."

Life returned to his clean-shaven face. A more relaxed posture replaced rigidity. Maybe her idea was connecting with him.

"Let's compromise," he said, resignation creeping into his voice. "You can go ahead and ignore my advice. But I'm only going to give up half of my share of profits from The Star."

No, this wasn't working. She needed more than half. Too much had gone wrong to fall short now. The farmer's death, Gaye's murder, all the years of desperation and disgusting survival could be put behind her with the security of the new Alverson House.

"Alex, please support my plan." Sophia tried to keep the frustration from her voice. "I couldn't have made it this far without your help. The sooner I open, the quicker we'll produce real profits. I need all the cash for only a month, maybe a little longer."

Alex remained fixed in his chair. No warmth emanated from eyes or lips. She was being beaten at a battle she couldn't afford to lose.

"Please. Please don't Jew me down on this deal."

Alex's expression turned to stone, his face lost all color. He spun toward his purchase order board with such violence the papers on his desk swirled onto the floor. Now what was wrong?

"Alex," Sophia pleaded. "Please."

"Of course," he answered, his body rigid as a frozen pine. "Whatever you want, Miss Alverson. But my price is 50 percent of your damn hotel, not 30."

"But"-Sophia straightened with alarm-"I'm putting up two-thirds of the money," Sophia said.

"And you still need me to make it work." He turned back to her. His angry glare knifed through her. "Fifty percent or nothing."

Why was he no longer rational? What had rekindled his anger? Why these unreasonable demands? And he'd called her Miss Alverson, not Sophia. What a child he was when he didn't get his way. And what exactly was he after? He'd feel better once the income from her new venture poured in. At least she now had enough capital committed to move forward.

"Any success of your Alverson House," Alex said, biting off the words, "will result from quantity purchases for both hotels. You'll be able to offer customers either the low-or high-priced spread."

No doubt such savings would occur but not enough to warrant Alex's demand for 50 percent ownership. What a greedy bastard. But where else could she go? Who else could she trust?

"All right." Sophia swallowed her confusion and resentment. "Thank you."

Sophia never dreamed he would be so irrational. Time to leave before he changed his mind. She slid her chair back and took several steps out of the office with hat and parka in her hands. The deed was done.

A quick turn to the left and she found her exit blocked. Her head jerked up. A man blocking her path. William Jefferson Smith. Lord. Even more trouble.

"Didn't mean to startle you, ma'am," Soapy Smith said, the sound of his words as slick as maple syrup.

A surprised gasp escaped her. What was that scoundrel doing in Stromberg's? She twisted her shoulder to him and pushed past toward the rear door. Were he and Alex in partnership? Was that why Alex had acted so strangely?

CHAPTER THIRTY-THREE

Alex stepped to the office doorway to see Soapy, slim and stylish in his usual perfect-fitting three-piece wool suit. The man tipped his immaculate light-gray Stetson. Bright, intelligent eyes turned from the retreating Sophia to Alex. An expression of interest and bemusement gave life to his undertaker pallor. How long had that sneaky son of a bitch been outside the office door? How much had he heard?

"What do you want?" Alex asked, smoothing his shirt front and trying to regain his composure. Courtesy was the last thing on Alex's mind.

Alex wheeled back into his crowded space to pick up the scattered purchase orders from the floor. How dare that bitch accuse him of Jewing her down. Did Sophia have any idea how her "Jew" remark ripped at his self-esteem? To say nothing of how risky and poorly timed her proposed venture was. He glanced with disgust at the multitude of unfilled merchandise demands on his order board, then turned to face Smith's cool, unreadable expression.

"Why are you here?" Alex said. "It's a little early for poker, isn't it?"

"Can't afford to play you right now," Soapy answered.

The man presented his usual pleasant, guileless grin. Right. The ever-loquacious Smith could slip into a stone-faced persona that gave new definition to the term "poker face." Soapy was as sly an individual as Alex had ever met. That very characteristic made the man's company more interesting than anyone else's in mud-clogged Skagway. Cards provided their only common denominator as far as

Alex knew. And the unspoken danger Soapy represented added to the challenges of their marathon games.

"Got a business proposition to discuss with you," the well-dressed hustler said.

"I've got more business than I can handle," Alex muttered, forcing a degree of civility he didn't feel.

"It's never too busy to pass up a good opportunity," Smith persisted.

"Let's be honest, Soapy," Alex said. "With all due respect, I don't know what kind of legitimate merchant you'd be. You know you can't threaten your customers into buying. We should stick to poker, which you play so well."

"Now, Alex," Soapy said, not appearing to be the least offended. "I've already proven my commercial prowess. I've developed a fine organization."

Warnings rang. Smith had materialized in Skagway in early September. No one knew who he was or where he'd come from. And no one questioned the rapid growth and scope of Soapy's dubious activities since he had arrived. But Soapy didn't seem bothered that Alex was a Jew. Maybe Soapy didn't discriminate when it came to fleecing people.

"Your fine organization?" Alex said, smiling to take the edge off his words. "Your minions of con men, thieves and alleged murderers perform your dirty work. Allows you to play the role of courtly, respectable citizen."

"My, my," Smith said, his fingers tracing the rim of his hat. "You're too good a friend to be hoodwinked by all those nasty rumors and innuendos."

"Sure," Alex answered. "We're friends. Like Lee and Grant. Willing to fight it out over the card table. But business together? Don't you have your hands full with your casino and scams?"

Alex turned again to retreat behind his desk. A mistake to turn his back on a snake-oil salesman like Smith. Alarms bristled on the hairs of his neck. Soapy was no less dangerous than Alex's old nemesis, Isaac Snyder. That thought pricked another of Alex's concerns—why hadn't that bastard Snyder made some move of retribution? Or did he already have agents in Skagway ready for revenge? But what could happen in his own office during business hours?

"Opportunity waits for no man," Soapy countered and stepped uninvited into the small room.

A bemused expression returned to his unwanted guest's face as his manicured fingers traced the tight, dark bristles of his short-trimmed beard. An infectious smile spread across Soapy's angular features. Smith resembled a kind preacher, not a hard-nosed, often vicious, swindler.

"I've never seen Miss Alverson," Soapy said, "without that ridiculous hat jammed down upon her ears." He directed a steady gaze at Alex, soulful gray eyes set against almost chalk-white skin. "Knew she had interesting looks. I'll gamble those baggy clothes cover a few secrets as well. Bet she's a hidden beauty."

Get to know her as closely as you like, Alex thought. Be my guest. You too will discover the many secrets to that woman, including bigotry and excessive acquisitiveness. He couldn't care less if Soapy attempted to move in on the bitch.

"I heard rumors you were associates," Smith said. "Why do you think she's so secretive?"

"I think she hates men," Alex answered, surprising himself. Sophia's slur had doused any romantic feelings he'd had for her. "We are business partners. Nothing more."

"You mean you're not friends like you and me?" Soapy said, the sparkle of a gold tooth visible within his broad smile.

Could Soapy be any more manipulative and devious than Sophia? Without The Star's profits, Alex would have to scramble to stay solvent. Why not listen to the man?

"Well?" Alex asked. "What are you offering?"

"You operate the finest and most respected outfitter in town," Smith said without trace of irony or disrespect. "And you do seem to be very well inventoried."

Growing piles of duplicate merchandise multiplied like rabbits. If Smith had a clue about Stromberg's business, the man would realize how imbalanced the store's inventory had become. Or did he somehow know? Still, he might as well play along and see where the con man headed.

"We have the most complete selection of goods in Alaska," Alex agreed. "You decided to head to Dawson? Need an outfit?"

Soapy traveling to the Klondike was as likely as Mordecai filling an order correctly. He couldn't picture Smith with his hands dirty and calloused. And he couldn't resist the jab.

"No, sir," the man said. "Actually, I'm selling. I know you have a full supply of new goods. I am impressed. I'd like to run a different idea by you, if I may?"

Great. All Alex needed was more product. If he had fire insurance, maybe he could convince his poker partner to torch the store. Alex straightened. Could Soapy be responsible for today's arson attempt? Could those bumbling drunks have been part of Smith's gang?

"What's on your mind, Soapy?" Alex asked, increased caution stoking a higher level of attention. "I apologize for being in a hurry. I've got lots to do."

"I understand perfectly," Soapy said. "My associates and I have accumulated quite an inventory of slightly used goods. Both clothing and equipment. We thought you would rather control this product than compete against it."

Alex tightened. Had a subtle threat filtered through the respectful delivery? A warning reinforced by today's near disaster? Now his curiosity was aroused. But why? If Soapy had wanted to burn down Stromberg's, he wouldn't have used such clumsy idiots. Or was Alex reading too much into this same-day coincidence of Smith's visit and the fire?

"You are a shrewd merchant," Soapy began, "one who will see the advantage of an unorthodox idea. I propose to supply you with a steady stream of this product for only pennies on the dollar. You open another location, perhaps on Main Street, several blocks from Stromberg's. I have a suitable site picked out where you would offer used but serviceable items at discount prices. You'd serve different types of customers than Stromberg's. Those that can't afford new items."

"Where do you obtain your 'steady stream' of merchandise?" Alex asked. Probably from theft, murder, and hopeless despair.

"From various sources, as you can imagine," Smith said, waving his long-fingered elegant hands in dismissal. "You interested?"

Perhaps this idea had potential, an insurance policy against the slow months ahead. Necessity muted his irritation and alarm. With rock-bottom pricing, he wouldn't need to worry about a complete selection of goods. He'd cherry-pick. But he had no excess cash, and with Sophia's damn plans, no prospects of any change in that position. Although dealing with Soapy would be no safer than sticking a finger in front of a rattlesnake.

"What would your payment terms be?" Alex asked. "And would you be my benevolent landlord as well?"

"Whatever you're comfortable with," Smith said, a benign grin accompanying his words. "How does the name 'Nearly New Emporium' sound?"

The name sounded like a sleazy business that Isaac Snyder would choose. But what the hell, he should consider Soapy's proposal. After all, this was a frontier town, not San Francisco.

"Let me give it some thought, Soapy."

The idea of becoming partners with the devil should trump any potential profits. Then again, one of his few areas of agreement with Mordecai was the fact that cash flow was king.

CHAPTER THIRTY-FOUR

Whatever animals had traveled this rough, overgrown rock-strewn path—bear, caribou, moose—had either fled or ended up as food or clothing for voracious gold seekers. Thick fir and hemlock boughs slapped Jared's cap-covered head. Dense bushes, ferns, salmonberry and other low growth assaulted ankles and feet. Devil's club was the worst, with sharp spines on the stems and undersides of its branches. Wind whispered through the trees, a living thing. Dripping-gray clouds smothered all.

Arms and legs worked equally well in the steep scramble up A B Mountain's game trails. Long legs bought precious traction. Brutus's chugging breaths faded in the dense foliage behind him. A long-absent emotion registered—pride. Jared had finally outrun the barrel-bodied Airedale.

Small patches of snow now littered the cluttered forest floor. Colder, frost-laced temperatures promised the imminent arrival of winter. Swelling fear of losing these runs thrashing up the mountain shrouded his thinking like the blackened skies above him. Then, as he gulped and gasped for air, the steady updraft from the canyon far below carried the pungent smell of death.

How many dead horses littered the canyons? Two thousand? Two thousand, five hundred? This morning a distraught packer loading Stromberg's deliveries put the number at three thousand. The wrangler's eyes had glazed in disbelief and sadness as he shared the appalling news. Unexpected tears formed in Jared's eyes. So much wasteful abuse and cruelty of man toward helpless animals.

A tragedy played out on the Pass. Jared had seen the pathetic condition of the horses. Helpless animals led by idiots who didn't know a horse from a cow, let alone mules, oxen and even reindeer. They possessed little or no experience packing the horses. Their negligence condemned the animals to die.

What had that newspaperman, Tappan Adney, written in late August when describing the battle up the Gold Trail? "Men were like wolves, they fed on each other." At least September had brought a welcome end to the insatiable mosquitoes and the more painful bites of no-see-ums. But the absence of irritating insects brought little consolation for those on the trail of terror.

The halfway point was within reach. Jared's path took him above the sickly sweet stench of the appropriately nicknamed Dead Horse Trail. Climbing became difficult work now. The stink of death subsided, but oxygen became harder to find. And Jared didn't want to break rhythm. One misstep and he'd slide two or three steps backwards. He had to keep building momentum up the steep wall.

Dense forests of pine and cypress would soon become firs, then thin out near the tree line of A B Mountain. Jared moved with growing power, comfortably light-headed. But dark shapes resembled monsters. Branches and boulders melded into a fantastical vista of Jules Verne creations. He could have dismissed the images if an occasional mound hadn't resembled Brother Tom. Strange that he couldn't create a clear picture of Tom's face, only his hulking body. For that matter, neither Morgan's nor William's features could be summoned from his memory.

What was wrong with him? Why had his family turned on him? Why Tom's viciousness? And then, of course, the ever-present image of Sophia danced just beyond reach. Ridiculous to even consider her in his dreams. Yet something rang familiar about her.

Firs thinned, and Jared burst beyond the well-delineated tree line. Filtered sunlight welcomed him to his normal turnaround point. He stopped a hundred yards onto the rocky ridgeline that, with a few extended dips back into pines, could take him all the way to the top of White Pass. This improbable route's one-way distance—Skagway to the pass—would take between five to seven hours. Eighty percent of the hapless fools who crossed the turquoise-blue Skagway River spent weeks on the slippery trail of death, never reaching the top with all their required gear. He'd save the complete trip for another day.

A ragged duet broke out between the high-pitched whistle of thick-furred marmots and the short, high peeps of rat-sized picas. A golden eagle soared hundreds of feet above the low-flying pipits, warblers and golden-crowned sparrows. Wildlife became more visible. Deep breaths sucked in cleanliness. Jared found himself much closer to a wished-for utopia and further from the hellhole of Skagway.

And where was Brutus? Now this was embarrassing, competing through life with his dog. And losing until now. Would his partner meet him on the way down? The full-bodied Brutus could soldier on forever, but not at the killing pace Jared set up the almost vertical flank of A B. Pride registered again. And why should he hurry back down to Stromberg's? Alex had plenty of help.

The lure of the Klondike beyond the Coast Mountain range became a powerful force, almost irresistible. But he couldn't overcome the pull back to duty and responsibility to his boss, Alex. Why? Wasn't he a free, well-educated man? Well, education was only another tool of the capitalists. Didn't they need literate workers? The entire educational system's true hypocritical motive was not to enlighten but rather instill strict discipline and crush children to the will of the teacher. Great. Now he too was nothing but a literate slave. He turned and began his descent.

Various-sized rocks painted with slippery moss littered the mountainside. The sole of his leather work boot skidded on a lichen-smeared stone. Jared crashed to the ground and smashed his knee, bringing instant, throbbing pain. He had better pay attention. Getting hurt up here was not a good idea, with or without Brutus.

The best way down was to jump and slide through the jumble of dense, grasping foliage and treacherous plant-covered rocks. Where was the game trail? He bounced and crashed, his rear end a platform more useful than arms. Now a rhythm developed, winding through the boulders and trees. Jared committed his entire body to navigate down the steep slope. Arms crossed his face for protection from the limbs and bushes whipping at him. He traveled at an insane level of speed. How far to the bottom? And would he meet up with Brutus when he landed on the trail at sea level?

CHAPTER THIRTY-FIVE

Sophia stepped from the cocoon of her private room into The Star's frantic kitchen. Even the chaos of The Star couldn't shake off the unsettling memories of last month's confrontation with Alex. She needed an escape other than the congested streets of Skagway. Time for the relative peacefulness of a horseback ride on the road to Dyea.

She dodged waiters serving nonstop meals prepared by the invaluable Jacob Tredaway. How would she staff the new Alverson House? Wouldn't she require employees with more skill and class than those at the rough-and-tumble Star? Alex's objections to her new hotel echoed in her mind. Could she keep running her original location once the new hotel opened? Would she—could she—move the crocky, but hard-working Jacob Tredaway from The Star or somehow find a new, fancy cook?

A tall man appeared at the Star's entrance. Soapy Smith. He materialized right in her face. She flinched backwards, unable to conceal her surprise. Unnerving the way the crook seemed to emerge out of thin air. Again. Had he been waiting for her, or was his arrival coincidence? The man stood impeccable before her, elegance unable to hide the threat that hung like ocean mist around him.

"Good afternoon, Miss Alverson," Soapy greeted her, hat tipped in courtly fashion. "We meet again."

Her trips around town had provided more than enough evidence of his strangling grip on the lifeblood of Skagway. His gentleman's manners and expensive clothes did nothing to mitigate her dislike and distrust of the man. His clean, slick sophistication repulsed her more than a drunk cheechakoe passed out in the mud. Smith never did anything without a reason.

"Your new enterprise nears completion," he said, a disturbing gleam reflecting from his eyes. "I have a proposition for you."

"I'm not interested in anything you have to offer," Sophia replied, her hand working into the oversize pocket of her mackinaw for the comfort of her large pistol.

He stroked his well-trimmed beard. His hand's sensual movement across his face produced a disturbing reminder of her father. A wave of revulsion filled her.

"I would like to invest in your new hotel," Smith said. "I realize you have a relationship with Alex Stromberg. Somewhat difficult though. I can provide a more respectful partnership with more substantial financial resources."

Who did this contemptible man think he was? Sophia would rather leave Skagway than be associated with such a rogue. This man represented danger, evil. She stood straighter and squared her shoulders. She wouldn't let this bastard intimidate her.

"My present situation is completely satisfactory."

"I have several ideas," he continued, ignoring her comment, "that could vastly increase the business and profits of your new venture. Alex is a fine merchant, but I doubt his experience in more complex endeavors."

Typical Soapy. Turning on a presumed friend and perhaps associate. Who the hell was this thief to criticize a hard-working businessman like Alex? He'd been a lurking presence when she'd argued with Alex on financing the Alverson House last month. Had he heard their entire conversation? She swallowed hard at the thought of dealing with Smith at any level.

"Have you considered incorporating a fine first-class sporting house into your new location?"

Fear roiled her stomach. Did he know about her past? Her hand tightened on the pistol. She glared at the man with disbelief. She stepped around him and headed for the stable and her horse.

"Your offer is unwelcome and offending," Sophia said, attempting to control her shaky voice. "I have no desire to do any kind of business with you."

"You should seriously consider my suggestion, Miss Alverson," he called out to her, but she would not respond to him.

* * *

Her horse stood alone in the stable, a baleful stare greeting her. Ragged black spots and scars disfigured the horse's broken brown hide. Many rips and gashes had only recently healed. The ugly horse proved strong and perhaps even grateful for Sophia's rescue from inexperienced, frustrated cheechakos. But not so grateful that Sophia didn't have to keep clear of the horse's occasional nips.

Sophia saddled her large mare, then ran a gloved hand, still quaking from her confrontation with Soapy Smith, over the animal's neck. She stepped into the stirrup, swung onto the saddle. The previous owner had no name for the miserable beast other than "Damn nasty sack of bones." Her name change to "Gaye" seemed natural, even poetic justice, until the news four weeks ago of Gaye's tragic slaying. Still, the name stuck.

The horse no longer fought the bridle. At least, she thought, the sturdy horse appreciated her. Could she develop the same sense of companionship and loyalty with Gaye that seemed to exist between Brutus and Jared? Was that why Sophia loved the slow-witted filly? Partnership with an animal brought honesty and trust, something sorely missing in her human relationships.

A gentle kick of her boot heels prodded the horse out the stable opening. Sophia sucked in the refreshing air, then exhaled a cloud of steam. The weather, wet and crisp, distanced her from the discomfort of her encounter with Soapy Smith.

The bitter chill of early mornings created frozen ridges dusted with white crystals. Now, hours later, the road had been ground into a midday morass of slop. The White Pass Trail was soon to close, mired in mud, impassable with boulders and the dead bodies of hapless pack animals. Sophia struggled against what had become a one-way stream of beaten men and beasts flowing in sad retreat back into town.

Activity on the treacherous street demanded her attention. Still no decrease in the number of gold seekers shipping into Skagway. The new arrivals would all be stuck in town until the trail froze and became passable again. Good for business, and her sparkling, luxurious Alderson House would open within weeks—the finest hotel in Alaska. But recurring concerns of Alex and Soapy forced out any sense of well-being.

So why had Alex become so angry? He had reacted just like a child. Perhaps he'd disliked being told by a woman what to do. Men. Still, she shuddered. She had made many mistakes without the benefit of Alex's expertise since he had slammed a door in her face.

As a successful businessman, why wouldn't he willingly invest one or two months' profits from The Star for the opportunity to earn a fortune with the Alverson House? Because his pride was hurt? There had to be something else. What had she done to so dramatically alter their relationship?

She urged Gaye to a trot and guided her over the bridge of the swift-flowing Skagway River, turning left toward Dyea. This route provided an escape from the sorrow and disappointment that straggled down from the Dead Horse Trail. So disconcerting to glance back at the motley parade. Then a shape the size of a small brown bear emerged from the trail's fork. Brutus.

The Airedale trotted toward Sophia, closing the space between them. His tongue, almost as large as his head, drooped from the side of his mouth. Rhythmic pants bursting from his wild-haired body could be heard even at this distance. Gaye jerked back. The horse danced sideways, steam rising from flared nostrils. The closer the dog jogged, the more Gaye reacted, throwing her head skyward, lunging backwards, shoulders arched.

"Hey, easy, Gaye." Sophia lowered her head, patted the mare's pitted neck. "It's okay, lady."

But her soft calls went unheeded. The horse focused on the approaching dog. Hoofs lifted and slammed into the soggy earth with jarring force. Gaye's erratic movements threw Sophia off balance. She tightened her knees, struggling to stay in the saddle.

Brutus stopped some twenty feet away, head pointed up the mountain toward a noisy crackling of underbrush. Sophia snatched at her hat, knocked loose from her horse's frantic jerks. A crash resounded above, branches flying. A man's body, arms swinging wildly, slid down the last few feet of growth onto the trail halfway between dog and horse. Gaye swiveled at the man's shattering arrival. Too much for the spooked animal. Sophia grasped at the reins.

The horse reared. The sudden movement threw Sophia's shoulders back, her hat flying. The reins slipped from her hands, and her fingers grasped for the saddle horn. Gaye continued her frantic dance. She snapped sideways. Sophia's feet lost connection with the stirrups. Again the horse reared, threatening to collapse backwards. How could she escape? She released her hands from the saddle horn and threw her body to one side. The flat of her back smacked the wet ground. All air forced from her lungs. Darkness blocked her vision. Gasping unconsciousness threatened to overwhelm her.

"Miss Alverson?" a man said.

A face appeared. She couldn't get a clear picture of the person, features a little cockeyed. Brutus's huge black nose took form above her. Sophia blinked several times. Jared materialized, his hand holding his dog to one side.

"I'm so sorry." Jared's irregular features twisted into pained chagrin.

Her shoulders lifted from the wet dirt as she propped herself on her elbows. Embarrassment built within Sophia almost as rapidly as soreness blanketed her body. Too vulnerable lying on her back like an upside-down turtle.

"Help me up," she demanded. What the hell was this maniac doing falling from the mountain like Icarus from the sun?

"Perhaps you should stay still," Jared said, his voice coming from far away. "You'll know in several minutes if you're seriously injured."

If she could just roll to her side and struggle to her feet. But a wave of light-headedness swept away her equilibrium. Tipping sideways, she again headed to moist ground. Strong hands caught her under her armpits, stabilized her, and eased her to her feet. Sophia took a tentative step and turned to Jared.

He appeared young and foolish. Then his expression tightened, eyes squinting, forehead furrowed. A shocked expression lit his damaged face.

"You're the boy on the train," he stammered. His discovery brought unanticipated animation to his sad countenance. "But you're no boy."

Oh, no. He'd finally recognized her. She'd become too confident and comfortable in Skagway. Didn't this discovery by Jared prove her vulnerability? She would have to return to her past vigilance. Didn't Hawk Face always creep through her dreams, his apparition still appearing among the crowds in town?

"No," she said, scrambling to find her protective hat. "I'm no boy. Now help me on my horse."

"Why didn't you let me know?" Jared stammered. "I owe you so much. Maybe my life."

Jared looked so silly and immature. What a difference between the confused, pathetic boy and the charged attractions and dangers surrounding Alex and Soapy. Jared presented no threat. In fact, he appeared almost comical with the complex swirl of his emotions—confusion, embarrassment but, yes, the same hungry eyes as Alex. She wanted no connections to her past life. The quicker Sophia could free herself from his presence the better.

"Don't be melodramatic." Sophia spied her hat and made a painful lunge to pick it up. "All you needed was a little aid getting to a hotel. Now all I need is help getting back onto my horse."

Jared helped place her foot in the stirrup and held the horse's head. She swung onto the saddle in a slow, careful arc. The pain of her bruised torso demanded her attention. Unrelenting pressure in her chest brought difficulty in breathing. But Sophia maintained her seat on Gaye, fighting off any threatening loss of consciousness.

"Did you ever finish *The Time Machine*?"

"Yes." What a silly question. Sophia turned her horse down the path to Dyea. "Several times. I'll return it this evening."

"No," Jared hollered. "Please keep it."

That was what the young man cared about? Literature? Hard to be too concerned that he had recognized her. Sophia smacked her heels harder than usual into the horse's side. Gaye jumped to a canter.

CHAPTER THIRTY-SIX

J ared remained rooted to the earth as Sophia rode toward Dyea. His hands tingled from the touch of her body, his fingers aflame from the inadvertent discovery of large, soft breasts hidden beneath layers of clothing. He slammed his mouth shut, too late to avoid exhibiting to her the look of a moronic dunce.

Why had she hidden her identity? She was the one who had saved him on the train. Why was she angry with him? Of course, knocking her off her horse might not have endeared him to her. But why wouldn't she allow him to express gratitude for her help? Why did she look through him, ignore him?

Jared staggered off the trail and collapsed at the base of a damaged cyprus tree. A jagged wound on the trunk next to his shoulder evidenced the brutal assault of a prospector's axe. A revelation registered—until now she had never looked Jared in the eye. She had always averted her gaze or avoided him, despite the fact that she must have known him immediately. She had been afraid of recognition. Why? She certainly had nothing to fear from him. Embarrassment faded.

The image of her helpless on the ground brought a surge of warmth and excitement. Sophia Alverson was no longer an aloof, untouchable ice princess. She was human, no different than Jared. He may never have a chance to satisfy his desire or develop even the fragment of a relationship. Still, the feel of her body vibrated through his limbs.

That night, excited emotions overcame the usual nighttime shadows of depression and sadness. Sophia. His thoughts of her might be ridiculous fantasies. But the image of her direct gaze and the burning touch of her body remained vivid. Jared yanked off his boots and burrowed into the bedding fully clothed. He reviewed their brief encounter in unending loops, always returning to that moment when his hands wrapped around her torso, fingers on fire from the softness of her breasts.

Gusts whipped the worn canvas tent. The fabric snapped with the random wind shifts. Where the heck was Brutus? Jared had left the flaps loose for his dog's return, but all that entered the tent was freezing air. When would his partner return from his evening rounds? Jared fiddled with his nest of blankets and bear hides. Sound sleep would evade him without the Airedale's presence. Why couldn't exhaustion alone allow him sweet escape into senselessness?

His body heat warmed the cocoon of covers, and images faded into darkness. The dreamy vision of the beautiful woman engulfed his consciousness. Jared again slipped his hands underneath her arms. Sophia leaned back against his chest. He lifted her upright, and increased pressure from her body thrust against him. His fingers once again sunk into sensual mounds, this time cutting through the fabric of her coat, blouse, underwear, to her silky flesh.

Her firm buttocks rubbed against Jared, up and down, again and again. A sense of urgency filled his loins. Sophia kept moving, rotating. She wouldn't stand still or turn around, kept leaning into him, generating strange sensations. Not uncomfortable but unsettling. Additional pressure built with each of her movements. Jared didn't know if he wanted her to continue, move faster or stop. Why was she doing this?

Too much excitement now. He needed relief, but Sophia wouldn't cease, and a growing passion swallowed Jared. He would burst if she didn't release him from this bizarre backwards embrace. And then he did explode. His eyes snapped open to a sensual release in his groin. Moisture soaked his underwear, then spread to his pants. An embarrassing hardness tented his blankets.

Hot shame blazed across his face. Whatever had happened was sinful, wasn't it? The release of his seed exquisite, but an act of disgusting evil. He swallowed his confusion, struggled to contain the sticky fluid saturating his crotch. This was not his first humiliation, but nothing had as clearly connected to a specific female. One whom he actually knew, one who inhabited his dreams most nights and days. His agitated breathing echoed in the tent as if he'd run a marathon.

Then he became aware of angry muffled voices rising from outside. A panicked scream, cut in half to a gurgle. Brutus let out a rumbling growl. The dog sprang to his feet from the bedding near Jared. When had the Airedale returned? The sound of men struggling in the alley on the other side of the canvas demanded his attention. Jared threw the covers to the side and dove for the tent flap, following Brutus toward the disturbance.

Shadows of two men pummeling a smaller figure danced against the muted light from the back of Stromberg's. One mugger's arm crushed the victim's neck from behind while the other slammed fists into the crumpling body. The little man had no chance.

"You're gonna tell us where your damn stake's hidden, you little bastard." The rasping voice held a mix of frustration and vicious menace.

"Stop," Jared cried in midstride. "What are you doing? Leave that man alone."

Both assailants wheeled toward Jared. The one with the death grip released his victim, then flung the short man to the ground. Jared flinched. The battered figure moaned and rolled on his side. The robber's partner kicked hard into the heap curled on the frozen mud. How much damage had the muggers already inflicted? Then for a second time two attackers made threatening moves toward Jared.

"Who the hell you think you are?" the larger thug cried out, throwing a wild swing at Jared's head.

Jared's forearm blocked the punch, but the speed and strength of the man's blow knocked Jared off balance. He staggered to the side, then regained his fighter's stance and warded off the next punch. The crook stepped into each swing, driving Jared back toward his tent. The man knew how to fight. Flashing images of Tom's sucker punch filled Jared with anger and energy. He wasn't going to underestimate these bullies. No more fancy jabbing or shuffling footwork. He wouldn't be caught by surprise this time.

Jared reacted with a flurry of uppercuts and overhead blows, dancing in the mud with stocking feet. Two, three, then four swings connected. His burly attacker hesitated, then wilted under the continued barrage. He stumbled to the ground from a final well-placed right cross. Jared shifted backwards.

The felled assailant scrambled on all fours into the darkness, regained his feet, then sprinted down the opposite end of the street. Jared let him escape, watching the man wheel around the corner onto Third Street. Screams came from the other thief, disappearing the other way down the frost-crusted alley, Brutus snapping at his heels.

The dog responded to Jared's call, trotting back toward the tent, head and tail erect. A surge of exhilaration shot through Jared, followed by questions. What had he done? Chilling temperature registered. Jared's shoeless feet had turned numb.

He bent over the small elderly figure huddled on the ground. Hands secured the man's armpits in the same way he had assisted Sophia. But the thought of his soiled pants brought heat to his face. Well, the man was in no condition to notice or care.

Jared dragged the beaten man into the tent, his weight unsubstantial despite the bulky clothing. Blood stained the old man's face. Hands hurt like hell, but Jared experienced a sense of empowerment. The Airedale sniffed the injured victim.

"More like partners now, Brutus?"

He lit a kerosene lantern and bent over the little man, an ancient, grizzled sourdough. Blood dripped from the corner of his mouth, large contusions sprouted from several blows on cheeks and forehead. The crooks had caused plenty of damage to the face of the old man. The injuries generated unexpected compassion. Jared too had suffered a similar fate. But tonight the confrontation had ended differently.

A soft moan rose from the rumpled figure. The gnarled old man's eyes flickered open, then widened. His weather-beaten features and fierce expression tugged at Jared's memory. The wounded man's hand flashed to his belt. He yanked out a huge Bowie knife as long as the prospector's arm. Jared rotated back on his heels.

"Easy, mister." Jared raised empty hands before the victim's wild eyes. Brutus stirred in the corner. "We're friends. My dog and I saved you from a couple of thieves."

"Bastards," the prospector spit out. "Would've sliced 'em into sausage if they hadn't jumped me from behind."

Blood continued to seep from broken skin above his eye and cheekbone. The small figure waved his enormous blade, sputtering an impressive string of curses. Lord. Cross an entire continent all the way to Alaska, and who does he meet? A sun-burned Duffy. A chuckle escaped his lips.

"What's so funny?" the old man asked, as belligerent as the crusty Irishman who had coached Jared at Yale.

The prospector glanced around the tent crowded with blankets and merchandise. The knife remained a shimmering threat, floating between them. Finally, he sheathed the weapon and made a rapid inventory of pockets and pouch. An evil laugh erupted from his split lips.

"Bastards only got what's left of my traveling gold. Where am I?"

"Stromberg's warehouse," Jared replied. "Store's next door. My dog and I heard you attacked. Drove off two men mugging you in the alley."

"You think I got more gold stashed nearby?" Suspicion glinted in the old man's eyes.

"I hope you do," Jared answered, "if gold's important to you. Doesn't seem to make everyone happy."

"You ever been starving?" the prospector asked, eyes again roving about the cluttered tent.

"No."

"Well," the injured man said. "I've starved, and I've had good meals. I prefer eating. Gold comes in handy when you're hungry. But you're right, gold don't solve all problems. Just most of them."

"My name's Jared Monroe." Jared reached for a blanket, then handed the coarse wool to the sourdough. "What's yours?"

"Friends call me Salt. That's all you need to know. That's all I am." Salt wiped his still bleeding lower lip with a filthy sleeve. "I kinda remember a dog jumping into the fight. Had one hell of a set of teeth. That him over there? Looks mean."

"Brutus, come here," Jared called to the dog. The Airedale only lifted his head. "Please."

The animal rose to its feet and took several measured steps to Jared. The massive, kinky-haired head poked at the prospector. The old man flinched. Brutus seemed satisfied. Must recognize an animal that smelled as bad as the dog did.

"He can be friendly," Jared answered the grizzled man's unasked question, then wrapped his hand around the dog's muzzle. His fingers lifted hair and jowls revealing a frightening set of teeth.

"Holy shit," Salt said. "Those are lion fangs."

Jared released his hold. The vicious-looking beast licked Jared's face until he put up his arm to ward off the Airedale. The old man watched, eyes reflecting both wonder and distaste.

"I better be gettin' on," Salt said, shrugging off the blanket.

He struggled to his knees, arms wrapped around his torso. The effort forced short gasps. Pain added creases to his already wrinkled features. Just how far did the injured man think he could go?

"You're banged up pretty bad," Jared said. "Bet you've got a couple of broken ribs. I know how that feels. Why don't you take it easy? Spend the night here. We've got the space. There's plenty of blankets."

The rough-edged prospector looked first confused, then grateful. He sunk back to the ground, closed his eyes and fell asleep within seconds. No thank you offered.

"Goodnight, Duffy," Jared whispered.

CHAPTER THIRTY-SEVEN

Jared followed Brutus into Stromberg's tent. The Airedale collapsed onto a tattered bear hide. Jared threw his steaming hat and gloves into a corner. Lightheaded physical satisfaction from his run registered despite fatigue and body aches. Then he noticed Salt lounging on a bundle of clothing inventory.

"What's the matter, boy?" The lantern light reflected an unsettling gleam from Salt's eyes. "Caught in an avalanche?"

Well, well. This was a first. Most times, the only conversation Jared could pull out of Salt would be a grunt. The man's dark moods would last for days. This grumpy old man across the cluttered tent held knowledge and experiences of the Yukon close to his vest. Too bad.

"Been out for a run." Jared rubbed his numb hands together.

"Again?" Salt asked. "You are one crazy boy. Where the hell you run to?"

"Top of A B Mountain." Jared peeled off his wet boots and socks, soaked with sweat and snow from his struggle up and down the disappearing game trails. Could Salt be in one of his rare talkative moods?

"Won't get far with wet feet," the miner said. "Toes freeze up and fall off. Always need a bag of extra socks when you head into the wilds."

Jared needed a lot more than socks. He removed his mackinaw and dirt-encrusted pants, leaving on only his stained long underwear. He was filthy and exhausted from his run. And his struggle up and down the mountain brought mental relief for only so long. How could he wipe away the frustration and disappointment that seeped into his mind?

Now off the mountain, he had no desire to return to work at Stromberg's. Depression engulfed him. In the dark clutter of the Stromberg warehouse tent he could only generate self-contempt for his fantastical infatuation with Miss Alverson. This entire futile Alaskan adventure had turned into a disaster. Time to return south, wiser but to a no less rotten world. He reached for one of the rabbit-fur blankets on his cot and wrapped the thick covering around his shoulders.

"How many times you been up that mountain?" Salt asked, directing a baleful glare at Jared. The old man's luminescent eyes dominated his pock-marked face.

"Fifteen, twenty." Jared said. "Not sure. I don't run all the way to the top. I stop at the tree line. Still a ways to the peak. But you could connect to White Pass working the high ridges."

Salt's eyes flashed and lips curled. The first smile to crack the miner's knotted features. He leaned forward, full attention on Jared.

"How the hell you get up that slope?" Salt asked. "It's covered with nasty brush. Low-hanging limbs that'll knock your head off. Broken branches grabbing at your ankles. Slippery fungus-covered rocks of all sizes. Naw. Not possible."

Why was the old man so curious? Jared didn't have to prove anything to Salt. And he definitely didn't have the energy to debate. In fact, he still couldn't even find the strength to dress for work. The temporary comfort beneath the warm fur blanket in his sweat-encrusted underwear offered further reason to stall.

And how much longer could he make the climb, or for that matter, run anywhere? Snow was beginning to stick to the rutted, muddy streets of Skagway. Jared shuddered at the warning signs—lowered temperatures, vanishing hours of daylight and nothing but threatening gray skies. The ever increasing gloom of winter in Alaska brought a tightening to Jared's chest as if the absence of light carried him closer to death. He glanced at the old man. The unwavering, inquisitive expression on Salt's face had become annoying.

"What are you looking at?" Jared's burst of unexpected belligerence startled him. His voice sounded strange to his own ears.

"Just figuring what you're made of," Salt said. "Tell me the truth, lad. How do you get up that damn mountain?"

"Follow old game trails most of the way," Jared said in a soft, self-conscious voice. "The biggest challenge is coming down. You generate too much momentum—go too fast—and lose the path."

"Take me up there," Salt said.

Where did that demand come from? The prospector had shown little interest in anything Jared did. He'd also shrugged off all of Jared's questions. The crocky SOB hadn't even thanked Jared for saving his life. Now he wanted to share Jared's forays up the mountain? Jared sat stunned.

"The whole way?"

"Naw," Salt said, wiping his hands on ragged pants. "Just want to get a feel for your so-called route."

"What for?" Skepticism and curiosity vied within Jared.

"Might have an idea."

Salt's vague answer further irritated Jared. If the prickly sourdough was so intent on asking questions, so would Jared.

"How long have you been prospecting?"

"Well, boy," Salt said, "longer than you've got time to listen."

"Try me," Jared said.

"It ain't that I've just been some old fart searching for a pot of gold," Salt began, lively eyes focused on Jared. "I've been journeying through the landscape of life. Been an ugly trip. Learned about man's evils. Even found peace."

"You don't look too peaceful to me," Jared said, shifting the rabbit-skin cloak. Salt's huge Bowie knife and his propensity to wave the weapon about contradicted the crusty man's statement of peace.

"I started out bitter and disillusioned, just like you," Salt said, an earnest expression on his sunburned face. "I first hit the gold trail in '58. Too young for California, not enough of a stake to head for

Australia or New Zealand. Went to Fraser Canyon south of here in British Columbia. Learned plenty about mankind. Don't know if gold makes all men evil, or if we're all just born bastards."

"How old were you?" Jared asked.

Hard to believe Salt had ever been young. This rough, edgy character probably came out of the womb creased and ornery. What kind of parents could have given birth to such a strange creature?

"Not sure," Salt replied. "Maybe eighteen or nineteen. Left the farm in Iowa pretty quick. Nothing there but work, dirt and misery. Along the Fraser River, white men stole claims from the Indians. Then white and black started battling. On Christmas Eve if you can imagine. The worst were the damn hypocritical British officials. Those sons of bitches stole from everybody."

"What finally happened?" Jared asked. His journey west paled in comparison to the old man's experiences.

"Official storyline had British Royal Marines and new administrative flunkies restoring order." Salt spit on the packed earth of the tent floor, just like Duffy's disgusting habit. "That's bullshit. Civil War's what did it. The most unruly and nasty prospectors were Americans. When the war broke out, they went back south to pick sides and kill each other."

"Why didn't you go back?" Jared questioned.

Could what the old man said be true? Jared thirsted for the knowledge Salt seemed to have soaked up in his travels. Jared inched forward, drawn by Salt's magnetic pull.

"First lesson," Salt said. "All men are the same, North or South. Mostly bad. A little good. That war didn't need me, and I wanted to get away from civilization, not die there. I worked my way up the Fraser to Quesnel. Headed east into the Cariboos and another strike."

Images of forested wilderness and frozen creeks filled Jared's mind. The Cariboos, a forbidding country of soaring mountains and impassable glaciers, couldn't be that different from the Yukon Territory.

"How'd you do there?"

"Lesson number two," Salt said. "You got to be the first one there. By the time I got to some decent color country, it was too late. Canadian bastards had beat everyone there. They proved men from all countries are mean and avaricious. I spent a few lean years panning low-yield creeks 'til I gave up."

"You've got a pretty good vocabulary for an illiterate miner," Jared said, unable to flush out his doubts. Still, even if the prospector was lying or exaggerating, he could spin one hell of a tale.

"Never said I was uneducated," Salt replied. "I've had plenty of time to read. That's one good thing about being holed up all winter."

Movement at the tent flap interrupted Salt's discourse. A rumbling growl came from Brutus in the corner. Horace's pale bald head poked in.

"I need help, Jared," the skinny clerk said. "Alex went stomping out of here an hour ago. No idea when he's coming back."

Jared didn't move. He wanted Salt to continue, afraid he wouldn't get the old man to open up again. The hell with Stromberg's and Alex and Horace. He'd paid his dues many times over. They'd have to survive without him.

"Sorry, Horace," Jared said after a pause. "Can't make it. Sprained my ankle. You'll have to run things without me the rest of the day."

A red flush blossomed on Horace's face. The skinny man muttered unintelligible phrases and backed out the tent flaps. Jared turned back to the prospector and settled deeper into the furs of his cot.

"Trouble in paradise for your boss?" Salt's sarcasm hung in the wet, frigid air.

"Yes," Jared answered. "The normal routine at Stromberg's changed since the trail's been closed. Used to be prospectors felt fortunate to find any supplies." How much should he confess of the changing dynamics? "Quality's become an issue. Customers are comparing prices to the competition down the street. People used to appreciate and accept the integrity of our selection. Now there's lots of haggling and arguing."

"White Pass will open soon as everything freezes and snow covers the dead horses," Salt said, pulling out his huge Bowie knife to clean filthy fingernails. "Business'll pick up again. Give all those fools an opportunity to freeze to death."

Salt put down his knife and pulled out two cigars and a bottle of rotgut. He took a swig and waved the bottle and wicked-looking cigars at Jared. Jared hesitated. Liquor had never passed his lips. He'd never smoked. Why not? What good had abstinence accomplished?

"Can't conduct serious business without the proper fixin's," Salt said. He took another healthy slug of whiskey, put a match to both cigars and handed a lit cheroot along with the bottle to Jared.

"Are we conducting serious business?" Jared asked.

"Might be. I'll finish my story. Then we'll decide. Take a drink."

Jared accepted the cigar in one hand and brown glass container in the other. He took a guarded puff. His mouth felt as if filled with foul ashes from a still-smoking hearth. He took a swallow of booze to wash away the terrible taste. The liquor blazed its own fire in his throat.

Why on earth would anyone poison themselves with such disgusting things? Jared shook his head, stubbed out the cigar, and passed the bottle and tobacco back to Salt. The sourdough smiled again. Twice in one day.

"I shall continue," the old man said with a slight bow. "After starving half to death in the Cariboos, I figured it was time to check out some rumors circulating about the Black Hills in the Dakotas. The white man was once again ripping off the Indians, this time the Sioux. Bad mistake. Went to Deadwood. Not much different from Skagway."

Salt spit twice and took a healthy swallow of booze. The same sour expression remained before and after his drink. The powerful liquor didn't seem to faze him.

"Staked a claim. Was hard-rock mining, so I teamed up with a couple of fellas. Hit a nice seam, and things were looking promising. Then we had the misfortune of catching the attention of a violent bloodsucker, George Hearst."

Salt couldn't have invented all these facts. There must be some truth in much of what he said. Jared had waited for him to open up. But there had to be a reason for all this unexpected shared information.

"Evil comes in many shapes, but mostly it shows up in nice clothes with a couple of thugs on each shoulder," Salt's disgust evidenced in both tone and expression. "I believe Mr. Soapy Smith is additional proof of that fact."

The mention of Smith added a new level of credibility to Salt's tale. Jared was well aware of Soapy and his hoodlums. Would the wilds of the Yukon interior be free of such monsters?

"Hearst offered us about one-third of the mine's value. We told him to butt out. That night Hearst's enforcers showed up. Killed Malcolm and Kelly, my partners. I was taking a crap in the trees when I heard the shots. Pulled my pants up and ran like hell."

Brutus rose from his spot in the corner. The dog came over to Jared and poked him with his muzzle. Brutus looked at Salt, sniffed, then slid from the tent for his late afternoon rounds. The miserable Skagway weather didn't seem to bother the dog. Amazing how graceful and silent the thick-bodied Airedale's movements.

"Dog seems to have a mind of his own," Salt said, his puffing creating a foul-smelling halo around his grizzled head. "Don't do much of value, but he did help save my ass."

About time Salt offered some form of thanks. The old man now swung between charming and irascible within the same sentence. Jared shook his head.

"Traveled to Cripple Creek," Salt continued, alternating puffs with hits off the whiskey bottle, "near Pike's Peak in Colorado. Then back north. Picked up a few pokes in Cayoosh Creek. Chinese there first. They dished out their own brand of intolerance. The yellow pig-tailed bastards drove out the whites. Even then, pissed as I was, I recognized the irony of the situation. Proved intolerance comes in all colors. I went a little further north to Tualmeen. Turned the tables on the Chinks. A goodly amount of us noble whites drove out the cocksuckers. This time stole their claims. Another lesson. Evil don't play favorites."

The image materialized of the slipper-encased foot of a lynched man twitching beneath a San Francisco light pole. The victim's shoe floated to the ground. The unlucky Chinaman. Difficult to believe

Chinese could hold their own against white men, based on the violent discrimination he had witnessed.

"For the last ten years," Salt began, then lay back on a pile of coats and hit the bottle again. "I finally found my place in the world. In this here great wilderness, to be precise. Too damn rugged for sleazy city folk or rich thieves. I've traveled all through the Yukon River basin. Mined enough gold to keep from starving. First at Fortymile, then Circle City. But things have gone to hell with the Klondike strike."

Salt had to have some motive for his performance. Did this mean the sourdough wanted to include Jared in some plan? Jared's heart jumped. He ached to travel the empty lands beyond Skagway and the Pacific Coast. Just hours before, he had cast a longing gaze at the ridges and mountains visible from A B's tree line. The siren call from the Yukon Territory had been almost overwhelming.

"Not much civilization beyond Dawson." Salt's voice hardened with anger. "Used to be honor among all us prospectors. Changed now. May have to find another wilderness paradise. World's gettin' smaller, but there'll always be another gold rush somewhere. Should be enough untracked country in Alaska and Canada to last my lifetime. You oughta consider giving the Yukon a try."

Could the wide-open Yukon finally be attainable? Salt had scored a direct hit. But Jared was all too familiar with his obvious shortcomings and limitations to attempt such a journey on his own. He needed a mentor, a guide, an old mountain man like Salt.

"What are you saying, old man?" Jared asked, not sure whether to be excited or frightened.

CHAPTER THIRTY-EIGHT

Salt was waiting for Jared when he and Brutus stumbled exhausted back to Stromberg's tent. The wizened prospector's face reflected myriad emotions, without his perpetual sour expression. What had possessed the little man to make today's brief venture with Jared into the tangled underbrush of A B Mountain? Salt's short, surprising foray had at least supplied new questions to distract Jared on his brutal climb, but not enough to block a more important claustrophobic concern. How much longer could Jared overcome the accumulating snow and plunging temperatures that made the struggle up A B increasingly difficult?

He collapsed onto his bed of hides. Lying on his back, Jared stripped off his filthy boots and steaming, soaked socks. Canvas walls rippled in the late-afternoon wind, whipping in confused gusts. Salt remained immobile, leaning against a pile of excess merchandise. Jared pulled off the rest of his clothes, self-conscious once he reached the last layer of underwear. The tent had become much smaller since Salt had taken up unofficial and, Jared hoped, temporary residence. The old man's uninterrupted glare irritated Jared.

"I'll tell you what," Salt said. "You're nothing but a dumb-ass greenhorn. But I'll bet those long legs could cover some ground."

This "dumb-ass greenhorn" was in no mood for a verbal flogging. He and Brutus should have left the old man to the mercies of the two thugs assaulting him in the alley behind Stromberg's. Life would have remained a lot more peaceful and less complicated.

"I'll take you where you should go," Salt said. The old man couldn't stand still. He spun in the tent's tight quarters, arms flailing, eyes flashing. "The Yukon's clean and vast. No one telling you what to do. I'll teach you to survive, live off the land, travel across rough country, and when to hole up so the weather don't kill you."

Jared slipped into dry clothes, avoiding his unwanted guest's baleful stare. Still, Salt's shift from sarcasm to selling piqued Jared's interest.

"It's a country," Salt said, "free of man's nasty footprints and evil ways."

"It'll be filled with the dregs of humanity," Jared mumbled in disgust, stretching clean, dry socks over numb feet. "Once the pass opens, these greedy Skagway scoundrels will flood the interior."

"Not too many are gonna make it," Salt stated.

Salt's features appeared carved from rough granite. Even his tough pock-marked skin evidenced a certain strength. Another shift of emotion from the sourdough to dead serious. So many similarities between the prospector and Duffy. And both of them difficult to be around.

"We'll be in Dawson 'fore those helpless idiots get their gear packed."

"How?" Jared asked, busying himself with the buttons on his flannel shirt. "The trail's still closed. Winter's almost here. Rivers in the interior are frozen, and food's short. Mounties are now stationed at the top of the Chilkoot and very soon the White Pass. Word is they won't be letting anyone through who doesn't have a year's supply of food and equipment. Then they'll demand payments for the duty tax. Quite a racket."

"That's where you come in, boy." Salt leaned closer to Jared. "Think you can get a couple of mules up A B Mountain? Horses wouldn't make it too far. We cut straight up the mountain. Sneak around those useless bloodsucking Canadians at the top of the pass. Follow the ridges and drop into Lake Lindman, then Bennett."

What the hell was the old man talking about? Jared had broken trail through the mounting snow on the game paths, but the footing remained treacherous. He and Brutus, and perhaps Salt, could make it. But mules? Salt's questions confused Jared but also awakened emotions buried beneath months of frustration and disappointments.

"Maybe," Jared said, and that was a stretch.

"Maybe don't cut it. Yes or no?"

Jared cringed. He wouldn't lie to himself. Yes, he yearned to escape into Salt's wild country. But Jared's previous failures and obvious inexperience overpowered his dreams. How should he answer? He had no idea if he could lead Salt, let alone mules, over such brutal terrain.

"I'm not sure." Jared's answer, gutless even to his own ears, brought heat to his face.

"Too bad," Salt said, a doleful expression emphasizing his melodramatic tone. "Guess I'll be moving on. I could have taken you where you truly want to go, once we're over the Pass. Well, at least you're a damn fine worker."

"I try," Jared answered, confused by Salt's change of subjects.

"I know you do the books for your boss, handle much of the heavy work, wait on customers, and with all your crazy running, you're in pretty fine shape. Make good money too, don't you?"

Jared focused on lacing his shoes. How much money was he making? Not that he cared. Living space in the storage tent and food at The Star were part of Jared's pay. Alex stashed his cash earnings in Stromberg's safe.

"So," Salt said in a neutral tone, "I guess being a clerk in this fine town is nice, soft and fulfilling. What you gonna do with your life? Follow Alex Stromberg around from town to town, gold rush to gold rush?"

"No." The word burst from Jared's lips. "What about our supplies? We can't lug all the stuff we'll need up over the mountains."

"Well, now," the old prospector said grinning, eyes afire. "You know the way to the top. You can mark a trail up those game paths you found. Bear, moose or deer made those trails—mules can surely make it. You said you been raised with mules and horses. Plus, you're a knowledgeable merchant. Food's what we'll be taking. Whatever's lightest and most valuable. You choose the best selection. Maybe Mr. Stromberg will give you a deal."

"Won't we need more than food?" Jared wanted to clamp down the transparency of his swelling interest in the conversation.

"Yep," Salt said. "But most of what we'll need already's been dumped along the way from the Pass to Lake Bennett. You know how much mining equipment, clothing and cooking kits been dumped by those hopeless tenderfeet. Hell, your boss could open a branch store on the far side of the Pass using all the crap left behind. Food's what we'll take. Worth more than gold in Dawson. They'll be close to starving by the time we show up."

Salt was talking to him as if Jared had made up his mind. This was insane. How could he trust his life to this old man? But what did he have to lose? He couldn't face many more days of slaving away at Stromberg's. And if he struck it rich, would Sophia Alverson continue to ignore him?

"I can get us over the pass," Jared blurted out.

"Good lad." Salt stepped to Jared with an outstretched hand. "Partners. I'll pay for what we'll need, you lead us over the Coastal Mountains. Need to purchase five good mules and a team of inside sled dogs. Carry about 1000 pounds. Plus our food. Mules 200 each, dogs 20, and you and me 50-pound packs. I got a freight sled stashed at Lake Bennett. Use it to travel to Dawson. Be there in no time."

"Inside sled dogs?" Jared asked.

"Born and raised in this northern snow country," Salt said. "Tough as nails. Dogs can survive any kind of weather, pull a sled all day. Got thick fur like a wolf. Mostly malamutes. Unlike those soft weaklings from the south." The old man's lips curled in disgust, yellow teeth exposed. "We're not taking your worthless animal," he spit out. "Brutus wouldn't last a week in the wilderness."

"He's going," Jared retorted, iron lacing his words, fingers curled into fists. "Or I'm staying."

Salt threw his arms in the air and spit. Jared looked on with revulsion. The prospector's filthy habit would soon turn the hammered dirt floor of the tent into a bigger swamp than Broadway.

"Laddie, you know how to handle a rifle and pistol?"

"Some," Jared said. He knew how to shoot a rifle. Had an old Sharps growing up, but he'd never shot a revolver.

"Your life may depend on how well you can shoot," Salt said, eyes narrowing. "All kinds of wolves in the wilderness. Two-and four-legged varieties. Do a little practicing before we head out. Keep your weapons oiled and handy. I'll get us a couple of Remington repeaters. Use the same load as our handguns."

This entire adventure with Salt was becoming both more real and more complicated by the minute. Was he tough enough to survive in the Yukon winter? Could he trust the old man with his life? Could he get them over the pass?

"Might want to leave some notice to your next of kin," the prospector said with a lowered voice.

"Don't have any," Jared said. Unwelcome memories of the family farm, rejection and his brother's evident hatred washed over him.

"You an orphan?"

"Might as well be," Jared said without emotion.

"Got any savings?" Salt asked and again rose to his feet, energy requiring action.

"Yes," Jared replied. Where was Salt going with this question? "In Mr. Stromberg's safe."

"Check with your boss. Make sure he's still got your money."

"I don't really care about the money," Jared said.

"You may not care now, but one day you will," Salt said with a look of pity. "I'd make sure it's safe."

"Do you need money for our outfit?" Jared asked. Was Salt going the long way around the mulberry bush to ask for a grub stake?

"No, lad. I told you our deal." Salt wiped his hands on his dirty pants. "Let's start putting our list of supplies together. Don't want to waste no more time."

* * *

Jared threw down another bag of flour onto the symmetrical pile on the selling floor. At one point the general store had provided him an oasis of sanity. No longer. Jared had practiced his resignation speech, but nerves overcame the comfort of any preparation. Why was it so difficult to face Alex? He couldn't put this off any longer. He walked to the small office at the back.

"What can I do for you, Jared?" Alex said, head hovering above a stack of invoices, all probably overdue. The speed with which business soared and crashed unsettled Jared.

"Mr. Stromberg," Jared began, "I'm going to be leaving. I'll be gone in a week."

Color rose on Alex's smooth-shaven face, his head seemed to swell. His boss swallowed hard and took a deep breath. Jared prepared himself for Alex's expected explosion. But instead of anger and a river of invective and protests, a surprising slender smile creased Alex's lips.

"I'm sorry, sir," Jared stammered. "I need to move on. I hope you're not too upset. I very much appreciate you helping me when I was down and out."

"Well..."

Alex's long hesitation stoked renewed concerns. Was Alex's initial response about to be replaced with a more predictable temper tantrum? Jared tightened, steeling himself for whatever might come next.

"Yes," Stromberg said with surprising calm, "I am very upset. I finally have you trained. Business is about to pick up. Trail should open in a couple of weeks. No way I can replace your intelligence and integrity. Nothing to choose from among the waves of disgusting humanity rolling through Skagway. But hell, there's more to life than this pisspot of a city. Where you headed?"

Jared had girded himself for battle. But the absence of resistance left him deflated, unprepared. Where had Alex's understanding and empathy come from?

"Salt and I are headed to Dawson," he muttered.

Alex's sour expression evidenced how unimpressed he was. He yanked open his bottom drawer, pulled out his liquor bottle and took a swig without offering any to Jared. The man's eyes locked on the young man.

"You're nuts," Alex said, head shaking from side to side. "You're leaving with winter coming? Thought you had a head on your shoulders. You should know by now that not only will few of these cheechakos reach Dawson, but all of the valuable claims are filed. Merchants and freight packers are the ones making money. You've learned enough to get rich without handling a shovel and pick axe. At least wait until spring, when you'll have half a chance of surviving."

"Salt's lived in the Yukon for years," Jared replied, not as confident as he sounded. "He's providing the grubstake and the experience. By the way, can you tell me how much money I've got saved?"

Alex's hard stare brought nervous sweat to Jared's face. Jared kept the books but didn't have the combination to Stromberg's safe. Was Salt right to be concerned about Jared's savings? Had Alex, in desperation, used all the cash he could get his hands on to satisfy his mounting debts?

"I don't know," Alex said. Once again he tilted the bottle to his lips. "But let's go count your stash."

Stromberg put his hand on Jared's shoulder and guided him over to one of the few secure safes in Skagway. Alex's serious expression transformed into his broad salesman smile. The sacrosanct steel box had always been off-limits. Alex twirled the dial until the tumblers gave a hard click. The door swung open. Alex rummaged through the bottom shelf and withdrew a small canvas drawstring bag. His fingers unlaced the pouch. A modest pile of gold coins and bills poured onto the desktop.

"Shall we count together?" Alex asked. "Looks to be close to what was stolen from you your first day in Skagway. About $500. Doesn't that coincidence give you something to think about? You made your stake back in a little over two months. In a year you'd make $3,000, assuming you continue to live like a hermit in a goddamn storage tent." Tight lips twisted in scorn. Eyes opened wide with pity. "Just what do you think you're going to find in the Yukon wilderness?"

Embarrassment brought heat to Jared's neck and face. Salt had sown doubts. Alex Stromberg may have sharp edges to his personality, but no question he was honest.

"Would you keep my earnings in the safe?" he asked, swallowing embarrassment.

"I'd be happy to, Jared," Alex answered. "But that Salt's a strange one, like many of the old sourdoughs. I wouldn't doubt he knows his way in rough country. He's shrewd and tough as frozen horseflesh. Hope you can trust him."

"The truth is," Jared replied, "I'm not sure. I do know I'm sick to death of Skagway. I've got no place else to go. What do I have to lose?"

"Just your life, Jared."

Alex returned to his paperwork, dismissing Jared with a flick of his wrist. Jared stood a moment longer, then turned, fighting back his apprehension.

CHAPTER THIRTY-NINE

The dim light of the lowered lantern flame bounced random shadows against the tent walls. Jared made a final check of his pack and glanced at his new partner. The old prospector sparkled with light and energy—appearing ten years younger, giddy as a bride, large, dominant eyes looming like beacons from his weathered face. Nothing could contain him. The man skipped around the tent smiling like a child. Astonishment filled Jared.

"Now you're sure you hid those trail markers?" Salt asked.

The question had been repeated ten times over the last two hours. Salt, with his dogged persistent repetition of already answered questions, again reminded Jared of Duffy. Was Salt uneasy? Why? The packing and loading of the mules and a team of rugged inside dogs were almost completed.

"What's the matter?" Jared said. "An old sourdough like you getting nervous?"

"Nervous?" Salt blew the word out in a whispered gasp. "I never been happier in my life. I'm headed back into the welcome wilderness. All we gotta do is finish packing up the dogs and get out to the street."

"It's pitch black. We've got half an hour before first light."

"Get moving, lad. I'll give you your first lesson of the day—how to travel in the dark."

"Brutus," Jared called.

He lifted a twenty-pound sack of dried fish off the scarred earthen floor of the tent and turned toward his dog. The Airedale appeared more massive than usual, pacing in the shadowed corner. Erratic steps seemed out of character for the self-assured animal.

"Brutus, come here."

Jared stepped in front of his dog, scratched the dog's scraggly chin, and eased the leather and canvas pouch on his back. Reaction came at once. Brutus made a violent sideways jerk. The dog shook off the pack, bolted to the tent door, then whirled to face Jared. Jared murmured the dog's name and again approached the Airedale. The dog's jaw nervously snapped, his body rigid. A growl? No, more of a throaty complaint.

Jared leaned forward, Brutus shifted backwards, his wide body half out of the Stromberg tent. Jared stood up straighter. Confusion and frustration joined already swirling emotions stoked by the dangerous plan in place. Jared had come to rely on Brutus's steadiness and strength, especially now with such dramatic changes ahead. What was this all about?

"Damn it, Brutus, come." Jared winced at his own use of profanity and at the explosion of sound he'd made in the empty alleyway.

"Hey," Salt snarled, grabbing Jared's arm. "Pipe down. We don't want nobody noticing us slip out of town."

Jared stomped toward the tent flap. Brutus dodged into the alley. A quick dash from the tent and Jared chased him into the darkness. The sled dogs erupted into chaotic barks and vicious snarls shattering the early morning stillness. The seven various-sized malamutes lunged as one at Brutus, testing their leather harnesses. The Airedale made a cautious circle beyond them, moving with calm dignity. Had the presence of these dogs been the reason Brutus had become so antsy in the tent?

"Goddamn it," Salt bellowed as he exited the tent. "I paid extra to get an experienced dog team that's been working together so I could control 'em. Wanted less trouble and fuss."

The dogs kept up their racket, even when Brutus blended into the darkness at the end of the alley. The prospector reached the second mule in line and untied his whip. A nasty snap announced the unfurling of the threatening cord.

"That no-good mutt of yours got the whole team riled," Salt complained. "Entire damn town might throw us a going-away parade this morning, now that we've waked 'em up." Salt cracked the moose-hide thongs close to the sled dogs' ears, bringing an end to the racket. "Should turn 'em loose to finish off your dog once and for all."

Jared knew Brutus could handle any one of the malamutes. The dog could hold his own against two, maybe even three. But the seven-dog pack would be too much. Yet another unexpected complication for their seven-hundred-mile trek. Jared would have to make sure the sled dogs were under control at all times. Who would present the greatest threat to the Airedale, the malamutes or Salt?

Jared stepped to the closest mule and slung Brutus's pack on top. He jerry-rigged the satchel to the mule's load with two sloppy knots. Salt pushed him aside and secured the pack tighter.

"Don't start making mistakes before we even leave town," Salt growled in disgust. "Good for nothing mutt," he said in a lower voice. "He don't carry his weight, the hell with him. He stays here."

"He's going with us." Jared's clenched jaw reflected a stubbornness he never knew he possessed. "Or I'm staying."

"Who the hell's the boss?" Salt thrust his face in front of Jared's. "Boy, where we're headed we'll be living life on a thin edge. You'll need every morsel of food we lug into the Yukon. I hate to worry you, but life and death got a close relationship in the wild."

"Brutus will pay his way. And soon."

Jared turned and walked back inside the tent, Salt on his heels. He shrugged into his pack, adjusting the fifty pounds of supplies. The old coot's glare was as uncomfortable as the cutting edge of some object buried in his knapsack. Just ignore the old man.

"Guess you're right," Salt considered out loud. "We can always eat him, if things get tight. Then use his hide to help us stay warm. He'll be a four-legged, one-way walking-pack. But just how, laddie, will that dog provide any value soon?"

"Do you want to pull five mules straight up A B Mountain, or do you want Brutus to herd them up?"

Salt spit on the tent floor. He moved to his pack, eased into it with a practiced movement and walked outside. Jared blew out the lantern and left the tent. The malamutes milled in a confused muddle lashed together in dog-sled order, their excited yips and barks muted with Brutus out of sight. Jared moved to his spot in the formation led by Salt, followed by the inside dogs, Jared, and five mules. The disgraced Brutus was lost in the rear.

The old man had planned and orchestrated the first phase from Skagway to Lake Bennett. He'd gone over the details for two weeks. But beyond Bennett, Salt had told Jared very little. Didn't matter. Excitement rekindled in Jared, despite the rutted street and strange behavior of his independent, yet usually predictable dog.

Frigid rain had fallen in varying and unending amounts for the last weeks of October and now the first half of November. Thick, grasping Skagway muck froze into ice-encrusted creases and ridges. Only cautious progress could be made down State Street to the bridge over the roiling Skagway River. The glowering promise of daylight was welcome, but it did little to aid the burdened party's departure.

* * *

Jared crouched with Salt amidst uneasy mules and sled dogs. He glimpsed patches of murky skies through occasional breaks in the dense canopy of cedars and spruces. There might be light and visibility in Skagway, but not here a mere hundred yards up the base of A B Mountain. An invisible high tide of leg-breaking booby traps littered the treacherous forest floor. Jared's confidence crumbled.

It had taken twenty minutes to progress this brief distance in the unrelenting blackness of early morning. What had he been thinking when he'd agreed to this insane gamble? All Jared's runs had been during daylight. Leading loaded mules and dogs up this precarious, clutching terrain with limited visibility was challenging enough in the planning stage but had at least seemed possible. Now the foolishness of the venture blossomed like the myriad mushrooms and lichen flourishing in the nightmare landscape.

"Time to wrap the mules," Jared said, using the chore to deflect growing fear.

He fumbled with thick cotton material cut into wide strips. Heat radiating from the closest animal provided direction. Chilled fingers wound cloth around the foreleg from hoof to hock. He secured the protective bundle with rawhide laces.

"Makes no damn sense," Salt said. Curses and stumbled steps evidenced his partner's reluctant cooperation in the task. "What the hell's some cuts and bruises?"

"We've been over this," Jared said finishing with the mule. For all of Salt's boastful talk, his ignorance of livestock was surprising and disconcerting. "You saw how treacherous all these rocks and branches are. One of these mules slices a tendon, and it's not moving another step."

"Now can we get underway?" Salt asked.

"You're asking me?" Jared replied. "This was your brilliant idea. You're the experienced mountain man. I do know this—these mules aren't moving another foot without more light."

Salt muttered a stream of curses, spit into the Medusas tangle that seemed to grow denser around their ankles as they stood shivering in the almost solid moist mist. Lord, what had Jared done when he'd agreed to partner with this bitter old man?

CHAPTER FORTY

J ared took several tentative, stumbling lunges forward. He couldn't see the first cloth strip or remember which of the infinite branches he'd secured the material to. The minimal light made the search for his hidden trail marker a severe test. Salt had insisted that the small pieces of dark flannel be invisible to anyone but Jared. He'd done his job too well. The almost perpendicular slope mocked his frantic, thrashing search. Now he felt swelling panic.

Another string of muted curses emanated from Salt, now lost from sight behind Jared. Would this become yet another failure in a life already littered with mistakes? He blinked back tears of frustration, redoubled his efforts, then fell face-first to the uneven ground. Jared rolled over on his side. A corner of limp flannel hung beneath a thick cedar branch. Relief.

It would have been impossible to struggle up A B without the faint game trail he had tagged earlier. May still be hopeless. A vague, translucent glow eased through the thick vegetation above them. Jared allowed a welcome sigh. At least they wouldn't end their journey into the Yukon Territory an embarrassing quarter mile from town.

Light increased, dim and bleak, but enough to give definition to the cluttered forest floor. Jared moved back to Salt and the animals. He took the reins of the most stubborn of the mules and tied the wet leather straps around his chest. He lunged forward and pulled the reluctant animal step by step up the breath-sucking mountain.

Salt whistled a low pitched "Hyia," and the dogs picked their way through the debris, following the lead mule and Jared. The old prospector had strung the other four pack animals together, fitted his reins against his body and pulled the mules forward. Now they were moving.

"Brutus, herd," Jared called out.

"Your damn dog won't even carry a pack." Salt let out a snort reflecting the sarcasm he wouldn't hide. The old man spit into the dense, thick air. "You think a silly-ass command like that's gonna mean anything?"

"Save your breath, you stubborn old goat," Jared hissed. "You'll need all the air you can suck in if you're going to pull those mules all the way over the top."

The crushing steps of the animals resounded as they inched upward through the wet earth. He knew Brutus. The dog would drive the last mule in line. He even thought he heard the growl and snap of the Airedale at the end of the scraggly train. Brutus would prove his value now.

The next piece of flannel hung forty feet up the indistinct path. Jared trudged forward. He had his bearings, no longer necessary to count his labored steps. He smothered an errant laugh. The slow-moving party smashed and crashed up the steep slope. The deafening clatter they made could probably be heard on the selling floor of Stromberg's, along with Salt's constant stream of profane screams. Salt's desire for secrecy seemed ridiculous.

Minutes clicked by. The wild keening of the wind stifled communication. Hours passed in painful, stumbling ascent. Two steps forward, one backwards, Jared jerked by the cautious mule he seemed to be dragging up the mountain. Heat built up under Jared's layers of clothing. Reluctant admiration grew for the old man striving upward with the responsibility of controlling dogs and four mules.

"Damnit, that's it." Salt's cries reached epic volumes. "We ain't gonna make it with these dogs tied together. Traces get tangled every other step. I'm turning 'em loose."

"No, Salt," Jared shouted.

Jared wheeled around, dropped the mule's reins and crashed down the slope toward Salt. Too late. Brownie, the lead dog, a large malamute dominant in size and aggressiveness, stood for a moment, back hairs raised skyward. A frightening snarl erupted from its throat, followed by the howls of the other six.

A lunge for one of the free animals failed. Then Jared watched in horror as they bounded down the broken terrain. They had to be after Brutus trailing the mules. Salt's desperate lurch kept the last four sled dogs under control. Jared stumbled by him, hesitating only long enough to grab the prospector's pistol from its scarred holster.

"Don't you shoot those dogs," Salt hollered. "We ain't getting beyond Lake Bennett without 'em. They're worth a hell of a lot more than that damn sack of fur of yours."

Jared hurled past the nervous mules, locked in place by the encroaching forest. He saw Brutus crouched, butt against a large boulder, a small clearing before him. Brownie charged, but slipped on a lichen-covered boulder. The twenty-pound pack on the dog's back caught on a thick, low-hanging hemlock limb, further restricting the animal's attack. The lead malamute arrived in front of Brutus, off balance. The Airedale crushed the smaller dog to the forest floor. Teeth ripped at the malamute's throat.

"Brutus, stop," Jared screamed.

Fur and blood flew into the frigid wet air. No way to reach the struggling animals in time. Only the rush of the next dog saved Brownie. Brutus released his hold on the defenseless husky just in time to meet the charge.

Brutus lowered his center of gravity, like a Roman army legion arraying itself in a defensive square. Sled dogs were slashers, ripping at their opponents. The attacker, encumbered by its pack, hit Brutus on his shoulder. The Airedale shifted to the side and flung his rear end against the aggressor. The sled dog lost its footing, tumbling beyond the huge rock covering Brutus's rear. Jared's concern shifted from his own dog to the overmatched malamutes.

One more dog piled into Brutus's clearing, momentum carrying the animal into a collision with Brownie, still attempting a quick exit from the jaws of Brutus. Once again the Airedale attacked, ripping an ear to shreds and bloodying the hapless dog's muzzle. Jared, ten yards from the fray, fired a single shot into the air.

"Brutus," he yelled, stumbling closer. "Brutus, no."

Either the cracking retort of the pistol or Jared's cries caught Brutus's attention. He released his latest victim. All three malamutes scattered into the underbrush. Brutus stood alone. Blood dripped from his shoulder and jaws.

Salt clattered toward them, cussing an unintelligible blue streak. The old man scrambled through the dense underbrush searching for his dogs. Gloved hands grabbed the smaller gray-brown malamute by its harness and neck. The poor animal, already cowed by Brutus, made little effort to resist the prospector.

Jared made a cursory check of Brutus. Several superficial cuts evidenced the short battle. Jared slumped against the large boulder that had protected his dog's back, listening to his partner thrash through the impenetrable forest. His emotions swept from proud awe at Brutus's fighting ability to worry over the other dogs' possible injuries.

What would they do if half the sled team disappeared or were injured? Jared swallowed an acid taste. He could already hear Salt berating him, see the irate old man shoot Brutus. He placed Salt's pistol on a half-buried rock, then dropped his face into gloved hands, torn and bruised. Lord, not even one day's progress.

Salt emerged minutes later with two of the dogs. Brownie was missing. The miner's huge eyes bulged from effort and anger.

"I told you that dog of yours was worthless," he said between gasps. "If that missing dog doesn't show up, I'm using your devil animal to pull the cotton-pickin' sled."

Salt jerked and yanked the two dogs back up toward their teammates. It had been a waste of time worrying about the sled dogs doing damage to Brutus. Jared worked his way up the steep hill to his place in the lead. Without another word he began the arduous climb leading his bedraggled party.

CHAPTER FORTY-ONE

Alex had been correct. Sophia hated to admit it. She had been swallowed alive by the demands and details of her new hotel. Bad enough his intransigence and lack of cooperation had cost them both hundreds of dollars. And even a more valuable commodity was being wasted—time. An unending series of decisions and problems kept her sleep-deprived and anxious. Latest dilemma: hiring a cook for the Alverson House dining room. Not a cook, she clarified in her mind, but a chef.

The Star's cook was as ornery and prickly as a disturbed old billy goat, but the man was a money machine. Old Jacob Tredaway produced cheap, filling meals. Unfortunately, ham, eggs and baked beans would not constitute a gourmet experience at the high-class Alverson House. Plus, finding a replacement for him wouldn't prove any easier than finding someone else to handle her new hotel's food service. Sophia could come up with only one solution. With that realization, a plan took shape.

The Great Northern Hotel, the prime competitor for the Alverson House and current candidate for best hotel in Skagway, boasted the most luxurious room accommodations and finest restaurant. The Great Northern's menu more resembled Delmonico's in New York than a frontier outpost eatery. Eric Legare ran the kitchen.

Legare had a reputation as an excellent, though temperamental, chef. She could either steal him for the Alverson House or find someone in Seattle, a long shot at best and a time commitment she could ill afford. No, she would visit the competition, sample a variety of dishes to confirm quality, then seduce Mr. Legare with charm and the offer to double his salary.

Another consideration, undesired and unexpected, pushed its way into her consciousness. When was the last time she had worn anything other than a rough man's clothing? How long had it been since Sophia had assumed the role of sophisticated lady? The thought of dressing up in her velveteen gown and dining at the Great Northern held an irresistible appeal. Anticipation generated a rare smile.

But what of the risks of being recognized as the murderous fugitive, Maggie Saunders? This danger could be avoided if Alex would be the one to approach Legare, but she was loath to request anything from him now. One night out at the edge of the civilized world shouldn't be too difficult. She'd been circumspect for months without a hint of discovery except for the harmless Jared. Time for a brief and important evening on the town.

* * *

The mirror hadn't lied. Every man's eyes at every table of the Great Northern's dining hall fixed on her when she made her entrance. Was coming here a stupid, arrogant mistake? A disconcerting combination of flashing alarms and long-suppressed satisfaction left her trembling. But it was too late. She followed a waiter to a corner table.

Drafts rippled through the large room. Cheap art that would embarrass a run-of-the-mill whorehouse hung from bare, unfinished walls. Her confidence soared at the frazzled tablecloths, chipped chairs and scarred wooden floors. The Alverson House was a comparative palace even in its unfinished state. Self-assurance surged along with the quiet pleasure of her fellow diners' attention.

Lord, men were so predictable. She could still dominate a room. Not as a whore but as a respectable and beautiful woman. Could she ever perform this role in public again? Certainly she would be a more effective asset as the stunning and charming hostess of the Alverson House then managing behind the scenes disguised as a man. Why couldn't life become this simple and straightforward?

"Are you ready to order, madame?"

A tall, thin man in white shirt and black vest with a well-trimmed mustache hovered above her table. Another reminder of hires needed. Maybe she would steal this waiter away as well as the cook, assuming the man treated her properly. Must have respectable help at the Alverson House, from servers to maids. The list of challenges grew as she looked into his solicitous brown eyes.

"I've never had the pleasure of visiting your establishment." She fixed him with a modest smile that still made the man blush. "I'm very hungry. Why don't you serve me a complete meal of those dishes you most recommend? Money is no object. I'm sure that you'll take very good care of me. And what is your name, sir?"

"Michael," he said, an earnest response conflicting with longing eyes that confirmed that she was a goddess gracing his area of the dining room. "Leave it to me, madame. I'll let the chef know your request. I'm sure he'll rise to the occasion. Could I bring you a bottle of wine? We have the finest selection in Alaska."

"No, thank you," she said, offering her most demure smile. "I'm saving myself for your fine food."

Then he was gone, scuttling back toward the kitchen. Back rigid, head held high, he pushed through the swinging door into the cooking area. She forgave the fact that he ignored the restaurant's other customers, whose attention had also been fixed on Sophia.

In the next hour and a half the bounties of the Great Northern flowed across her table. Crème of artichoke Morlais soup, stuffed olives, anchovies on toast, and bittersweet pickles flooded the table. Then came plates of halibut with hollandaise sauce, glazed ham with Madeira, sweetbread Neapolitan style, terrine de foie gras, and potatoes gastrome. Finally, a trio of desserts was presented— cream meringue, ice cream Charlotte, and kirsch sorbet, and French coffee to wash it down. The food proved far superior to the hotel's construction.

The fine cuisine was a complete departure from her basic meals at The Star. Could she even digest the rich offerings? Sophia inhaled the dishes, consuming more in one sitting than she'd eaten the previous several days. The challenges of producing such an array of quality dishes here in the middle of nowhere had to be daunting.

"Your reputation is well deserved," Sophia said, sipping her coffee. With each course she lavished more and more attention on her server, Michael. "I would very much like to commend your chef, if he has but a moment."

"Yes, madame," her waiter said with a proud smile. "Monsieur Legare would be honored to make your acquaintance."

She nodded, and he was gone in a flash. Michael returned with a man more caricature than cook. Eric Legare's full belly and fat arms and legs advertised the intake of sumptuous epicurean delights. His white chef's hat bobbed dangerously atop a fat-cheeked smile that was the antithesis of the curmudgeon Jacob Tredaway. Only Michael's arms could be seen behind Legare's bulk.

"Madame," the chef gushed. "I'm so pleased you enjoyed our humble offerings. I don't know how you can eat so much and still look so lovely. I hope you will return often—daily—to our establishment."

Legare spoke with hands punctuating his words. The chef's cheeks glowed with emotion and sincerity. Stealing a chef might be simpler than she had thought. Then an uneasy glance around the dining room made her aware of the increased attention the chef's visit had generated, more unwelcome and dangerous. Her ego had desired the focus on herself, and successful she had been. Time to complete her mission.

"May I ask you something personal, Mr. Legare?" Sophia said, lowering her voice, interrupting what seemed to be an endless flow of compliments and platitudes. "It would seem to me that a chef of your fantastic abilities is somewhat wasted in a rather common restaurant such as the Great Northern."

Legare's wide mouth dropped open, eyes reflecting confusion. He attempted a stammered response, but the words refused to form on his full pink lips. Sophia could read his questioning gaze—was she complimenting his cooking or criticizing his restaurant or both?

"How would you like to work in the finest dining room on the entire West Coast of the United States?" Sophia said, directing an enchanting smile at the chef. "And at double whatever salary you are now making? I am opening such a place, the Alverson House, in several weeks. I would enjoy very much working with a man of your outstanding abilities."

Confusion transformed to sly pleasure. The gleam on Legare's face answered her question. Sophia held her tongue.

"When can I start?" he asked, dropping his voice to a whisper.

"I will contact you shortly," Sophia said, transfixing him with a seductive smile she hadn't used since her first critical meeting with Alex in San Francisco.

Strange that she felt no discomfort using the same guile she had employed as a high-class hooker. There seemed a fine line between using her face and body for money and the same assets to accomplish goals less carnal. Sophia rose from the table. Legare grabbed her chair, then her hand on which he planted a wet kiss.

"Until then, my lady."

He tore his eyes off Sophia and with hesitation retreated to his kitchen. She couldn't help but think about the Great Northern's unfilled orders that had stacked up during the chef's avid attention to her.

When she reached the entry, she made one final satisfied sweep of the dining hall. All the customers followed her movements with pleasure. But one man's face held what could only be described as a smirk. His hard, soulless eyes and thick wet lips would never be forgotten. She knew him.

Terror punched a physical blow. Air escaped her chest like a punctured balloon. No name came to mind. But she could never cleanse her memory of her former customers at the Prairie Flower. Had he recognized her? What kind of jeopardy had she put herself in?

She hurried into the lobby, wrapping her fur-lined coat around her body. Was the man's expression recognition, appreciation, or a reaction to the obsequious behavior of Legare? Sweat sprang to her face despite the frigid temperatures on Broadway. Would this one moment of vanity destroy her?

CHAPTER FORTY-TWO

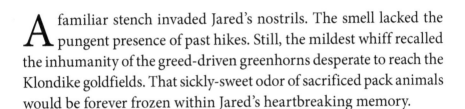

A familiar stench invaded Jared's nostrils. The smell lacked the pungent presence of past hikes. Still, the mildest whiff recalled the inhumanity of the greed-driven greenhorns desperate to reach the Klondike goldfields. That sickly-sweet odor of sacrificed pack animals would be forever frozen within Jared's heartbreaking memory.

The temperature continued to drop. Plumes of vapor rose from Jared's mouth. The cloud of moisture mingled with the ground mist and light snow dribbling through the solid network of limbs above them. Much easier to run up the darn mountain, in rhythm, using both feet and hands. Tougher with the irregular progress of the animals and encumbering pack. A dull, consistent daylight filled the congested universe of foliage. At least Jared could see beyond his hands.

He staggered to a stop, their first rest in several hours after a discouraging lack of progress. Of the hidden trail markers, he had counted only ten of thirty. Had Jared once fought his way to the top of this monster mountain in only a little over an hour?

"Salt," he called down, "you okay?"

"Couldn't be finer, young man." Salt's gasps betrayed the extent of his struggles. "We're away from that murderous, thief-infested hellhole."

"Not too far away. We're less than a third of the way up," Jared called back. "Might not make the top before dark."

"Got to."

Salt's words mirrored Jared's fear. The slow, erratic pace was taking far more time and energy than Jared had expected. Neither man wanted to spend the night in this claustrophobic prison. Jared considered alternatives. There weren't any.

"We've got to pick up the pace, Salt. Untie the reins. You'll make better progress leaning forward, using both hands and legs."

"Who's gonna keep these damn pigheaded excuses for horses moving?"

"Brutus." Jared sighed at Salt's intransigence. "I told you once before. Trust me." Jared heard Salt spit. "I was raised with mules. They don't like dogs nipping at their heels. If we don't try, we'll never get to the top by nightfall."

Again he leaned forward, gloved hands grabbing branches and jagged rocks, pulling as much as pushing. His own mule's traces remained wrapped around his chest, but he played out more length in the leather straps. The mule jerked back, but Jared yanked forward, using the weight of his entire body. The animal stepped after him, a slight increase in speed.

"Brutus, pick it up," Jared called back, his tone communicating a new sense of urgency.

The train stumbled into action. Jared could sense additional activity by the increased snapping and crackling of underbrush. No doubt about Brutus's snarls and barks at the end of the line. The Airedale drove the herd with constant pressure of sharp teeth and loud snarls. Jared felt better, forward momentum pushing him quicker.

"You gonna make it, Salt?" Jared asked after about thirty minutes.

"Yeah, but that damn dog's driving these mules up my rear end."

"Then start moving faster," Jared said, a smile creasing his lips. "What do you think of Brutus now, you old coot?"

The increased pace generated a cacophony of snorts, growls, snaps and crashes. Progress was much easier leaning uphill, far better than the step-by-slow-step stumble of earlier hours. Light flakes of wet snow continued to slip through the thick overhead canopy. Their cool touch and taste fueled more energy.

The day's struggles, the imprisonment of Skagway, his doubts and insecurities drained away. Even the unknown had to be better than the road he had traveled. A past he might discard like a snake sheds its skin. Only sporadic visions of Sophia Alverson's exotic beauty remained.

Why? What could he accomplish in her eyes? Just another foolish, avaricious man cruelly sacrificing animals and common sense for rumored riches. No. Jared searched for freedom of his soul, some justification that life held higher meaning. And Sophia epitomized that hope.

* * *

Several rest breaks later Jared sensed a slight thinning of the grasping forest. He'd quit counting the markers but knew they were over two thirds up A B Mountain. They'd made decent progress. Joy infused his arms and legs with more power and vitality.

"Brutus, pick it up," Jared insisted.

Tension from the traces eased, air from the mule's labored breathing warmed the back of Jared's neck. Brutus pushed the entire train a half-step faster. Jared laughed out loud at the increased cursing from Salt. Confidence surged. He knew they would emerge above the treeless ridge top soon. Before the early Alaskan sunset, he hoped.

But the temperature had dropped at least thirty degrees from Skagway's already bitter cold. In the open spaces, the growing accumulation of snow, unchecked by dense forest, would hide even greater leg-breaking dangers. Escalating wind whistled through the remaining treetops like a madman's symphony. There would be no relief in this last leg before darkness forced a halt.

"Jared." Salt's rare use of his name caught Jared's attention. "I like the way you're pushing. Come in handy where we're headed."

The compliment swept over Jared like a warm breeze. Duffy had never once passed a supportive or kind word Jared's way. Could he have misjudged Salt?

"What about the snow?" Jared asked. "Can't see what's underneath us."

"Don't worry," Salt answered. "Need some weather. And old Brownie just showed up, tail 'tween his legs. Got to have frozen lakes and deep snow if we're gonna sled to Dawson. Let's camp. No way to travel in the dark up here."

A grove of wind-bent stunted spruces beckoned. Jared turned toward them. He entered the minimal but welcome protection of the gnarled trees with their huge trunks and stunted tops no more than ten feet tall. Large boulders provided an additional windbreak. Jared secured his mule and unstrapped the supplies.

"What are you doing?" Salt cried out.

"What's it look like?" Jared replied.

Jared continued to pile the packs between rocks several yards from the tethered animals. He then moved to the dogs to unload their burdens. Each animal gave grateful shakes with the freedom from their burdens.

"Take us an hour to repack in the morning," Salt almost whined. "Just leave 'em for the night."

"No way," Jared insisted. "Don't know how far we still have to Lake Bennett. We've pushed these poor animals to the edge of their endurance. We're unpacking and rubbing them down. You said we're selling them at the lake. We'll get a better price if they're in decent shape."

Salt clamped his jaws together, then helped Jared with the rest of the dogs. Salt dug out their furs. Jared fed rolled oats to the mules and dried fish to the dogs. Darkness dropped like a rock. There was barely enough time to anchor their tent with small boulders. These blizzard-like conditions would force an unpleasant cold camp—no fire.

Freezing chill invaded Jared's senses once the chores were done. He crawled after Salt into the flimsy, wind-whipped canvas shelter. Jared burrowed under white rabbit furs and munched on hardtack. Little comfort in such surroundings, but he had survived a brutal first day.

"How far to Lake Bennett?" Jared asked.

"I figure 'bout ten to fifteen miles," Salt said. "Jared, we could become a pretty good team. We done covered some ground. I figured for sure we'd spend the first night buried on the side of that damn mountain. At least we got the easy part out of the way."

Salt had once again used his name. Jared hid his pleasure in the invisible blackness of the tent and the enveloping freezing evening. But Salt's last words gripped Jared in a cruel vice of fatigue and fear. There had been no "easy part." If Jared was to survive, it would be better to focus on the positive.

CHAPTER FORTY-THREE

This couldn't be true. Alex stood at Stromberg's rear entrance. Cases of evaporated peaches and apples as well as dried apricots swamped the store's small warehouse area, overflowing onto the selling floor. Dizziness competed with nausea. This contribution from California's fertile Central Valley was as useless as the mud clogging the streets of Skagway. Death of a business by fruit.

How much gold had Alex sent down to Mordecai in three months? Over $20,000. And what had over two years of normal profits in San Francisco gotten him? Not saws, nails, bits or braces. No flour, bacon or beans. Just one ton of useless fruit. His father had once again shipped whatever product he could purchase at a cut-rate price. If only Alex could bury Mordecai under this useless pile of produce.

Alex staggered back into his office. The walls closed in around him. Heat built beneath his layered clothing. Fear flushed his face. He'd stacked empty boxes on the selling floor to fool customers. The camouflage reflected the emptiness of his future prospects. How could he fight back? Gaping holes in Stromberg's inventory could no longer be hidden.

The imminent opening of the trail and endless flow of new clueless treasure hunters would bring no profits if he had the wrong mix of product. And The Star's flow of cash poured not into Alex's desperate hands but into the bottomless pit of Sophia Alverson's hotel fantasy. No way to work out of the deepening hole of insolvency.

Trembling fingers pulled open the bottom desk drawer and yanked out a half-full bottle of whiskey. At least Skagway had no shortage of cheap booze. He gulped a generous swig. But the strangling sensation in his throat remained unrelieved.

And Sophia? No one should ever make a large capital investment in a transitory location, and Skagway served as a prime example. Did Sophia understand the damage she wreaked on him both financially and emotionally? How could he ever hope to make her understand?

He shouldn't have refused her. He had overreacted. She had wounded him deeply at the time. Her Jewish slur had never registered to her as bigoted or cruel. It was her ignorance—not prejudice—that had come between them. Now he could no longer generate much anger or hostility toward the woman. Yes, his own damn fault.

To her credit she had overcome her inexperience, unfortunately by wasting their shares of The Star's profits. Only one avenue of escape remained—a dangerous partnership with the Devil, Mr. Soapy Smith. Alex would have to borrow operating funds for Stromberg's and commit to the gangster's proposal of a used-goods store. At a usurious rate. He'd be better off bolting from Skagway. Steal Jared's meager $500 and gather whatever other cash he could scrape up to use as traveling funds.

"Well, hello, Mr. Stromberg." An oily voice interrupted the depressing quiet of the deserted store. "Thought I'd travel up north to this den of iniquity and check out the neighborhood."

Elijah Cummings filled the door frame with his well-fed bulk. Elijah. Aptly named. His unexpected appearance offered deliverance. No one else in the world could better offer salvation in this situation than Mr. Elijah Cummings, western salesman for Brooks & Bundy. Alex welcomed the sly smile of his unlikely messiah, but a savior just the same.

Stromberg's had long done business with the slippery wholesaler. B & B represented over fifty manufacturers supplying everything from nails to rice, mackinaws to condensed milk. And Stromberg's enjoyed a line of credit with the distributor. Alex might fill his needs through Elijah without having to deal with his father in San Francisco. Avoiding the old man's interference could save him.

"Lord, am I glad to see you," Alex gasped.

"How's life and business on the edge of the world?" Elijah asked, fat cheeks squeezed hard blue eyes into smiling slits.

The salesman stood over six feet and 250 pounds. Cummings would crush a man's nuts as he patted him on the back. But compared to Soapy Smith, Elijah was a lamb.

"Doing great," Alex lied. "Business is booming. But I'm needing fill-in merchandise quickly. You know how difficult it is dealing with Mordecai."

"Oh, yes, I do." Elijah gave a solicitous nod with his oversize head. "I can help you out. Though freight costs up to Skagway will put a dent in your margins. We're shipping out of Seattle now, so at least it's cheaper than San Francisco. Let's go have a few snorts. We can write up your orders first thing tomorrow."

Elijah's smile and outstretched hand belied the flip side to B & B's fine offerings. Better dot the *i*'s and cross the *t*'s if the buyer didn't want to be taken to the cleaners by this man. He was a gouger. But not a destroyer. The man would squeeze margins, not put Alex out of business. A bankrupt client was of no use to B & B. That was, unless there could be something in it for Cummings.

Alex allowed a smile to escape. He could place his orders from memory. Why wait until tomorrow? Finally a way out of this mess.

"And I've got some very interesting news," Elijah said with a self-satisfied smirk. "Good and bad."

God only knew what sordid news the salesman had uncovered. His information was rarely uplifting. Still, listening to Elijah's good and bad news would be a small price to pay to escape Soapy's clutches.

"Got a bottle right here," Alex said extending the whiskey. "No need for a glass."

Elijah grinned, snatched the brown container and swallowed two liquor-diminishing gulps. Liquid dripped from the corner of his capacious mouth. He flashed a scheming smile and wiped his chin with fat fingers.

"I guess we should cover the bad news first," the salesman offered with a sigh.

Elijah settled his massive bulk into the chair opposite Alex's desk. A look of sadness distorted the salesman's features. Alex couldn't imagine any bad news worse than his present predicament. Jesus. Had the man's best friend died?

"You remember," Elijah began with a mournful downturn of his lips, "that cute little red-headed package at Bertha's we was all so fond of. Well, some crazy son of a bitch sliced her up something ugly."

"What...how..." Alex rocked back in his chair—a body blow.

"Bertha herself found the little whore dead," Cummings said. "Tied to the headboard and gagged. Why would anyone do that to sweet little Gaye?"

Alex tried to shut out the image of Gaye desecrated. Always smiling, wanting to please. He still carried a warmth and tenderness for the woman. The generous, fun-loving Gaye still had a hold on his heart.

"You don't look so good, Alex," Elijah said. "How come you're taking this so hard? I know you were fond of the girl, but she was only a whore."

"No, she was a woman." Alex struggled for air. "That's the trouble with you, Elijah. Whores are there to please you. They only take the money they charge. Don't suck you dry like the society bitches I've had to deal with in San Francisco."

Where did he find the presence of mind to get philosophical about women? Especially with Sophia draining him. Maybe she wasn't the normal society leech, with her men's clothing and hard work. Still, the financial effect had proved the same.

"Sorry you're so undone," Elijah said, reaching out to pat Alex's arm. "Never seen this soft, romantic side of you Alex. Let's drink to good old Gaye."

* * *

"Now, the good news," he said. "A whore in St. Louis butchered a rich slob of a customer and took off with his money. A lot of money."

A whore murdered a customer? The fool probably deserved it. Alex didn't give a damn. Why would Elijah think he would? Alex had much bigger problems.

"Four or five months ago," Cummings continued, "this high-priced hooker named Maggie Saunders, the star attraction at the city's famous Prairie Flower, slit this customer's throat ear to ear. The poor bastard happened to be the richest damn farmer in Minnesota. Rich but dumb. The fool carried around quite a bit of gold, and Miss Maggie ripped it right out of the seams of the farmer's overalls."

"Fascinating," Alex said. "How the hell does this news mean anything to me? Good or bad?"

"Well, you won't believe this." A greedy gleam brought a sparkle to the salesman's eyes. "That cold-blooded killer's living right here in Skagway." A disconcerting leer colored his broad features. "In fact, you know her. Calls herself Sophia Alverson. She's your partner."

"Sophia?" What was this idiot talking about? "Elijah, you're mistaken. I know her well. A little eccentric, yes, but a respectable lady all the same. Certainly not capable of murder."

Could Elijah be correct? Speaking the words opened Alex's mind. Had Sophia buffaloed him so totally? Was this the reason she acted so strangely? No social contact, hiding her sex and identity dressed like a man. True, the woman had never spoken about herself, her past. And a crime such as murder could explain why she'd chosen Skagway, so isolated a destination. Sophia's hidden beauty and allure masked a killer?

"Alex, I am sure," Elijah said, a grin stretching his full lips. "I been a customer. And I must say, ole Maggie gave me my money's worth. Yes, sir. Good enough to partake several times. It's her all right."

Confusion swirled within him. His instincts had never failed him. He couldn't have misjudged her so completely. A jagged rock of emotion wreaked damage with each bounce. Elijah placed a solicitous hand on Alex's arm.

"There's a $1,000 reward for the lady." Elijah lowered his voice to a conspiratorial whisper. "Biggest damn reward I've ever heard of."

Alex jerked away, tried to stand, stumbled and collapsed back into the chair. Walls again tightened around him in the tiny office. Elijah was often as full of bullshit as he was facts. Why should this story be any different? This couldn't be true. Alex knew Sophia. Worked with her. Needed her.

"Just where did you see her?"

"At the Great Northern at dinner in all her glory."

The thought of her forced out of his life brought another unexpected wrenching of his heart. He couldn't operate The Star, finish the cash-sucking Alverson House without Sophia. And his emotions toward her far transcended their business relationship. Had he been repressing his true feelings for her? No, he wouldn't be party to extortion.

"I'll pay you the reward," Alex blurted out.

"Come on, Alex." The fat man looked down on Alex with an unsettling combination of pity and excitement. "The reward's peanuts. I'm surprised a crackerjack businessman like you don't see a much more profitable angle."

And this was the good news? Were all his business associates of questionable character? Alex hadn't felt this trapped since his last visit to Mordecai's goddamn green chair.

"You and I are gonna become partners," Elijah beamed. "We're gonna blackmail Maggie or Sophia or whoever the hell she is. Get control of her share of the business. I grant you I'm not as pretty, and she's got to be putting out for you, eh? But at least you'll have a partner that knows what's up."

A gleeful cackle split the man's ugly lips. Damn. He had to have some time to sort out this whirlwind of a disaster. How should he respond? Alex fought back an urge to smash Elijah in the face. Shock kept his mouth shut. He had to find a way to protect Sophia. That much he knew.

Alex sipped at the bottle and passed it to Cummings. Too much tragedy and destructive news. He prayed for the alcohol's numbing effect. Nothing he could do about Gaye except mourn her. But Sophia? God, could Elijah be right? What should he do? What could he do? Both he and Sophia were no better than rats in a trap if Elijah was right.

"I've got to get outside," Alex gasped. "Need air. And the bottle." He stood, shaking, and struggled into a thick mackinaw, then added his bulky parka. "Come on, Elijah."

"It's too damn cold out there," Elijah said. "Just calm down. You want air, just open the damn door. It's freezing outside."

Alex pulled on gloves, flipped the hood of his parka over his head and grabbed the bottle.

"Let's go, partner." The words almost choked Alex. "If I don't clear my head, I'm going to pass out. I don't ever want to hear any more news from you, good or bad. Remember, in some places they shoot the messenger."

CHAPTER FORTY-FOUR

Clarity arrived with the Alaskan chill. Alex shook off the cloying paralysis that had engulfed him in Stromberg's. But the unwelcome, threatening presence of Elijah could not be as easily discarded. Something different in the evening, though. An off-shore breeze scoured the skies of fog and mist above Skagway. Yet an impenetrable wall of thick roiling clouds sat atop the Coastal Range. A nasty storm must be roaring through the peaks above.

Alex walked north toward the mouth of the Skagway River, where it met the waters of the Lynn Canal. Translucent light from a three-quarter moon lit the ragged side streets. A star-studded canopy hovered seemingly within hand's reach, the usual whistling winds reduced to a mere whisper. Elijah stumbled through the crusted snow, arms swinging to maintain Alex's determined pace.

"Damn. Slow down," Elijah complained. "What's the big rush?"

Elijah Cummings as a partner? Untrustworthy. Always on the road. No help at all. How could he trade Elijah for Sophia? She worked night and day operating The Star and opening the Alverson House. That woman got things done. And maybe she was as ruthless as Alex. He lifted the whiskey to his mouth. But no liquid passed his lips. He needed his wits about him.

"Here, take the bottle," Alex said, handing it off to Elijah.

Elijah snatched the liquor and floundered forward to the edge of town, every step taking Alex closer to the demand for some decision. Another hundred yards and Cummings grabbed Alex's arm.

"Enough, dammit," the winded salesman panted. "This is ridiculous. Let's head back."

"Elijah," Alex said, striving for patience and a calm voice. "I need the walk. And I'm going to show you something beautiful. Something you've never seen before. Something very appropriate for our new partnership."

Once again Alex marched toward the confluence of the river and bay. He couldn't let Cummings know the powerful and conflicting relationship he had with Sophia. That he both needed and desired her. He also couldn't entice the reluctant fat man much further, couldn't stall him much longer.

"You make good sense, Elijah," Alex said over his shoulder. "That woman has become very difficult. Got too many quirks. One hell of a temper. You're right. Time to get a new partner."

"Now you're talking," Elijah said, and with audible effort pulled abreast of Alex. "I knew you'd see the advantages of my proposal. There's much more to gain than just the reward."

His words evidenced relief even as he skidded on the slippery terrain. The unexpected clear skies allowed refracted light to bounce off the large man's eyes. His brief smile competed with a desperate need for air.

"Can't partner with women," he wheezed. "They just don't understand how the world works. Alex, I look forward to our partnership, but I ain't going no further."

Cumming's gasping breaths echoed in the beautiful but sharp-edged evening. How could Alex protect Sophia? Elijah was like a hound dog locked onto the scent of a 'coon. Not only was the man capable of blackmailing Sophia, but Alex could also be discarded at the earliest convenience. No compromising with Cummings, no flexibility, no compassion. The salesman was forcing Alex to play his cards now. Would Alex trust this slippery opportunist to cover his back? Never. The man had sealed his own fate.

"Look," Elijah said in a whine. "I'm turning back."

Alex wheeled on the salesman. Perspiration coated the large man's forehead, despite the freezing temperatures. His bulging eyes flashed from Alex back to the dim glow of Skagway.

"No, you're not," Alex answered. The large Colt rose from his holster by complete reflex. "I'm going to show you something whether you want to or not."

"What the hell are you doing, pointing a gun at me?" Disbelief tinged Elijah's voice. "You gonna shoot me because I gave you some bad news? You need to handle your sorrow."

"And just what do you know about sorrow?" Alex asked. "Do you mourn Gaye's death? Hell, the closest thing to sorrow you've experienced is losing at poker or arriving at a whorehouse with no women available."

"Have you gone mad?" Elijah cried in panic. "Put that gun away."

Did Cummings really think Alex was going to kill him? Did Alex's face reveal a willingness to muder? How easy it had been to crush a beer mug against the head of Snyder's henchman. No regret had registered with either the shooting of the rough thug at the Empire or Sizemore's death in the Barbary Coast alley. And hadn't Mordecai always implied that Alex had been responsible for his brother's death? Had it been an accident? Was it terror and sadness that fueled the unending nightmares, or the guilty conscience of a boy who'd contributed to the drowning of his favored brother?

"You pull that trigger, and the whole town'll come running."

"Elijah." Alex laughed. "This must be your first day in the saintly little hamlet of Skagway."

The thunderous clap of the revolver erupted. The bullet whistled past Elijah's bundled head. The fat man lifted off the ground in surprise and shock. How easy it would be to end this dilemma right now with a bullet. And why not?

"What the hell you doing?" he shrieked. "Look, we can work out some kind of arrangement."

An arrangement with this unprincipled schemer? Alex pushed Cummings forward with the long, threatening barrel of the massive pistol. Killing Elijah might save Sophia, but without B &

B's merchandise and credit, he'd be back dealing with that cut-throat Soapy Smith. Why did he always find himself in these no-win situations? Now wasn't the time to deal with that dilemma.

"Don't stop, Elijah. Keep moving if you know what's good for you."

Alex prodded Cummings to the edge of land, where the river mixed with the solid bulk of the Lynn Canal. The salesman whimpered. Moonlight reflected off the slight chop created by the merging of the two watery elements, sparkling lights as numerous as the crystal-lit stars.

Such a rare evening, cloudless and almost windless. If San Francisco Bay had been this calm years ago, his brother wouldn't have died. But choppy waters had swamped their fragile craft. The expected stab of guilt sliced through him. He shuddered. He couldn't escape the horrors of his past. But the present—this threat to Sophia, their businesses and his conflicting emotions—provided its own justification.

Sophia. He'd suppressed his true feelings long enough. Even the revelation that she might be a whore excited him. And there must be another side to the story of the St. Louis murder. He wouldn't lose her. This woman was worth saving. He turned his attention back to the disheveled supplicant before him.

"I told you I'd take you somewhere beautiful, Elijah," he said, "You don't seem too appreciative of this incredible spectacle."

Elijah twisted his head back toward Alex, his face a kaleidoscope of emotion. Then he spun his body, hurling the whiskey bottle at Alex's head. Not even close. Alex gave silent thanks. The man had given him an excuse to fire. He squeezed the trigger with a sense of relief.

Two shots punched into Cummings' broad chest. The salesman tipped back into the inky water, feet still anchored on the sandy shore. The body undulated as if still living. Then the dead man swung at an angle, connected to the shore but pulled by the retreating tide and fast-flowing Skagway River.

"You know, you'd still be alive, Elijah," Alex said, experiencing only a lifting of pressure. "But you're just too damn greedy." He'd had no choice, had he?

Alex waded knee-deep into the freezing surge. He grasped the bobbing body. His fingers clutched Elijah's broad bloodied chest. He knelt forward on one knee, water to his waist, and pushed the corpse into the river's strong current and retreating tide. The half submerged hulk floated like an uprooted cedar log and soon disappeared below the sparkling surface.

Alex had only done what he'd been forced to. Finished. No more doubts. Then the raw power of the flowing forces tore at Alex, almost ripping him off his feet. He fought back a sudden terror and struggled to regain his balance. Temporary footing allowed him to dive headlong for the shore. Freezing water covered his head, sucking the air from his lungs, soaking his clothes. Fear of the gripping surge fueled a horror absent since the disaster on San Francisco Bay. He flailed in panic, fingers finally digging into the soft sand, arms in frantic action. He clawed back to dry land.

CHAPTER FORTY-FIVE

S alt seemed to have little trouble sleeping. But the howling wind made Jared feel like he'd spent the night atop a roaring freight train. Better to be on the trail than lying cramped in their ineffective shelter.

"Gonna be tough going for a while," Salt said as he and Jared repacked the animals. "Snow covers miles of rocks we won't see 'til we trip on 'em. Might make only a mile an hour. Jared, you break trail with the mules. Put your mutt back to work. I'll lay back a bit. Don't call me 'til you get desperate, then I'll trade places with you."

Was Salt parceling out positive encouragement in niggardly amounts? At least he was more positive than Duffy. Jared was glad to be moving again, treacherous footing or not.

"Take your time, boy," Salt said. "Five or six miles to the top of the Coastal Range, then it'll be firmer ground. Once we reach Lake Lindman, we'll hook up with the main trail. With luck, the way to Bennett won't be too clogged. I figure two days to the lake, where we'll dump the mules and pick up the freight sled I stashed."

Jared forced himself up sharp rises that dropped down into depressions several hundred feet deep. Their path skirted the highest of the peaks. The bare, unforested slopes near the peak of A B Mountain no longer deflected the powerful blasts of air that roared across unprotected ridges. The wind became as fearsome a barrier as the unmerciful climb through tangled underbrush. The trudging pace was brutal. Any thrill of the journey was soon beaten out of Jared.

Progress slowed even further as man and beast fought for balance, picking their way through a deceptive surface, sharp rocks lurking below. Salt's predicted mile-an-hour pace now looked good to Jared. He lacked the strength to rewrap the mules' leggings, now only tattered banners. But they had served their purpose up 'til now. The animals showed few scrapes or injuries.

Jared thrashed through the thick snow and dangerous rocks. He'd had enough. Salt made no attempt to relieve him. He threw the reins over the lead mule, which halted. Jared worked his way back past the fourth mule, then heard Brutus's bark erupt. No violent edge to the sound but a definite warning. Jared cleared the last mule and saw the problem. Salt and the malamutes had gotten too close to the halted mules. Brutus's snarls held Salt and the dogs frozen in their tracks. The Airedale ceased his noise at Jared's arrival and lay down, eyes glued to the sled dogs and Salt.

"You take the lead or we rest," Jared called out.

Jared panted, then collapsed onto the snow. The prospector pushed past Jared, handing him the leather leads of the sled dogs. The old man seemed more surly than usual. Jared was beyond giving a damn.

* * *

Another ridge to stumble down. The misery of his Boston Marathon paled in comparison to this struggle with the imminent threat of freezing to death. The crushing force of the wind blew Jared off balance every few steps along the high route from A B Mountain to the rumored crest of the Coastal Range. An unnecessary handicap, considering the treacherous footing and his numb stumps for feet.

Pellets of ice came inexplicably from all directions, whipping his exposed face. Unwelcome moisture soaked him both inside and out— sweat beneath his layered clothing, incessant snowfall soaking through his parka and pants. Would he ever be dry again? And nothing to see beyond one hundred feet in thick, eternal clouds. Jared could be winter traveling with Salt in New York's Adirondack Mountains.

Jared was too exhausted to make the effort to trade places with the surly Salt, who again labored at the end of their small pack train. The old man had uttered little more than undecipherable grunts and curses, each swept away from his lips by overwhelming blasts of arctic air. What were the chances they would wander forever, never reaching Lake Bennett?

This current descent seemed to go on forever, snow thicker and deeper with each step. Multiple ridges mocked his previous simplistic view of the distance from A B Mountain's tree line to the summit of White Pass. One step at a time had the hypnotic effect of leveling the terrain—up or down no different at the snail's pace he could barely muster.

The weather grew calmer yet even colder. Jared glanced up at the sky's eternal gray canopy and spied cracks of cobalt blue. The solid murk above had turned to delineated, individual clouds. A subtle shift in wind and temperature wound its way into Jared's clogged senses. He staggered to a stop and shook his head to clear the confusion. Wind still slapped his exposed cheeks, but not with the vicious gusts of only an hour ago.

Salt had convinced him of the value of a full beard as protection against the brutal Yukon conditions, but the scraggly mess decorating Jared's face looked more like a failed wheat crop. A bandana would serve him better, but the cloth was buried in his pack.

He put his head down and resumed slogging down the endless ridge. Then no new mountain shoulders rose to impede him. Within several hours, welcome crystal-blue sky dominated above and to the far horizons to the north and east. The increased chill couldn't be ignored, sensation now absent from fingers as well as toes. But powerful winds had settled into a milder, consistent breeze. He didn't need to ask Salt. They had made it over the crest of the Coastal Range.

* * *

The short day bled light into fast-approaching dusk at the intersection of the well-tramped trail to Lakes Bennett and Lindman.

Salt remained taciturn and silent, following Jared, the mules, and Brutus. That night was spent with greater comfort thanks to the absence of the brutal wind. A roaring fire created a welcome wall against the frigid weather. Matches and fire-starting moss were worth much more than gold in the Yukon wilderness.

Salt broke his silence only once that evening. They would reach Lake Bennett and his stashed dogsled mid-morning. Only four or five miles of easier traveling to go.

The next morning the mules and dogs were packed, and Jared followed Salt down the trail. Salt acted no different than the previous day. The benign terrain should have lightened Salt's spirit, but the old curmudgeon remained in a nasty mood. What had happened to make the sourdough such a miserable traveling companion? Jared racked his brain. Nothing Jared had done could account for Salt's foul humor.

Evidence of the packed trail, but still no one in sight. Then a mild rise revealed the rough camp of Bennett sprawled along the lake's edge. Snow blanketed frozen waters, and only the absence of foliage delineated the shoreline. The lake stretched east in a thick, elongated finger as far as Jared could see. But the relief of reaching their first destination compensated for the bedraggled appearance of the settlement.

Men, dogs, and a few emaciated pack horses meandered among the village of well over one hundred tents of all sizes and shapes. The sound of axes, howls of dogs and curses of bundled men echoed through the thin chill air. Still no comment from Salt. What was the old man's problem?

Salt stayed in the front and led the party to the edge of camp, where he gathered the mules and secured them to a fir stump. The trees around the camp had long ago been harvested to construct boats, that activity seeming to be the only project underway. Grunts and nods made up the greetings of other campers, camaraderie seemed to Jared submerged beneath an ever-present tension and competition.

"Unpack the mules and stay here," Salt grunted. "I'll be back in a couple of hours."

Salt gathered the sled dogs. He secured their harnesses and traces and led them on foot away from the lake. Jared fought back a swelling uneasiness. What the heck was going on with the old coot?

CHAPTER FORTY-SIX

The sharp snap of Brutus's teeth brought attention to a fast-approaching dog team. The boxy frame of a freight sled careened behind a team of seven malamutes. Jared recognized Brownie in the lead. Excited, gleeful barks echoed against the wooded hills surrounding the frozen lakeshore. Salt crouched low on the back runners of the sled, clinging tight to the short handlebars. Jared's eyes focused on the figure driving the team. Without cargo, the empty freighter bounced from the powerful pull of the dogs.

Brownie broke trail, proud in his traces. The large lead husky slowed one hundred yards from Jared and the mules. But Salt cracked his moose-hide whip above the team, and they bolted back to full speed. Salt's hoarse cry turned them in an arc. Then he stepped on the brake, the outfit coming to a stop in a spray of wet snow only a few feet from Jared. The old man moved with a surprising sprightliness, considering the last few days' brutal struggle over the Coastal Range. Salt could be quite the showman.

The trip across the mountain ridges had been a walk in the park for the dogs, all the hard work done by Jared and the mules. Now the dog team jumped and twitched in their harnesses, stimulated after the boredom and humiliation of their journey. Brownie howled a piercing request for more action.

"Stay here," Salt commanded Jared but with perhaps a somewhat lighter tone. "I'm going to try and sell these mules for a decent price."

Packers had large tents here at Lake Bennett, smokestacks protruding through the tops. Salt moved between tents and skeletons of mainly flat-bottomed boats in various stages of construction. Salt paused and talked to a few of the bundled workers.

A sad, scattered assortment of sore and starving animals hauled timber from nearby forests. Not much use for them until the trail opened. Would this be the fate of his faithful mules? A pang of pity sliced through Jared, knowing the murderous Dead Horse Trail would soon open to resumed carnage.

Salt trudged back with a burly, full-bearded man. A bloodstained apron draped across his broad chest and belly. He had to be the only butcher in Lake Bennett. The mules stirred at the men's approach.

"Got um sold," Salt said, spitting. "Ain't been much meat available here for quite a spell. Got a hell of a price."

Salt untied the halter on the black mule, the most stubborn of the bunch. Salt jerked the animal and steered it toward the butcher. No love was lost between Jared and the intransigent animal after spending three brutal days battling with the mule.

"Best-looking beasts I seen since before the trail closed," the large man said. A smile as broad as his body allowed black teeth to appear from behind the man's wild beard. "There's enough meat here for weeks or until the trail opens. Then they'll get swallowed by the new swarm of starving fools in a couple of days. Wouldn't even have to feed these mules they'd be eaten so fast. How'd you get these animals up here, sourdough?"

Salt thrust the mule's reins toward the butcher. The burly man grabbed at the offered straps. The black mule jerked back. The nervous animal threw its head and body back, hooves flying, grazing the chest of the butcher. The large man staggered back.

"You nasty son of a bitch!" the butcher roared.

The mountain of a man reached across his body and slid a sparkling blade as large as an axe from a scabbard. In the same motion the furious man sliced open the mule's throat. The hapless animal fell forward onto the ground. A dark spurt of arterial blood painted a random pattern of color on the dirty white snow.

Air rushed from Jared's lungs, the drama a solid punch to the solar plexus. But he didn't lose his composure. Instead, a weight seemed to drop from his body, replaced by resignation. Life was no different at Lake Bennett than Skagway and most certainly Dawson. He couldn't change the brutality and callousness of life, the injustice, avarice and inhumanity in the world. Now Jared would not be bound by any rules from his past. He could make up his own, just like the barbarians surrounding him.

No wonder Salt hadn't given a damn about wrapping the pack animals' legs or unloading them at the end of each day. The mules were on a one-way trip to the top. Jared shouldn't have been surprised. Better to slaughter them now than have the poor animals brutalized for weeks while they starved to death.

The butcher gathered all the remaining harnesses and led the live animals away. Why had the man killed the black mule only to have to drag the carcass all the way to the butcher's tent? It seemed stupid to Jared.

"Your plan was to sell them to packers," Jared said, amazed at the calmness enveloping him.

"No buyers," Salt answered, stepping into Jared's face. "And I'm not interested in what you thought. I'm done with you and that useless mutt."

Salt's comments had not caught Jared by surprise. The old man's perfidy and lack of integrity now seemed predictable. But Jared had no intention of releasing Salt from their agreement.

"You said we were going to Dawson." Jared's tone remained even and subdued. His dispassionate attitude remained in place.

"No way a whiny, gawky flatlander is going to keep up with a good sled." Salt spit into the snow. "And despite your damn dog's interference and attacks, I still got a fine sled team."

"Yes," Jared said. "But you'd still be on the wrong side of White Pass without me and Brutus."

"True." Salt nodded, scratching his beard. "Must admit you're a tough bastard. Broke trail and served as a sixth mule. But I ain't babysitting no cheechako for over six hundred miles. I aim to travel twenty to twenty-five miles a day."

"Let me try," Jared said.

Salt had unfurled his true colors. Jared felt like a spectator to a staged drama. If he had to, he'd resort to the same violent methods as the rest of mankind. Now Jared would try to deal with Salt as rationally as possible, even though he knew it would be a waste of time.

"You gave me your word," Jared said.

"Don't owe you nothing."

"Yes, you do," Jared said. "There is some honor in this godforsaken country. Didn't you say you had some? You're paying your debt to me. You're going to do the right thing."

"Ain't no right or wrong," Salt said. "You get away with what you can get away with. That's the law of the Yukon. You ever been shot at? Ever starved? Been powerless? Held in contempt and disgust? No, you haven't. I don't even need to ask. You ain't lived that much."

Salt was wrong. What would he think if he knew the miseries and disasters Jared had experienced the last six months? What would the old codger say to Jared's rejection by his family, beating by his brother, survival on drugs, witnessing a brutal hanging, theft of his money? But why waste his breath.

"You never intended to take me to Dawson, did you?"

A swelling filled him with righteous anger and energy. Jared welcomed the building pressure. He could—no, he would—break this scraggly rooster's neck. But could he commit murder? Would he lower himself into the cesspool of immorality that defined Skagway and the trail to the Klondike? But he'd crossed the line into a new world. And he knew he needed Salt.

"Sharp boy, ain't you?" Salt said, sarcasm lacing his words. "Have to say, as well as you done getting us across the mountains, you won't have any trouble getting back to the fine metropolis of Skagway. You got your clothes, and I'll cut out food for you. But what about your dog? Good opportunity to get rid of that worthless hairball. Let him starve."

"I can keep up with you," Jared said, now almost hoping for an excuse to rip into the deceitful prospector.

"How?" Salt spit before starting to load the sled.

"Use the snowshoes we packed."

"Snowshoes?" Salt stopped packing freight, looked up at Jared. "You think you know how to use snowshoes?"

Training for three winters in New England had required certain skills. Jared had mastered both the huge, ungainly hunting shoes and the smaller more efficient trail snowshoes. Could he keep up with Salt's sled on the flats of Lake Bennett and the several even larger lakes ahead? No. Salt would just have to slow down, pace himself and the dogs. Jared would make that happen. The savagery of the butcher had opened his eyes to violent options he'd never considered before.

"You are taking me."

And what about Brutus? Could the dog keep up? He glanced down at the Airedale, who had tracked the increasingly intense exchange. Balls of snow clogged his kinky coat. Yes.

"All right, hot shot," Salt said, separating the dogs from the sled. "We'll finish loading the freighter and take off before dawn. See if you can keep up."

The prospector wouldn't sneak out without him. Jared would sleep by the sled on his canvas bedcover wrapped in his bear robe. And when and if necessary, he'd provide a little persuasion to slow Salt down. Let's just see how well the little bastard dealt with Jared's new laws.

* * *

Daylight was but a faint promise when Salt cracked his whip above the malamutes and set off across the lightly tracked snowfields lying on top of Lake Bennett. Jared followed with long, ground-eating strides, parka hood tight around his face and a flannel bandana to warm and filter the sharp-edged frozen air he gulped.

He had practiced on the trail snowshoes the previous afternoon. It hadn't taken him long to regain the required rhythm. He'd even given thought to what he should carry on his back, in case he found himself left behind by the treacherous Salt. Nothing too heavy if he was to keep up. Dried fish for Brutus and bacon and enough rice for himself to last over a week. Also, plenty of socks, second pair of boots, an extra mackinaw, bear robe and ground cloth.

Jared had also secured leather moccasins on Brutus's paws. The old sourdough had spit in disdain. And Salt's earlier admonitions to keep Jared's repeating Remington handy had become better advice than the prospector could imagine. He'd use it on Salt if he had to.

"Don't go too fast, Salt," Jared yelled as the dogs strained forward at a loud, energetic clip. "I'm warning you."

Salt's laugh echoed across the empty expanse. The laden freighter skimmed across the flat frozen lake, dogs fresh and excited. Jared stepped after the sled with efficient steps. Within a half mile, Salt had outdistanced Jared and Brutus by some fifty yards.

"Slow down," Jared called out, knowing the caution was a waste of time.

He allowed Salt to pull ahead another twenty yards before he stopped, pulled off his gloves and levered a shell into the Remington's breach. Early morning gloom reduced the prospector and the freighter to indistinct shadow. The first shot kicked up a puff of powder to the left of the sled. Salt cracked his whip and the malamutes reached for another gear. Okay, old man, time to live by the new laws.

The freighter jerked to the right just as Jared fired a second bullet aimed at the other side of Salt. The bullet shattered the rear stanchion of the sled. The heavy freighter swerved and toppled over. Salt flew off the rear traces and tumbled into the snow.

The old man jumped to his feet and whirled back toward Jared. Jared lowered the rifle. My God, he could have just as easily hit Salt as the sled. But his hands remained steady. Jared closed the gap between them and pointed the gun at the prospector's grizzled head. He'd never experienced such a sense of control.

"You be careful, you son of a bitch," Salt growled. "Could kill someone acting like that."

"What makes you think I wasn't trying to kill you?" Jared said, flashing Salt his crooked smile.

"You ain't got the balls to kill me."

"Maybe," Jared agreed, "but I've got no problem putting a slug in your leg. You either leave with me, or you don't leave at all."

Salt pulled his mouth free of the parka hood and bandana and spit into the untracked snow. His luminous eyes darted between Jared and the upended sled. Jared almost laughed at the confused expression on the prospector's face.

"We're only four days from Skagway," the old man said, a plume of steam enshrouding his wild head, "but seems like a lifetime of changes in you. Still, you're gonna slow me down by at least a week or two. I won't have you holding me back, boy."

Jared remained planted before Salt. He appeared hesitant, unable to meet Jared's stubborn gaze. Jared no longer gave a damn about the old man's plans. This time Jared would follow his own destiny.

"I guess you're not such a bad lad," the prospector said after several minutes of puzzled silence. "I'll make you a deal. There's nothing in Dawson you ain't seen in Skagway, just smaller, crazier and more desperate. Ain't nothing there for gold to buy. Nothing, that is, unless you're interested in drinking, dancing, whoring, or winter mining in some godforsaken hole."

Jared stood anchored to his snowshoes, numb hands gripping his rifle. He had nowhere to go and nothing left to lose. Nothing would change his mind.

"I'm going to pay you for a fine job of trail breaking," Salt said with a note of wheedling. "I figured it would take well over a week to reach Bennett. Not three days. And I'll give you a bonus for what you did."

"I don't care about your blood money," Jared said. "You said the value of the trip was in the journey. Remember, old man? I'm going to Dawson, and I'm setting the pace. I'll be sleeping by the sled every night. Build a nice fire and sleep well because I've got this worthless mutt by my side. He'll rip your throat out after one false move."

"Twenty thousand in gold," Salt said. A hard cold stare accompanied the outrageous bribe. "Safely stashed in Skagway."

That amount of gold was a fortune, a life-changing amount. Jared should put this dangerous journey in perspective. Consider all sides.

But any considerations were a waste of time. The deceitful sourdough lied anyway.

"No thanks," Jared replied. "Let's hit the trail. If we travel slower, we'll be able to mush longer in the dark. Night driving, as you described it."

The sourdough might have covered up to twenty-five miles a day in the daylight hours. Jared would be lucky to make twenty. Could he pick up the difference night driving, several hours on each side of sunrise and sunset? Close enough. That would be his commitment to Salt.

What if he couldn't maintain a killer pace like that for four or five weeks? He'd take it a day at a time. He couldn't escape the final and most probable outcome—that he wouldn't survive. But either Salt slowed down, or Jared would shoot him, no longer fazed at the thought of violence. If the butcher could slaughter a mule because it reacted in fear, then putting a bullet in Salt to survive hardly registered on the scale of brutality. Adapt or die. So be it.

A new expression of wariness wrinkled the old man's eyes. He nodded at Jared, then mushed into the glowing birth of a brief Yukon morning. Jared cast a comforting glance behind to the trotting, mist-shrouded Brutus. The dog was worth his kinky-haired weight in gold, though maybe not $20,000. The probability of Jared strolling into Skagway and somehow receiving that amount of money was the stuff of paperback novels.

CHAPTER FORTY-SEVEN

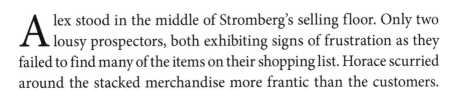

Alex stood in the middle of Stromberg's selling floor. Only two lousy prospectors, both exhibiting signs of frustration as they failed to find many of the items on their shopping list. Horace scurried around the stacked merchandise more frantic than the customers. Evidence of Alex's disintegrating dream.

What the hell had he done? He'd killed the only man who could have saved Stromberg's. Not only had he committed murder—the flimsy veneer of self-defense hadn't lasted a minute—but he had just as effectively committed financial suicide. The potential deal with Soapy Smith grew into a more frightening specter without Elijah Cummings.

The bell above the front door rang an ironic cheerful tinkle, and two bundled ladies entered. Morganna Everett, the wife of Skagway's one and only baker, led the way. She was as dumpy and doughy as her husband's products. A gangly, blue-eyed lady followed behind her at a sheepish pace.

"Mr. Stromberg," Morganna gushed. "I'm so glad you're here. I want you to meet a dear friend of mine, Susan Neusom, just arrived from Seattle."

Susan Neusom looked closer to a broomstick than the plump loaf of bread that best described her companion, despite the heavy coat, thick dress and unseen petticoats. She did possess attractive eyes, but it would take much more than clear blue eyes to compete with Sophia's many assets. Alex fixed a smile on his face and wished he was any place other than Stromberg's.

"Miss Neusom will be working with us at the bakery," Morganna said. "I so wanted her to meet the most eligible bachelor in town."

A blossoming redness colored the sharp-featured face of the new arrival. More and more women were finding their way to Alaska, the great land of opportunity. With a ratio of one hundred to one, even this plain-faced woman had a chance to claim a husband. But Susan Neusom held no attraction for Alex. Alex clung to an image of Sophia, his high-strung, sleek Arabian mare.

Sophia. Where was she? She had cancelled their last meeting. And Elijah's news had changed everything. Sophia guilty of cutting someone's throat? No cold-blooded killer would slave as hard as Sophia. And would a whore be so resistant to any physical contact? Elijah couldn't have had all the facts. There had to be another side to the story.

Still, images of Sophia performing duties as a working girl brought a level of arousal Alex had trouble controlling. Could she now refuse his advances with the facts he possessed, assuming they were true? He had glimpsed more than enough sexual promise behind that ever-present wide-brimmed hat, scrubbed face and baggy clothing. No comparison possible with the two women standing before him.

The baker's wife ended her spiel in support of Susan Neusom, but chitchatted on. Alex offered no response other than a respectful, but distracted, demeanor. Frustration contorted her face. Morgana whirled and made a noisy exit, purchasing not even one can of Mordecai's goddamn peaches. Should he have offered some encouragement? They might have bought something. Still, Alex exhaled in relief when the door closed behind the women.

Why was he fighting so hard to hang on? Yes, the Klondike's allure would bring many more greedy and star-crossed souls to Skagway, but for how much longer? And if an end to the gold rush was so imminent, why not fold up his own business and head south? The answer could be found in Stromberg's astronomical profits the last few months before the White Pass closed. And before Mordecai quit shipping the merchandise Alex needed. With six to ten more good months, Alex might be freed of his father forever. That was worth some risk, wasn't it?

But now his inventory was too full of holes, even if he coerced his share of The Star's profits from Sophia to buy more goods. Besides, the promise of Sophia proved a far greater allure than mere gold. He needed breathing room. Time to cut his deal with the Devil, then tend to his relationship with Sophia.

* * *

Soapy slouched on the scarred visitor's chair in Stromberg's cramped office. A fresh bottle of whiskey sat untouched on the desk top. A gut-churning reaction bubbled within Alex. Negotiating with Soapy required a clear head, especially as he dealt from weakness.

"But I think 'Nearly New Emporium' is a great name," Soapy protested. His beguiling earnestness gave the impression of honesty as far from reality as California from Alaska. "You won't need to explain the various conditions of your inventory. Customer walks in the door and understands why he's getting such a good deal. It's the old truth in advertising."

The goods Smith offered came from every conceivable illegal activity, from theft to murder. Yet he spoke of truth in advertising as if it mattered. Alex couldn't believe the man's gall. But what difference did it make? Soapy fronted the merchandise, the store and the minimal fixtures required. All Alex had to do was hire and supervise some played-out miners so down on their luck they had no options. Their predicaments weren't that different from Alex's. The sour thought caught in his throat.

"Okay, fine, Soapy," he agreed. "The Nearly New Emporium it is. But if you want me as a partner in this new venture, I need to cut another deal with you."

"What did you have in mind, partner?"

Soapy went from excited entrepreneur to flint-eyed shark in a flash. Alex stifled a nervous laugh at the transformation. Extracting a loan from Smith was such a desperate move on Alex's part. His rash act at the mouth of the Skagway River would cost him dearly now. On second thought, a shot of liquor now would actually be beneficial.

"I need some temporary financing." Alex forced the words out. "Stromberg's, due to unfortunate errors by my father, requires a rebalancing of its inventory."

"How much rebalancing are we talking about?" Soapy asked, fingers tracing his precisely cut beard.

Alex had worked with great diligence to keep the number as low as possible, but without a reliable wholesaler like B & B, he'd be forced to overpay for fill-in product.

"Ten thousand dollars."

"No problem," Soapy said, hands up, fingers splayed. He looked like he was ready to reach into Alex's pockets, not supply working capital. "What kind of collateral would you like to offer?"

"Collateral?" Alex said. Just how deep a hole was he willing to dig? "We're partners. Isn't my word good enough?"

"Please," Soapy said. Sad eyes and a disappointed grimace greeted Alex. "I'm a businessman. I do lend money. Because we're partners, I'll charge only 10 percent interest per month. But not without some form of security."

Jesus. Ten percent a month was usurious beyond belief. That was 120 percent a year. Ridiculous even if he did pay Soapy back in a month after the Pass reopened. No way he'd borrow at that rate. But now he had to at least play out this charade.

"I'll pay 5 percent a month and put up Stromberg's as collateral," Alex offered.

He felt like he was in another poker game with Soapy. Only Smith had all the cards. Next time, you son of a bitch, the game will be fair and honest. Let's see then how well the hustler did.

"I don't think so, Alex," Smith said. "You're borrowing money to keep your store afloat. If things are so precarious and you need my money to stay in business, only a fool would accept security already at such high risk."

"Well, no loan, no second-hand store," Alex said. He gave an elaborate shrug and laid both palms flat on the desk.

Soapy studied the ceiling, steepled his fingers and pursed his thin lips. A respectable banker dealing with a difficult, risky customer. The silence that filled the small room made the space even more cramped. Alex glanced at the brown liquor bottle perched on the edge of his desk. No. Another drink wouldn't improve his situation.

"I might offer 7 1/2 percent," Soapy said, "with proper collateral."

The man knew Alex had no children, so it couldn't be his first born. And without a loan, Alex might as well head back to San Francisco and the nightmare of his father's judgmental disapproval— Sophia or no Sophia.

"What do you have in mind?"

"How about your interest in The Star and the Alverson House?"

That son of a bitch. How did Soapy know about his partnership with Sophia? Did that bastard also know Sophia's past? Probably not, or he would have already threatened blackmail. And what would Sophia do if she discovered Alex's deal with the biggest crook in Skagway? Of course, she wouldn't really have a choice after Elijah Cummings' revelations. But who the hell was Alex to get so righteous? Hadn't he just killed a man to keep him quiet?

"Would you like to think about this?" Soapy asked, reverting to compassionate capitalist.

What was there to think about? Either he sold his soul to Satan, or he gave up any hopes of independence from Mordecai. Perhaps he should consider folding Stromberg's. He could tell Soapy to stick the Nearly New Emporium up his ass and become operational partners with Sophia. Though up to now, she had made all the decisions concerning the two hotels. He'd have either to gain her consent to be an active partner or use her past as leverage. Neither option boded well for a better relationship to come. But why put the horse before the cart?

"My interests in The Star and Alverson House far exceed $10,000," Alex said. "You drop to 5 percent, and we keep this loan completely confidential. This arrangement is between you and me only."

"Six percent," Soapy said, sticking out his well-manicured hand. "And we'll keep this little secret from everyone. Including Miss Alverson."

Alex stuck out his hand. He had to believe this deal with the Devil would work out in his favor. If the gangster betrayed him, he'd shoot the prick quicker than he'd disposed of Elijah. He'd at least bought more time.

CHAPTER FORTY-EIGHT

Her fingers traced the no longer comforting outline of her man-sized revolver. How long could she stay huddled in the cocoon of her room behind The Star? One week and she still panicked at every sound. Wouldn't some disaster of discovery have occurred if her ex-customer made a move to expose or arrest her? Of course, there were no lawmen in Skagway. But there was also no real secret to where Sophia cowered.

"Miss Alverson." The voice of Malcolm Stenson accompanied an annoying knuckle-rapping on the door.

Sophia gasped for air and waited for her throbbing heart to slow enough for words to form on dry, cracked lips. Stenson had done a fine job serving as general manager for her new hotel. But without her direction, the man couldn't put his boots on the correct feet.

"Miss Alverson," Stenson called again. "The new brass fixtures don't hold enough candles to light the stairway. What do we do? Too late to order different ones."

"Use wood," Sophia said.

Why couldn't she be left alone? Of course, she knew the answer—the imminent opening of the Alverson House.

"Have the carpenters throw something together that holds three or four candles," she shouted at the door.

"Miss Alverson," Stenson said. "If you want to open in two weeks, you've got to make some decisions. Candleholders aren't our only challenge."

Yes, the grand opening neared. Sophia knew she was out of time. But the Alverson House's birth now held more dread than dream. How could one glimpse from the outside world bring her fantasy life crashing down? How could all the intricate walls of defense, the flimsy rationalizations, the painstaking planning, disguises and sacrifices, be shattered so quickly? She couldn't give up now. She wasn't even sure she had been discovered.

"I know, Mr. Stenson," Sophia said, forcing calm into her words. "I'll soon be up and about. Go take care of the candelabras."

Stenson's snort of disgust registered through the locked door. She could imagine his thoughts, none of which she could argue with. Just another weak-willed woman succumbing to the pressure of a business challenge. All that money invested now at risk. Her disappearing when she was most needed.

And no Alex. Not a single querulous peep. She'd cancelled their last meeting, and he still hadn't questioned her absence. Strange, since he appeared so desperate to get the Alverson House open and regain his precious cash flow. She had always been able to read men, but Alex was as unpredictable as a roulette wheel.

"We've only got half the staff hired." Stenson continued his impatient banging on the door. "We're short on linens for the dining room. And you said you had a cook lined up. It's time for him to get his kitchen and supplies in order—"

"Mr. Stenson," Sophia barked at the wood barrier, anger overcoming fear. "You employ who we need and get the tablecloths from Seattle. I know we'll have to pay more, but just do it. I hired you as the Alverson's general manager. Manage. And quit hammering on my door. I'll be out soon enough."

Disgruntled curses faded away as Stenson stomped off.

She buried her face in her pillow, hand grasping the Colt .44. Would she go out in a blaze of gunfire when her past came roaring through the door? Or would she be only a whimpering pile of broken spirit and shattered dreams? Wasn't cringing in her room as bad as any prison? The role of frightened damsel in distress would solve no problems. What she needed was a knight in shining armor to rescue her. Why did Alex have to be such a stone-cold creature? Lord, why was she always so alone?

After all these weeks of fear and trepidation of discovery by Hawk Face, she'd been identified by some pudgy-faced businessman. Perhaps the man at the Great Northern did not recognize her at all. Maybe she was grossly overreacting. But she'd die before facing her accusers in St. Louis.

Another smack on the door. Her heart again raced to painful levels. She had to overcome her crippling terror.

"What now?" she called out.

"Miss Alverson." Now Jacob Tredaway's irritating voice reverberated. "Supplies just arrived. Don't you want to inspect them?"

She hadn't personally checked on The Star's supplies in weeks. Old Jacob had resented her interference. Why the change now? Her cook had to be concerned at her hermitlike existence this last week. Tredway might not be any knight in shining armor, but at least he worried about her.

"Jacob, you don't need me to receive the supplies." Sophia focused on each word, fighting for control.

"You ain't eaten much of anything either," her faithful, stubborn cook said.

"I'll be fine. Soon. Just leave me in peace. Please."

Silence returned. Peace did not. Sophia lifted her face to the mirror, hardly recognizing the swollen, bloodshot eyes, puffy, blotched face, and hair in witchlike disarray. She had bills to pay. People to hire. Decisions on furnishings, hotel menu, paint colors. An endless flow. God, what role could she assume that would save her now?

She needed Alex. But he was disgusted with her. What an idiot she'd been. She knew nothing about business, buildings, investments. Her dream had become a nightmare.

She couldn't hide in her room much longer. She could ignore the danger and reemerge in disguise once more. She could hunt down the man who may or may not have recognized her. And then what? Shoot him? Bribe him? Or she could slink out of Skagway and run in fear for the rest of her life. Great choices.

She would have to swallow her pride and ask Alex for help. But it was one thing to beg for aid with the Alverson House, quite another to request protection from murder charges. Would he help her or arrest her himself? He could collect the reward and end up owning 100 percent of both The Star and the Alverson House. She'd failed miserably at manipulating Alex, let alone understanding him.

CHAPTER FORTY-NINE

The trail had reopened. Canadian Mounties now controlled the White Pass, requiring every prospector to possess enough supplies to survive in the interior. That list cost around $500 and probably weighed 1,000 pounds. But where was Alex's expected surge of volume? All four clerks were busy. Stromberg's did have some customers. Far too few, though. Shouldn't those strict regulations have stimulated business? Where was the pent-up demand?

Yes, there was a hell of a lot more competition. But Alex had worked his ass off to present a balanced inventory for those fools still heading to the Klondike gold fields. A month of excellent business would build his margins back to a profitable level. That hadn't happened, wasn't happening. Now he worked hard to stay in the same place and pay Soapy Smith's exorbitant interest rates.

"Mr. Stromberg." A scruffy, frazzled young man burst through the front door, shouting, "Horace is in deep trouble at Nearly New. A mob's destroying the store. We can't move, let alone sell anything."

Just what he needed—another goddamn debacle. Alex had turned the entire operation of the used-goods store to his seemingly capable assistant. How hard could it have been for Horace to set up Nearly New? But if Smith's store became a disastrous failure, Soapy would make Alex pay one way or another.

"Jamison, you're in charge," Alex called out to his most experienced employee and headed out the door with the frightened young man. Damn. He sorely missed that cock-eyed Jared.

Alex pushed through the crowded traffic of men and animals. A slight warming trend had turned the once-frozen streets of Skagway into a morass of mud and manure. Splintered wooden sidewalks with rotten planks and sharp edges were more dangerous than the slop of the streets. He approached the Nearly New Emporium, only to be blocked by a throng of prospectors and cheechakoos at the doorway. Alex fought against the mob. Harsh words and hard stares greeted his efforts, then the chaos he confronted inside stopped him cold.

Customers flung merchandise over their heads, stomped through two to three feet of goods strewn over the floor, yelling for prices. A sea of long underwear, shirts, parkas, mackinaws, pants, boots, shovels and canteens covered the floor. Price signs on walls had no relationship to the jumbled disorder of scattered goods. A few lucky patrons pushed for position to pay for their purchases.

Horace struggled at the cash box. The overwhelmed man crouched behind the counter, the only furniture or fixture in the store. A disorderly line of ten to fifteen miners harangued him with questions and curses. Two other clerks stood backed up against the rough wood walls, terrified, helpless and useless. The scene was more riot than retail. Had Nearly New taken all these potential customers from Stromberg's? Alex's stomach tightened into a knot at the thought.

"Listen up," he screamed. "Everyone out."

The howling mob continued filling their arms with dirt-cheap merchandise. Alex yanked his Colt from its holster and fired several shots into the cluttered floor. Heads whipped toward him, bodies froze in place. The deafening rounds caught everyone's attention.

"We're closed," he shouted, eyes on his incompetent clerk. "We'll open again tomorrow morning at nine. If you've picked out purchases and are already in line, we'll take your money. Otherwise, out." Alex motioned to the shell-shocked clerks pressed against the wall. "You two block the door. Now. Get on the outside and shut the damn door behind you. Tell everyone to come back tomorrow. Anyone gives you trouble, scream and I'll help you out."

The two men pushed to the door, scrambling over the jumbled piles of merchandise. Alex holstered his weapon and herded the remaining customers out of the store. The line of prospectors waiting to pay Horace held their ground.

Alex surveyed the mayhem in disgust. Better this ridiculous dream of Soapy's should be named Completely Useless. How fast could he put this mess back together?

"What the hell happened?" he asked, struggling to control his temper.

"I...I'm not sure," Horace stuttered. "We opened the door, and all hell broke loose. We never had this much business at Stromberg's."

Alex didn't need to be reminded of that uncomfortable observation. He should have stopped by, helped with the planning and displays. Now he couldn't let Soapy discover how negligent he'd been. A little direction could have solved a lot of problems. So much for Stromberg's promoting quality.

And, of course, the same could be said for his lack of cooperation with Sophia and the Alverson House. Alex swallowed a bitter taste of bile. He had no one to blame but himself. But surely that idiot Horace could have done a better job than this.

"I had everything separated in piles by price," Horace said, a quiver in his voice, hands shaking. "Shirts for fifty cents, one dollar, dollar fifty, two dollars, two fifty. Price stacks for all the different products." Horace waved his arms above his head, perspiration dripping off his forehead. "Signs on the walls listed them. We opened early for a dry run so we could iron out any problems."

"You had five or more different price points? Why?" Alex asked, wondering why he wasted his time pounding on Horace's empty head. "You just piled them on the floor and hoped for the best?"

"These goods were in all conditions from plumb-wore-out to brand-new," Horace answered, grabbing a worn pair of pants and a new ugly yellow mackinaw from the pile at his feet. "Thought you'd want to squeeze out as much profit as possible."

How had Horace planned on keeping the goods separated? The signs on the wall had become worthless as soon as the first customers dove into the pile of merchandise. Horace proved far too limited. Alex suppressed a desire to rip into his assistant. Not worth the effort, and he'd already expended excessive amounts of energy on his own store.

"Okay, Horace," Alex said, his brain reeling off the required steps to making the store functional. "Make a sign for the front door saying we'll open tomorrow morning.

"Mr. Stromberg," Horace whined, avoiding eye contact with Alex. "We can't clean up this mess and be in business by tomorrow morning."

"We'd better be." The steel-laced words left no room for argument.

Alex took off his coat, rolled up his sleeves, and unbuckled his gun belt. Energy flooded his body. Finally a straight-forward problem he could solve with hard physical work and no unanswerable, complex challenges.

"We're going to separate this merchandise again." Alex felt back in his element, shutting out his financial pressures and the unsettling ambiguities of his feelings for Sophia. "This time only two price points per type of item. We'll build bins and nail price signs onto each display. Now get off your ass, Horace, and start hustling. Send two of your boys to pick up one hundred wooden planks four feet by one-half to one inches. Have them pick up a bag of nails, hammers and saws at Stromberg's."

He had planned to confront Sophia this very evening when Stromberg's was fully functional. Now this. But he didn't know how to approach her. What to say. How to best use Elijah's information. He could postpone dealing with Sophia for another day. And based on the chaos surrounding him, another night.

* * *

Alex pushed Horace and the three clerks through the rest of the day and all night. Food from The Star's kitchen sustained them. No whiskey to slow them down. The work required little thought, only physical effort. Then well after midnight, Alex's thoughts returned to Sophia. The image of his mysterious partner burned bright.

The last week, once he'd received Soapy's $10,000 loan, he'd spent every waking hour getting Stromberg's back in shape. The twenty-hour days kept sleep to a minimum. The good news—few nightmares had penetrated his exhaustion. Yet the puzzle of Sophia Alverson had never left his consciousness. She was in hiding. She must have recognized Elijah or realized he'd recognized her. Only that could explain her disappearance. But he shouldn't think about her now.

Now Alex had to open the doors of the Nearly New Emporium at nine in the morning. The winter sun, skirting the ridge of the horizon and diluted by Skagway's air-polluting fires and marine cloud layer provided weak evidence of a new day. An impatient crowd, double from the previous day, awaited the reopening. Word must have spread through Skagway about the rock-bottom prices offered. Well-ordered and clearly priced bins would make shopping simpler and contain the product. There would be no repeat of the chaos and confusion of the day before.

Alex positioned one of the clerks by the door to allow no more than twenty-five customers in at one time. Horace and another clerk worked the cash box. Another two men were hired on the spot to do nothing but keep the merchandise in order and refill the bins from the back room.

Nine o'clock. Show time. Alex swung open the door, glared at the anxious crowd with one hand on his .45. He took a step back, thrusting his clerk into the opening, partially blocking the flow of men. At twenty-five shoppers he again stepped forward, palms out halting the surge.

"You got this mob under control now," he said to his nervous helper. "Remember, no more than twenty-five at a time. You can do the math, can't you?"

Too bad everything was so cheap. No matter how successful Nearly New would become, Alex's half of the limited profits would solve few problems. At least he wouldn't have Soapy on his ass for any failure to open Completely Useless.

Murky skies outside prompted a return to his bewildering, perplexing questions surrounding Sophia. And the unsettling reality of his financial position. Business kept dropping below expectations at Stromberg's. He was headed for disaster. Now the contributions from The Star and soon-to-open Alverson House were even more critical. He could no longer postpone the inevitable confrontation with his partner. And that would be nowhere near as simple as putting Nearly New back together.

CHAPTER FIFTY

G reed. Of course. Greed and envy. Why had the realization of his brothers' motives taken so long to register? The belated revelation, though welcome, brought Jared no corresponding flash of physical warmth. Jared had certainly given his family's crushing rejection enough thought. But exhilaration charged his body. Jared strode with a lighter, more fluid step across frozen Tagish Lake.

The leather-webbed snowshoes rebounded off the powder-packed surface created by the dogs and sled. Long legs swallowed distance, keeping him never less than thirty yards behind the treacherous Salt. Jared's body had been built for this kind of challenge. A painful smile split his frost-bitten lips.

The biting arctic air seared his lungs. An endless spinning review of the tragedy at the Monroe farm had focused on what he had done wrong. He had been unable to identify his sin. Now he knew he hadn't committed one, certainly nothing to deserve banishment. Relief swept Jared. William and Tom had cast away Jared for one simple reason. His brothers had had no intention of allowing Jared to claim his third ownership in the property. Father Monroe had been bullied from control, the old man's helplessness clear under the fading Yukon afternoon. What a fool he'd been to waste so much time flagellating himself.

Jared shifted his rifle to his left hand, swinging the right to regain some sensation in deadened fingers. Twice the prospector had put too much distance between them, forcing Jared to drop his gloves and fire a warning shot. Fear of being left behind kept Jared alert and on edge. He trusted Salt as much as he trusted brother Tom.

The prospector reached the edge of Tagish Lake and mushed the dogs up its bank. The old man pointed to the front of the dogsled without a word. Jared struggled to follow. He had little choice except to work his way around the sled and team. He began the arduous task of breaking trail. At least he now served a valuable function for Salt. Jared should have felt safer, but exposing his back to the unpredictable sourdough created a discomforting tightness in his neck. His strength faded in small increments with the more difficult terrain.

* * *

The next morning flatter surfaces returned, this time Marsh Lake, the third day out of Bennett, fifth day of the journey. The easier traveling along Marsh Lake's ice ended too soon when the source of the Yukon River had been reached. Only a wide frozen stream evidenced the birth of the mighty, mythical waterway. The first few miles progressed in benign, manageable consistency, not much different than previous lake traveling. Jared followed the sled and Salt.

The unending review of his previous life that had swirled through his mind on his march through the wastelands no longer flowed in complete thoughts. Jared now only concentrated on form. Each step he took demanded clearance above the ragged track of the dogsled. He looked up to see Salt again disappearing. Another bullet by Salt's ear seemed required. A monumental effort was required to pull off his thick glove, chamber a round, cram his frozen finger against the trigger and place a shot at the old man's feet.

Several more miles downriver, jagged snow-covered blocks of ice appeared. A multitude of shapes and sizes littered the river in increasing bulk and frequency. What raw force had created such chaos? Salt was forced to drive the team from the river course, and Jared found himself once again struggling through untracked snow.

* * *

Two days later, brutal trail breaking for the sled had drained his remaining strength. Jared could no longer form any rational thought.

They had again reached the simpler lake travel over the relatively smooth surfaces of twenty-mile Lake Laberge. Still, Jared felt like he was trudging up A B Mountain with a load of rocks. He staggered forward, wondering which step would be his last. No question of if. Only when.

He tripped over the tip of his snowshoe, unable to lift his foot high enough to clear the trampled track of preceding dogs and sled. The effects of ten energy-sapping days on the Klondike Trail, cold so bitter each gasping breath possessed as much pain as oxygen, had reduced him to desperation. No matter how deeply he inhaled air, his legs demanded more.

Most sensation had left his hands. Had the temperature continued to drop or had all warmth-sustaining vitality been sucked from his body? He had to keep swinging his arms, switching the rifle back and forth, flexing fingers that seemed to belong to another person. The damn Remington felt like a log, inhibiting the required manipulation of his hands. Then the weapon fell to the snow, his hand unable to close around the wooden stock. His useless fingers couldn't pull the trigger even if his life depended on it. Now he was at Salt's mercy.

The miner pushed ahead, oblivious to the brutal conditions. How could the old man ignore the crushing blanket of arctic air? Was he immune to the debilitating elements? Would the sourdough keep traveling when Jared collapsed? That question could be answered without doubt.

"Salt." Panic drove the word through his frost-coated lips.

Salt pulled the dogs to a halt, stepped off the runner of the freight sled and stumbled to his knees. The old man regained his feet with obvious effort and threw his arms around his body, beating circulation back into his hands. Maybe the sourdough was human after all. Jared retrieved his gun and cradled it in the crooks of his arms. He tottered the remaining steps to the old man.

"Need to rest," Jared said, mist from his breath shrouding the man.

Salt gave him an appraising stare, but Jared no longer cared what the sourdough thought. The prospector didn't look much better than Jared felt. The grizzled miner couldn't even generate the energy to punctuate his expression with the usual spit. He swung one arm toward Jared, knocking the Remington from his hand.

"No reason to worry anymore, laddie," Salt said, the jet of steam from his mouth more impressive than the low volume of the words. "We're going to hole up. When it drops below minus fifty, you never want to be alone. Since you never know when that's gonna happen again, you're safe 'til we reach Dawson. Besides, can't drive the dogs more than five days in a row."

A growing uneasiness surfaced when he considered the killing temperature. Did Salt mean what he said? And what would happen when Salt no longer needed Jared? The sourdough had tried several times to discard Jared like an empty whiskey bottle. Salt might not be able to spit, but there was no change in the cold remorselessness of his eyes.

"How do you know it's that cold now?" Jared asked.

"It's too damn cold when my balance goes," Salt said, "and I can't seem to stay on the runners. Don't need no mercury thermometer. Better build a fire before it's too late to light a match."

Were they really in that much danger? Jared overcame the energy-draining chill and joined Salt gathering wood. The sourdough kicked snow from a mound bordering the nearby creek bed to reveal a pile of valuable fuel. Jared assembled as much wood as possible and followed Salt back to their camp. The old man laid large limbs on the snow to serve as a hearth and assembled an array of twigs and small branches. He yanked off a mitten. Fingers white as snow pried dried moss from his parka pocket.

Jared watched the prospector snap off the heads of invaluable sulpher matches attempting to light the moss. After four failed attempts, a different kind of chill raced down Jared's spine. Yukon travelers told of freezing to death for want of a fire. Weak as he was, Jared refused to die here, less than a third of the way to his destination. Jared pulled out matches from his inside pocket and brushed Salt aside. He struck a match against the barrel of his rifle. The match flared, and Jared lit the precious moss. God still existed.

Salt fed the feeble sparks with small twigs. Stick by stick, branch by branch, the life-giving flames grew until a large crackling blaze roared in the otherwise silent wilderness. Brutus stuck his snow-shrouded muzzle toward the fire. Salt didn't bother to push him away. Jared resisted an overpowering desire to roll into a fetal position beside the blossoming heat.

"We got to prepare camp," Salt said. "Gonna be here a couple of days. Yukon freezes always last a couple of days."

"Shouldn't we move into those trees for more shelter?" Jared asked.

"Got to keep the fire in the open," Salt said, enough life stirring in his body to bring expression to his words, in this case, condescension. "Heat melts the snow from the tree limbs. Drops onto the fire and snuffs it out. We'll unpack the sled, dig out a space and set up the tent facing the fire. Collect a pile of wood that'll last awhile."

The danger of freezing to death had to be real for Salt to call a halt. Could Jared have struggled even another one hundred yards? Thank God he wouldn't have to find out.

"Every living thing is burrowed in until this cold spell breaks," Salt said, confirming Jared's thoughts. "Only a fool would try to travel in this weather. And he wouldn't last long."

* * *

Salt tipped the sled and gear on its side to better block the wind and contain the fire's heat. For once the small drill tent seemed a comfortable size, even with Brutus jammed into the space. Jared had welcomed him inside. He paid no attention to Salt's animated complaints when the Airedale pushed into the cramped tent.

The malamutes had moved closer to the flames once Brutus had shifted his location. The native dogs burrowed into the snow, curled into tight balls and seemed quite content, ignoring the deadly cold. Jared felt no such sense of security, even safely ensconced in the drill tent. The frightening frigid air served as a constant reminder that death loomed close by.

The old man spread out his fur blanket, stepped on Jared's foot and elicited a growl from Brutus. Salt ignored both Jared and the dog, turning to exit the shelter. The sourdough returned with a brown bottle of liquor.

"Got two more 'sides this one," Salt said with proud defiance. "Tucked 'em in for just such an occasion. Can't drink when I'm traveling. Alcohol slows the blood, numbs the senses. But we ain't going anywhere for a spell."

Salt opened the bottle and swallowed a mouthful. He offered the whiskey to Jared. Jared flinched. His first and last drink remained a clear memory as sharp and bright as the campfire. Instead, Jared pulled out his small notebook and entered the estimated mileage of the day.

Cold had forced them to hole up several hours before darkness, limiting today's progress to twelve to fourteen miles. Jared had increasing difficulty determining distance, despite his New England experience clocking winter snowshoe workouts and his many spring and summer long-distance runs. Still, he felt confident in his estimate.

Close to two hundred miles had been covered in ten days, by his primitive calculations. The absence of Salt's bitching evidenced the excellent progress they must have accomplished. But Jared had snowshoed into complete exhaustion. Without several days rest, Salt could have left him to die in the Yukon outback without a whimper. Ironic that the killer frost had saved his life.

Salt contented himself with small sips after the first hearty slug, giving a satisfied belch that echoed in the small tent. Jared focused on the prospector. Unexpected moist warmth had replaced the normal aggressiveness of the old man's expressive eyes.

"You're not such a pain in the ass," Salt said, his inescapable breath thick with the odor of alcohol. "Turned out to be a passable companion 'stead of the dead weight I had you pegged for."

The booze twisted his diction, his statement slurred but distinct enough. This was as talkative as the surly Salt had been since Lake Bennett. Most men became aggressive, nasty when drunk, but Salt turned mellow and loquacious. Maybe the sourdough should have brought a case of whiskey on their journey. And maybe he had. Jared's ignorance became more evident every day.

"So many fools struggling to the Klondike," Salt said. "They're already over a year late. Every claim with color's long gone. Me and my partners staked early on Bonanza when it was still called Rabbit Creek. Picked up a second claim up on the hill above El Dorado Creek. Other miners say we're crazy digging so far from the water. We'll see. I figure we got another payoff coming."

Salt lapsed into a dreamy silence. A huge grin plastered his usually grim, scarred face. The old man took a couple more nips, then looked at Jared as if he'd seen him for the first time. Very strange, considering they squatted only a foot apart.

"My partners," Salt said with a chuckle. "That worthless mutt of yours got more brains than Lizard and Thorton combined. They're dumb as stumps. They been wandering the wilderness and digging holes as long as me. They ain't in it for the gold. Poor souls'll just keep on drifting 'til they die."

"What about you?" Jared asked. "You might be deceitful and ornery, but you're not stupid."

"Why, thank you for your kind words, laddie," Salt said with an incongruous giggle. "I keep telling you the value of life is in the journey. Unlike mine, yours ain't ending in the Yukon."

What did that comment mean? Had Salt given him a compliment or a threat?

"I ain't all that interested in gold either," Salt mumbled on. "Got plenty. Since you don't have a future as a miner—not that you're not tough enough—I should give you the $20,000 I offered you back in Bennett in case I don't make it. All ya gotta do is look up that crazy preacher, Alonyious Perkins. Lives in a shack, 'tween the edge of town and the river. Safer than that sham of a bank in town."

The concept of a banking establishment in that hellhole did seem preposterous. Nothing could be secure in that infested den of crooks. Alex Stromberg would never trust a bank in Skagway. He kept his money in his office safe. Soapy Smith probably owned the company,

The First Bank of Alaska, the business no more legitimate than the fake telegraph office that had no telegraph wires.

The prospector dug under his layers of clothing, exposing several leather thongs, and jerked one of the shoelace-size cords free. Salt's stubby, battered fingers pulled out a stained hide pouch. When he loosened the mouth of the bag Jared caught the unmistakable glitter of gold. The old man grunted, then crammed the poke back under his matted clothing.

"Ain't got that much gold on me," Salt said. "I'll give ya an IOU."

Salt's generosity only appeared with excessive amounts of whiskey. If only Jared could believe the old man. But that would never happen, not after what Jared had experienced at Lake Bennett. Salt could stay drunk the rest of his life, and Jared would still never trust the back-stabbing gnome. Nothing the old man said could be believed, except the dangers of the deathly freeze that gripped them. The two-faced sourdough could serve as the model for the character in Robert Louis Stevenson's recent novella, *Dr. Jekyll and Mr. Hyde.*

"Let's write up an IOU," Salt stuttered, "from me to you."

"I told you," Jared said, keeping his hands snug under his armpits. "I don't care about your blood money."

"Listen to me, Jared," Salt said. "Weren't easy sneak'n that gold all the way from Dawson. Had to carry it upriver and across that damned pass. Fighting those idiots thrashing up White Pass the toughest part. Barely got the gold to Alonyious 'fore those varmints ambushed me behind Stromberg's. Good thing that lunatic preacher man owes me his life. Twice."

He looked hard at Jared. Salt's eyes now burned liquid bright. His voice had firmed, and he took another swig from the seemingly bottomless bottle. Salt's philosophical expressions seemed as incongruous in the primitive Yukon as a church service in Skagway.

"Dammit," he demanded, anger surfacing, large eyes flashing. "I told ya to write up an IOU. Twenty thousand dollars."

What a waste of valuable paper. Salt had to be too drunk to think straight. How could the prospector believe Jared would buy into the sourdough's bull? Jared picked up the pad just to calm the old man down.

"How much gold did you bring out of the Klondike?" Jared asked as he scribbled out the IOU.

"Enough to pay you $20,000 and not miss it." Salt grabbed the pad and scratched his name at the bottom.

This time Jared wanted to spit in disbelief and mistrust.

"You're angry and frustrated with your life," the old man said, "'cause you're impotent, got no control of things. You want to accomplish something with your life? Or you want to spend your days slaving away at places like Stromberg's? Boy, with money you can get things done. Won't be a victim. You'll have choices. Maybe do some good in the world."

What the hell did Salt know about good in the world? That side of his nature only appeared with whiskey, then vanished with a night's sleep. Even if wisdom lay in Salt's words, Jared doubted the old man practiced what he preached.

CHAPTER FIFTY-ONE

Diners and lodgers crowded primitive wood-plank tables swaying under the weight of Jacob Tredaway's basic stomach-sticking dishes. Alex entered The Star with his mind in turmoil. This place was more productive than most Klondike gold mines. If all he had to worry about was The Star, there'd be no financial issues.

"Jacob," Alex called to the crusty cook, "where's Sophia?"

"She's back in her room," Jacob answered, poking his head out of the kitchen doorway. "Not feeling too good, I guess."

"What do you mean?" Alex asked.

"She's been holed up back there for almost ten days," Jacob said. "Don't eat much. Hard as hell gettin' any words outta her. Me and Stenson been on our own. Don't know how the Alverson House will ever get finished."

"Let's see if we can't flush her out," Alex said, adjusting his coat with hands more nervous than he cared to acknowledge.

He strode by the cook and approached the door to Sophia's sanctuary. What the hell was behind that door? In all the months they'd worked together, he'd never been this close to where she lived. His hand poised, ready to knock. But what to say? After almost two weeks hiding in her room, what kind of shape would she be in?

Shouldn't there be some idea as to how he would confront her? Hell, what were his feelings—anger, frustration, lust, love? Should his strategy be to calm or coerce? Would more control of The Star and Alverson House be the goal or sexual satisfaction? Maybe both. Elijah would have chosen blackmail. What a mess.

Skagway's intrusive hum filled the hallway. Cries came from men unloading in the alley. Horses snorted from effort, nerves and discomfort. The collage of sounds reflected the nonstop, frenetic night-and-day energy of the frontier city. For a moment, Alex was unable to form his words. He could stall no longer.

"Sophia," Alex called, rapping on the door. "We need to talk."

He heard nothing from within the room. He knocked again, impatience overcoming indecision. He needed to see her, talk to her. What would he do if she refused to let him in? Kick the door down?

"Not now, Alex." Her voice, even muffled by the barrier, sent a surge of emotion through his body.

"Now, Sophia." Alex's voice rose in volume.

"No, Alex. I'll be out soon. I'm not ready. Maybe tomorrow."

"Goddamn it," Alex cursed, and pounded harder. "We're out of time."

"Mr. Stromberg." Jacob's tone had its own sense of urgency. "Miss Alverson said not now. I think you better respect her wishes."

Alex wheeled around ready to crush the impudent cook. A double-barreled shotgun stared Alex in the face. Jacob Tredaway and two other Star employees stood shoulder to shoulder with their boss. A weapon that deadly in such close quarters represented a serious threat. Alex took a deep breath, searching for calm.

What the hell was going on? He only had the intention of confronting Sophia with Elijah's accusations. Or so he had told himself. Were his motives as pure as these three men? Apparently not. They were prepared to shoot him to protect her.

There had to be more than just Sophia's beauty for these men to make such a stand. Hadn't Alex proved the same commitment? He had. Were they also willing to murder for her? Did they also love Sophia? Yes, he admitted. He loved her. Revelation swept away all of the ambiguity of his emotions. The last of his denials and doubts evaporated.

"You don't understand," Alex said, staring at the stubborn cook. "Miss Alverson is in danger. I only want to protect her."

Jacob didn't move, a rock of determination. Alex turned back to the door. The hell with that shotgun and Sophia's faithful bodyguards. One way or another he was going to face her.

"Sophia," he called out, struggling to keep the edge out of his voice. "Please let me talk to you. I'm waiting right here."

Alex clenched and unclenched his fists more in anxiety than anger. He counted the seconds, stopping at two hundred. He'd always relied on his wits, quick with his tongue as well as his fists. Now he drew a blank. Then Sophia opened the door.

Her hollowed-out cheeks added more emphasis to her prominent cheekbones. Stress and strain reflected in her death-white face. Swollen lips without makeup. Huge eyes mesmerized despite red-tinged whites.

"It's okay, Jacob." Sophia's tone softened. She gave the three men a wan smile. "Please get back to work. I'll be fine."

The cook lowered the shotgun, then turned back toward the kitchen with his two partners. Alex had to respect the men's protective instincts. He doubted he generated that kind of loyalty from any of his employees. He had thought only pay created loyalty. Even Jared had chosen Salt over him. His respect for Sophia ratcheted up another notch.

Sophia motioned him into her room, then closed the door. She wore a man's trousers and work shirt. They did little to hide her voluptuous body. Curly auburn hair flowed loose below her shoulders. She still appeared beautiful beyond belief.

"I know what happened in St. Louis," Alex blurted.

"Do you?" A trickling of color appeared on her face.

"Let me rephrase that," Alex replied, retreating. "I was told a story by a merchant named Elijah Cummings. Said he was an ex-customer of yours."

"And what was that story?" Sophia asked, averting her eyes.

She held her hands in tight fists at her waist, knuckles white. She took a half-step back, putting some space between them. He stood frozen. Hypnotized. For once a woman controlled him.

"I don't believe you robbed and stabbed a man," Alex said. "There must be another side to Elijah's allegations. Assuming the whole story isn't just some wild tale."

A shudder rippled through Sophia's body. Her knees folded, and she slumped onto the bed. Alex hovered above her. She appeared so helpless. How could he comfort her? What did she expect him to do?

"Alex," Sophia said in a muted voice, "please sit down by the desk."

He wanted to reach for her, hold her tightly in his arms. Instead, he reached for the small chair next to a narrow writing desk in one of the corners. Minutes passed. He prayed for words from Sophia that would defend her against Elijah's lies, and, in turn, his own precipitous actions. Words that would allow him to console her. Alex waited, no longer impatient.

"This man. This rich bastard farmer hurt me." Her words seemed drawn from a deep abyss. Her pleading eyes betrayed a vulnerability he had never seen. "He ripped me apart. Almost killed me. I couldn't work for weeks."

Sophia had confirmed Elijah's indictment. She had been a whore. A whore. Her confession erased any doubt.

What terrible events had forced her into a life of prostitution? Did all the ladies of Bertha's house have tragic tales? In his self-absorbed search for carnal pleasure, he had ignored the possible suffering and humiliation that must have destroyed the lives of these women. Lives stained beyond redemption by events he couldn't imagine.

His physical satisfaction had been enhanced by bringing those women pleasure. Had he? How would he discern such fact from act? Even Gaye could have easily deceived him. Sophia opened his eyes. Her once impervious shell had crumbled, revealing a defenselessness that had to be embedded in every whore. How blind could he be?

"You don't have to tell me any more," Alex said.

CHAPTER FIFTY-TWO

Sophia tore her gaze from the floor. She looked into Alex's eyes and glimpsed emotions she had never seen before. Feelings that instilled within her a glimmer of hope. Alex often visited whores. Did he feel compassion or disgust during these encounters?

"Alex," Sophia insisted. "I've been accused of murder. I've never told anyone what happened. I need to tell somebody—you—the truth."

Fate had treated her without pity. Now fate had delivered her this man. This could be her only chance to go back in time and face her demons. Only with honesty could there be a secure and rewarding future.

Breathlessness gripped her chest, choked her thoughts. First words came out in an awkward jumble. But as Sophia picked up momentum, her past flowed with growing clarity. Initial cramps in her stomach eased. Alex's face blurred. Her story took her from her sanctuary in The Star to a world only she had inhabited the last ten months.

* * *

She left out no details from her confession. Grasping at an opportunity to earn the last necessary funds for her escape from the Prairie Flower. The soulless farmer ripping her body apart and forcing a miscarriage. The theft of a few lousy gold coins. Her exile to the oppressive, stifling closet of a room. The farmer's return. His threats and attack. Her desperate struggle to survive and the accidental death of the bastard farmer from Minnesota.

Then realization. There would be no justice for a whore claiming self-defense. She had somehow gathered her wits and begun her panicked escape from the Midwest. Depots, trains, disguises and raw terror. All to deliver her from a hangman's noose. Sentences tumbled out. With each word Sophia's burden of guilt and fear shrunk.

Then she refocused on Alex's hard stare and tight lips. Sophia strained to read the enigmatic expression on his face. He didn't look judgmental. Rather, undecided. Did he even believe her? What had she expected? Unconditional forgiveness? Damn it. She needed more of a reaction. How long would this uncomfortable calm last?

Still, her confession lifted an incredible weight. The truth, ugly though it might be, had been shared. An almost peaceful silence pervaded the small room. But Sophia was still a criminal in the eyes of the world. Hadn't her old customer, Elijah Cummings, confirmed her status as a guilty fugitive?

"Please say something, Alex."

"What happened, Sophia?" Alex asked, his tone neither critical nor accusatory. "You're obviously well educated. How did you end up working at a brothel?"

Lord, enough. These were not the words she wanted to hear. Then the hard lines on Alex's face relaxed. The first evidence of his understanding? So why not tell him the rest of her story? What did she have to lose? Maybe she'd find compassion as well. But would there be any advantage in telling Alex everything? The true story was more melodrama than fiction. Would he think more or less of her?

"I was born Maggie Saunders. Life was wonderful until my father went broke in the Panic of '93. I was sent to a friend of my father's in Cincinnati, then an aunt in St. Louis."

Second thoughts flooded her before she could continue. The sordid details would do no more than generate unwanted pity, make her appear weak and pathetic. Alex didn't need to know about her family's tragic disintegration. Her father forcing her to an associate who used her as an unpaid house whore. Her mother frozen to the dirt floor of their shotgun shack, never to rise again. Her brother and sister probably sold into slavery like her. And the belated news of her drunken father's death beneath the wheels of a milk cart.

Sophia felt herself again drifting from her room in The Star, from Skagway, Alaska, back in time. Could Alex hear the distance in her words? She kept her eyes fixed to a far wall. Painful memories and emotions flashed before her.

"I started working in a shirt factory. Conditions were not good. I became ill. Couldn't get my strength back. They fired me. Without my wages, my aunt forced me out into the streets."

That was all she was willing to share. Alex could put the rest of the pieces together himself. Her eyes filled with moisture, but no tears escaped. She flashed a quick glance at Alex. An unexpected, animated gleam reflected from his eyes. Still no betrayal of opinion or judgment. Sophia wiped her nose with her sleeve. Alex was hardly breathing. She wanted to challenge his silence. But the words wouldn't come.

"Let's get the Alverson House opened," Alex said.

His voice sounded strange, strangled. An interminable silence followed. She couldn't read him. Did he feel guilty for abandoning her project? Or was he so desperate for cash he had no choice but to get the Alverson House up and running?

"I'll do what I can to help you finish." His voice now soft, even kind. "You'll need someone to help handle the remaining details before opening, hire the balance of your staff, a budget, a promotional plan."

Sophia blinked back unexpected tears. His words had to evidence an acceptance of her. He must believe her. She hadn't lied. She'd told him as much as she was willing to share. And he had listened.

For the first time Alex might prove a true ally. And if she could trust the warmth swelling within her body, much more. But nothing had been said to lessen her concerns. Nothing about the dangerous threats from the outside world. What about Elijah Cummings?

"The man," she stuttered. "The one who said he knew me from St. Louis. What do I do about him?"

"He'll no longer bother us," Alex whispered, soft eyes locked on hers. "He's now with your Minnesota farmer."

Sophia gasped. "Oh my God."

The man was dead? Had Alex killed him? And what would he now demand from her? What would it cost her? Fear returned, swelling within her. Yet how could she explain her pounding heart, her overwhelming desire to be cradled in this man's strength?

Alex rose from the chair and leaned toward her. His hand cupped her chin. She felt his lips, warm, firm, passionate. Turmoil swirled through her. She'd never been kissed like this. Such intimacy. An unknown flush of pleasure suffused her body. Did she really desire this man's touch? Hadn't she sworn off anything that would expose her to emotional dependency? Hadn't she pledged never to welcome a man's physical contact again?

"Let's get to work, Sophia." Alex released her, his eyes aflame with a complexity still undefined. A never-before-seen smile thawed the features of his normally hard-edged face. "I'll meet you at the Alverson House at noon."

Then he turned and walked toward the door. Sophia fought an impulse to grab his arm, pull him back to her. She didn't know what she had expected, but it definitely wasn't a forgiving kiss and quick exit. She sat on the bed. Her fingers touched her lips, traced his kiss. Confusion overwhelmed her racing heart. Why had he left?

CHAPTER FIFTY-THREE

Two and a half days and nights in a ten-foot tent with the crusty Salt had proved penance enough. Frigid air, though far from comfortable, provided welcome release from the claustrophobic confinement. Jared thanked a Lord he was no longer sure existed. The extended rest had saved him. Now he paid the price of his immobility as he worked off the accumulated stiffness. He focused on the rhythm required to control his awkward snowshoes.

Scattered spruce, fir and lodgepole pine littered the surrounding lifeless landscape. Salt and the dogs broke trail before Jared, no worries about the prospector's shenanigans behind his back. His Remington rested in the straps of his backpack but could still be reached within seconds if needed. Although his stiff, half-frozen fingers would be hard-pressed to fire the weapon.

Jared concentrated on working the tightness from his abused muscles while keeping a wary eye on Salt. The old coot's temporary drunken civility hadn't lasted beyond this morning. Hadn't Salt told him danger would be a constant companion on their trek? What the miner hadn't told him was that the threat would come from Salt.

Brutus closed on Jared's heels, snapping and growling. What was this all about? Unlike Brutus to be so unsettled. The Airedale even had his tail tucked between his legs. Jared scanned the terrain, woods to the left, the Yukon River meandering through Alaskan wilderness to his right. A deep canyon had been carved between the bluffs bordering the river.

Rare movement flashed at the periphery of his vision. Something shifted a hundred yards from their path. Wolves? He trudged forward,

Brutus whining and snapping with increased urgency. Were those four-legged creatures traveling parallel to Jared and Salt? Yes.

"Salt," Jared called out.

The freight sled ground to a halt, and the old prospector turned back to Jared. Even at a distance Jared could sense the old man's impatience.

"What's the problem?" Salt asked. "Two days of rest and you're already soft?"

"There's a pack of wolves after us," Jared said, pointing to four or five large animals now frozen in place, muzzles testing the air.

"Relax, boy. They been following us since we started this morning," Salt said. "Probably holed up as long as us, and they're hungry. Even wolves got more sense than to hunt at fifty below."

Faint fingers of death tickled at Jared's neck. What would kill him? The treacherous Salt? Brutal, unforgiving temperatures? Voracious wolves? Even the ferocious Brutus showed signs of dismay. A multitude of life-threatening perils swamped what little confidence he had constructed. How much more vulnerable could Jared be?

Salt pried his rifle from the top of the freight sled. He yanked off a mitten, chambered a round and fired first one, then a second shot at the shadowing wolves. The bullets didn't come close. But the wild animals took off.

"They won't mess with us," Salt said and repacked his rifle. "Damn varmints are only good for pelts. They'd pick off a straggler, though. That useless hair ball of yours would make 'em a fine meal. Let's move."

Jared watched the wolves' unmistakable lope in the distance. The thick-furred animals moved with fluid grace despite the deep snow. Even from afar the ominous creatures exhibited beauty and power. No wonder Brutus had become so antsy.

* * *

The sky remained a threatening gray, the resulting light an imitation of day. Ice caked his eyebrows and sparse, splotchy beard, the balance of his exposed skin clawed raw from the unrelenting elements. But the killer freeze had not reappeared. Jared high-stepped his way fifteen feet behind Salt and the loaded freight sled. The degree of rhythm that Jared had developed on the cumbersome snowshoes provided a level of control more illusionary than real.

For the second time Salt cut away from the ice-encrusted Yukon River, which now veered to the south or southwest, where the rumor of a winter sun lightened the horizon. How did Salt know where he headed without the security of the twisting Yukon? An even higher degree of uneasiness filled Jared, more than ever at the mercy of the nasty prospector.

* * *

Salt halted the party in semidarkness. Jared shrugged off his pack and performed his nightly task of gathering wood while Salt pitched their tent. The world beyond the protective light of the fire faded into threatening darkness. Jared took an inventory of his battered body. Not too bad, considering.

How long had they cut cross-country without sight of the river? Did Salt really know where the hell he was headed? The gray cloud-choked sky gave few hints. Today's path away from the river generated curiosity as well as suspicion. Was Salt using a compass hidden from Jared along with the prospector's cache of secrets? Jared wanted answers from the sullen old man.

"How do we reconnect with the river?"

Salt poked at the newly lit blaze with a frozen branch. Without whiskey, the old man had retreated back into morose silence. In a way, this attitude was more comfortable than dealing with the verbal abuse that constituted most of Salt's conversations.

"Salt," Jared said, impatience fueling his need for real information. "Talk to me."

"Just keep heading ten degrees west of due north," he answered in a low tone, never turning his head toward Jared.

"How do you know we're headed northwest?" Jared said, pushing for more specific information.

What if something happened to Salt? The old man appeared as unbreakable as granite, but terrible events could happen in such unforgiving territory. And nothing had changed Jared's distrust for the man, certainly not the empty gesture of Salt offering an IOU hundreds of miles from civilization. He would dump Jared and Brutus whenever it became convenient.

"Compass."

"Show me," Jared insisted.

Salt pulled at the leather thongs around his neck. He produced a once silver compass discolored by the elements. First fire-starting moss, then a pouch of gold, now a compass. What else did the prospector keep around his neck?

"If we only follow the river," Salt said, "it could take an extra ten days to get to Dawson. We'll run into the Yukon tomorrow afternoon where the Little Salmon feeds in."

Salt stuffed the compass back beneath his clothes and crawled into the tent. End of discussion. Jared had been told that all he needed to do was trace the course of the Yukon. No one had said anything about a compass. Jared's defenselessness had never been clearer. And he had as much faith in Salt's good intentions as he did a New England capitalist.

* * *

The dogsled intercepted the river the next day as the old man had promised. Three weeks into their journey. Hard to believe.

Today they had traveled for miles along an extended bluff above the frozen Yukon. The river lay one hundred feet below, littered by fractured chunks of ice in sizes ranging from small, irregular mounds to building-sized blocks.

Impenetrable stands of spruce ebbed and flowed to their left. At times the groves of trees ranged a quarter mile away, offering vistas of white-shrouded wilderness, other times squeezing men and dogs into a narrow twenty-foot corridor on the precipice overlooking the river. Seductive silence surrounded them, welcome quiet free of man's selfish, destructive imprint. And no sign of wolves.

Salt bobbed off and on the rear runners in front of Jared, a delighted elf, happy with their progress. Few challenges other than mileage lay between them and Dawson. Jared strode after the sled in a land as unreal as the last six months of his life. The steady pant of Brutus served as a metronome for Jared's pace. The absence of shadow created a one-dimensional, dreamlike tableau.

Last night Salt had assured they'd reach Dawson in a little over one week, two-thirds of their journey behind them. What then? Salt had promised to take care of Jared. But that pledge was as worthless as house cats pulling a sled. The old man kept pounding away that the lesson was in the journey, not the rough-and-tumble town they headed for. True. The journey stretched Jared far beyond his preconceived limits, instilling a degree of welcome confidence. Again, what did that mean? Maybe he and the Airedale would just keep going deeper into the wilds forever.

Then Brownie lurched to the left, the lead dog's sharp cut drawing the team with him. The heavy freight sled fishtailed toward the canyon edge. Salt's arm snapped back, the whip poised to crack above the team's heads and straighten the swerving animals. Too late. Ground crumbled to within a few feet of Jared. The snow-covered bluff tracing the river's path collapsed. The sled dropped into space.

Salt released the moose hide, arms flailing. Jared flopped spread-eagled onto his chest at the edge of the chasm, head extended just beyond the newly cut canyon.

"Salt!" The desperate, mournful sigh was all Jared could muster.

Salt fell free, dropping, thrashing, then smacking flat on his back on a wind-blown ledge a quarter of the way down the steep wall. The sled seemed to hover in the air above him. The malamutes were snapped backwards, dragged into space, tumbling in a graceful arc. Then the 1000 pounds of sled and supplies smashed onto Salt and bounced into free fall, dogs' legs wind-milling helplessly. Snow flakes hung in the frozen air, then the sled team emitted howls of fear. Jared remained frozen in place, terrified of moving a finger.

The dogs dropped another seventy-five feet in concert with the sled and slammed onto the Yukon's rock-solid river banks.

The cushion of accumulated snow along the river provided no soft landing for the densely packed freighter. A shattering noise echoed from below.

Jared lifted an arm with extreme caution, then shifted a leg. The ground held. He rolled over sideways onto his back, a careful move with snowshoe-encumbered legs. Jared raised his lower body high enough to clear the snow, then scooted a few feet to a safer vantage. Quivering fingers stripped the laces of his snowshoes. The pack fell from his shoulders.

Jared inched back to the precipice and peeked over the edge. Salt sprawled lifeless, a colorful smudge against the cliff's wall. Jared hesitated. Could he reach Salt on his precarious perch? Could the sled dogs have survived? He extended both arms and chest over the edge. A small waterfall of snow, rock and dirt dislodged beneath him. A litany of good reasons to stay put flashed through his mind. None of the thoughts, though, worked to keep him safely on the lip of the cliff.

Rigid tree roots decorated the first third of the dun-colored cliff face. He grabbed the roots with mittened hands and lowered himself. Just pretend to climb down a ladder. Ignore the increased shaking of hands and an inability to keep air flowing through his lungs. Fight off the emerging hopelessness if Salt proved severely injured or dead. And disregard the dizzying vertigo from the immediate threat of a hundred-foot fall to his own death.

First one trembling step, then another, each footstep lodged with care against the face of the wall. Confidence brought increased speed. But the easier than expected descent did nothing to calm hands, lungs or mind. A foot landed on the ledge, a skinny three feet wide. Jared clung to the cliff face with one arm, his body hovering above Salt.

Unnatural indentations from the crushing damage of the sled gave the old man's body the look of a sparsely packed scarecrow. Blood already solidified into hard crystals, lacing lips and ears. Salt's eyes, huge, luminescent and expressive in life, stared out in a lifeless gaze already stripped of light. The crushing weight of the sled had imbedded the prospector into the earth.

Jared clung with one arm to an exposed root and used his teeth to remove the glove from his free hand. Tentative fingers stretched to the still-red cheeks of the old man. Did he hear whimpers from the dogs below, or was it just the wind whistling through the fractured surface of a hibernating Yukon? No sound from Salt. Never another sound out of Salt. Panic clutched Jared so tight he could barely hang on.

A rational thought stabbed through the hysteria—get the compass. Jared reached for Salt's neck. Exposed fingers ripped at the miner's clothes, the effort threatening his perilous balance. But fear provided strength. He tore open the parka, snapped the buttons at Salt's neck exposing the compass and two other pouches tied around the dead man's throat.

Jared's hold on the exposed roots of the cliff slipped. He needed both hands to adjust his grip. He released the leather straps and made a frantic grab against the ragged dirt wall with both hands. Debris showered upon him, but he maintained his handhold. Then with one hand he again snatched at the leather thongs. Numb fingers wrapped around the straps. Success.

He wedged the leather over Salt's head and slipped them around his own neck. Air returned to his lungs, and with the momentary relief, a different concern. What should he do with Salt? No way could Jared haul the dead man up the cliff. He would have to leave the broken body on the ledge. He had no choice.

Now Jared had to move to safety before the freezing air stole what little control he still possessed. His face pressed against the rough surface of the cliff. He gathered his remaining energy and clambered up the roots.

Brutus met him at the rim with tongue darting over Jared's face. Thank God his dog had survived. Now what? Jared stuck the frozen stump of his hand back into his mitten. He flung his arms in the air with manic force, jumping in place to force blood into frigid feet. An unexpected calm appeared as life-giving circulation returned to his system.

With shaking hands, Jared removed the compass and two leather pouches from around his neck. He loosened the straps around the heavier of the two bags. Even in the murky daylight, gold dust sparkled. How much? Several hundred dollars. Worthless on the Yukon Trail. But the gold would be of value in Dawson. Assuming he made it to Dawson.

He clawed open the larger, surprisingly lighter second pouch. He peered into the bag and saw something much more valuable than gold—dried moss for fire starter. He would die without fire. He'd been so careful to pack matches in several places, but he hadn't known enough to pack the equally imperative moss. What else would he need if he were to survive?

At least he had his ground cover, one fur blanket and a hand axe. No tent. He wore all his clothes except the bag of socks Salt had insisted on. He carried some food, but how long would it last? Thank God he had some dried fish for Brutus. He had his rifle, but he hadn't seen a living creature since the wolves. And his only ammunition was the ten or twelve shells still in the weapon. Everything else was on the sled, the supplies now scattered along the frozen Yukon.

Could some of the dogs still be alive? How injured would they be? Did he have either time or extra bullets to put the animals out of their misery? The bleak landscape lay deathly quiet and unforgiving. They had traveled along the steep bluff for two days. How much longer would they have to go before they could drop to the river level and backtrack? No. Nothing he could do about Salt or the dogs. Or even the lost supplies. He had only one option—keep trudging toward Dawson and hope for the best.

Jared reattached his snowshoes and shouldered his pack. He couldn't waste another moment. The sooner he and Brutus set off, the better their chances of surviving. He glanced at his dog with a flash of anger.

"Next time, damn it, you're carrying a saddle bag."

CHAPTER FIFTY-FOUR

A light wind blew down the river course, more than enough to cut deep into Jared's tattered, insufficient clothing. How long had he been trudging through the barren Yukon wilderness? Days? Weeks? Yesterday he had forced the last piece of pemmican down his constricted throat. One more portion of dried salmon remained for Brutus. Jared would now have to survive on pine-needle tea. If only he had more food, he could travel forever, body wire-strong.

Before, his free hands had been needed to cope with the ever-present danger of Salt's treachery. Now, without the old prospector's threat, he gripped fir branches as polelike levers. The straps of his pack held his useless rifle. No sensation in his fingers and only a few bullets left. Fresh game would solve many problems, but he couldn't shoot a moose if one ran into him. And dressing the large animal with his hatchet would be ugly.

His long, rhythmic strides ate up the miles. Only the sky changed. One day crystal blue, the next, menacing clouds shifting from white to black with infinite shades of gray. Previous snowy days had brought warmer temperatures and refreshing moisture to frozen, split lips. The constant was the black ravens wheeling above, oblivious to the killing cold.

He traveled well into the fast-closing evenings, then gathered wood before dark. But lighting the fire was a life-threatening challenge. He couldn't use the matches without removing his gloves, and every time he exposed his fingers to the vicious elements, he risked frostbite.

Jared huddled each evening with the once massive Brutus. Now the large dog shrank with each passing day.

Yet he felt so complete, so confident, though he had so little. Did his light-headedness come from hunger, the unending chill, or his arrival at a spiritual peacefulness? Would death bring him total freedom? Was he ready to die?

The hell with Salt, his brothers, Skagway, Alex, all mankind. Even the image of Sophia Alverson had become tarnished and faded. Still, he made efficient progress beside the fractured ice sculptures littering the slumbering Yukon River. If only he knew how much farther to Dawson.

A sharp, gunshotlike crack interrupted his thoughts. His head snapped up. Only tree sap, freezing and expanding. Then he noticed a splotchy brown stain on the horizon. Another traveler's fire? Would there be food, shelter?

Jared plodded on toward the unnatural cloud and the promise of safety and security. Minutes passed. The dirty brown shadow grew. More ravens than usual wheeled under the harsh winter sky. How did these sleek, death-colored birds survive? How did they maintain body heat? What did they eat? Did he need answers? No, and he refused to give up. He wouldn't just burrow into the snow, end his suffering. He had become a raven.

The sound of Brutus's heavy breathing came closer. His dog had been falling farther behind. The struggle through unbroken snow proved more difficult for the animal than for long-legged Jared on snowshoes. Now Brutus pushed past Jared. Animation had returned to the Airedale. And ahead, the alien smudge filled a respectable chunk of the horizon.

More than the smoke from a single fire. Much more. Long-absent excitement spread within Jared. He followed Brutus and topped a mild rise. Tents. Rough cabins. Movement. Dawson.

* * *

Heavy steps took Jared down Dawson's rough snow-encrusted streets. The building facades in this central part of the frontier town promised much more than the boxes crouched behind them. A plethora of bars and gambling houses filled both sides of the street. Men's faces reflected hunger and hopelessness, an absence of permanence. The avaricious, frenetic desperation of the denizens of Skagway to hit the trail for the gold country was replaced in Dawson by a different, foreboding characteristic—a struggle for survival.

Missing boardwalks, crude, haphazard construction and lack of purpose in the prospectors as they passed by in silence stoked Jared's concern. Dawson, the heart of the fabled Klondike gold rush, reflected the grim stare of starvation and despondency. This was Salt's "promised land"?

Jared pushed into one of the first establishments offering food and lodging, the Pioneer Saloon. Overwhelming sensations bled energy from him. His battered body melted beneath the sensuous waves of warmth and smells. He stood dumbstruck inside the door.

"Hey," a burly bartender yelled from behind a primitive bar. "No dogs."

Jared gave the man a blank stare, then slid along the wall until he wedged into a corner, paralyzed by the seduction of warmth. His knees buckled. The weight of his backpack dragged him to the floor.

"Need food." His words struggled through cracked lips.

"Told you to get that damn animal outta here," the bartender said.

The hulking man moved from behind the wood planks, fierce beard bristling with aggressiveness. He towered over the slumped Jared, who could barely raise his gaze to the man's angry eyes.

"Where you come from?" someone nearby asked, features rough-edged from winters of unforgiving elements.

Jared's iron discipline faded into passive exhaustion. He'd been stronger in the cold, more in control. Now each word required a focus he no longer possessed.

"Skagway," he murmured.

"Just you and your dog?"

"Started with a sourdough named Salt," Jared said. "He died on the trail."

"Salt?" the same man said. "That old geezer's tougher than frozen rawhide."

"He's frozen now," Jared answered, eyes drooping.

Energy dissipated. All resistance fled like the wind. Conversations flitted around him. Words came in bits and pieces. A welcome avalanche of contentment and safety swallowed him.

"You go ahead and try to kick out that dog, Barney," a disembodied voice said. "I seen him in action back in Skagway."

"Let him lay," another man said. "They're both played out."

Bread appeared before Jared on a tin plate. He took a bite, but couldn't swallow. He gave the food to Brutus. The dog had no trouble swallowing. Jared hung tight to his partner and gave into the pleasant, unthreatening blackness of sleep.

* * *

That first evening in Dawson, twelve hours in a corner of the Pioneer passed without incident or memory. Jared had slept like the dead through raucous drinking, dancing and gambling, confident that Brutus would protect him if necessary. He found simple meals upon awakening. Oats and dried salmon for the dog. Beans, desiccated potatoes, stewed apples and coffee for Jared. The feast couldn't be matched by Delmonico's in New York. But the price, $15, took a chunk out of Salt's pouch. The old man had been right—food was worth far more than gold.

The second night found Jared crammed into a low-clearance bunk bed in the Alexander Hotel. Vermin infested blankets, foul smoke and worse odors from his fellow lodgers were his companions that night. Compared to this dump, The Star was a first-class hotel. Still, he'd slept close to twenty hours. Rising again famished, he'd spent another fifteen dollars on meals for himself and his dog. The room charge—only one dollar. Brutus, stomach full, hung close to the Alexander, though free to roam the streets of Dawson if instinct prompted him.

The third evening jammed into so-called civilization proved too much. The next morning Jared purchased a one-man sled, ground cover, small tent and a moth-eaten bear fur. Gear cost less than food, but Salt's pouch had now been cut in half. Still, he was drawn to the open and free wilderness.

Sleeping in the frigid air seemed a much better option than the last three nights in Dawson. He traveled to the base of Moosehide Mountain to the east of Dawson in search of the perfect camping spot. Some sheltered alcove Salt would approve of. He came across a pile of large boulders cluttering the base of a short, steep ridge.

An open space, a large fissure-shaped canyon hemmed in on three sides by snow encrusted rock walls worked well. He scraped the snow off the stone walls framing the wind-protected area and used snowshoes to compress the powdered floor. Cut fir boughs layered the ground. The one-man tent and ground cloth finished off the shelter. Then Jared struggled two hours gathering firewood, which he stacked on one side of his wind-free encampment.

A curious awareness of well-being enveloped him as he worked. He lit a fire positioned at the tent entrance, then fed the flames into a roaring blaze. No way would he retreat back to depressing Dawson to sleep. Jared understood the sensation. He would never be labeled a cheechakoo again.

But how would he escape back to Skagway and then south? Few jobs were available other than winter mining. Slow starvation, frostbit fingers and toes held no future. Every possible escape required funds. Salt's traveling stash now held less than $100 in gold. The outrageous prices of this wilderness city would make short work of that meager amount.

Tomorrow he'd search out Salt's partners up on Bonanza Creek. Some internal duty demanded that he personally present notification of the old sourdough's death. Then he had to figure a way out of the Yukon. Well, he'd worry about that tomorrow. Now flames warmed his hands. He tilted his gaze up to the day's brittle blue sky, unsullied by Dawson's brown cloud of pollution and depression. Nothing seemed impossible after surviving the brutal, death-defying trek through the Yukon.

* * *

Jared entered the rough-edged settlement of Dawson the next morning, Brutus at his side. Log barracks of the Canadian Mounted Police bordered the main street in the north end of town. Police. Now there was a unique concept. Too bad Skagway hadn't been annexed by Canada.

Front Street continued on, lined with hovels, buildings and tents stretched for over a mile south to the mouth of the Klondike River. Paradise Alley, clogged with cribs, tents and lean-tos, ran parallel, separating the main drag from the Yukon River. Jared, the dog still close by him, traveled on.

Dawson appeared larger than it was. The vast majority, newcomers, eyes glazed, features frazzled, were easy to identify by their mackinaws and thick cloth caps. Twill parkas or deerskin coats, fur caps and bulky fur-lined moose-hide mittens clothed the more animated old timers. Jared fit in with this latter group, thanks to Salt's direction in Skagway. But the few better-off ones mocked the helplessness of the vast majority. No different from every other community Jared had visited in his now extensive travels.

He passed minimal earth-covered dwellings that gradually gave way to more substantial log structures. Hotels, bars, gambling dens and sparsely inventoried retail establishments predominated, tents and smaller cabins filling the spaces between commercial buildings. Farther south sat the several blocks dominated by the two major trading companies, the Alaska Commercial Company and the North American Transportation & Trading Company. Their solid storehouses constructed of logs and corrugated metal were the largest buildings in Dawson. And all were as empty as the city inhabitants' eyes.

Jared needed something to eat and enough food for several days while he searched for Salt's partners. He left the Airedale outside to fend for himself and entered the Pioneer. Early-morning movement inside gave the appearance of purpose and meaningful activity. Another mirage.

"Where ya been?" a voice from the corner asked. Pauly Addison beckoned Jared. The gnarled sourdough had been one of the few willing to exchange information with Jared.

"Camping out of town," Jared answered, moving by men huddled around one of several stoves placed around the Pioneer's main room. "Heading up to El Dorado Creek."

"Hope you ain't lookin' for work."

"No," Jared said. "Want to notify Salt's partners of what happened. Then I'm moving on."

"Thorton and Lizard are two of the craziest prospectors in Alaska. Watch your back." Pauly's cackle rose above the muted conversations. "Then just where the hell you gonna go and what you gonna eat?"

"Those are the right questions," Jared acknowledged. He now possessed less than fifty dollars.

"You might find some mining work out in the digs," Pauly said. "Could pull in fifteen to twenty dollars a day. Enough to survive. But you don't look like no miner."

Jared nodded. The thought of wintering in this Yukon frontier town frightened him more than the threat of freezing to death on the wilderness trail. Dawson made Skagway look like the land of milk and honey. One didn't starve to death on the coast. He wanted out. But how would he and Brutus break away?

"There is one possible way out for you," Pauly said in a conspiratorial tone. "I seen that dog of yours in action in Skagway. Mean son of a bitch. Could whip most any dog in town. Big money in dog fights. I know a promoter could help you get set up against Harrington's wolf dog."

The memory of Brutus ripping the throat of the large mongrel on the shores of the Lynn Canal almost killed his appetite. How desperate would Jared be after another week of dwindling resources? Something would turn up. Some way to escape. Had to.

"Thanks," Jared said. Despondency and desperation hung over Dawson as thick as the wood smoke of a thousand fires. "I'll think about it after I get back from the claims."

CHAPTER FIFTY-FIVE

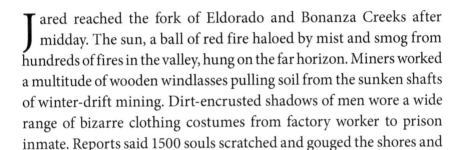

J ared reached the fork of Eldorado and Bonanza Creeks after midday. The sun, a ball of red fire haloed by mist and smog from hundreds of fires in the valley, hung on the far horizon. Miners worked a multitude of wooden windlasses pulling soil from the sunken shafts of winter-drift mining. Dirt-encrusted shadows of men wore a wide range of bizarre clothing costumes from factory worker to prison inmate. Reports said 1500 souls scratched and gouged the shores and hillside benches above the snow-filled creek beds. Amazement swept over Jared. This was the home of millionaires?

Surrounding country resembled a shattered and denuded Civil War battlefield rather than wilderness outpost. Much of the timber had been roughly ripped from the nearby forests. Now, as cords of firewood, the lumber smothered the primitive tents and cabins built on the tightly clustered claims, each approximately 500 feet in width. Could this foul, thick smoke curling from rough cabins and deep cuts in the earth be even more polluting than the factories of eastern cities?

Many of the visible claims, some of the richest in the Yukon, had ten to twenty laborers clawing for gold in the now-frozen earth. But Jared could see only one scrawny miner at Eldorado Number 8. The man dressed in an old red-striped cloth parka, ragged mittens and feet wrapped in sacking perched atop a pile of dirt. Creaks echoed in the dense air from the scarred wooden arms of a crude windlass he worked. Sooty vapors and curses drifted from the four-by-six hole beneath the primitive crane. All movement seemed in slow motion, the complete opposite of the deceased Salt's constant, frenetic energy.

The miner caught sight of Jared and ceased his desultory labors. The ferret-faced sourdough wiped a filthy sleeve across his face and cast a suspicious glance at Jared. Without breaking eye contact, he called down into the mine. An equally dirty head with a feral expression popped to the surface.

"Are either of you Mr. Lizard or Mr. Thornton?" Jared asked the two filthy prospectors.

Neither made any greeting or response. Had conversation become a long-lost art for these two? Jared stared with misgivings at ferocious yellow eyes, sunk deep within black faces layered with months of dirt and grime. Stuck atop their pile of earth, they resembled oversized, deranged prairie dogs.

"Got some bad news for you," Jared said and approached the two men. "I was traveling with Salt from Skagway. Had an accident a week from Dawson. Salt went over the river bank. Freight sled crushed him."

The two miners greeted the news stone-faced. No curiosity about Salt's death, no interest in the outside world, no warmth or concern for Jared. Also no offer of food, drink or shelter. So much for hospitality. No wonder Salt preferred traveling. And if the interior of their cabin reflected the men, Jared would rather spend the night in a snowdrift.

Nothing left for him to do now. He had discharged whatever convoluted duty he had felt and had wasted a day and much valued energy. Jared shook his head in disgust and wheeled away from Salt's pathetic partners. He didn't bother calling out to Brutus. The Airedale would have no more desire to stick around than he did.

Back at the fork, Jared looked longingly at the only two-story building this side of Dawson. The Grand Fork Hotel didn't look too grand, but it advertised a hot meal for $3.50 or meals and bed for a day at $12. Far too rich for his shrinking bankroll.

Instead, Jared pulled out several pieces of jerky and a doughnut of baked flour. Brutus received a ration of dried salmon. Then Jared started the twelve-mile trek back to town. Night traveling would be dangerous and draining but would beat anything tainted by the presence of Lizard and Thornton. Ironic that Salt's training would help Jared distance himself from these subhuman creatures.

* * *

Boots twisted beneath him with each step on the icy surface. He was halfway between the Eldorado claim of Salt's partners and Dawson. The ice-encrusted path along Bonanza Creek grew more treacherous than slogging through deep, untracked wilds on snowshoes. An inability to focus proved the real problem, though.

Must be close to midnight. Yet bright translucent moonlight flooded the wilderness landscape. Cloud-clearing wind bit deep beneath his layered clothing but not enough to dislodge disconcerting thoughts. Demonic visions of Lizard and Thornton lurking behind rocks and stumps dominated his consciousness. Jared struggled to clear his mind. Then another misstep, and Jared struggled for balance. Frustration replaced unsettling images.

Enough of the constant litany of trials and tribulations. Trouble, even anguish, were as much a part of life as air and water. Time to accept the reality of the world's random mean-spiritedness. Enough of the impossible idealism that opened him to crushed expectations and overwhelmed values. One thing was certain. He had to escape this winter's imprisonment in Dawson. Escape from Alaska also. But how, without resources?

Then the bright, virginal light of the winter moon took on an eerie glow. Distinct color shaded the snowfields surrounding him. He glanced skyward at the night sky, now a luminescent, vibrant pink. Pink? Something must be taking a toll on his senses. Certainly his concentration. His feet skidded out from beneath his body, and he collapsed onto the frozen ground, gaze forced skyward.

Curtains of pink and pulsing red shimmered across the heavens. Colors blossomed more brilliant with each passing second. The Alaskan wilderness evening became a fantasy land of color and movement. Was he losing his mind? Jared lay where he had fallen, mouth gaping open to the night sky.

What was this incredible light show? Hadn't this miserable world proven incapable of producing such beauty? Now Fourth of July fireworks paled in comparison. Blinking eyes couldn't dislodge the drama before him. How long until reality returned? Frigid air crept beneath his protective clothing. He couldn't sprawl motionless on the frozen tundra much longer.

Scenes from his life appeared, intermingled with the wavering lights. Each shimmering curtain parted to reveal a brief glimpse of his past, rippling from early life on the Monroe farm, through college, to this desperate, disillusioning trek into Alaska. Surrealistic reds and pinks flowed from chapter to chapter. This frantic retreat from the Klondike claims and the demented miners scraping for promised gold was just another such chapter. Jared sunk into calm peacefulness for the first time in months. Life would go on.

Brutus's icicle-like tongue against Jared's face snapped him back to the present. An overpowering pressure to escape this frozen prison replaced the euphoria of brilliant heavens. Wild rumors concerning his dog reverberated in his ears. Could Brutus provide the means to escape? Yes, the Airedale could fight like no animal Jared had ever seen. Yes, dog fighting was barbaric, despicable even. But the last six months had proved necessity superseded principles if one wanted to survive.

Jared tore his eyes from the heavens and fastened them on his dog. Brutus stood above him, light snaps of his teeth reflecting mounting impatience. His thoughts coalesced like the clarity of the frigid Arctic sky. Jared scrambled to his feet, the supernatural pinkish-red glow promising to light the way back to Dawson, Skagway and the mainland. Let Brutus finally pay his way.

CHAPTER FIFTY-SIX

Only a few beaten-down prospectors hung out at the Pioneer, Northern, and Monte Carlo saloons. Jared next entered the Gold Hill Saloon. At ten in the morning the dance floor was empty, but there was his man. The focus of his search sat at the bar sipping coffee and reading a stained and torn months' old newspaper.

"Excuse me, sir." Jared approached the familiar face, name lost in the exhaustion of his Dawson arrival.

"Well, well." The gentleman offered a wide-open, disarming smile that creased a well-trimmed, bearded face.

"Good morning," Jared said. "I believe we met several days ago."

"Oliver McClain." Clear, sparkling blue eyes stood out in a town of inhabitants draped in fear and threatened starvation. A clean extended hand proved him no miner. "At your service, Mr. Jared Monroe."

Had Jared told the man his name? Had to be a hustler or gambler, waistcoat and vest as out of place as his effusive greeting. Didn't matter. This incongruous character could provide a ticket out of Dawson. Or so Jared hoped.

"I'll bet you've come to talk about dogfights," McClain said. "And of course I am a bettin' man."

His prescient remark confirmed Jared's strategy. Who better to approach than a gambler? Jared would do whatever it took to escape this frozen hell. And he'd deal with whomever it took.

"You said to talk to you if I was interested in fighting Brutus," Jared said, squaring his shoulders as he crossed an invisible line of commitment. "Well, I am."

"You have come to the right man."

McClain jumped from his seat at the primitive plank bar. Several scraggly customers of the Gold Hill Saloon stirred from their semicomatose states at McClain's animation. The gambler turned to them, his contagious grin bringing energy to the early-morning drinkers.

"Gentlemen," he bellowed. "Get the word out. The meanest, nastiest, toughest mutt in Skagway is looking to challenge the baddest, biggest, most vicious four-legged creature in the Yukon."

"Harrington's wolf dog?" A haggard prospector spit out the words through a mouth missing half its teeth.

"You bet," McClain said, winking at Jared. "I'll take care of everything. Drum up the biggest pot 'a gold this backwater hole-in-the-wall ever seen."

"How does this work?" Jared stammered, off balance by the speed of McClain's offer.

"Young man," the gambler said, "all you got to do is show up. Let's say four days from now. We'll use the Alaskan Trading Company's warehouse. Biggest building in town. Damn near empty, and I know the local manager. Winner—most likely your intimidating animal— earns 15 percent of the purse. The loser, poor old Harrington and his mangy wolf mongrel, gets five."

The percentages made little sense. But Jared no longer had any illusions as to the charity of mankind. He would enter this partnership with eyes open. Why should he trust McClain any more than Salt?

"What's in it for you?"

"Ah," McClain said, his smile threatening to split open his face. "My fee is only 5 percent. I contact Mr. Harrington, secure the warehouse and do all the promoting to get the word out. Seventy-five percent goes to the gamblers."

"Why wait four days?" Jared asked.

"Need a few days to notify the backbone of our betting community," Oliver said. "Those prospectors along Eldorado and Bonanza Creeks got the real money. I figure we can fire up potential bets of well over $100,000."

A gasp escaped Jared at the size of the promised pot of gold. Fifteen percent of $100,000 would get him and Brutus back to the Mainland in first-class fashion with enough left over to head in any direction they chose. And Brutus could also use a couple of days' rest and a few more meals to put him in tip-top shape.

"What do I need to do?"

"You just parade around town with that dog of yours," McClain answered. "Maybe have that hound pick a few fights to whet everyone's appetite."

"Brutus fights only when he has to," Jared objected with only a slight stretch of the truth.

"He'll have to when he meets up with Harrington's wolf dog. I don't know who's more dangerous, the animal or Harrington. That mean son of a bitch was a professional pugilist. Lasted twenty-two rounds with John L. Sullivan. Before those pantywaist Queensberry rules. We're talking bare-knuckle boxing."

Was he supposed to be impressed? So what if Harrington was a bare-knuckle boxer. The man's fighting exploits meant nothing to Jared. Brutus would be battling the dog, not the man. And 15 percent meant an escape in a style Jared couldn't have imagined.

CHAPTER FIFTY-SEVEN

Screaming prospectors, townsfolk and lost souls packed the building. Deafening roars greeted Jared. High-pitched shrieking from a swarm of dancehall girls and whores added an additional layer of chaos. Heat from packed bodies and unfettered emotions added surreal warmth to the Arctic world. Jared's eyes adjusted to the murky surroundings and dim confines of the trading company's cavernous warehouse. Brutus stood at his heel, ears perked, tail erect.

"I told you." McClain bounded to greet Brutus and his owner. "You can depend on me. The pot's rising like the Yukon River in early spring thaw. We're well over a hundred grand."

McClain turned his attention back to the frantic wagering taking place. Gold flew from hand to hand, the clamor overpowering McClain's words. The disconcerting visages of Lizard and Thorton sprang to mind. They would fit in just fine with such a crowd of crazed heathens. Brutus remained unfazed, offering only an occasional growl to create more space around him. Jared felt himself swept into the excitement, despite his distaste for the blood sport.

"Place your bets, boys," McClain cried out, his voice lifted in a futile attempt to rise above the tumult.

Jared stood on his toes and craned his neck, looking for Brutus's opponent. Only random movement could be seen on the far side of the dirt-floored storage area. Then Jared spotted a large slatted crate, observers maintaining a measured distance. What kind of animal required caging? Had he done the right thing pushing for this fight?

A glance down at Brutus's curly-haired mass made the questions unnecessary. The Airedale had met every challenge.

McClain slapped Jared on the back, the gambler's eyes gleaming at the frantic miners struggling to place their wagers. With his fists full of gold, the man kicked an empty shipping container to the center of a cleared area. He mounted the box, and the overwhelming roar ebbed to a muted murmuring.

"I present Jared Monroe," McClain called out, "and his fighting brute, the Scourge of Skagway. There's still plenty of time to get your bets placed."

Jared led Brutus to the open area. Cheers and shouts reached a new level. Still no opponent in sight, though a crowd continued to cautiously circle the slatted crate. He patted Brutus's head and leaned over his dog.

"Brutus," he spoke into the animal's ear. "Time to pay your dues. Sorry it's come to this, but it's our only hope. Besides, you've been practicing for this moment your whole life."

Images filled his mind. Brutus destroying the attacking dog on the Skagway beach. The blood-soaked scoundrel prone on the streets of San Francisco. Hoodlums scattering from Brutus's snapping charge in the Barbary Coast. He even remembered the pile of rats on the family farm and his dog's angry face-off with Brother Tom. And then an unexpected, unsettling thought: How far down the scale of civilized man had he fallen to force his faithful partner into the merciless world of dog fighting?

Bedlam retreated to excited whispers, catching Jared's attention. A tall man, Jared's height, clothed in a bulky parka, entered the warehouse and yanked the crate toward the center of the building. The wood planks screeched in protest against the hard-packed earth. Then a ferocious, primeval howl rose from the cage.

The crate rocked from the animal thrashing inside. The terrifying wail of the massive imprisoned creature sent a shock of alarm through Jared and quieted the crowd. Jared took a tentative step forward to shake hands, Brutus at his side. The tall man's battered face showed nothing, and he refused to offer his hand to Jared.

Several men cleared space around the crate providing an unobstructed view of the captive wolf dog. A fetid-smelling froth dripped from the muzzle of the imprisoned beast. Brutus stopped, frozen in place. The Airedale even took a step back, a tremor visible in the dog's broad shoulders. Brutus couldn't be frightened. Neither man nor beast had ever cowed the Airedale.

The huge wolf dog fell silent, body filling the cage. Brutus took yet another step backwards. Jared gaped in disbelief at his dog's drooping tail and increased panting. Only fear could explain such behavior. Then Jared took a harder look at the savage creature straining to get at Brutus and understood why.

Orange-tinged eyes bored into the Airedale. Not much domestic dog could be seen in the wild animal. The monster looked fifty pounds heavier than his Brutus. Hadn't his dog reacted with uncharacteristic uneasiness on the trail when the pack of wolves had shadowed him and Salt? Jared had never considered the animal's vulnerability, thought the dog indestructible. Until now.

Jared again placed a hand on Brutus's kinky-haired head. A familiar rumbling vibrated through Jared's fingers, the sound overwhelmed by a rebirth of the mob's cries. Brutus stiffened into attack mode, tail straight out, teeth snapping. Still, something had changed in his dog's demeanor.

"That mutt ain't got much chance." The comment came from a nearby spectator and found support from others. "I want to change my bet."

"You haven't seen this dog in action," McClain's voice boomed. "He's taken on three huge mongrels at once. Killed them all on the beach in Skagway."

Jared accepted the lie from the promoter, as well as an additional stream of exaggerations. If this was what it took to create more betting, so be it. Too much at stake to back down now.

A new, frightening howl erupted from the imprisoned wolf dog. The cage rocked from his powerful surges against the wooden slats. The bundled owner stepped from behind the box and slammed a club against the bars. The wolf dog stopped its struggle. But an unsettling wail remained, echoing off the wood-beamed ceiling.

Jared glanced at the ferocious penned animal and focused on Brutus with new insight. Could his valiant dog survive a battle with this creature? He had never considered that Brutus wouldn't prevail. Was even the loser's five 5 percent of $100,000 worth his dog's death?

"You ready?" McClain screamed over the deafening racket, the crowd gaining even more energy.

The Airedale was his partner, his only family, friend and defender, a vital component to Jared's well-being. An unexpected surge of protective emotion swept through Jared. He would rather risk his own life than Brutus's.

"Fight's off," Jared cried out, captured by impulse. His voice rang above the chaos with a surprising determination.

"What'd you say?" McClain flashed an uncomprehending look at Jared.

"I'm not letting my dog fight," Jared answered, louder, resolve strengthening his voice.

"Too late," McClain cried out. "This crowd's put down their money. Their blood's up."

Panic registered in the promoter's words despite the uproar around him, an atmosphere textured with violence. The gambler's eyes grew large. Jared grabbed Brutus by the neck and pulled him back. Disbelief registered on dirty, weathered faces. Excitement shifted to screams of anger. The crowd closed around Brutus, Jared and McClain, locking them in place.

"You can't walk away, boy," McClain shrieked, snatching at Jared's arm.

Brutus came back to life, snarling, teeth snapping, surging toward the gambler. Jared's quick hands and iron grip held the dog back. The mob grew more frenzied. Swelling danger radiated from the crowd, their impatience and anger incendiary. Jared swallowed his own fears and hung tighter to Brutus.

"There's got to be a fight," McClain screamed in Jared's ear, "or all hell's going to break loose. They'll not only rip you to pieces, but me too. Your dog won't be worth a nickel either."

Furious faces thrust toward him, sound becoming a crushing, impenetrable wall. The massed bodies squeezed ever tighter. Jared had to maintain his composure against growing claustrophobia. Let this maniacal mob beat him. He wouldn't sacrifice his dog.

He glanced at the wolf dog's owner, Harrington. The so-called ex-professional pugilist appeared unruffled, his misshapen features and ridged scar tissue a mask of calm. The man's ruined face certainly resembled a fighter. His own damaged features must look almost normal in comparison.

Could Jared hold his own against a professed professional? At least he didn't have to worry about further injury to his already distorted appearance. Maybe bulky clothes masked an overweight body. And did he have a choice? Unexpected confidence swept away doubts. He had never felt stronger. He could dance and dodge forever. So, Duffy, how well did you train me?

"I'll fight Harrington," Jared cried to McClain.

The promoter's expression flashed to incredulous. His shock then faded to relief. That emotion didn't last long, though, turning to dubious in seconds.

"Why would anyone put money on you against Harrington?" McClain yelled over the noise. "Got to be a reason to bet. No competition, no way to generate interest."

CHAPTER FIFTY-EIGHT

A lex moved with purpose through the snow and mud-clogged street half a block from Sophia's new pride and joy. Where had he found the energy to add the hotel opening to his existing list of challenges? His eyes focused on Sophia, not the hard-edged realities and uncertainties of the new venture. And there she stood before her sparkling creation with an unmistakable expression of pride and pleasure. Today was a time for celebration and, he hoped, much more.

Strong gusts whipped the canvas Grand Opening banner nailed beneath the block-lettered, royal-blue Alverson House sign. A large crowd, well-dressed businessmen to ragged prospectors, flooded through the elegant beveled-glass front doors of her long-awaited dream. Free beer and food never failed to attract a mob in Skagway.

Sophia's and his accomplishments of the last week had been herculean—fixtures installed, wallpaper hung, carpets laid, dining room and kitchen equipment located, staff hired, a Grand-Opening celebration that attracted more participants than could be accommodated. Alex had been true to his word. He had attacked the complicated obstacles threatening the opening. Strangely, he'd never felt happier.

Overlook the realities uncovered by Alex's budget for the Alverson House operation. Forget about the number of dangerous shortcomings exposed. Alex approached her with a smile he couldn't contain, disregarding the difficulties lined up against her hotel becoming profitable. They would have to fill both the hotel's rooms and dining room to eke out even a small initial profit. Still, the pleased expression on Sophia's beautiful face blew away all his negative thoughts.

"Well," he said without a trace of irony or sarcasm. "Your dream come true. I hope you're satisfied."

Standing beside her, almost touching, he could feel a depth of emotion and intensity radiating from the woman. He was now ready to open up his soul to her. So why had he kissed her only once—a kiss so passionate, yet gentle, that he still felt the soft press of her lips on his a week later?

She reached for his hand. The shock of connection snapped his eyes toward hers. He wasn't going to take advantage of his secret knowledge of her past. No. He wanted her to respond without coercion. She had to desire him as much as he hungered for her.

Her smile transcended all barriers. Close inspection reflected the same extreme fatigue in her as his mirror had shown him earlier this morning. A fresh, lightly scented smell floated from her. She might be dressed like a man, but today she looked and acted like a lady. Did she have the same hopes as he for overdue consummation?

"It's time we celebrated, Sophia."

Alex tightened his grip on her hand and guided her through the entrance of the Alverson House. She must trust him. Must know what he anxiously anticipated. Alex led her up the polished stairs, past the blue flocked wallpaper and cedar wainscoting. They ignored the frantic activity in the lobby. The Alverson House was now open. Uncontrollable desire demanded instant gratification. Alex could wait no longer.

He followed Sophia into her new room. The accommodation stood in antiseptic cleanliness, little evidence of Sophia's possessions yet in place. But the double-wide bed, a luxury previously unseen in rough-and-tumble Skagway, sat against the far wall, its blue checkered comforter spread across its breadth.

Staring at her brought an unsettling dizziness. Was it her exquisite face? Her sumptuous figure distorting her man's clothing? Her scent, as welcome and refreshing as a mountain breeze? Didn't matter. When the door closed, he locked his attention on her.

How long had he waited for this moment—to share his own passion with a woman willing to accept his gifts of attention? Certainly long before he had met Sophia. His body quivered, his hands shook. Not the worldly, sophisticated man-about-town now. What should he do? Lust gave way to a confusing, overpowering desire to protect her.

Sophia moved first, stepping into his arms. She lifted her face. Her radiance filled Alex with renewed confidence. He met her lips with a tenderness unlike any emotion he had ever experienced. Her full breasts crushed against his chest, creating instant arousal. He welcomed her kiss, exhilarated as it transcended a mutual warm embrace. He clung to her in a tightening grip. His lips now moved over her flawless features—prominent cheekbones, regal forehead, strong chin—to her throat, where her shirt interrupted the progress of his mouth.

He lifted his head, gazing into Sophia's bewitching eyes. They reflected an array of emotions from excitement to tenderness to yearning. He had no doubt she was willing to physically commit. More than that. He sensed a need that encompassed passion, respect, perhaps love. And love was exactly what he offered.

His shaking hands slipped the deerskin parka off her shoulders. Clumsy fingers took forever to unbutton her shirt. Alex fought a surge of desire to rip it off, but the garment finally came undone, revealing thick long underwear. The swell of her breasts expanded the fabric.

Alex lifted the ribbed cloth over her head. Sophia reached to cover her exposed bosom, crossing her arms over her chest. An impossible task. Alex would have chuckled if his throat hadn't constricted with tightening desire.

Sophia stepped back away from him, to the bed. Alex roughly ripped at his own clothes. In his haste to pull off his boots he lost his balance and stumbled sideways. Sophia's laughter provided a moment of perspective. Then she pulled off her boots and pants, and all perspective evaporated.

Alex took off the rest of his clothing and took several unsure steps toward Sophia. His next kiss became more urgent, exerting more pressure. Take it easy, he told himself. Stay soft and gentle. His lips moved again to her throat, then her deep cleavage. He could spend forever embracing breasts that defied gravity.

As he stood, her hands caressed the back of his head and neck. His tongue massaged the large areolas surrounding rock-hard nipples. Yet no murmur or moans escaped her lips. He forced himself to be patient, stay slow and tender. He moved below her breast, sinking to his knees. His tongue traced the path to her navel, then to the trail of dark, fine hairs until he arrived at the top of her thick pubic hair.

Sophia's body turned rigid. This wouldn't work. He stood, fully embraced her and pushed her onto the bed. His next kiss brought renewed intensity. Once more he slipped down her body, struggling to maintain calm. Sophia's body again clenched.

Alex couldn't stop. He no longer had the power to slow down. And Sophia smelled so fresh and clean. He had dreamed for years of bringing pleasure to a woman with his mouth in just such a manner. He found the moist spot through Sophia's tangle of curly hair. His hands tucked beneath her full buttocks, forcing Sophia to arch her body. His tongue entered, and Sophia's rigidity melted into fluid, dancelike gyrations.

Finally, uninhibited cries of pleasure filled the room. Alex knew she had never been treated like this, despite all the men she had been forced to lie with. He lost all restraint. Alex crawled back up her body, his erection a momentary awkward obstacle until he entered her. Gentle and soft became actions of the past. Pure, feverish passion consumed him.

CHAPTER FIFTY-NINE

J ared pushed the gambler off the crate and jumped up in his place. Sight and sound blended into a swirling mixture, a forest of faces and waving arms. But the extra height atop the crate achieved a degree of separation from the angry mob. The gamblers had been caught off guard by the change of opponents, from dogs to humans.

"You want a fight?" Jared cried, raising his own fists into the dense, pungent air of the warehouse. "I challenge you, Mr. Harrington."

Jared flung what he hoped to be a pugnacious stare at his proposed adversary. His fist punched the air. Harrington's battered, scarred face gave nothing away, eyes only slits, lips a tight crease.

"Who the hell are you?" came one distinct shout out of the chaos. A cascade of curses and threats followed in another wave of inflamed emotions. "Give me my money back, you son-of-a-bitchin' swindler."

Furious bettors surged toward McClain, forcing the frightened gambler against Jared and the crate he stood on. At least he had their undivided attention.

"Hold on," Jared cried out.

His arms again rose, carving out a moment of relative quiet. He needed to gain enough support to keep the betting alive. If he had allowed McClain to stretch the truth about Brutus, why not now exaggerate his own feeble accomplishments?

"I'll tell you who I am." The strength of his voice carried to all corners of the warehouse. "The undefeated Ivy League Heavyweight Boxing Champ. Worked with the most famous trainer in America. Duffy Wentworth. And I won the championship not once but twice."

The crowd's mood shifted to attentiveness. All these dirty faces had come for a fight, any fight. And they would root for the underdog, even if their money was on the expected winner. Jared had his opportunity.

"Harrington's been in the ring with the great John L. Sullivan," a bearded miner screamed out. "He's only been whipped by the best. Punk kid like you won't last one round."

Roaring consent echoed throughout the warehouse. Cries again rose for wagers to be returned. The emotional riptide now tugged against Jared. He glanced over at Harrington, saw a smirk blossom on his fragmented features. The man's evident confidence could work in Jared's favor.

"Exactly," Jared shouted against the sea of agitated passion. "He's been beaten, whipped by many. I'm undefeated. Harrington's a has-been. Probably a never-was. Mr. Harrington, you afraid to fight me? I guarantee you've never faced a man in the condition I'm in."

Jared kept eye contact with Harrington, the man seemingly bored despite the crackling emotion surrounding him. Was his potential foe made of stone? Voices shifted from threats of frustration, anger, violence to animated conversations. Interest again swelled in the tight confines of the warehouse. Wouldn't the boxer's pride force him into the ring? Time to seal the deal.

"You all know what a marathon is?" Jared shouted. "I took second place in the Boston Marathon. Over twenty-six miles of running. Fast."

The ex-fighter's face evolved into a bright crimson crisscrossed by ridges of stark-white scar tissue. Now, finally, some emotion from Harrington. Jared kept the artificial sneer frozen on his face.

"How far can you run, Mr. Harrington?" Jared taunted. "I just snowshoed in from Skagway. Thirty-two days. How tough was that winter crossing? You could ask Salt, who many of you knew, if he hadn't died on the trail."

"This was supposed to be a dogfight," Harrington snapped in a strange scratchy voice, the probable result of a punch to the throat, an overmatched boxer pummeled by the best. "Since your dog ain't ready to fight, maybe you should take his place. You fight my wolf dog."

"As you can see," Jared said, lacing his words with sarcasm, "this so-called professional pugilist is too far over the hill to box an Ivy League champ. I don't blame you folks for being upset. Mr. Harrington's a barbarian. He can't stand up against the boxing skills of a proven winner."

How easily the barbed, aggressive words flowed from Jared's mouth. But he had to create enough doubt in the bettors' minds to leave their hard-earned gold on the table. This was still his only opportunity to escape Dawson's deadly, interminable winter.

"Well, Mr. Harrington?" Jared pointed his finger at the boxer. "You in or are you and your wolf dog going to slide out the back door?"

Again, where had this newborn confidence come from? Who was this man challenging an obvious professional? Could he survive against Harrington? A now familiar answer came to him—fear could transcend into courage when one had no choice.

Harrington glared at Jared. He answered by shrugging out of his bulky parka, then unbuttoning his thick wool shirt. Harrington displayed a rangy, broad-shouldered frame. His opponent carried no fat. So much for Jared's first assumption of an overweight, over-the-hill ex-fighter. The crowd's thundering cheers resumed. They had come for a battle, a fight to the death. Dogs or men. Made little difference.

McClain muscled his way back onto the crate, back in control. Jared stepped down. The promoter's confidence and composure returned as he regained his position on the box.

"All right, ladies and gentlemen," the gambler called out. "Any more bets?"

Jared dug his fingers into the thick, kinky hair of his Airedale. Well, Brutus, we're finally full-fledged partners. For better or for worse. And if Jared didn't survive, Brutus would face the worst.

* * *

Jared stretched his neck, flexed his shoulders and bounced on legs as strong as twisted steel wire. He threw his parka aside and stripped down to one layer of underwear, self-consciousness discarded as easily as clothing. Only his heavy boots seemed to keep him from floating in the murky darkness of the Alaska Commercial Company's warehouse. Harrington faced him with the advantage of lightweight native mukluks on his feet. Jared couldn't care less.

Rules of the fight presented few surprises. Three-minute rounds, crates placed for the two fighters for two-minute breaks, bare knuckles, no need for a ten-second count after a knockdown, unlimited number of rounds. Last man standing won.

"Last chance to run," McClain said, leaning forward, lips close to Jared's ear. "Afraid you've got less of a chance against Harrington than your animal had against the wolf dog."

Jared shrugged and tried to swallow his trepidation. No room for doubt now. Focus on the strength of his legs, the confidence in his conditioning. Have faith that his Ivy League ring experience would be enough to carry him through.

McClain smacked a frying pan with a large metal spoon, and the fight was on. Jared moved to his toes, dancing to his right, quick on his feet. Harrington remained flat-footed, turning his body as Jared flitted in a circle. What kind of strategy was Harrington employing?

Watch out for his jabs, Duffy would have warned. That would be the boxer's lead weapon. Keep moving. Memories from Yale flooded through his mind, not necessarily good ones. But the minimal boxing skills he had exhibited in college should carry him against this plodder.

Jared threw a few jabs, catching nothing but air. Then he only sensed his opponent's lightning right cross. Time only to duck out of the direct line of fire. The vicious punch still caught the top of his head. Jared toppled to the hard-packed dirt. He rolled to his knees, both hands anchored to the ground to keep his body from collapsing. Less than a minute into the fight, and he was already on the ground. Where had that punch come from?

He rose to face Harrington, who still stood flat-footed. Now two painful jabs to the face before he could clear his head. Each hit cracked into Jared with authority. Lord, this man was quicker than a snake. This fight could end before it had started, with Jared humiliated and beaten.

Down again from another unseen right cross. This one brought images of the aurora borealis. Jared rose slower with more caution. Legs morphed from steel to weak-kneed butter. He scrambled to survive, finding it difficult to avoid the flat-footed punches of the pugilist.

Could he even last the first round? Jared's senses vibrated from the trauma of Harrington's hits, each bare-knuckled blow drawing blood. Harrington's rain of blows smacked out any thoughts of an easy victory. The welcome clang of the frying pan sounded in the packed space. Jared had at least regained his footing.

Two minutes rest was nowhere near enough time to recover. One round and Jared felt his confidence shredded. How had this man ever lost a fight? His opponent's speed and power proved overwhelming. How would Jared defend himself if he couldn't even see the punches coming? Hard to even distinguish the bang of the frying pan for round two. His head still rang from the first-round beating.

Jared rose from the crate. A series of jabs and a crunching upper cut brought a flow of blood in his mouth, salty and bitter. And another visit to the floor. Jared rose again, dazed but determined. He would not give up. His only hope was to stay out of the range of his opponent's flashing punches. The crowd dissolved beyond the makeshift ring. Jeers and screams muted to a soft hum as he focused on Harrington.

The boxer's lightning blows kept coming with unrelenting speed. Somehow Jared avoided his antagonist until the saving peal of the frying pan. Then round three.

He couldn't match Harrington's boxing skills. No doubt about that. What else could he do? Jared shook off several hits, then charged straight at his enemy, smacking his torso with solid blows. Jared swung with everything he could muster, leaning his body into

Harrington's. Anger and humiliation fueled the blasts. The pugilist took two quick steps back. And then nothing but air.

Jared staggered into empty space, and an unseen, painful rabbit punch whacked the back of his neck, driving him once again into the dirt. Jared lay motionless, stunned. He didn't have a chance. He should just accept the loser's 5 percent of the pot. That would be enough to at least get him back to Skagway and the Mainland. Jared rolled to his side, struggled to his knees, and staggered to his feet, searching for balance.

No. No more passive acceptance of fate. No more groveling on the ground. Jared propelled his body forward into Harrington, driving him into a crowd Jared had forgotten existed. The frying pan sounded a welcome end to round three.

Now what? Nothing left but his legs. Keep his feet moving on the hard-packed dirt floor. Keep focused. Jared spent the fourth round dodging and feinting, anything to stay beyond the reach of the professional's blasts. But another round survived.

Boos cascaded into his ears. Where had all these angry people come from? Curses and ridicule registered in his battered brain during the brief break before round five. He had to shake the dizziness, dispel the thickening cobwebs, remember what was at stake—life or death.

The unwelcome bang of the frying pan announcing another new round again coming too soon. Jared resumed his scrambling, desperate escapes from Harrington's attacks. Now the mob moved in on the fighters. The encroaching crowd stole precious maneuverability from Jared.

"Quit running, you coward," one of the spectators screamed.

"What's the matter?" another voice answered. "You got some place to go this winter?"

What did the crowd's taunts matter? Jared just needed to stay out of Harrington's reach. Use those iron-laced legs. He poked at the grizzled fighter with ineffectual punches.

Then every other jab or two, his opponent became sloppy. A mounting impatience showed on Harrington's scarred face at Jared's continued shucking and jiving. Something shifted, unidentifiable, but subtle, like the changing tides.

* * *

Jared soon lost count of the rounds. But he drew on his deep reservoir of strength. Confidence surged from his hard work at Stromberg's, his maniacal assaults on A B Mountain, and the brutal battle to survive the Yukon wilderness. And Harrington's frustration seemed to be growing. He threw fewer and fewer punches. Still the man stood flat-footed, anchored to the stamped-earth floor.

Jared scored more blows of his own. First, two or three a round, then sequences of clouts that rocked his antagonist. Was a frustrated Mr. Harrington tiring? Did Jared have a chance? The first sprouts of belief brought renewed energy.

Round fifteen, eighteen, twenty—Jared no longer knew or cared. He held fatigue at bay. Arms sluggish but still capable of painful pops to Harrington's head and body. In a clinch, Harrington breathed hard, his blood now mixing with Jared's. But Jared couldn't free himself from the desperate man's clutching grasp.

"Let's call it a draw," the ex-professional whispered into Jared's ear as they wrestled together. "We'll split the pot."

Surprise surged through Jared. Had he heard the man correctly? He took two quick steps back, a move Harrington had taught him in an earlier round, an earlier lifetime. Harrington stumbled forward, dropping his arms, defenseless for a moment. And there it was, an opening as wide as Alaska. Jared gathered strength and balance.

Frustration, disillusionment and pure fury coalesced into a flood of power. No more being pounded into the earth. No more unexpected tricky punches from brother Tom. No more meek cringing from physical threats. Jared's world tilted.

His haymakers, flat-footed crushing blows, smacked into the boxer. Jared moved in for the kill, slugging and blasting the man toward the dirt of the warehouse floor. His opponent's knees folded, the man's body collapsing, slumping to the ground.

Harrington attempted to rise. Jared pounded him again with an unrecognizable ferocity. Without mercy. Blood coursed through his head. Fists flew in an unknown, ecstatic rhythm. His ears picked up an escalating roar. Then the red veil of fury lifted from Jared's vision. Harrington lay immobile in the dirt. For once Jared stood above a beaten victim.

The Dawson crowd went wild. He glanced at the screaming gamblers, Brutus, a shocked McClain and back at the humbled Harrington. The big man huddled in a fetal position, arms protecting his head from punches that had already landed. The crowd had gotten their money's worth.

Jared slumped upon his crate, too exhausted to smile. Too unfamiliar with victory to raise his arms.

CHAPTER SIXTY

Jared awakened to a world of pain—an aching head, swollen hands and throbbing ribs. Memories jostled him. His brother's merciless fists. The excruciating train ride west. Dwarfs and drugs in a San Francisco hotel. Sled dogs dropping like dying birds. Confusion merged with agony. Was he still lying in the rich soil of Ohio? Did his brother lurk outside his hampered vision in the evening twilight? He squinted through puffed eyelids. No, but reality wasn't a lot better—Dawson in midwinter.

How much of his life had he spent bruised and beaten, struggling for survival? An image materialized: A large man possessed of enormous strength and lightning speed closing in on him. A professional boxer. Then the threatening fighter lay helpless in the dirt.

A muffled laugh seeped through his split lips. No more squirming in the mud. He had finally won. He had overcome daunting odds. The triumph was his, although a victory more painful than most defeats.

Had it been only two days? Lord, he hurt so bad. He felt as if he had just limped from the makeshift ring minutes ago. But he'd won. Calming warmth filtered through his body. He'd earned enough gold to be carried across the frozen wilderness of Alaska. He could spit at Skagway as he was lifted off the beach into a first-class cabin on the ship of his choice. He hadn't just outfought an experienced fighter, he had exceeded all expectations.

Pleasure swept through him. He rolled on his side and swung his legs off the bed in slow motion. Nausea and throbbing muscles encompassed his body like a shroud. He planted his feet on the dented wooden floor. Unadulterated joy thrust him upright.

He staggered out of the small room. Then a stairway, narrow and steep. No challenge too big now. He could overcome any obstacle. He stumbled down the stairs one at a time.

The last step descended onto the main floor of the rustic Pioneer. A sea of startled faces turned toward him. The crowd broke into enthusiastic cheers.

"Jared, you iron-fisted son of a bitch." McClain was the first to reach him. "Been waiting two days to congratulate you, boy. What a fight. Never seen anyone survive a beating like that."

Shouted praises and tributes overwhelmed whatever the promoter had yet to say. The adulation was nothing Jared had ever dreamed of experiencing. Certainly not all winners paid such a high price for victory. But victorious he was. His head swam with an onslaught of pride and pain.

"Mr. McClain." Jared shrunk back from the offered pats on his back, attempted handshakes and McClain's proffered bear hug. Too much, too soon. "I think I need a little more rest before we start celebrating. How about helping me back upstairs."

* * *

Another twenty-four hours provided major progress in healing. This time when Jared stepped down to the Pioneer's main room, he maintained better physical control of his body. And there awaiting him was the same cast of characters greeting him with the same effusive congratulations. Had they spent the night in this dump?

"Here's your winnings." McClain again was the first to welcome him, handing Jared a bulging moose-hide pouch. "Twenty-four thousand dollars, plus a few flakes. Biggest pot I ever been associated with. Knew you'd whip Harrington."

"You hid that fact well," Jared said in a low voice.

"Ah, lad." The gambler's signature smile cracked his face wide open. "Fear is by far the best motivator. That mob would have ripped both you and me to shreds if we'd tried to escape. They're like a pack of dogs. Would've attacked us at the first scent of fright."

The Pioneer's front door opened, and a ragged miner stepped in. Jared looked past the man and glimpsed the usual ceiling of gray-black frozen mist that lay oppressively upon Dawson. The thought of escaping this miserable town brightened the murk. He could use more time to mend, but opportunity beckoned.

"How am I supposed to free myself from this miserable town?" Jared took a seat next to the promoter. "You promised me."

"I told you I'd find a way to get you back to Skagway," McClain said, a sour look on his face. "But it's a mistake for you to leave now. Don't walk away. Might be tough getting you a fight until spring, but then it's Katie-bar-the-door."

An earnest expression took over the gambler's face. The Pioneer patrons echoed McClain's arguments. These bored prisoners of winter would pay to see two cockroaches fight. But Jared needed to move on.

"Can you imagine the number of fools, braggarts and bullshitters flooding into the Yukon from the coast?" McClain inflated with emotion. "They'll supply enough cannon fodder for fights that will make you a fortune."

"I've already got a fortune," Jared said, cupping the pouch of gold in his damaged hands as if it were the last egg in Dawson. "And we've already had this conversation."

"No, Jared," the promoter wheedled. "I mean real money."

Jared offered only a cold stare. He'd leave with or without this man's help, buying his way out of Dawson. He had the money.

"All right, all right," the gambler said, waving his arms in disgust. "In five days you'll head out with Jonny Tuglit, the Taglish Indian musher. He'll be carrying the mail to the coast."

Thank God the mail had to be delivered through rain, snow, sleet and danger. All those elements would be present during the projected three week trip back to Skagway. Carrying only the mail would allow rapid progress in the wilderness. But he did still have one piece of unfinished business in Dawson.

"I want to check on Mr. Harrington," Jared said, his voice assuming an earnest, almost pleading tone.

"You what?" McClain said, his look of confusion showing on the only clean-shaven face in the Pioneer.

"I want to see if he's all right," Jared answered, hands placed on the table between them. "Been three days since the fight. I owe him a lot."

"You owe him nothing," McClain blustered. "He damn near killed you. Not sure he wants to see you either. Might just pull out a pistol and shoot you."

Jared pushed himself upright with effort, using swollen fists as levers. The table provided support. Queasiness and debilitating pain still gripped him, but some unknown need drove him to meet the boxer. Good thing there were five more days to heal before heading out.

"He's over at the Silver Pan." Resignation was evident in the gambler's voice. "He's lickin' his wounds. I'd approach that man with care."

"Help me with my parka," Jared said to McClain.

Good thing the Silver Pan was only a short block away. Jared shrugged into the welcoming warmth of the garment, then weaved toward the door. McClain's grip on his jacket steadied him.

"Hey," McClain said, "I saw your dog out and about this morning."

"He'll be fine," Jared said, waving away McClain.

* * *

He entered the log building, a twin to the Pioneer. Locals sat and milled around the haze-filled room. Jared's eyes adjusted to the dim light. Every hotel-bar in Dawson reeked of smoke and men long unwashed. Several dance-hall girls in garish costumes circulated among the desultory men. They made half-hearted flirting attempts to get attention. The men ignored them, keeping to their drinks and card games. Too early in the day to stir up interest. Yet the crowd acknowledged Jared with salutes and murmured compliments.

The boxer sat slouched alone on a chair in the farthest, darkest corner of the Silver Pan. A ring of clear space surrounded him, no one willing to get too close. An unexpected tightening squeezed Jared's chest. What kind of reception would he receive from the fighter? Jared approached with measured steps, boots scuffling across the wooden floor.

Harrington looked up. His face showed a fair share of cuts and bruises. Bloodshot eyes met Jared's.

"What the hell do you want?" the battered pugilist grunted and turned his attention back to his whiskey, bent and broken fingers in an awkward grasp around the shot glass.

"Just wanted to see how you were doing," Jared said, the heat of self-consciousness prickling his face. "You put up a heck of a fight. Wanted to thank you for saving my dog. Don't think he would've done too well against your wolf."

The beaten man stared at Jared. Blackened eyes swept up and down. Then Harrington burst out laughing.

"What's so funny?" Sparks of anger awakened within Jared.

The crowd pressed in around him and the boxer. What the hell did they want? Curiosity or hoping for another battle? Jared bit down on his growing temper. He'd come here with good intentions.

"You look in the mirror lately?" Harrington wheezed. "You're the most beat-to-shit winner I've ever seen. Hard to believe you're still breathing as many times as I hit you. I been in many fights, but never seen nobody take the beating you did."

Harrington stood with effort, using the chair for assistance. He stuck out his hand, as swollen as Jared's. Jared accepted. The fighter collapsed back on his chair and emptied his glass with a quick swig. A morose expression returned to his face, and he broke eye contact with Jared.

"Now go about your business," the fighter said, staring at the half-full bottle. "Let me have my peace."

Jared turned away, not quite satisfied with the meeting. One of the dance-hall girls appeared before him. Curly black hair tumbled to her shoulders, bright red ribbons adding welcome brightness to the gloomy bar. He attempted to step around her. She stood her ground—pouty lips and dark eyes a little too small for her square face. Sturdy and tough—best kind of woman for the Klondike. She flashed a conspiratal smile.

"To the victor go the spoils." Her fingers played with the buttons on his parka. "You look real battered, but I'll bet I could get a rise out of you."

The encroaching crowd broke into a chorus of howls, cackles and lewd comments. Heat returned to his cheeks. He had no clue what to say or do. He'd rather face Harrington again than deal with this intimidating woman.

"Please," he mumbled.

She ran a finger from under his chin, down his chest, stopping an inch above his belt. Her sparkling eyes skewered his. Restless energy snaked through him.

"My name's Mandy, and I'm the best there ever was."

Raucous snorts and shouts again erupted. Jared swung his head around the room, searching for an escape. An image of his bright red face caught his attention in the cracked mirror behind the bar. A wave of humiliation engulfed him. He tucked his head and tried to move around her again. She grabbed his arm and held on with an iron grip. Where did this woman get such strength?

"Give us some space, dammit," she spit at the crowd, dragging Jared into a corner. "Tell you what, champ," her husky voice and red lips inches from his. "I saw the fight. You're quite the man. I'll do you for free."

Mandy planted a soft, wet kiss on his battered lips. An urge Jared only experienced in the dead of night forced the blood from his face to between his legs. Confusion and indecision clouded his senses.

He'd never kissed a woman. Never held a lady in his arms. Maybe now was the time he became a complete man. Shouldn't he learn about the act between a man and a woman? What if he could accomplish the unthinkable with Sophia? What if he offered her his heart and soul, and she accepted?

Then a clear vision of Sophia slid between Jared and his uncomfortable arousal. The sculpted elegance of Sophia's high-cheek boned beauty, her presence more real than the dance-hall girl before him. Sophia offered the chance of true love. How could he cast away such a dream? The uninhibited urge in his groin dissipated like rain on hot paving stones.

He'd never received one ounce of encouragement from Miss Alverson. Maybe all was illusion. But no. He would remain faithful and pure, even if he was only to be rejected by Sophia. Even if he might act the bumbling fool.

"No thank you, madam," he said returning his attention to Mandy.

She put her hands on her hips. An expression wavering between pity and disgust twisted her pretty face. Jared backed away. He only wanted out. He moved toward the door, as desperate as reaching for the finish line of a marathon. His panicked retreat took him to the street. For once he welcomed the freezing chill of the Yukon.

CHAPTER SIXTY-ONE

Predawn mornings on the Yukon Trail had been the toughest of the initial brutal journey from Skagway to Dawson. This first awakening on the return trip proved no different. Pain, stiffness and bitter cold once again enveloped Jared. He struggled to his feet. But the day's promised beauty, solitude and cleanliness soon submerged the discomfort.

Jonny Tiglet wasted no time feeding, then harnessing the dogs. No cheery greeting, no morning fire, no life-giving hot coffee. The man's stone-faced visage reflected no emotion. The Indian spoke less than Salt on a bad day. Could he even speak more than ten words of English? Did it matter? The Mounties trusted Jonny to deliver the mail across this forbidding wilderness. That had to be credibility enough.

Jared, the fish-filled saddlebag draped over one arm, called out to Brutus. He had surprised his dog yesterday when he had slapped the pack on Brutus's back before the animal could react. Today the Airedale kept his distance, wary of being trapped a second time.

"Brutus," Jared said again, voice rising. "Let's get loaded up."

The Airedale stood motionless twenty feet from him. Jared took several steps forward. Brutus moved backward an equal number of paces.

"What is this, Brutus?" Jared said. "We're wasting time. Come here."

No movement from the dog. Jared stepped forward, Brutus inched away. Jared lunged, the Airedale danced to the side, landing in a tripod position, head resting on his front paws, large butt thrust upwards. Again Jared took several awkward steps toward the dog. And Brutus kept the same space between them. Now each attempt was met with a growling bark and snapping teeth.

"Dammit, Brutus," Jared whined into the crisp emptiness. "I thought we were done with this nonsense."

Jonny appeared at Jared's side. He grabbed the pack and pushed Jared out of the way. Jared lost his balance and stumbled down into the deep snow.

"I show you how handle dog," the Indian grunted.

Jared struggled upward. Jonny pushed him back down with one hand. Then a billy club materialized in the Indian's other hand. He wouldn't strike Brutus, would he? How would his dog react to such a threat?

"Stop, Jonny," Jared yelled, scrambling upright.

Too late. A large brown-bodied blur crashed into Jonny. A ferocious roar erupted. Brutus's iron jaws clamped around the man's throat. The explosion of action slammed Jonny onto his back.

Jared got his legs beneath him and dove headlong into his dog. Both arms wrapped around the Airedale, Jared clinging to the dog's broad chest. Heels dug into the snowy terrain provided leverage. The weight of his body ripped Brutus away from Jonny. The animal's empty sharklike jaws snapped in the air. Only the thick fur of the Indian's parka had saved the man from Brutus's slashing fangs.

"No!" Jared howled, holding tight to the powerful animal. "No!"

Jonny scrambled to his feet, took two frantic steps backward and stumbled to the snow again. He crabbed away from Jared and Brutus, stopping behind the sled. The Airedale shook off Jared's arms and stood quivering, attention locked on the retreating Indian.

"Jesus," was the only word Jared could muster.

Had the dog reacted to protect Jared or to Jonny and his threatened aggression? Or had the animal become as wild as the surrounding countryside? Enough. Jared picked up the discarded saddlebag and strapped it on the sled. Forget about Brutus carrying the dried fish.

"Still a partnership, eh?" he said with disgust. "Just not an equal one." He glanced at the Taglish Indian. "Stay away from my dog. Got a mind of his own."

* * *

Skagway appeared out of the mist large, loud, and nasty. Just as Jared expected. Gone less than three months and the distasteful hellhole proved to be as unchanged as the day he had departed. The good news this time was his visit to Skagway would only be a short layover.

Twenty-three days of brutal cold, traveling much of the time in the dark to get here. And he still didn't know how he would approach Sophia or where he would go when he escaped this dump. He'd check in with Alex, not sure why. And if he could find the courage, meet with Miss Alverson. And say exactly what? The absence of answers didn't prove too disturbing. To his surprise, a new self-assurance existed comfortably within his confusion. A new reality.

Salt's deceit and then death had led to self-reliance in the wilderness. An inability to find a meaningful life in Dawson had led to unknown strength and perseverance in whipping a professional boxer. Things didn't work out for the best. Rather, one made the best out of what happened. He might not know where he was headed, but he now had the tools to meet most any challenge. Or so his newfound confidence promised.

At the entrance to the general store, Brutus separated from Jared and disappeared down the crowded street. A step over the threshold, and familiar smells and colors assaulted Jared's senses. The store appeared well-ordered, well-stocked and filled with customers picking through the offered merchandise. A light buzz of activity greeted him. Today seemed a visit to a past life.

But the level of business seemed somehow muted. Still, no comparison to the bleak, empty shelves of Dawson. Had he left Stromberg's only two and a half months ago? The world had shifted since he had last passed through this doorway. Were the changes only superficial, or would he forever view the world differently?

Jared made his way to the back office. Alex sat surrounded by his ledgers and stacks of papers. Jared had once spent most of his days there. He knocked on the door frame. Alex glanced up from his desk.

"Well, I'll be damned." Alex leaped to his feet, swung around his desk, and gave Jared an unexpected engulfing hug. "Didn't think I'd ever see you again. How the hell did you survive? Weren't even gone that long. Lord, am I glad to see you. This definitely calls for a drink."

Alex returned behind his desk and pulled the ever-present bottle of whiskey from the drawer. This effusive, emotional greeting from the always cool, collected Alex threw Jared off balance. What events had occurred during Jared's absence? He stood speechless.

"Don't have much time," Alex said, "but tell me what happened. Where's Salt? Why are you back so soon? Did you make it to Dawson? Jesus, you look more beat up than when you left. Sit down. Have a drink."

Jared sat as directed but waved away the drink. He ran his fingers over his cheeks, his lips, then his chin. He could only imagine how rough he must appear, grizzled beard, lumps and bumps. Three weeks in the frigid wilderness should have brought down the swelling in his face, heal the cuts and bruises. Alex wasn't looking too good either. The man had never appeared so exhausted, nervous and disheveled. And swigging a large whiskey in the middle of the day was a shock. The Alex that Jared knew never lost control in any situation.

"Jared, your arrival here is a godsend," Alex said, fingers dancing on the glass of the liquor bottle. "I've got to get to San Francisco. Goddamn Mordecai is squeezing the life out of me. But I'm real curious about your journey."

Deep black pouches spread below Alex's bloodshot eyes. Pale skin stretched across cheek bones more prominent than Jared remembered. A subtle yet persistent twitch flickered on one side of drawn lips. The question wasn't what had happened to Jared in the Klondike, but what had happened to Alex here in Skagway? His former boss appeared to be the one who had spent brutal weeks in the wilds of Alaska.

"Salt and I made pretty good time—"

"I'll bet you're here to pick up your savings," Alex blurted, a shadow crossing the man's features. "Well, you got here just in the nick of time. I was sorely tempted to temporarily borrow your funds to get to San Francisco. But your little stash is still here."

Jared had forgotten about the earnings he'd left with Alex. He had over twenty thousand dollars in the pack at his feet. He had no need of his past wages. Salt had been right about one thing. Money was the key to choices and opportunities.

Alex turned to his safe, twirled the dials, opened the heavy door and pulled out a small pouch. He slapped Jared's gold on the desk, then looked up. Alex's expression was one of relief.

"You won't believe the deep shit I'm in," Alex wailed, hands flapping the air with futility. "Goddamn Mordecai's strangling me. Seems like there's new competition opening up every week. Since you left, I haven't been able to hire any decent help. Soapy Smith's got me entangled in a used-goods store that's selling everything ten cents on the dollar. Never get any cash from that useless operation. And I've got other problems with that crook, Soapy. Also, the newly opened Alverson House is sucking cash like a newborn sucks at his mother's tit."

Alex paused, breathless. Amazing how distraught and disturbed the once dominant, impenetrable Alex had become. Jared fought to cover his shock at Alex's agitated behavior.

"I've got a great opportunity for you," Alex began again, eyes narrowing, mouth pulled into an unnatural smile. "I'll double your stake for three weeks of your time. Must catch a boat down to California. Shake my money out of my old man and get back to Skagway. You run Stromberg's while I'm gone. Just three weeks and you'll have another $500. Only three weeks."

Three weeks? He'd give Skagway three hours, and that time would be spent on one foolish attempt to approach Sophia. Otherwise, he would be out of town even sooner.

"I'm sorry," Jared said rising from his chair. "I'm not interested. I plan to leave Skagway in a day or two. I'm only going to give my regards to Miss Alverson. Then I'm getting as far from this evil pit as I possibly can."

Panic, then resignation twisted Alex's features. Finally, an unexpected crafty expression appeared. Jared didn't know what Alex wanted but sat up straighter with tightened resolve.

"Listen, Jared," Alex said, holding up his hand. "The job I'm offering is more than just taking care of Stromberg's. I want you to work with Sophia. She needs help getting the Alverson House profitable. You'd have to spend time with her."

That certainly changed things. He glanced down at Alex, who looked up with a smile laced with sincerity. Was he being manipulated? Probably, but so what? He'd been struggling for some plan of action the entire trip from Dawson. Any legitimate excuse to spend moments with Sophia would serve as a golden opportunity. He could now spend time with her and with a purpose.

"I hate this city, Alex," Jared said, addressing Stromberg by his first name for the first time. "I'll stay for three weeks and that's it. If you're not back, you'll have to rely on Horace."

But what was the relationship between Alex and Sophia? When Jared had left for Dawson, the two seemed often at odds with each other. Had anything changed that association? Whatever had occurred, Alex out of town would provide Jared with the chance to approach Sophia with fewer distractions.

"That's great. That's just fine," Alex said, relief painting his features. "We'll get you one of the finest rooms in the Alverson House."

"I'd prefer my old spot in the warehouse tent," Jared said. "I would like a bath, though."

"No problem," Alex almost shouted. "Bath, meal—hell, a feast. Whatever you want. Let's get over to the Alverson House and tell Sophia our plan. She knows I have to go to San Francisco as soon as possible. By the way, where's that ferocious mutt of yours?"

"He's out exploring," Jared answered. "I don't think he wants out of Skagway as bad as I do."

CHAPTER SIXTY-TWO

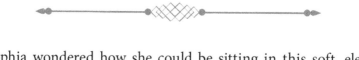

Sophia wondered how she could be sitting in this soft, elegant armchair in this sparkling lobby completely alone. Beautiful furnishings and the best workmanship Skagway could supply. But the hotel was only one-third full. Her dream was turning into a nightmare.

At least the restaurant was busy. And her cook, Eric Legare, was firmly wrapped around her finger. Still, she knew meals alone could not lift the Alverson House to profitability. The front door opened. Lord, about time a customer showed up. Sophia rose from her chair. No, not a customer but an even more welcome sight.

"Alex," she called out.

Alex's eyes darted around the vacant lobby, hands fiddling with his coat buttons. The poor man looked exhausted. And she, rather the Alverson House, was a major cause of his deteriorating condition. She moved toward him, then noticed a second figure, lingering behind Alex.

"My God," she exclaimed. "Jared."

He stood tall, eyes fixed on her. His disjointed features had once given him the appearance of a goofy, self-conscious young man. Now his face appeared even more battered. But the additional injuries and serious expression projected a new worldliness. Yes, even a toughness. She squashed her desire to comfort and embrace Alex. Instead, her eyes locked on Jared.

"Look who I ran into," Alex said, relief and irony lacing his words. "Young Jared just returned from the wilderness to save us."

Jared remained behind Alex but no longer seemed obsequious or uncomfortable in her presence. Sophia had treated him less than graciously in the past. Now she felt ill at ease.

"Really," Sophia said, then directing a coquettish smile toward the new arrival. "Welcome back, Jared. How do you plan on saving us?"

A full-blooming blush spread over Jared's damaged face, but he remained silent, his expression serious. Well, some things hadn't changed with the ex-clerk. Just what could Jared offer? Why did Alex appear so uneasy?

"Jared's going to run Stromberg's for a few weeks." Alex's nervous hands jumped from the lapels of his coat to the butt of his holstered pistol. "Free me to go to San Francisco. He's also offered to help you with the Alverson House."

So Alex had found a way to travel south. How would she survive without his strong arms around her? Lord, the very thought of his threatened trip to San Francisco left a hollowness in her heart. If only she hadn't created additional financial pressures for him with her hotel. This was her fault.

"You're sure there's no alternative to you leaving?" Sophia asked, her voice crackling with anxiety.

"No," Alex answered, irritation creeping into his voice. "We've been over this. Many times. You know the numbers as well as I do. It's the Alverson House that's sucking us dry."

"We're doing better each week in the restaurant," Sophia said. Why couldn't her dream be given the time it needed? "Can't you hold out a little longer? Business will definitely pick up."

"Sophia." Alex threw his arms in the air. A grimace gave clear evidence of his mounting frustration. "I've got enough cash for two or three weeks, maybe four. That gives me just enough time to travel to San Francisco, shake my money out of Father." His voice lowered but took on an angry edge. "The goddamn interest charges I'm paying Soapy are killing me."

"What?" A sickening lump expanded within her chest. "What interest charges?"

"I told you," Alex said, waving a hand in a dismissive gesture. "Needed some capital to get Stromberg's back on track."

"No, Alex. No, you didn't tell me." Sophia jammed a hand into a coat pocket, searching for comfort from her revolver. "Please, not Soapy Smith?"

Soapy frightened her as much as the ever-present threat of Hawk Face. His vicious absence of scruples and lack of mercy. Alex just stood there, his silence answering her question. Yes, that despicable crook, Soapy Smith.

"You never mentioned any loan from that criminal," she hissed. "How much?"

His eyes darted around the room. Sophia's heart beat faster. What else had her partner not shared with her? Why couldn't he meet her wide-eyed stare?

"Ten thousand," Alex replied,

"Ten thousand?" she shrieked with astonishment. "What happens if you can't pay?"

Shadows had always surrounded Alex, questions unanswered. He'd never told her what had happened to Elijah Cummings. Of course, she hadn't wanted to know. He played his cards too close. But borrowing money from that cutthroat, Soapy Smith? Chills radiated through her.

"He takes Stromberg's," Alex said, his voice growing louder. "But that's not going to happen. There's plenty of money in San Francisco. I guarantee you I will get it. I just need a little more time."

"Why didn't you tell me?" Sophia asked, biting back a sense of betrayal.

"Because it's no concern of yours." Alex slammed a fist into his palm. "Look, goddammit, there wouldn't be any problems if it wasn't for your cash-draining hotel."

Sophia took a step back, warning signals ringing in her ears. Would he even return from California? All he had in Skagway was debt and pressure. Was she enough to bring him back? Was this the real Alex?

"When are you leaving?" Anger drove her words out in a croak.

Jared cleared his throat. She had forgotten about him. The young man's eyes whipped between Alex and her. Confusion and embarrassment painted his face.

"Now, thanks to Jared," Alex grabbed her shoulders, "I'll be back soon as I can. You think I want to take that miserable fucking boat ride to California and back? You know I hate traveling on the water, to say nothing of dealing with Mordecai. Don't worry. I know what I'm doing."

His fingers dug into her flesh. Her hands flew to his wrists, and she struggled against his grip. Alex yanked her to him. He planted a hard kiss on her mouth. Sophia's lips felt the imprint of his and the absence of any heat or affection. Where had this roughness come from?

"I owe you a lot, Jared," Alex said over his shoulder. "Take care of Sophia and Stromberg's. I won't forget what you're doing for us."

For us? Is that what he had said? Was she really still part of his plans? That was his goodbye after everything they'd been through? Leaving her alone to face the daunting challenges crushing her? No warm, loving farewell? One lousy kiss?

* * *

Her weeks with Alex had flown by like a dream, distorting reality, squeezing out her past doubts about her partner. Now he was gone. Sophia should have been more cautious, more realistic. Hadn't she promised herself over and over to never lose control of her life? People didn't change, despite all her wishful thinking.

She had expected Alex's departure to San Francisco, but the loan from Soapy Smith? Damn, what a naïve fool. Now even more doubt flooded her. What circumstances could possibly bring him back? No, their relationship, whatever it might have been, had ended. She could kid herself all she wanted, but that was the truth of the matter.

"Sophia?" Jared's voice was soft with concern.

She looked up. He still stood across from her. An aura of calm surrounded the young man, solid, understanding. A gentle smile appeared on his scarred and swollen face.

"He'll be back," Jared said. "Alex might be difficult at times. But I've never met anyone more capable. When he gives his word, he keeps it."

He pursed his lips, took a deep breath. No longer any embarrassment, just no more to say. Air returned to her lungs. She mustered a smile. Jared was making a valiant attempt to comfort her.

What had happened to Jared on his journey to the Klondike? What had brought such a notable change in the man in only a few months? Could Jared solve any of the troubling outstanding issues of the Alverson House? That possibility seemed laughable. But curiosity filled Sophia.

"The Alverson House, in trouble though it may be," she said, hands checking for loose strands of hair poking from beneath her slouch hat, "can still buy you a meal." She stood, for one of the rare times, uncomfortable in her bulky men's clothing. "Follow me."

She led Jared through an adjoining door, away from the funereal atmosphere of the lobby to the large dining room, where activity hummed. Royal blue-patterned flocked wallpaper covered the walls floor to ceiling. Elegant tablecloths, fine china and silverware, and polished maple chairs from back East filled the room. Harassed, white-coated waiters flitted between customers and kitchen just as she had always envisioned. How could such a fine operation not be successful?

At one of the few empty tables, Jared stepped forward and pulled out her chair. His courtesy in the barbaric environment of Skagway took her by surprise. She offered another smile, this one without as much effort. Jared sat opposite her and produced his own fractured kaleidoscope of a smile. Had he ever smiled before in her presence?

"What do you recommend?" Jared asked, ignoring the menu before him. "Why don't you order for me?"

"Fine," she said, a finger tapping her lower lip. "We'll both order fresh halibut."

The fish arrived with new potatoes and asparagus tips. Jared inhaled the seductive aromas and devoured his serving. No conversation, just serious consuming. She suppressed a chuckle at

Jared's obvious excitement. His gusto took Sophia's mind off Alex and stimulated her own ever-present appetite. When he had finished, she couldn't keep her eyes off the complex expression on his face.

"Not many decent meals on the trail?" she asked.

"None," Jared said. Another dazzling smile cracked his lopsided face. "This might be the finest meal I've ever had."

"Would you like something else?" she asked, an eyebrow arched.

"No, thank you," Jared said, resting a hand on his flat belly. "My stomach's pretty shrunk up. Not used to either quantity or quality. I wish I could eat more."

"I'm real curious," Sophia said, leaning toward Jared. "How'd you do on your trek?"

"Tough at first," Jared answered, "but got into a rhythm. Real cold. Brutal. Learned a lot about survival. Especially after Salt's accident."

"What happened to him?" Her fingers drew patterns on the fabric. Salt had always been a distant, prickly character.

"Sled went over a bluff above the Yukon River," Jared said, voice flat. "Landed on Salt. Killed him. The dogs too."

Salt dead? She straightened. The old buzzard seemed too tough to die. Jesus. How could such an experienced wilderness traveler have such a terrible accident? How could Jared have survived without the prospector? Sophia realized her mouth was open and clamped it shut.

"What did you do?" she asked. "How long were you on your own?"

"Brutus and I made it to Dawson in a little over a week," he said. "Didn't have many supplies, but the weather held. We made pretty good time."

But how had he endured? How could one so inexperienced escape death when on his own? There had to be much more to this story than Jared was describing. Yet here he was, alive and well. This was the crippled boy she'd rescued on the train to San Francisco? She struggled to hide her irritation and impatience at Jared's lack of details.

"Didn't stay long in the Klondike, did you?" Sophia probed.

"Dawson's a lot like Skagway," Jared said, his eyes meeting Sofia's. "Only worse. People starving. No way out. Nothing to do. Dirty, nasty town full of disillusioned, trapped, desperate fools."

Could Alex have survived such a brutal chain of events? Maybe. He sure wasn't doing too well under the current pressures. Perhaps there was some divine hand in Jared's appearance. Now her partner might never return. Could this young man help her face the predicament Alex had left her in? And if Jared had escaped injury in the sled accident and life-threatening solo journey to Dawson, what had happened to his face?

"I don't mean to be rude," Sophia said, "but it looks like your face took another beating."

"I needed money to get out of Dawson. Heck, I wanted out of Alaska. I made a deal with a gambler. Brutus was going to fight a wolf for money."

Once again color rose in Jared's face. He fidgeted in his chair. My God, things must have been desperate for this boy to resort to fighting Brutus. Was this the reason he was so uncomfortable sharing his experiences? Had he done something else he was ashamed of? Break the law? Was Brutus still alive?

"Please, Jared. Continue."

"But I couldn't let Brutus fight." Jared used his napkin to wipe away a thin film of perspiration from his forehead. "I stepped in and fought the wolf's owner. And I won."

"Lord, Jared." Sophia's interest overcame courtesy. "Tell me the whole story, dammit."

"This wolf dog would have killed Brutus," his voice dropping almost to a whisper. "Brutus was willing to fight, but he wouldn't have had much of a chance. The animal's owner was a professional fighter. Actually, I think he was a professional loser. He'd fought some great boxers, but he hadn't won many matches. I wouldn't have had a chance against a good pugilist."

CHAPTER SIXTY-THREE

A sour taste accompanied Alex when he turned into Second Avenue. He carried his valise packed with a minimum of items for his voyage. Where was his self-confidence, and worse, his self-esteem? Why had he left Sophia so abruptly? Hell, he knew the answer. He was only weeks—days—away from bankruptcy. Hadn't he been the one who had captivated Sophia Alverson? Earned her trust and respect? The one who had brought her to a new level of physical passion? Now he was but a shadow of himself.

He kicked at the clods of frozen mud cluttering the street, sending chunks flying down the avenue before him. The thought of weeks on the water, vulnerable to the whims of a merciless ocean, brought instant nausea. But there was no escape from the reality of Soapy Smith's debt and the negative cash flow of the Alverson House. He needed a miracle.

His desperation disgusted him. And he had put a bullet through the chest of his most recent possible messiah, the one man who could have brought him relief from this financial pressure. Elijah Cummings. Now he needed another chance, another divine intervention.

Alex shifted his valise to his other hand and walked toward the shoreline. The crowd of new arrivals and old hustlers mobbed the beach in ever-greater numbers. Two large men materialized from the horde slamming against Alex, each one grabbing an arm. They locked him in place. Someone poked a hard object in his back. Alex couldn't move, couldn't reach his holstered gun or use the derringer hidden in his sleeve. Sweat broke out on his forehead. Panic tightened his chest.

"Mr. Smith would like to see you," the third man behind him said. "Please come with us quietly."

No question who these goons were—Soapy's thugs. Both giants restraining him were familiar. He knew their faces and their brutal reputations. Calm down. Smith couldn't get money from a dead man. Just go along and see how this little drama played out. Then a laugh burst from his lips. Damn. Another miracle after all. He wouldn't be heading to San Francisco today.

"Of course," Alex said, "I'll go with you."

What choice did he have? In fact, he welcomed the excuse to postpone his cruise. Just relax and wait for an opportunity to regain control. This physical intimidation was a challenge he could relate to. Odds stacked against him. Danger and violence part of the equation. He had been here before. Threats generated familiar alertness and heightened sensations.

Strange the way life worked. Five more minutes and he would have been on his miserable mission to San Francisco. Let's just see what Mr. Soapy Smith had in mind. His confidence blossomed.

"Gentlemen, relax, take it easy," Alex said, allowing a tense smile to appear. "I'd be happy to see my dear partner."

He took a deep breath and relaxed his body. The men holding him released some of the pressure on his arms, then twisted him into a neat about-face with military precision. The rocky beach forced uneven steps, the two men working hard to keep Alex trapped. With each step Alex gained a little more maneuverability.

Some more freedom and he could shake his derringer free. Make a fight of it. Hope surfaced. No. Soapy had more cohorts than Alex had bullets. Be patient and see what happens. They had to be headed for Soapy's hole-in-the-wall den of iniquity on Third Avenue.

* * *

Ten of Soapy's evil minions filled the small clubhouse Soapy called home. Smoke created a density thicker than air. The plankboard bar supported a dozen elbows. Alex met their stares. Soapy sat at his usual round felt-covered table, back to the wall, eyes gleaming in the murk of the cabin.

"Alex," Soapy said, "thanks for stopping by."

A ripple of laughter greeted Soapy's sarcasm. His escorts pushed him toward their boss. Alex shook his arms loose, making sure he had easy access to his derringer.

"Certainly, Soapy," Alex replied, forcing a smile.

With his arms free, the derringer was available. A light-headed surge of energy brought Alex's reflexes to a bright sharpness. He may be a man beaten and close to bankruptcy, but his survival instincts remained strong.

Maybe he should just flick his wrist and put Smith out of his misery. Do the world a favor. He had no prayer against the whole gang, but Soapy would be the first to die. Soapy's hired guns had no brains. Would these animals, like a wolf pack, flip their allegiance to lead dog Alex if he killed their leader? Giddiness and anger, an oddly coupled play of emotions, filled him with long absent energy.

"You weren't planning on leaving our fair metropolis, were you?" Soapy asked. His slender, well-kept fingers played a self-satisfied beat on the table.

"I thought you wanted to get your loan repaid," Alex said, anger swelling. Soapy couldn't get it both ways, the bastard.

"The thought crossed my mind that you might not return," Soapy said.

"If I didn't return," Alex said, his voice reflecting a calm he didn't feel, "you'd take possession of Stromberg's and my half of Nearly New."

"Based on what I can see," Soapy said, "the combined value of those two ventures are far from equaling the $11,000 you now owe me. I just added the latest interest charges."

Soapy and his accomplices would run the two businesses into the ground in no time. All of Alex's hard work down the drain. Again the urge to shoot Smith took hold. But Alex's desire to survive also demanded caution.

"You're going to find out the value of those businesses if you don't let me go to San Francisco."

"Not a chance, Alex." Soapy's fingers clenched into tight fists.

"Soapy," Alex said, forcing himself to focus. Lose his temper now, and the game would be over. "If you had a clue how to run an honest business, you'd realize how wrong you are about Stromberg's."

Smith's body relaxed in his chair, shoulders dropping and a tooth-filled smile replacing his frown. Soapy's change eased Alex's tension as well as the men's surrounding him.

"You know, I've missed you at our poker games," Soapy said. "You presented one of the few challenges in town."

"I've been a little preoccupied," Alex replied. What was this slimy son of a bitch angling toward? Soapy's shift of subject had to be planned. Stay on guard or be run over. But he too missed the adrenaline rush of high stakes poker. "Look, Soapy, I'd be more than happy to play against you. Just you and me. None of your sycophantic henchmen around. But, as you know, I'm a bit stretched."

There had to be a more complex scheme at work than just preventing Alex from going to San Francisco. How would those plans change if Smith realized how grateful Alex was to avoid the nightmare of an ocean voyage?

"What if I lend you another $1,000?" Soapy offered in his most sleazy voice, one he must think came out sincere. "You can use that as a stake."

"Sure," Alex said. Was he sure? Could he take the risk of adding to his debt? Why not? Soapy's offer brought both excitement and a tightening in his stomach. But somewhere there had to be a trap. "What the hell. But as I said, there's certain conditions."

"That's what I like about you, Alex," Soapy said, stroking his well-kept beard. "I lend you money, and you set conditions. Sir, you have iron balls."

The men in the room erupted in laughter. Alex didn't laugh. Were they truly that entertained by Soapy's comment? Or were they only observing the protocol of laughing at the boss's jokes?

"Just you and me, Soapy," Alex said. "We'll take a room in the Great Northern. Make sure you bring enough money and a couple of brand-new decks of cards. I wouldn't want you to get your hands dirty."

Soapy nodded agreement. A swell of confidence swept through him. Then a shred of caution registered with Alex. When things were too good to be true, they weren't. No question in his mind that he could take the crook in an honest game. But that was the key—an honest game.

CHAPTER SIXTY-FOUR

Ceaseless winds buffeted the corner room in the Great Northern. Drafts whistled through the poorly constructed hotel. Alex felt the creakiness. The nondescript, bare-bones room seemed too understated for the promised drama to come.

Soapy counted out the chips with steady hands and gleaming eyes. Well-manicured fingernail slit open the first deck. Time to get down to business.

"Reds are one hundred dollars," Soapy said, "blues five."

Just Alex and Soapy. A couple of friendly poker players sitting across from each other for a game of five card stud. Nothing serious. Just financial life or death. And possibly more.

"Fine," Alex replied. "Better give me ten reds. You're the man with all the money."

Soapy distributed the chips. Alex counted the small pile he received from Soapy. Alex would check every chip, every card, every movement of his crooked opponent.

"You ready, Mr. Stromberg?" Soapy said in his most formal tone. "One hundred dollar ante, no betting limit."

Alex's and Soapy's revolvers had been left at the Great Northern's front desk. A useless gesture. Soapy had to have a hidden weapon. And Smith's men lurked in the hallway. One call from Soapy and they would crash through the flimsy door, the lock more decoration than substance. Alex had loosened the cuff of his sleeve on the way to the hotel to free up his deadly little pistol. Alex would bet his life he could put a bullet in Soapy's head before his enemy could react.

"Good by me," Alex answered.

First hand, Soapy folded after three cards and $500. Second hand, Soapy folded after four cards and $600. Too easy. Alex won three out of the next four hands. Up over $2,500. If this was some kind of trap, Alex was more than happy to cooperate. But the threat of an ambush stayed with him.

After an hour, Alex had won close to $5,000. It wasn't that Alex was getting great hands, more Smith's being dealt lousy ones. His opponent seemed oblivious. His poker face in place, no words and a stone-cold silence greeted every hand. Alex's energy and excitement grew with each victory.

Could he possibly win enough to pay off Soapy? Would the scoundrel keep playing that long? Would Alex's luck hold? Or was it luck? And if there was a swindle, surely he'd have seen signs by now.

"You know, Soapy," Alex said, unable to suppress a smile, "I've got enough winnings here to buy you dinner. The Alverson House serves great food. How long do you want to play?"

"I'm well aware of Miss Sophia's theft of Eric Legare," Soapy said, keeping his eyes on his hands, shuffling his chips on the table. "But it's rude and poor sportsmanship to walk out without giving your opponent a chance to get his money back."

Alex searched the man's expression, weighed each of his words. Nothing except a tightening around the man's mouth and an ever more piercing stare. Just let the game continue.

The pots grew larger. Alex gained another thousand dollars. He now had more blue $500 chips than $100 reds, the piles of tokens so tall they threatened to collapse. Soapy had no one to help him cheat or distract Alex's concentration. All the hours, all Alex's experience playing high-stakes poker, coalesced into a growing confidence. But again, was this too good to be true?

No question Lady Luck could turn on a dime and destroy an overconfident player. The flip side to the equation was that if he didn't think he could win, he wouldn't. If Alex walked away now, he could give his $6,000 in winnings to Soapy and cut his interest burden in half. That would eliminate the immediate necessity of sailing to San

Francisco. But with the roll he was on, he could possibly wipe out the entire debt. What kind of freak was he to embrace such risk and danger?

Alex now held the deck. First card, the hole card, face down, then one face up. He had an ace in the hole and a ten showing. Soapy showed an eight of hearts, then bet one thousand dollars. Alarms rang.

Alex wasn't about to be bluffed by the threat of a couple of eights. He pushed out two blue chips and added a third. Soapy called Alex's raise and waited for the next card.

Alex dealt a jack to Soapy and an ace to himself.

Damn. The perfect card. Two aces to Soapy's potential pair of eights or jacks. Not much of a contest yet. Just keep Smith in the game. Alex bet only $500. Soapy raised an additional thousand, pulling off another surprise. This move made no sense. Either Soapy was off his game, or Alex was just flat-out winning. For once he could ignore financial problems, his perilous relationship with Sophia and his father's lack of cooperation. Alex hadn't felt this invigorated in months. This was even better than sex with Sophia.

Could he squeeze $12,000 from Soapy? Was this the miracle he so needed? But something didn't add up. Smith was neither a fool nor an amateur. The crook couldn't be cheating if Alex was dealing the cards. Could he? And Alex had to use care if he was to coax that much money out of Smith.

With two aces, Alex couldn't resist meeting Soapy's bet and raising another thousand. Alex held his breath, and Smith didn't disappoint. Two more blue chips hit the table. Alex kept the smile off his face. The pot reached $4,100. How long could this go on?

Alex flipped the fourth card face up. Holy shit. Another ace for him, another eight for Soapy. Three aces, two showing. His hand would crush the swindler, even assuming the man's hole card was an eight. Alex caught himself nervously tapping his foot on the floor.

If he was to win enough with this incredible hand to pay off his debt, now was the time. But he had only a few chips left in front of him. He would soon be out of money. Would Soapy come up with a satisfactory solution to keep Alex in the game? Or would this be the point Soapy would fold and walk?

Alex tossed his last four blue chips on the pile. They landed with a satisfying clink. He had used up his entire stake. The one thousand Soapy had lent him and the five thousand he had previously won. Well, Mr. Smith, just how crazy are you?

With neither blink nor flinch his opponent called Alex's $2,000 and raised another $2,000. What could Soapy possibly have to make him bet so irresponsibly? Alex stared at the face cards. Blood pounded a wild rhythm in Alex's head. Alarms rang yet again. Then he pushed all concerns aside. He just needed the contest to continue. But how was he supposed to come up with another $2,000?

This was the game, the hand Alex had practiced for his entire life. He had Soapy beat three aces to a potential three eights. Soapy stared at the table, let minutes pass. One chance in forty-two Soapy would get a fourth eight on the last card that would be dealt face down. The same odds that Alex would confront to get a fourth ace. He'd take those odds all day long.

"As you can see, I'm out of money, Soapy," he said. "How do you expect me to meet your raise?"

"Do you really want to continue?" Soapy asked, his face an expressionless mask. He shuffled the chips on his side of the table. "Tell you what, my friend, I'll add $2,000 to what you owe me. Deal the last card, and let's see where we stand."

Alex felt alive and confident. Where was the fear and doubt that had infected him only hours ago on Skagway's beach? He nodded his consent and dealt the last two cards face down. Alex tabled the deck and rubbed his hands together waiting for Smith to look at his final card.

Soapy was in no hurry. Alex stared at his adversary. Someone had to break the stalemate. Alex lifted the corner of his down card and bit hard on his tongue. The taste of blood and pain couldn't suppress a satisfied sigh. His down card had to make him a winner—a second ten. An ace-ten full house.

Every once in a while an incredible opportunity presented itself if one could gather enough courage. Time to bet the farm, or, in this case, his hotel partnerships. Alex looked across the table at Soapy and worked hard to suppress a grin. He ignored the first smile of the two-hour session that flickered across Soapy's face.

"Well?" Smith said.

"What value," Alex asked, "would you place on my 50 percent interest in The Star and Alverson House?"

The Star was worth plenty. The Alverson House, despite the massive investment, was an unproven commodity. Did Soapy know the true worth of the two businesses? Alex had to assume he did. Let Smith throw out a number.

"Based on what I know?" Soapy said. The wicked gleam in the crook's eyes couldn't be hidden, nor could the expectant tremor in Alex's hands. "I'd say $5,000."

"Ten thousand dollars," Alex countered, expecting the low-ball value. "And I'll wager it all on this hand."

The amount didn't matter too much. The pot stood at $8,100. Any amount over $6,000 would free Alex from Soapy's clutches and usurious interest rates. But why was Soapy still in the game? He hadn't even looked at his last card. Had Soapy been dealing, Alex would be suspicious. He'd pull his derringer and yank his money off the table.

"All right, Alex," Soapy said, and peeked at his last card. "We'll compromise. $7,500 for your interests in both establishments."

"Done." Alex exhaled and flipped over his ten. "Full house. Aces and tens."

Relief swept through Alex. He was out of debt. No nightmare, puke-filled voyage to and from California. No embarrassment or loss of face with Sophia. He could fully embrace their relationship, give of himself completely. He choked back a cry of joy. Wanted to kiss Soapy for the unexplainable intransigence that had kept him in the game.

But Soapy remained impassive. Then a look of pity flashed across the gambler's face, followed by a grin so avaricious it made Alex shudder in confusion. Smith turned his two down cards over. Four eights trumped his full house. Stunned disbelief gave way to fear.

How had Soapy done it? Had this son of a bitch somehow palmed cards? Could Soapy be such a great cheater that he'd pulled off a swindle right before Alex's eyes? But he'd given the bastard his total attention. Panic swept away any answers.

What would he tell Sophia? How could he face her? She despised Soapy, and now he would be her partner. The small room squeezed even tighter. Fingers tore at his shirt collar searching for more air. That had to be what Smith had been after the whole time.

"Give me forty-eight hours to come up with cash rather than my interests in the hotels," Alex said, unaccustomed sweat dripping down his back.

"Twenty-four, partner," Soapy answered. His grin displayed all his teeth. "Twenty-four."

What chance did Alex have to raise $18,000? There would be no mercy from Smith. Did an additional twenty-four hours matter one way or another? Might as well end his misery right now.

"Live like an asshole," Alex spit out, "die like an asshole."

Did it matter anymore whether Alex lived or died? At least he could take this slimeball with him. Alex cocked his arm to snap the derringer into his hand, but got no further. The hotel door burst from its hinges. Soapy's men flooded the room, weapons fixed on Alex.

"Just which asshole were you talking about, Alex? You best make the most of your twenty-four hours."

CHAPTER SIXTY-FIVE

A starched white tablecloth and clean silverware separated them. For the second day in a row, Jared sat across the table from Sophia. How could this be true? She smiled. She talked. She was indeed human. He had to wipe away the silly grin stretching his lips. Had to focus on her sentences, answer her questions. Such intimacy was unsettling and thrilling at the same time. Her beauty, the welcome attention, and the intelligence of her comments created an aura so bright he just couldn't concentrate.

"Jared, you seem miles away," she said. "Am I boring you?"

A shift in the tone of her voice demanded his full attention. Well, he wasn't as far away as Alex must be at this time.

"Heavens, no," Jared almost shouted. "I spent so many days on the trail, I'm just not quite adjusted to conversations. The Indian musher never opened his mouth. And Brutus and I communicate without words."

Sophia's laugh tinkled like fine crystal. He had no business lunching with this goddess. But why not? No woman would pick him as her first choice, unlike his old boss, who attracted women like bees to honey. And Alex's shadow lurked everywhere around them. Yet she seemed interested in what he said, comfortable in his company. He certainly had nothing to lose.

Lunch arrived. Loin of lamb with mint sauce. Fresh asparagus and potatoes hashed and baked in cream. Had it truly been only two days ago that he'd been chewing hardtack in the wilderness? So confusing. He dug into his lamb and potatoes like a drowning man grasping a life ring.

"Are you planning to stay in Skagway?" Sophia asked, her voice a curious combination of interest and concern. "That is, once you've performed your duty to Alex."

Jared stopped, fork hovering above his plate. How should he answer that question? Tell the truth? Be ambiguous? Even lie? What would keep alive Sophia's interest in him? Who was he kidding? He couldn't compete with Alex. He had no prayer to capture a woman of this quality. But if he could survive Salt and the Yukon in winter, floor an opponent like Harrington, why not shoot for the moon?

"I'm not sure." Jared looked down at his plate, unable to stare into those incredible chestnut eyes and be dishonest. "I guess I've got three weeks to make up my mind. Truth is, I hate this place. This city is disgusting and immoral. Brings out the worst in people." Heat rose on his face. "With the exception of you."

"My, my," Sophia said. Her sparkling laughter rang through the crowded dining room. "I'm glad you find me the exception. Glad you decided to take a room here in the Alverson House. You make delightful company. According to Alex, you'll help save our business. I now understand where those expectations came from after listening to your Klondike adventures."

Unexpected excitement crackled through Jared. One sure thought, it hadn't taken much to convince him to trade his old spot in Stromberg's drafty tent for a room in Sophia's hotel. But the challenge—rather, the responsibility—to help save Sophia's Alverson House, panicked him. And the mention of Alex disturbed him.

"Nothing could keep you here?" she asked, eyes crinkling with amusement. "Not even the love of a woman?"

Jared choked on his mouthful of food. Somehow he swallowed. He stole a glance at Sophia. A quizzical smile lifted the corners of her full lips. Thank God she wasn't laughing at him.

"Are you in love with Alex?" he asked.

Sophia's mouth opened, but no words came forth. Satisfaction filled Jared at her confusion. Then guilt swept through him. He'd put her in an uncomfortable position. But why not ask? End his fantasy now before more disappointment. Serve his three-week, self-imposed prison term in this wasteland and move on. Let him get on with his life.

Then her eyes popped wide open, staring at a spot over his shoulder. He twisted around to see what had grabbed her attention. Alex appeared at their table.

"Alex, you look terrible," Sophia stuttered, her voice trembling. "What are you doing here? You're supposed to be headed to San Francisco."

Alex's face did indeed look ravaged. He hadn't seemed well when Jared had seen him yesterday. Now his former boss resembled a man who had spent the last twenty-four hours a victim of the Spanish Inquisition. Jared rose to his feet in respect. And alarm.

"Why aren't you taking care of Stromberg's?" Alex accused.

His eyes fixed on Jared. Even fatigue couldn't mute Alex's anger. Was his reappearance some kind of a trap his old boss had prepared to test Jared's honor and Sophia's fidelity?

"I wish there was enough business to warrant my constant presence there," Jared replied.

Who was Alex to doubt Jared's commitment to look after the general store? His own anger flamed to life. Alex had begged him to watch the business. Jared glanced at Sophia. Her expression was one of irritation as much as shock.

"I must speak with Sophia," Alex said in a choked voice. "Leave us alone."

Jared remained motionless. He was through taking orders. From anyone. He met Sophia's gaze, hoping for some insight into this unexpected turn of events. What did she want?

"Jared can stay," Sophia said.

She waved Jared back into his chair, eyes reflecting a steely resolve. Jared exhaled. He wasn't sure she needed either Alex or him. This lady could take care of herself.

"Let's at least go into the lobby," Alex said with resignation. "There's no one there. As usual."

Alex's comment came without force or sarcasm, exhibiting a deference never before witnessed by Jared. Sophia flung her napkin on the table, knocking over her cup of tea. Her face transformed from confusion to anger, even fury.

Alex turned and moved to the connecting door, head down, shoulders slumped, steps hesitant. Couldn't be the Alex Jared knew. The old Alex was dangerous, quick to strike, not this hollow-eyed scarecrow. And Sophia. She'd always been calm, aloof and cautious, hidden behind her bulky men's clothing. Who the hell were these people?

* * *

"I've been up all night," Alex said, eyes fixed on the polished wood floor, "wandering around town."

"Dammit, Alex," Sophia hissed. "What's going on?"

"Soapy Smith waylaid me on the way to the ship."

Alex glanced up, then stared above Sophia's head toward the stairs. His eyes seemed to focus on some far away place. Jared took a half step closer to Sophia. He could feel her strain and anxiety, see the nervous twitch on her lips. An ominous stab of emotion sliced through him. Nothing good would come from this drama.

"That cheating son-of-a-bitch Soapy," Alex said a notch above a whisper. "I lost everything in a poker game."

"How much did you lose?" Sophia's voice trembled with dread.

"Everything." His voice dropped even lower. "Everything."

"What the hell do you mean, 'everything'?" Sophia's entire body quivered.

"Stromberg's. Nearly New." Alex's words came out strangled, distorted. "My share of The Star and the Alverson House."

Sophia stumbled. Jared caught his breath and grabbed her. She recovered her balance, snapped her wrists from Jared's helping hands and freed herself. But after only one step she slumped back against Jared. He directed her toward a chair across from Alex, and she collapsed into the cushions like a crumbling mannequin.

"Soapy will be your new partner by five this afternoon," Alex mumbled, a death mask for a face.

"You son of a bitch!" Sophia's screech ripped through the empty lobby. "You bastard. He'll turn the Alverson House into a brothel. Crush me."

The Alverson a whorehouse? Sophia and Soapy partners? Nothing made any sense. The world spun too fast for Jared. What did Alex's disastrous actions mean to Sophia? His confusion froze him in place.

"How much exactly did you lose?" Sophia asked, spots of color reappearing on her regal cheekbones. "Tell me, dammit."

"If you've any money stashed away that I don't know about," Alex began weakly, "now's the time to use it. You must have some funds hidden."

Sophia answered with a seething "No." Her hand jerked a lace handkerchief from her coat pocket. She dabbed her eyes, then drew the white fabric to her mouth.

Jared placed a tentative hand on her shoulder. He wanted to offer consolation or protection. Something that would ease her obvious anger and anxiety. But what? Helplessness and frustration washed over him.

"Then we're doomed." Alex sighed and massaged his forehead.

"How could you do this?" Her hands twisted the handkerchief in her lap. "How much did you lose?"

"Part of this mess is your own fault," Alex said without much conviction. He met her furious stare with vacant eyes. "This cash-sucking Alverson House put us over the edge."

A surprising look of guilt flashed across her face. What could possibly generate such an expression from Sophia? How much information was Jared missing? What he witnessed shattered all his preconceived notions about Alex and Sophia's relationship. He could only stand there a useless spectator.

"No, Alex," Sophia said with bitterness. "You can't blame me. Tell me. How much did you lose?"

"Eighteen thousand dollars," Alex said, deflating like a balloon, then sinking deeper into his chair.

"Goddamn you!" Sophia's howl echoed against the walls of the deserted room. "You've sold me to Soapy son-of-a-bitch Smith."

Surprise lit Jared up like an electric shock. The overwhelming amount of the poker losses might crush both Alex and Sophia, but the dragging weight of his money belt put $18,000 into new perspective. Salt's words kept reverberating—money provided opportunities. And the opportunities were all now Jared's.

"I'm sure you'll wrap Soapy around your finger," Alex said, sounding a little more like the old Alex.

Recriminations flew between Alex and Sophia, growing in volume and viciousness. A plan formulated in Jared's mind. He could save the day. Drive Alex out of the picture. Become Sophia's champion. What an incredible gift he had received from the boxer Harrington—gold, the life of his dog, and now, perhaps, the woman of his dreams.

"I have a solution," Jared said.

Couldn't Jared pay off Alex's debt? He'd then own interests in The Star and the Alverson House. Give it all back to Sophia. Let Alex keep Stromberg's—he couldn't care less about the general store.

Sophia and Alex had run out of steam. Both slouched exhausted in their respective chairs. Dammit. Why were they ignoring him when he had the answer to their misery and despair?

"I tell you, I can get $18,000," Jared's voice rising.

They looked up at Jared with blank expressions, no comprehension. An alien surge of power gave him strength and confidence. Jared savored the moment. He didn't know what would happen, but for once he was in control.

CHAPTER SIXTY-SIX

Jared's words drifted through the thick fog of Alex's consciousness. Meaningless. He was crushed. Hopeless. Much worse than any humiliation dealt him by father Mordecai. Alex searched inside himself for any island of redemption. But he was adrift in the same dark-gray sea that had swallowed his brother. And he had lost Sophia. Lost all shreds of honor, confidence and reputation.

Jared kept repeating the same incomprehensible message. Why wouldn't the cock-eyed clerk shut up and allow Alex to sink into complete, unavoidable despair? But Sophia must have heard something. Life returned to her features. Animation reflected in her eyes. She stared at Jared, lips parted. What was he yakking about? Something about gold. Alex fought to regain focus.

"Jared," Sophia said in a whisper. "Please don't taunt us with wishful thinking."

"I'm telling you," Jared repeated, "I have $18,000 in gold."

This was ridiculous. A flimsy offer with no connection to reality. Why was this young punk spouting such nonsense? Making a mockery of Alex's tragedy? Anger overcame the web of misery gripping him.

"What the hell are you talking about?" Alex said, air returning to his lungs.

Red-ridged fingers reached below Jared's flannel shirt and pulled out a canvas money belt with seams stretched to near splitting. The belt dropped on a nearby table with a loud thud. Jared released a self-satisfied sigh.

"Take a look, Miss Alverson," he said.

She reached for the belt. With shaking hands she opened the pouch. Alex couldn't see the contents, but Sophia's gasp shook off the remnants of his crippling depression.

"That's filled with gold," Jared said, pointing with pride.

"Jared," she blurted out. Sophia's body trembled as she poured out yellow nuggets and a smaller leather bag filled with gold dust. "How did you get this? Is it real? You're offering this to us?"

"I'm offering this gold to you, Sophia," Jared said, jaw now clenched. "No one else."

Alex looked up, startled. Jared's words and expression made it clear that Sophia was the beneficiary of Jared's generosity. But wasn't it Alex who was in debt to Soapy? It wasn't Jared's obligation that needed to be paid to save Sophia. Alex should be the one to confront Smith. He glanced at the rosewood grandfather clock in the lobby—3:10. Less than two hours to pay back the loan.

But what was the hook? Could Jared be that devious? The young man was too transparent. Too honest. Wasn't he also too naïve?

"What do you want for your gold?" Alex asked.

"Nothing," Jared said loud and clear, no uncertainty. "The money is to free Sophia from Soapy. And from you."

Sophia stood by the table, mouth still open, face flushed, long, shapely fingers tracing patterns among the scattered gold nuggets. The only way to save Sophia would be to pay back Alex's debt. That action would save Alex also—a miracle that had never entered his mind. But it wouldn't save Alex's relationship with Sophia.

"I'll take the gold to Soapy," Alex said. "I don't have that much time."

"No," Jared said, gathering the gold back into the money belt. "I'll take the gold to an assay office to count out $18,000. Then I'll pay off Smith."

Was he in a dream? The world no longer made any sense. But Alex would do anything to evade Soapy's deadly grasp, even accept the ironic position of backing up his ex-clerk.

"It's not that simple," Alex insisted. "You'll need me to go with you. Soapy isn't going to be pleased to get money instead of my interest in The Star and Alverson House. Someone is going to have to cover your back."

* * *

The cruel, wet wind of Skagway tore at all exposed flesh. Night had fallen like a club to the back of the head. Alex swore as he tripped over the frozen runs of Broadway. But all his senses fired, excitement returning after a long dormancy. This should be interesting. Jared had no idea what he faced, dealing with a low-life scoundrel like Soapy. No clue what a back-stabbing crook like Smith was capable of—fraud, theft, murder. At this point, Alex had nothing to lose, including his life. Be a shame for young Jared to get cut down on an errand of mercy.

"You got a weapon?" Alex asked, striding beside Jared.

"Don't need one," Jared answered. He searched up and down the street. "Brutus."

Alex detected a tremor in Jared's voice. So did Brutus. The Airedale appeared, jaw snapping, tail sticking straight out. The dog trotted close to Jared's legs. Alex was amazed. The animal must have picked up the scent of tension radiating from his master. Alex would rather depend on his guns, but the dog served as an excellent second choice.

Despite Brutus, he wished Jared had some weapon that he could use in the clutch. Surprise would be an asset. If they moved fast enough, they might be able to drop the gold and get out of Soapy's headquarters in one piece. Alex loosened his .45 in his holster, then released his shirt cuff for clear access to his derringer. Alex stopped at the door to Soapy's playpen. Now or never.

"You ready?" Alex asked his one-time assistant.

Jared didn't hesitate. He pushed open the door and stepped in, Brutus at his side. Alex followed him inside, one step behind, hand on his pistol butt.

"Whoa there, boy." The voice came from a large man leaning against the wall to the right of the door. "Where ya think you're going? And get that smelly mutt out of here before I plug him."

Alex recognized the thug. Did Jared? The same man that threatened Jared and his dog on his first day in Skagway. Soapy sat in his regular spot at his felt-covered table. The usual assortment of criminals littered the smelly, smoke-filled room. Alex counted six plus Smith.

"I'm here to see Soapy Smith," Jared said. "And the dog stays with me."

"Is that right?" The big talker pushed off from the wall and reached toward Jared.

Brutus snarled a warning, poised to leap at the threatening man. Jared moved faster. He shot out a long arm, grabbing the bully by the throat. His knee jammed into the man's groin. The huge hoodlum slumped to the floor.

"Nice work, Jared," Alex said, amazed at Jared's quick attack. Alex turned his attention back to Soapy. "This young man has some business to settle with you."

Alex pulled out his large pistol, hoping for an opportunity to waste one or more of Soapy's henchmen. Too many enemies for one man to cover, so focus on the leader. He rotated his revolver toward Soapy. No one moved. Alex felt in control for the first time in many days.

He prayed for an excuse to kill Smith but was more interested in Soapy's reaction to Jared's payoff. Jared took the few steps to the gambler's table. He released the money belt from his waist and slapped the heavy canvas onto the table without any evidence of fear or trepidation.

"Eighteen thousand in gold," Jared said. "Had it weighted at Yukon Assay. This settles your debt with Mr. Stromberg." He stepped back. "You're the disease that infects Skagway."

Jesus. The expression on Smith's face was priceless. First astonishment. Then confusion, followed by anger. The first time Alex had seen any loss of control in the man. The gambler turned bright red. Alex stifled a laugh.

Jared turned and walked to the door. Still no movement from any of Smith's associates. But one couldn't push Soapy too hard. Alex backed out behind Jared, revolver still pivoting around the room. Alex only wished he'd been the one to dump the gold in front of Smith. Or that Brutus had taken a pee in Soapy's temple.

CHAPTER SIXTY-SEVEN

Alex trudged down Broadway. Wet, freezing wind whistled against his face. Humiliation still hung heavy upon him. He had betrayed Sophia. But he'd survive. Hadn't he learned to live with the death of his brother? And no sleep in over forty-eight hours. No nightmares. How much longer could he function before physical collapse? This must be what a condemned man felt walking to his execution.

Thank God he'd been able to sell Stromberg's building, fixtures and inventory. He might have received only fifty cents on the dollar, but he now had enough cash to get the hell out of Skagway. Start something new. Somewhere else.

Anger still stoked a desire to confront his father and shake loose the profits the stubborn old goat owed him. But he just didn't have the energy to go to San Francisco. Seattle was also not an option, thanks to his father undermining Alex's negotiations for a store there. Would the Podunk town of Portland prove the right decision?

Damn. The hard gusts off the bay blasted him. He felt like he was climbing a mountain, even though Skagway's muddy, potholed streets were as flat as his spirits. The Alverson House would appear in another block. He ratcheted his pace down another level. He hadn't the stomach to face Sophia. But he felt compelled to meet her and Jared one last time. He stopped, muscles tightening. Quit stalling. Face them and get this last embarrassing goodbye over.

At least the past ruinous events were working out better than he could have imagined. The stunned expression on Soapy's face when Jared had handed over $18,000 in gold glowed in his mind and warmed his soul. He chuckled for the first time in weeks. Still, not a good idea to piss off Smith. If he didn't leave town soon, Soapy's disconcerting failure to take over The Star and Alverson House would very possibly be soothed by a fatal accident—to Alex. And Soapy could take Alex's share of Nearly New and stick it up his ass. Alex needed to keep alert.

A tall, thin stranger moved in front of him, also with a measured pace. The man carried himself with a degree of watchfulness. Black wool suit, no overcoat or even a hat. Dressed too lightly for Alaska. Didn't look like one of Soapy's minions. Must be a recent arrival. The man paused in a jewelry store doorway, and Alex passed, noting his face. Nobody Alex knew. No threat. Time to complete his mission.

One hundred yards more and Alex entered the lobby of the Alverson House. Jared and Sophia stood in conversation in the middle of the empty room. Jesus, the place was like a morgue, although the hum of voices and clatter of dishes resonated from the dining room. Still too many keys hung on hooks waiting for customers. He sure wouldn't miss this disastrous investment.

Sophia glanced at him. Her customer-welcoming smile turned to a sneer, as if he were spoiled meat. He shuddered at her glare. Once she had greeted him with pleasure. Never again. Still, he would miss this woman. Now wasn't there a new world awaiting Alex? Certainly Sophia Alverson could be replaced in his heart and in his bed. Couldn't she?

"I know you paid the money for Sophia," Alex said to Jared. He fiddled with the sleeve hiding his derringer. "Thank you anyway, Jared. I may not deserve it, but I appreciate what you did."

Jared seemed to be wasting no time moving in on Sophia. He hovered by her. Alex's departure would probably be appreciated. Was she really attracted to this gawky, lopsided savior? Amazing what money could accomplish. Certainly for Sophia.

"What are you going to do now?" Jared asked, stepping closer to Sophia, her hand snaking out to grip his forearm.

"Man like me," Alex said, "has done too many evil and irresponsible acts to be rehabilitated. I've got to go somewhere new. Start fresh." He faced Sophia. "I don't deserve your forgiveness. But, Sophia, I'll never forget you."

A gust of frigid air blew in from the front door, hitting Alex's back. Sophia's eyes looked past Alex and widened in surprise, then alarm. Alex turned to the entrance. The tall, gaunt man Alex had seen in the street stood in the open doorway, his face dominated by a large hook nose and a grin more snarl than smile. Alex stepped back beside Sophia.

The man remained just inside the threshold, leaving the door behind him ajar. Hairs rose on the back of Alex's neck. Something ominous about this character. Then Sophia gasped. One thing was damn sure, the man represented some kind of danger.

"Don't nobody move," Hawk Face growled.

What the hell was this all about? Who was he? Alex loosened the cuff of his shirt in a smooth movement. The stranger reacted in a flash. He drew a .45 from his holster and aimed the nasty-looking weapon at Sophia. Memories of Elijah's story flooded back. The man was after Sophia.

"Maggie Saunders," the man said. "I'm arresting you for the murder of Swen Nadar, as well as the theft of his money."

Alex caught movement at his side. Sophia's arm reached toward the revolver she kept in her coat pocket. The ugly, intimidating man took several steps closer, fingers tightening on his pistol.

"I said don't move," Hawk Face threatened. "Thought you'd lost me on the train, didn't you? You can't outrun the law."

No lawman could afford to spend months looking for this woman. Had to be a bounty hunter. Must be a big reward involved, just as Elijah had said. One thing for certain: Anyone who traveled this far to track a fugitive down was not to be underestimated.

"Ah, sir," Jared interjected.

"Do they know you're a vicious, thieving whore?" the man hissed, interrupting Jared, thrusting his chin toward Alex. "Wanted dead or alive. And dead would be a whole lot easier."

"Hold on," Alex said. Sudden energy and excitement swept away humiliation and self-disgust. Sophia might still need him. "You can't come in here and snatch this woman."

"Shut the fuck up," Hawk Face snarled and refocused on Sophia. "Told you not to move."

Sophia's hand dove for her pocket. Hawk Face cocked the revolver, the snap echoing in the empty lobby. Then Alex caught sight of the fast-closing shadow of Brutus. The big dog, snarling, charged through the open front door into the Alverson House.

"No," Jared screamed and dove at the bounty hunter.

Hawk Face swiveled the pistol away from Sophia toward Jared. His gun fired. Events compressed into a rapid blur. A bullet slammed into Jared. The force of the shot crumpled the young man to the floor. The bounty hunter then wheeled toward the attacking dog. Brutus went airborne. Hawk Face fired again. The shot caught the Airedale in midflight. But the animal's flying trajectory continued unimpeded toward the dark man.

Alex snapped his wrist to free his weapon. The derringer's smooth handle slipped into his hand. Thank God. He aimed and pulled the trigger of his small pistol at Hawk Face's head an instant before the momentum of Brutus's muscular body collided with the man. A shocking explosion erupted near Alex's ear. Sophia had fired at the same moment, using her large revolver.

The bounty hunter's head disintegrated into a spray of red and gray, his knees buckling as Brutus crashed into him, his pistol dropping from his fingers to the ground. Both man and dog collapsed to the floor, Brutus rolling off the bounty hunter.

Sophia glanced at Alex, indefinable emotion contorting her beautiful features. Alex's heart constricted. Then she took a step toward the fallen Jared. A guttural moan emerged from her mouth. She dropped to her knees. Alex had to save her.

"No, Sophia," he commanded. "Get out the back. Circle the block. Come in the front door like you're trying to find out what's happening."

Sophia froze, still gripping her pistol. Her gaze moved from one body to the other. Then her shocked stare turned to Alex.

"Now, Sophia! Now!" he cried out. "And give me your gun."

Alex grabbed her shoulder. He snatched at the smoking barrel of the .44. Sophia's hold tightened. She wouldn't let go.

"I'm not giving up my gun," she cried.

Jesus, this woman was stubborn. How many seconds before customers came storming in from the dining room? He snatched his own revolver from its holster and thrust it at Sophia. She released her weapon. Alex yanked her to her feet, turning her from the mayhem on the floor. His firm hand on her back pushed her toward the rear of the hotel and the door to the alley. She locked eyes with Alex.

"What about Jared?" she said.

"Nothing you can do," Alex said. He pointed to the back of the lobby. "Go before it's too late. And put my pistol in your pocket."

She sprinted toward the back of the hotel. Alex took two quick steps to Hawk Face. The small hole above his right eye from the derringer looked insignificant compared to the back of his head, a mass of blood and gore from Sophia's shot.

Damn, he couldn't let anyone discover the bounty hunter's mission. Alex dropped to the body. His hands ripped open the dead man's coat. He yanked out folded papers, telegrams and wanted posters of Sophia and crushed them into his own coat pocket. Just in time. The connecting door to the restaurant burst open. A wave of customers and waiters fought each other through the clogged entrance.

Alex scrambled to Jared. The young man lay in his own pool of blood. Was Jared also dead? A soft moan answered the question. Dark fluid stained Jared's shoulder. How bad? Alex couldn't tell for sure, but there was hope.

Shrill screams at the front door registered above the chaos in the Alverson House lobby, full of people for once. Sophia rushed to Jared and cradled his head in her arms. His eyes opened, and a weak smile twisted his lips.

Alex glanced over at the crumpled form of Brutus. The dog had bought critical seconds for Alex and Sophia. Now the Airedale lay motionless, like a pile of discarded carpet. Too damn bad. Brutus had been one tough animal.

"This son of a bitch," Alex told the crowd pressing around the bodies, "stormed in here and shot Jared for no reason. Had no choice but to shoot him."

Sophia jerked her head from Jared to Alex. What was she thinking? She directed a nod at him. Maybe her expression reflected forgiveness.

CHAPTER SIXTY-EIGHT

Sophia entered her back bedroom in the Alverson House. Jared lay in her large bed, propped up on pillows, eyes closed, shoulder swathed in bandages. She approached the bed, then went over to the corner of the room. Her hand stroked the kinky head of Brutus, sprawled on several blankets. An eye opened, the only sign of life from the Airedale. The poor dog was in worse shape than Jared, but Brutus would pull through. The animal's need to recover gave her an additional excuse to keep Jared in Skagway.

Time to wake up the young man. She eased down beside him on the bed and placed a light kiss on Jared's feverish brow. His eyes opened with a start, still reflecting the drugs Conner Samuelson had forced him to take. Her next move on Jared would be tricky.

Her former lover's unpredictable highs and lows had shown a man with too many edges—prickly, violent, passionate. But missing a key ingredient. His betrayal provided the proof of that. But what the hell did she know about tenderness and faithful commitment? Now before her lay a man as different from Alex as fire from water. Jared, placid on the outside, possessed depths of character discovered under extreme pressure and duress.

Too bad she didn't love Jared. But she did need him. He could provide more money and safety and become a hard-working, stable partner. Couldn't that be the first steps toward a loving partnership?

"How do you feel?" she asked.

"How's Brutus?" Jared turned toward his dog, wincing in pain.

"He'll survive," Sophia answered, reaching for his hand. "Take a while for him to heal, though. How are you feeling?"

"Tell you the truth," Jared said, smiling his lopsided grin, "I'm not sure. Didn't want to take Dr. Samuelson's medicine. Had a bad experience last time I took drugs back in San Francisco. In fact, it was right after you helped me on the train."

Calling Samuelson a doctor was like calling Soapy Smith a model citizen. The old man was in reality only a mediocre veterinarian, but all Skagway had. No reason to burden Jared with that knowledge. And Samuelson had saved Brutus.

"Doc told me you'll both need a while before you start moving around," she said, unbuttoning first Jared's shirt, then his long underwear top.

"The doctor said I'm damn lucky," Jared said, a blush blossoming on his face. "Good chance I'll be able to use my arm and shoulder like normal."

Amazing the different emotions Jared's disjointed features reflected. Well, she planned on bringing him to a level of pleasure he never dreamed of. This was just the foreplay.

She rubbed his chest, working her way down to his stomach in tight circles. The poor boy squirmed under her touch. He had to be a virgin. How many young men had she introduced into the world of sex at the Prairie Flower? They might have started out loud, obnoxious, full of themselves, usually fortified by alcohol, but oh, how quickly they had melted under her ministrations. Now Jared's erection tented the comforter. She'd have to be gentle or he'd explode.

Sophia reached out for his groin, fingers tracing a pattern in his pubic hair. A glazed expression painted his face. Only the combination of drugs and physical stimulation could produce such a look of bewildering ecstasy. Sophia fought back a giggle and kept a seductive smile on her face. She grasped him tighter and lowered her mouth. Too much. His hips spasmed, followed by an eruption. Too soon.

His face turned bright red, eyes clenched shut. How much more tender or subtle could she have been? She shifted forward, kissed his convoluted features. Her physical power over him gave her more time to develop a relationship, to convince the young man to stay in Skagway. Next time she'd be more careful.

"Relax, Jared," she whispered in his ear. "First time's always the quickest. You're not going anywhere." She cleaned him with a corner of the sheet. "We have plenty of time."

* * *

Sophia returned to Jared after several hours. Had she given him enough time to recover? She kissed his lips and stroked his cheek. She smiled at the sweet young man whose eyes widened inches from hers. A twinge of doubt crept through her. Then Jared mumbled unintelligible words, garbled by emotion, pleasure and laudanum. She doubted Jared would mind if they tried again. Her hands again massaged his chest, then stomach. His good arm snaked out and grabbed her.

"What are you doing?" he stammered. "God, I am so ashamed."

"Hush," she answered, and returned her lips and tongue to work on his nipples.

"Why?" Jared again stuttered. "Why are you treating me like this?"

She watched his eyes flutter. Deep, ragged gulps of air inflated his chest. Her fingers teased his swelling manhood.

"Why?" Sophia said. "You're the kindest, most compassionate man I've ever met. I want to make you happy."

Jared appeared helpless but hungry. Her experience told her the time had come to again get back to serious business. No better way to control a man than through his cock. Sophia pulled back the sheets and comforter. She kicked out of her boots and stripped off her pants. She'd planned for this moment.

Her supple fingers unbuttoned her shirt and released her full breasts. As she expected, Jared was rigid and ready once more. She straddled him, gentle, avoiding any jostling. Pain would be the one thing that could destroy this opportunity. She lowered herself on top of him, feeling the tightness inside. No disgust or revulsion with this man. He was no Alex and no customer either. She moved slowly but firmly. The performance was no longer dirty or demeaning. This act with Jared was surprisingly satisfying.

Jared muttered something.

"What did you say?" Sophia asked.

"You're certainly no ugly dwarf."

* * *

Sophia awoke startled. Hawk Face. He was in Skagway. Her heart pounded a painful rhythm. The events of the previous day came rushing back. Then she saw Jared beside her. Sophia took a deep breath, squeezed her eyes shut, then opened them. Had she really fallen asleep?

Yesterday's events confirmed she couldn't leave this rough-edged sanctuary. Hawk Face's unexpected appearance proved the threat of discovery was constant. Did his death mean an end to the danger? Was the bounty hunter one of a kind? One day she might become safe, but she'd never know when that would be.

She lay beside Jared's good shoulder and turned her head toward his. A sheepish grin greeted her. He certainly looked satisfied. She must have accomplished her goal. She stretched out. A series of new, questioning emotions played over his face. Sophia steeled herself for what she knew would soon surface. She should tell him the truth. Now.

"That man..." she began.

"That man made some terrible accusations," Jared said, his statement thick from drugs.

Wouldn't she be best off laying out the facts with her own words rather than responding defensively to questions? He was young and inexperienced but no fool. He'd have to realize that only a whore could bring him enjoyment with such skilled technique.

"I was a prostitute," she said with a firm voice. "But the man who I was accused of killing? That bastard attacked me. Hurt me badly. It was self-defense."

Jared looked troubled, then serious. How was this confession going to play out? Sophia had to be cautious. Whatever truth she shared couldn't turn the man against her. She needed Jared, certainly for a while.

"Whatever happened to force you into such a situation?" Jared asked with a degree of compassion.

Again the question she'd heard too many times. And a tone of judgmental righteousness tinged his words. Anger flashed through her. Men were all the same. Sanctimonious hypocrites. Yet she had to temper her wrath and answer Jared's unspoken accusations with an element of calm. Let her reinforce her role as victim, play on his kindness and romantic illusions.

"Several reasons, Jared. None of them my choice." She bit her lip, unable to control a degree of sarcasm. "Let's start with exposure, disease and starvation. How would you face those problems? What would you do to survive in an unforgiving city slum? Tell me."

Jared cringed. Seemed to shrink within himself. Sophia let his emotions play out. Now all she had to do was threaten to leave. Add some drama. She jerked upright, ready to exit the bed.

"No. Wait, please," Jared said. "I'm sorry. Don't go yet."

"Someday," Sophia relented, "I will prove to you how innocent I am of that bastard bounty hunter's slurs."

"I believe you, Sophia," Jared said, laying his good hand on her shoulder. "Leave this hellhole with me. We can start a new life. I still have money. We can go anywhere."

His capitulation was easier than she thought. At some point she'd tell him the entire story, just as she had Alex. And with each tragic piece of her past, she would attempt to wrap Jared into a web of dedication and subservience. But could she really control him that easily? She had no choice. Leaving this city was not an option.

"Jared, I can't leave," she said. "Believe it or not, the anarchy and absence of authority in this town is what will keep me safe."

"Skagway is doomed," Jared said with disgust.

"No, not at all," she whispered, her voice warm, convincing. "Alaska and the Klondike are huge. There's much more gold and other riches here for the taking. People are still pouring in, searching for their dreams. The railroad is coming to this city. Construction over the White Pass starts in the early spring. And when that happens, the Alverson House will prosper. Skagway will flourish, and Dyea will die a quick death."

"I despise this place, Sophia," Jared said, his tone pleading. "The scum of the earth has settled here. Dreams aren't realized in this pit of inhumanity, they're destroyed."

"Is that right, Jared?" Anger overcame her cautious manipulations. "Does that make me scum? Is that what you think of me?"

"No." Jared jerked upright. "That's not what I meant."

Pain creased his fractured features from his abrupt movement. Sophia calmed down. She'd use his romanticism and idealism, enhanced by the novels she read, to cement their relationship.

"We've time to discuss this, Jared," she said. "You're here for a while, until you and Brutus have healed. We have much to talk about."

And Sophia did have time. Time enough to capture him completely. She looked forward to the campaign, one she should easily win. But an inconvenient notion intruded—don't underestimate him. Jared was not the same man she had earlier discarded and ignored.

CHAPTER SIXTY-NINE

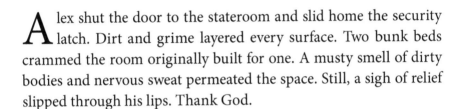

Alex shut the door to the stateroom and slid home the security latch. Dirt and grime layered every surface. Two bunk beds crammed the room originally built for one. A musty smell of dirty bodies and nervous sweat permeated the space. Still, a sigh of relief slipped through his lips. Thank God.

He dropped his only piece of luggage at the base of one of the bunks. Shouldn't be any more threat from Soapy Smith and his thugs. Slim odds that the crooked gambler would have Alex followed onto the *Grizzly*, a rust bucket of a ship headed for Portland. Should have shot the son of a bitch when he had the chance. Then again, he wouldn't be alive if he had.

The tight cabin created a peaceful cocoon. Alex wrapped the closeness around him. No sleep for how long? Going on three days. Had he ever been more exhausted? Stretching his neck and shoulders eased the tension in his body.

Even the menacing intimidation of his inescapable nightmares could not keep him from scrambling up on a top bunk. He stretched out on his back. The ceiling pressed down inches from his body. He placed his splayed fingers against the smooth surface. How could he be experiencing so much freedom in such cramped quarters?

Damn, he was tired, too tired for another journey crumpled on the deck puking his guts out. But rumor had it that sailing south was much easier. Just shut his eyes, pray for a calm voyage. Wouldn't it be wonderful to sleep and not wake up until docking in Portland? He had to get some rest. Had to close his eyes and hope for the best.

* * *

He wiped away a thin film of perspiration from his forehead. Had the stuffiness within the cabin made him so dizzy and disoriented? How long had he lain in bed? Had he slept at all? Couldn't have slept—no nightmares. Would have been the first time in years he'd experienced dreamless sleep.

He again placed his hands on the ceiling above him. Movement. Vibrations shocked him out of his semicomatose state. The boat was underway, swaying gently. Had the ship left Skagway? Where were they? Heat surged within his body. Now he struggled for air in the tight quarters. Relax. No reason to panic. Probably still cruising down the relatively calm Lynn Canal. The moment of truth would occur when the ship reached open water.

What a difference from the packed, frenetic trip north seven months ago. What naïve expectations he'd had. What an exciting future he'd plotted out. Only seven months, but felt like seven years. He'd lost more than just time. Some part of him hadn't survived his disastrous misadventures in Skagway. Might as well get some air, check out the *Grizzly*.

He swung his legs off the bed and dropped to the floor. Ship movement became more evident standing. He slipped back into his fur-collared coat, leaving the buttons undone so he could better reach his .45. Must be prepared for anything. He opened the cabin door and peeked out. Several figures moved away from his stateroom. Otherwise, the open deck seemed empty. The absence of any large group of travelers proved comforting.

He shut the door behind him and walked with uneasy steps toward the stern of the boat. A deep breath brought the clear, cold smell of the sea, laced with scents of unseen pine forests that crowded the waterway's shore. Sensations consistent with a new start in life.

A few other figures appeared and passed him on the deck. A quarter moon provided enough light for edged shadows, but no depth to the several other passengers. Only profiles and the outline of the vessel. Nothing threatening. Everything calm and quiet. Danger seemed far away in another life. Still, Alex could not let down his guard.

He stopped on the fantail at the stern of the *Grizzly*. Fresh air proved invigorating. Couldn't he look forward to a new beginning? He could jettison some old baggage, though his betrayal of Sophia might be the hardest to overcome. And this Skagway catastrophe would never have happened if not for that cheating bastard Soapy, not to mention dear Dad. His mind flitted from thought to thought, accompanied by a kaleidoscope of faces from the past months.

An image of Sophia rose before his eyes. She floated above the black waters and in front of the dark shadowed cliffs. Beautiful. Alluring. Full of contradictions. Just shake off the memory. He might never find another Sophia, but there would be other women in his future. Still, hard to believe Sophia loved Jared. Use him? Maybe. Love him? No way.

An ancient miner trudged by Alex. The man slogged along the deck head down, oblivious to anything around him. Empty of hope. Could have been Alex if not for Jared's $18,000 gift. But how had Soapy won that poker game? How had that gambler cheated him? And Sophia. Jesus. She'd shot that bounty hunter without hesitation. Who would have thought such a beautiful woman had the iron balls to do that?

But what about him? If he was to move forward into a new life, could he justify the killings he'd been forced into? Forced was the operative word. Each death had been an accident or at least a form of self-defense. Yes, self-defense. And under the same circumstances, wouldn't he kill again?

He turned from the water, leaned back against the railing. Clean air washed over him. The refreshing breeze continued to clear his head. Ocean travel wouldn't be that bad if conditions were always like this.

Two men walked toward Alex. He stiffened. His hand grasped the butt of his pistol. The men wore expensive overcoats similar to Alex's. No danger. Just two more vampires sucking the wealth from unsuspecting cheechakos. And who was he to judge? Was he any different? Yes. He had provided quality goods at fair prices. Relatively fair, anyway.

Cigar smoke wreathed the two men, their heads together, deep in conversation. Both men looked over at him when they had drawn abreast. Nodded. Alex released his grip on his weapon. Relaxed. Felt a smile on his lips. Maybe during the passage he'd learn who they were, what their story was. Perhaps even an opportunity to take advantage of these stodgy-looking passengers. He acknowledged their greeting with a nod of his own.

Then the two men stopped, whirled toward Alex, one to each side of him. Powerful hands gripped him under his armpits. What the hell was happening? In one fluid motion his feet left the deck. He was in the air, then over the railing. Grab something. Anything. Nothing but empty space. So fast. He floated through the air, back in a dream, body performing a slow twist. Where was he headed. Why?

"Mr. Isaac Snyder says goodbye," a disembodied voice called out.

The words echoed from a world away. Isaac Snyder. Alex saw the man's fat, wet lips and merciless pig eyes. The bastard had tracked him all the way from San Francisco. After all this time?

The floating sensation ended with a painful smack to his back. The rock-hard waters of the Lynn Canal engulfed him. His body was driven down, pulled by the momentum of the fall. Clothing gathered weight, immersed in freezing water. No air. No way to breathe. Raw fear as dense as the water enveloping him.

An unwelcome image sprang into his mind. His brother's frantic grip of blue-white fingers tilting the open vessel into the bay. Water pouring into the fragile boat. Let go, Samuel, or we'll both drown. The flash of his oar crashing down on hands hanging onto the gunnels of the small boat.

Darkness overpowered him. Open his mouth and he would drown. Let in the ocean waters and no more guilt. His lungs burned. His lips parted. No time left. Would he find his brother beneath the sea? Could he be headed to hell?

Or was this only another of the thousands of nightmares he had lived through every time he closed his eyes? Would he wake up in time? When would he know? He felt oblivion greeting him with unforgiving arms.

CHAPTER SEVENTY

J ared entered the Alverson House lobby after four hours inspecting The Star. Sophia stood behind the reception desk, checking in several well-dressed businessmen. Still, the activity level couldn't be described as booming, but things were buzzing. And she looked proud and professional, dealing with her new customers.

Sophia still wore men's clothing and her ever-present slouch hat crammed over now close-cropped lustrous auburn hair. But the clothes were no longer extra-large garments hanging on her body like oversize grain sacks. Beneath her clothing lurked a full-figured body that left him breathless. And nothing could hide the high cheekbones, bottomless chestnut eyes, and flawless complexion. Lord, he would miss her.

He took a seat in a comfortable armchair and waited for her to wrap up her transaction. The two men seemed in no hurry. She, on the other hand, couldn't hide her impatience. They were cutting into her efficiency. Jared had to smile. Even on a good day and fully recovered, he'd never match her concentrated energy and common sense.

Sophia could accomplish more in a day than anyone he'd ever met, including Alex. And unlike Jared's former boss, Sophia possessed no uncomfortable, unpredictable edges. The Alverson House was headed for success. And if Sophia incorporated Jared's few recommendations, The Star would continue to pour out profits as well. Smart. The woman was just plain sharp. He couldn't take his eyes off her as she walked from the reception desk to his chair.

"Have you got a report on The Star for me?" Sophia asked.

"Only a couple of suggestions," Jared answered.

Her smile brought instant arousal. Would he always melt in her presence? Every day they made love. What she had done last night with her lips, tongue and mouth had driven him to ecstasy. Each day a new physical revelation.

He was willing to accept the fact that she had been a professional sporting lady. But a killer? Not possible. Could she kill in self-defense? Maybe, but that wasn't murder. And of course it would be immoral for him to ever pay for sex. Then he realized how ridiculous that thought was. Hadn't he paid $18,000 for her attentions?

"You should consider cleaning up The Star," he said, suppressing an inappropriate smile. "The whole place needs to be scrubbed and repainted. The blanket dividers upstairs are as disgusting as the rags hanging in Dawson's pathetic excuse for hotels. Also, the kitchen could use new equipment. The quality of food seems to be slipping. The Star would pay back your costs to make those changes in a week or two."

"Very good, Jared," Sophia said, the serious expression on her face failing to mute her beauty. "I've been so caught up in the Alverson House I've ignored the Star. I'll have Horace handle all that immediately."

As if on cue, Horace scuttled through the connecting door from the dining room. The skinny little man was scattered, self-conscious, inefficient, homely. But give him a defined task, and he was unstoppable. And he'd take a bullet for his mistress quicker than even Jared.

"Sorenson's making his fish delivery," Horace said, breathless. "You told me to tell you as soon as he got here."

"Thank you, Horace," Sophia said and turned toward the rear of the building. Over her shoulder she called out to Jared, "Sorenson has been slipping in halibut that's a day old. Might be all right for The Star, but not here."

"Wait a minute," Jared said, standing up with a grin. "You can't leave me. I'm still recovering and need constant therapy."

Sophia hesitated, smiled, and stepped back to Jared. The sweet, soft kiss she planted on Jared's lips increased his excitement. Damn, he would miss her, but would she miss him?

"I'll see you tonight for dinner," she promised, then whirled and was gone.

That was also part of the problem. Sophia had less and less time for him. He had to break away from her sensual grip or forever be imprisoned in this disgusting excuse for a city. An involuntary shudder jerked him back to the moment. Horace still stood there like he'd missed his train.

"Jared, will you help get my ledgers in order tomorrow?" the nervous man asked.

"No," Jared said, his tone soft, but firm. "I'm headed south tomorrow morning."

The clerk looked as if someone had snatched off his trousers. His mouth worked like a fish out of water. He struggled for words.

"Why?" he stuttered. "You and Sophia are a great team. You've got everything a man could want here in Skagway."

"No," Jared said without much energy. "I don't have Sophia."

"What are you talking about?" Horace almost yelled.

"Calm down, Horace."

"Does Sophia know?"

"No," Jared said, sorry he had brought up the subject. "I'm going to tell her at dinner. If she has time for dinner."

That statement was a lie. He couldn't say good-bye to Sophia's face. He couldn't be rational or that honest. Her lure was overpowering. Better to write her a farewell letter.

"Where are you going to go?" Horace asked, distress coloring his face.

Good question. Jared had no clue other than somewhere south. Boats left for every destination daily. No problem finding space. He was surprised at the absence of the usual discomfort from his uncertainty. Where were the old disconcerting emotions of confusion, indecision and pessimism? Life had become an adventure.

"Why?" Horace began again. "Why would you leave a woman like Sophia?"

Horace blushed a color Jared had never previously seen on a man. He swallowed a smile. The poor clerk was even more captivated by Sophia than Jared.

"She doesn't love me," Jared said in a soft voice. He realized he had said the words aloud. He had revealed too much to Horace. "And I hate Skagway."

"As much as you despise Skagway," Horace said, also dropping his voice to a low, somber tone, "would you stay if Miss Alverson loved you?"

"Absolutely."

CHAPTER SEVENTY-ONE

Sophia's eyes failed to focus on the book Jared had given her. *The Adventures of Sherlock Holmes.* Why did she even want to read about crime? And Holmes at least had his Dr. Watson. Who did she have? No one.

Alone. Well, not completely alone. Still, Sophia's campaign of seduction had failed. What more could she have done? Well, she'd just have to make the best of this unexpected turn of events.

The street below her second-floor window bustled with activity, despite the fierce wind and heavy grey mist. A soft knock gave evidence that her workday had begun. Had to be Horace presenting himself for the day's instructions. She put down her book, then walked to the door and unlocked it.

"Good morning, Horace," she said as the timid clerk made his way into the well-furnished hotel room.

"Been two weeks." Horace spoke with his eyes cast to the floor. "Guess Jared's gone for good."

"You didn't think he'd really come back, did you?" she said.

"He's a good man," Horace said with a faint hint of reproach. "Thought you said he might stay."

"Might, Horace, might," she said biting back her own disappointment.

Sophia had been shocked and saddened when she'd read Jared's farewell letter. The lily-livered boy hadn't the nerve to tell her to her face. She had done everything within her ample powers to keep Jared in Skagway, certain she could capture his heart and soul. And didn't he love her? She thought she could see it every time he came near her. Unfortunately, she didn't love Jared. He must have sensed the lack of her romantic commitment. Add that to his extreme loathing for Skagway, and he had made his decision. In reality she never had much of a chance at keeping him. Now she was surprised at the depth of her regret.

Lines from Jared's message played through her mind. At least the man was honest, even if he was a coward. And he'd left the door open for her to meet him in the states—an empty offer. But no words of love. How had she misjudged him so completely?

"We'll get along just fine without him," she said and smiled.

"I hope so," Horace said. "Business is picking up fast. Don't forget your ten o'clock appointment with those railroad fellas."

"You couldn't possibly think," she said, "that I'd forget about renting six rooms for six months to those White Pass executives."

"But we only have four vacancies," Horace whined.

"Don't worry," Sophia said, welcoming such a simple problem. "They won't want all six rooms today."

Light vibrations rippling the floorboards beneath her feet testified to the escalating activities within the Alverson House. Fools continued to flood into Skagway. The White Pass Railroad would begin construction in several weeks. And Dyea was already dead and didn't know it. Her predictions to Jared had all come true.

"I'll see you downstairs shortly," she said to Horace, urging him to the door with both hands.

Now cash rolled in like dense, wet fog from the Lynn Canal. Poor Alex. If only he hadn't been so impatient, so impulsive. Sophia missed his energy, decisiveness and occasional charm. Her ex-lover wasn't evil or dishonest. He just couldn't avoid bad judgment. Where had he ended up? Could he find happiness there?

She glanced at the full-length mirror. What the hell did she need with such a reflection? To display her forever frumpy disguise? At least her choice of costume continued to deflect most men's unwanted advances. And did she even want another man in her life? Besides, how could she build an honest relationship on hidden lies? And now she had something else to hide under her bulky clothing. She'd just have to take life a month, a year, at a time.

A wave of queasiness overwhelmed her. Sophia stumbled forward, grabbed the back of her desk chair and smiled. It was a good queasy. Whose child was it? Alex's or Jared's? Would she know once the baby was born? Certainly she'd be able to tell right away, wouldn't she? Or would identification take weeks, months, years? Maybe she'd never be sure. Whoever the father, she would welcome it willingly, without question.

If she had known two weeks ago, would she have used her pregnancy to ensnare Jared? Probably not. This baby would be hers alone. She'd miss Jared's dog as much as she missed him. What great protection Brutus would have provided for her baby. But did she really want to share her child with anyone? Unlikely.

Strange. Alex had used her, and she had used Jared. Both men were now gone, neither expected to return. And one of them had planted the seed of a child. Given her the opportunity to bestow unequivocal love. Maybe she wasn't so trapped in Skagway after all. Finally, a future.

THE END

ACKNOWLEDGEMENTS

I would like to acknowledge and thank the following:

Our Airedale, Teton, who was the coolest, toughest, most loyal dog in the world and served as the template for Brutus, the true hero of this story.

Charlotte Cook who performed the heroic task of editing and inspiring this book while fighting for her life.

Sioban Boyer who worked harder to produce the cover than she did giving birth to her beautiful daughter.

Anne Fox and Joyce Mirabito, proof readers extraordinaire – 500 pages of perfection.

To the memory and inspiration of Jack London, the first writer to bring the Alaskan wilderness to life.

My wife Marilyn with whom all things are possible and my son, Matthew, proof of a better world ahead.

AUTHOR BIOGRAPHY

Chasing Klondike Dreams is Marc Paul Kaplan's first historical novel. His previous novel, *Over The Edge*, published by KOMENAR Publishing, is a thriller set in 1969 Jackson Hole, Wyoming, and garnered industry kudos and strong sales. Mr. Kaplan's long interest in wildlife and wilderness has led him to serve thirty years on the board of The Lindsay Wildlife Experience, an educational and wildlife rehab institution in Walnut Creek, California. He and his wife, Marilyn, have a son and live in Lafayette, California. He enjoys skiing, hiking and his beloved Airedale Terriers.